THE HUNTING TRIP

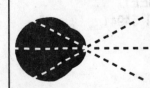

LIBRARY OF CONGRESS CATALOGING-IN-PUBLICATION DATA

Names: Butterworth, W. E. (William Edmund), 1929-
Title: The hunting trip : a novel of love and war / William E. Butterworth, III.
Description: Waterville, Maine : Thorndike Press Large Print, 2016. | Series:
  Thorndike Press large print core | Series: A novel of love and war
Identifiers: LCCN 2015038362 | ISBN 9781410480316 (hardback) | ISBN 1410480313
  (hardcover)
Subjects: LCSH: Intelligence officers—United States—Fiction. | Large type books. |
  BISAC: FICTION / Action & Adventure. | GSAFD: Adventure fiction.
Classification: LCC PS3557.R489137 H86 2015b | DDC 813/.54—dc23
LC record available at http://lccn.loc.gov/2015038362

Published in 2015 by arrangement with G. P. Putnam and Sons, an imprint of Penguin Publishing Group, a division of Penguin Random House LLC

in the United States of America
5 6 7 19 18 17 16 15

THE HUNTING TRIP

A NOVEL OF LOVE AND WAR

WILLIAM E. BUTTERWORTH III

THORNDIKE PRESS
A part of Gale, Cengage Learning

GALE
CENGAGE

Farmington Hills, Mich • San Francis'
Meriden, Conn • M'

Printed
1 2 3 4

AUTHOR'S NOTE

There will be those who are aware that in various lives, I am not only W.E.B. Griffin, author of books for those interested in the military, the police, and spies and counter-spies, but I am also Blakely St. James, authoress of first-person tales for those interested in lesbian romances, and coauthor with Richard Hooker of twelve-thirteenths of the *M*A*S*H* saga, and, using my given name and thirteen other *noms de plume,* have written somewhere around two hundred "published works." And from that they may conclude that this work is autobiographical in nature.

It is not. It is a romance novel. Or at least mostly.

This author's note is written because my mentor, late distinguished novelist and journalist William Bradford Huie, author of *The Americanization of Emily* and a great deal else, told me that he truly regretted not having appended such a *This is fiction!* disclaimer to *Emily*.

The male protagonist in *Emily* was a naval officer who, as Bill had been, was one of the very first Americans to land on Utah Beach on D-Day, June 6, 1944. Because of this, many people thought that *Emily* was an autobiographical account of his conquests, military and romantic, during World War II.

"Nothing could be further from the truth," Mr. Huie declared emphatically. "*Emily* was an entirely fictional romance novel, period."

Mr. Huie told me this at my home in Point Clear, Alabama, where he and a good friend of his had come for a visit. His good friend was a stunning blond British lady he had met during his naval service in England during World War II.

My wife and I agreed that Mr. Huie's friend, whose name was Emily, was even more spectacularly beautiful than Julie Andrews, who some may recall was nominated for an Oscar for her portrayal of Emily in the film adaptation of Mr. Huie's novel *The Americanization of Emily.*

Which was, as this book is, at the risk of repeating myself, a purely fictional story of love and war, and in no sense autobiographical.

Mostly, anyway.

— *William E. Butterworth III*

I
THE PLOT TO FOOL AROUND IN SCOTLAND

[One]

Main Dining Room
The Muddiebay Country Club
Muddiebay, Mississippi
1:20 p.m. Tuesday, September 2, 1975

Mrs. Homer C. (Carol-Anne) Crandall, a very good-looking, trim, silver-haired forty-two-year-old who was the wife of the president of the First National Bank of Muddiebay and president of The Tuesday Luncheon Club, took a second and last teaspoon of her Chocolate Volcano — all she allowed herself; a girl had to have the moral strength to resist the forbidden — consumed it, and then rose to her feet.

After thirty or so seconds, the other women — fifteen of them — stopped talking and looked to the head of the table. With a few exceptions, the women — who usually referred to themselves as "the girls," although just about all of them were as old as Carol-Anne and some older — were dressed much like their president, that is to say in simple black dresses, with a string of pearls, "a bodice piece" of jewelry, and both wedding bands and diamond engagement rings on the third fingers of their left hands.

"I declare this meeting of The Tuesday Luncheon Club open for business," Carol-Anne declared. "Martha-Sue will now lead us in the Pledge of Allegiance."

The girls dutifully rose to their feet, put their right hands on their left bosoms — these ranged in size from monumental to practically nonexistent — and then mumbled along with Mrs. Frederick H. (Martha-Sue) Castleberry as she recited the Pledge of Allegiance.

Mrs. Castleberry, whose husband was a partner in Muddiebay's most prestigious law firm, Tancey, Castleberry, Porter & Lipshutz, then sat down. The girls then, taking their cue from Martha-Sue, resumed their seats.

"Elizabeth-Ann," Carol-Anne asked, "will you please read the minutes of our last meeting?"

Mrs. Cadwallader (Elizabeth-Anne) Howard III — whose husband was president of the Muddiebay Mercantile Company —

rose to her feet and did so. It didn't take her long. Very little had happened at the last meeting.

"Hearing no objection, the minutes are accepted as read," President Carol-Anne announced. "Rachel, honey, will you give us the Treasurer's Report?"

Mrs. Moses (Rachel) Lipshutz, whose husband was also a partner in the Tancey, Castleberry, Porter & Lipshutz law firm, rose to her feet and did so.

As her husband was the only member of Tancey, Castleberry, Porter & Lipshutz of the Hebrew persuasion, Rachel was the only member of The Tuesday Luncheon Club to be so religiously classified.

There were those, generally those who were nursing resentment that they had not been asked to join either Tancey, Castleberry, Porter & Lipshutz or The Tuesday Luncheon Club, who unkindly referred to Moses and Rachel as the "token Jews" of those organizations.

Nothing could be further from the truth, the ladies and the lawyers replied, the latter asking if the name-callers were unfamiliar with Judah Philip Benjamin, who happened to be Jewish, and had been both Secretary of State and Secretary of War of the Confederate States of America and, after narrowly escaping capture with Confederate President Jefferson Davis, Benjamin had made his way to England, where he became legal counsel to the Queen, and the ladies suggesting the name-callers remember that Rachel (then Rachel Cohen) had not only been president of Alfa Phi Omega sorority but also homecoming queen at the beloved alma mater of most Mississippians, "Ole Miss."

Moses Lipshutz found praise among members of a secret organization called the Flat Earth Society, who whispered that Tancey, Castleberry, Porter & Lipshutz were damned lucky to have Lipshutz as a partner, because he was not only smarter than any of the partners but also arguably the smartest lawyer on the Gulf Coast.

The Flat Earth Society, which believes newspapers always tell the truth, that all politicians are honest, and of course that the earth is flat, had a similar opinion about treasurer Rachel Lipshutz of The Tuesday Luncheon Club: She was a natural for the position of money-watcher, as not one of the other girls had ever successfully managed to do a monthly balance of her personal checkbook without professional help.

When Rachel had finished giving the Treasurer's Report, she sat down.

"Hearing no objection, the Treasurer's

Report is accepted as read," President Carol-Anne announced. "We turn now to Old Business. Anyone got anything?"

No one had anything.

"And now, New Business," Carol-Anne said. "Anyone have New Business?"

When she asked that question, the ladies started gathering up their things. Usually asking for New Business signaled the end of the meeting. One of the complaints about The Tuesday Luncheon Club was that the girls never learned about New Business until it was reported as Old Business.

Today was to be different.

"I do, Madam President," one of the ladies said, raising her hand as if seeking permission to use the restroom.

"Yes, Bobbie-Sue?" President Crandall said. "What is it?"

Mrs. Ferdinand J. (Bobbie-Sue) Smith, who was married to the manager of the local branch of Schott & Swabbed, Stockbrokers, was at twenty-seven one of the younger members of The Tuesday Luncheon Club and not considered to be one of the brighter lights in its chandelier.

Bobbie-Sue consulted the notes in her hand, then said, "Carol-Anne — I mean Madam President — I move that The Tuesday Luncheon Club go shopping."

13

That caught the attention of the girls. Many of them immediately sat down.

Carol-Anne made a movement of her hands that suggested she thought Bobbie-Sue hadn't said all she had meant to say.

Bobbie-Sue looked at Carol-Anne for a moment, and then said, "Oh! I mean England. I move that The Tuesday Luncheon Club go shopping in London. London, *England . . .* not the one in Kansas."

The girls who had remained standing now sat down.

"Discussion?" President Crandall said.

Mrs. "King" (Nancy-Jane) Kingman — wife of the proprietor of the King Cadillac, Buick, Chevrolet, and Harley-Davidson Auto Mall — rose to her feet and proclaimed, "My husband is not going to let me go shopping in London. I have to catch ol' King doing something *really* wicked before I get to take my credit card as far as New Orleans."

Carol-Anne made another signal with her hands and again Bobbie-Sue consulted the notes in her hand, shuffling through them until she found what she wanted.

"I have considered that possible obstacle to The Tuesday Luncheon Club going shopping in London, England," she read, "and have come up with the solution to get around that obstacle."

"What?" Nancy-Jane challenged.

Bobbie-Sue again — for a good thirty seconds, which seemed longer — searched her notes for the answer.

"Most of our husbands are wildfowl hunters," Bobbie-Sue read, when she finally found them. "The finest wildfowl, specifically pheasant and grouse, hunting in the world is in Scotland. I suggest that we go to our wildfowl-hunting husbands and tell them that, because of their untiring labors on our behalf, we feel they are entitled to a twelve-day, plus travel time, vacation shooting pheasants and grouse in Scotland, and that we would love for them to do so, providing we are allowed to go with them at least as far as London."

"I didn't think she was that smart," Mrs. Jackson ("Bitsy") Skyler whispered to Nancy-Jane. Bitsy was forty-three, five feet ten, weighed 178 pounds, and was married to Muddiebay's most prestigious ophthalmologist, who stood five-three and barely got the scale needle to touch 130.

"You mean the idea," Nancy-Jane whispered back, "or her using words of more than one syllable?"

"Both."

"Bitsy, even the dimmest bulb provides

some light."

"Well, she's right about this," Bitsy replied. "If there's anything in the world that'd get my Jack out of his office — and me to London — it's him getting to shoot pheasants in Scotland. He's almost as bad as Randy Bruce. If it's got feathers on it, he wants to shoot it."

"Yeah."

The phrase *almost as bad as Randy Bruce,* making reference to Randolph C. Bruce, chairman of the board of RCB Holdings, Inc., was often used around Muddiebay's upper social circles, and it was not only used to describe his fondness for hunting.

"What the hell, let's give it a shot," Bitsy said, and raised her hand.

"Yes, Bitsy?" President Crandall called.

"Carol-Anne, I think Bobbie-Sue has a wonderful idea, and I move that a committee be appointed herewith, with you, Madam President, as chairperson, to get The Tuesday Luncheon Club to London."

"Second the motion, call for the vote," Nancy-Jane called.

The motion carried.

So did the motion to adjourn.

[Two]

Some of the ladies went home.

Bitsy and Nancy-Jane went to the bar, where both ordered gin martinis, no vegetables.

President Crandall walked out of the building onto the veranda and then off the veranda onto the golf course driving range. There was no one on the driving range, but she walked to the end of it anyway, and once there found a telephone.

It was answered on the second ring: "What?"

"I thought you would want to know, my precious, that I have just been appointed chairperson of The Tuesday Luncheon Club Committee to Arrange the Hunt in Scotland."

"Well, I'll be a monkey's EXPLETIVE DELETED!! uncle," Randy Bruce, with whom Carol-Anne was having her very first affair *ever,* replied. "You and the dimwit carried it off, eh? You get both ears and the EXPLETIVE DELETED!! tail, baby!"

Carol-Anne just tingled when Randy talked dirty, as he often did. And when he talked her into talking dirty — which she was now doing with far less self-consciousness than when she started — she tingled even more.

"I was thinking, Precious, that maybe we could get together and celebrate."

"You mean today?" Randy asked incredulously. "This afternoon?"

"No, next June," Carol-Anne said, a bit petulantly.

"No EXPLETIVE DELETED!! way, baby. I'm going over to Foggy Point to bust some birds with Phil."

Mr. Bruce spent at least one afternoon a week — and sometimes two or three — shooting skeet, trap, Crazy Quail, or all three, with his good friend Philip W. Williams III, who resided on the grounds of the Foggy Point Country Club, which was some forty miles distant across Muddiebay Bay.

Carol-Anne did not much like Mr. Williams, and not only because he was a EXPLETIVE DELETED!! Yankee.

"I'd really like to see you, my precious," she said.

"Yeah, me too, but that's the way the EXPLETIVE DELETED!! ball bounces."

Carol-Anne decided to be gracious.

"Well, I'm sure Phil will be happy when you tell him I got your plan to go to Scotland off to a good start."

"Are you out of your EXPLETIVE DELETED!! mind? If Phil even suspected that

18

just one woman was going along, even to do the laundry, I couldn't get him on the EXPLETIVE DELETED!! airplane at the point of a EXPLETIVE DELETED!! bayonet."

"Sorry, my darling. I forgot that."

"Give me a ring tomorrow and I'll see if I can fit you into my schedule."

Randy hung up.

Carol-Anne then went to the bar and ordered a vodka martini — "Stir, don't shake" — with itsy-bitsy white onions.

[Three]

The Warren

2700 Muddiebay International Airport
  Boulevard

Muddiebay, Mississippi

1:30 p.m. Friday, September 5, 1975

Three days after The Tuesday Luncheon Club's Tuesday Luncheon, Carol-Anne turned the nose of her Mercedes-Benz off Muddiebay International Airport Boulevard and onto the ramp leading to the underground garage of The Warren.

She desperately hoped that no one she knew had seen her doing so. She would have been severely taxed to explain what she was doing at The Warren, an enormous (eight-hundred-odd apartments) complex built to service the employees and customers of Muddiebay Ship Building & Dry Dock & Cruise Ship Repair & Fumigation Company, Inc. (MSB&DD&CSR&FC, Inc.).

MSB&DD&CSR&FC, Inc., was a fairly recent addition to the industrial base of Muddiebay, but its predecessor company, the Muddiebay Ship Building & Dry Dock Company, Inc. (MSB&DDC, Inc.) dated back to the First World War, and its predecessor company, the Muddiebay Ship Building Company (MSB), traced its history back to the War for Southern Independence, sometimes called The Civil War.

MSB&DDC, Inc., had gone belly-up twenty-five years ago, at which time it had fallen into the hands of RCB Holdings, Inc., which bought out the stockholders for peanuts. RCB Holdings, in turn, had sold the stock to Mr. Randolph C. Bruce for peanut shells, permitting RCB Holdings, which was wholly owned by Mr. Bruce, to take a very nice tax loss.

Mr. Bruce was not at all interested in shipbuilding or, truth to tell, that much interested in legally questionable tax dodges, but rather in the several hundred acres of tidal lands surrounding the shipyard that had been in the hands of the company since the days of the MSB Company.

They were absolutely useless for any commercial purpose, consisting as they did of hundreds of tiny islands that the waters of Muddiebay Bay inundated twice daily with the tides.

The one thing the tiny islands were good for was as construction sites for duck blinds, which is why Mr. Bruce had bought MSB& DDC, Inc.

He proceeded to build blinds and make other improvements, which gave him the largest private duck-shooting area in North America.

He thought that eventually some innocent soul would come along onto whom he could unload MSB&DDC, Inc. — less the tidewater acreage — and recoup his initial investment. Whatever could be said about Mr. Bruce, and a good deal was, no one ever suggested that ol' Randy didn't know how to turn a buck.

Four years previous to the events to be chronicled in this romance novel, he thought such an innocent soul had indeed come.

Señor Pancho Gonzales of Miami contacted him and said that if the price was right, he might be induced to take the ruins of what had been the physical plant of MSB&DDC, Inc., off Mr. Bruce's hands.

No one ever justly accused ol' Randy of

ever being asleep at the switch, either. Randy had the greatest admiration for the ethnic minority — of which he suspected Pancho was a member — which now owned eighty percent of Florida from Key West to Palm Beach — the Miami-Cubans who had escaped their Communist homeland with nothing but five-dollar bills and the shirts on their backs.

Randy put Tancey, Castleberry, Porter & Lipshutz to work finding out just who Pancho was.

A week later, Moses Lipshutz bought Randy lunch at the Muddiebay International Trade Club and announced that in exchange for a check in an amount that made Randy wince, he would tell him what he had learned about Señor Gonzales.

Randy promptly wrote the check. Moses's advice had always been more than worth the money Randy had paid for it in the past.

"Don't look so unhappy, Randy," Moses said. "When I do your income taxes this year, my fees will appear thereon as a fully deductible business expense."

Moses then told Randy that he had learned that Señor Gonzales had indeed escaped Castro with nothing but a five-dollar bill and the shirt on his back. And that he now owned a shipyard in Miami, engaged almost entirely in the maintenance, repair, and fumigation of the armada of cruise ships now plying the Gulf of Mexico and the Caribbean Sea.

The enterprise was profitable, Moses reported, but not as profitable as Mr. Gonzales thought it could be if he could move the operation elsewhere, and get out from under the taxes of the City of Miami, Broward County, and the Sovereign State of Florida. Not to mention the outrageous wages he had to pay his unionized workers for standing around with their thumbs inserted in their ears, noses, and other bodily orifices.

Due diligence on Mr. Gonzales's part had revealed there was a derelict shipyard perfectly suited for his needs in Muddiebay, Mississippi, which he could probably steal, as its owner would most likely be some ignorant Mississippi shit-kicker.

"Moses, why don't you and Rachel take a few days' vacation in Palm Beach? As my guests. And while you're there have a chat with Pancho. I'll go along with anything you come up with so long as I get to keep my duck blinds. And if you can make a deal, take ten percent from my end for your trouble."

"Fifteen percent, and I'll take care of incidentals."

"Done."

The result of that luncheon meeting was the Muddiebay Ship Building & Dry Dock & Cruise Ship Repair & Fumigation Company, Inc., Pancho Gonzales, president and chief executive officer, Randolph C. Bruce, treasurer, and Moses Lipshutz, vice president and general counsel.

The dry details of who now owned how much of this new enterprise would little interest those who purchased this tome for its romance, so they will not be chronicled here.

But it should be noted that Mr. Moses told his wife, in the privacy of their bedroom, that while it was true a Jew could outwit an Arab at the bargaining table, the Jew she was married to had all of his legal and negotiating skills taxed almost to the breaking point when he sat down with Randy's Miami-Cuban to play Let's Make a Deal!

It had immediately become apparent to the executives of MSB&DD&CSR&FC, Inc., that one of their first problems was going to be housing for the many employees of the shipyard and for the crews of the cruise ships who could not stay aboard their vessels while they were being serviced, repaired, and/or fumigated.

The Bruce Construction Company almost immediately began construction of the enormous apartment complex built on land acquired by RCB Holdings from the Bruce Land & Timber Company, Incorporated.

The precise details of this similarly would be of little interest to those hoping to read of romance, and will not be recounted here.

But, *en passant,* the architect of the project prepared his plans by going to the nearest 8 Dollar Motel, which was thirty-seven miles distant from Muddiebay. He took careful measurements of the 8 Dollar Motel's "Luxury Suites" that rented for $10.95 per night. He reduced the room dimensions by twenty-five percent and used them for the plans of the apartment complex.

In doing so, he hadn't considered the ramifications of reducing the size of the bathrooms by twenty-five percent. The result of this oversight was that while the restrooms in the apartment complex did provide the necessary sanitary accommodations, they did so in a rather crowded environment like those of the unisex facilities on airliners.

The executives of MSB&DD&CSR&FC,

Inc., on reviewing the plans, instructed the architect to make a few minor changes.

In order to explain this, the reader must think of the project as a three-story structure in the shape of the letter *E* lying on its side, the open side facing the waters of Muddiebay Bay. Three stories only because four or more stories would require elevators and elevators cost money.

The architect was instructed to merge the six suites on the third-floor bay side of each part of the *E* into one suite. In other words, where there had been eighteen "Bay Side Apartments" there would now be three. There were now to be elevators running from the basement garage to what were going to be the three Executive Apartments. They would not stop at intermediate floors, but serve only the Executive Apartments.

One of these was assigned to Señor Gonzales, the second to Mr. Lipshutz, and the third to Mr. Bruce. They provided a place for the MSB&DD&CSR&FC, Inc., executives to discreetly entertain their guests. Señor Gonzales's and Mr. Bruce's guests were almost invariably of the gentle sex, while Mr. Lipshutz's guests were invariably gentlemen in their middle years who liked to get together for a few friendly hands of high-stakes poker and could see no good reason why they should have to give a cut of their pots to the EXPLETIVE DELETED!! Yankees and Cowboys who operated the casinos in Biloxi and Ocean Springs in order to do so.

The Executive Apartments were furnished on a "cost be damned" basis. In Señor Gonzales's case, this meant — in addition to other amenities — a mirror ceiling in the master bedroom. Mr. Lipshutz's apartment had a pool table. And Mr. Bruce's had an indoor range at which he could fire .22 caliber shot cartridges at moving duck targets.

On Carol-Anne's third visit to Mr. Bruce's apartment — the first two had been both brief and entirely devoted to the satisfaction of what the Book of Common Prayer terms "the sinful lusts of the flesh" — she asked Randy why the apartment complex was called The Warren.

"It fits," he replied.

"I don't understand."

Randy had exhaled audibly in resignation.

"Okay," he said. "One day I was researching CuNi —"

Carol-Anne felt a tingle.

"Oh, you *wicked* boy, you!" she said, and stuck her tongue in his ear.

Carol-Anne thought that she understood

what her lover was researching: instruction in the techniques of an absolutely wicked sexual practice that she would never have dreamed, before Randy, of allowing anyone to practice on her body but now seemed a quite attractive activity.

She erred.

Randy was researching a supplier of piping with a certain percentage of copper and nickel in its makeup at a lesser price than he was now paying for it. Such piping, called CuNi in the construction business, resists the corrosive effects of seawater more effectively than non-CuNi piping.

"Control yourself," Randy ordered. "You want me to answer your question or not?"

"I can hardly wait, my precious, imaginative lover!"

"And there it was, Cuniculture."

"I don't know what that means, Precious, but from the way it sounds, I'm all for it," Carol-Anne, now tingling all over, said. "Culture is my middle name."

"It means commercial trade in rabbits," Randy explained. "And you know what they call a place where a lot of rabbits live?"

Carol-Anne confessed her ignorance.

"A warren," Randy said. "Get it?"

Carol-Anne had felt the tingling stop and quickly excused herself to go to the restroom. She was determined that Randy not see the tears of disappointment roll down her cheeks.

[Four]

Carol-Anne had a dual mission at The Warren today.

After bouncing around on the waterbed with Randy for twenty-two exciting minutes, Carol-Anne turned to the second.

"All the arrangements for our trip to Scotland are in place, my precious."

"It's about EXPLETIVE DELETED!! time," Randy replied.

In truth, Carol-Anne was rather well-known for her skill in organizing things. This was in large measure due to her ability to get people who knew how to do things to do them for her, whereupon she would take the credit.

She explained to Randy that she had had a word with Mary-Louise Frathingham, whose husband, Amos, was proprietor of Muddiebay Exotic & Exciting Vacations Travel, Inc. Mary-Louise had long hungered to be asked to join the Ladies of The Tuesday Luncheon Club. Amos had long lusted after more business from both the First National Bank of Muddiebay and the MSB&DD&CSR&FC, Inc.

Carol-Anne did not have to remind Mary-Louise that she was president of The Tuesday Luncheon Club, or that her husband was president of First National, as she already knew.

But Carol-Anne did say that all three of the senior executives of MSB&DD& CSR&FC, Inc. — Mr. Moses Lipshutz, Señor Pancho Gonzales, and Mr. Randolph C. Bruce — would be going to Scotland. Mr. Lipshutz would be accompanied by his wife, Señor Gonzales by a niece, and Mr. Bruce by an unnamed friend, gender not specified, who was going to get the trip as a birthday present.

ME&EVT, Inc., rose to the challenge Carol-Anne gave them.

With the exception of arrangements for the actual pheasant and grouse shooting, which would take place on the property of friends of Mr. Bruce, ME&EVT, Inc., would handle every other detail of the jaunt from the moment the travelers arrived at Muddiebay International Airport until they went the other way through the airport doors on their return.

Although there would not actually be twenty persons on the trip, ME&EVT, Inc., had planned the trip as if there would be. Using a trick known to the travel trade as a

Twenty-Plus-Two, ME&EVT, Inc., would guarantee the purchase of twenty business-class seats on all airliners involved, ten double-occupancy rooms in the five-star Claridge's Hotel in London, ten double-occupancy rooms in the two-star Dungaress Royal Hotel in Dungaress, Scotland — the best available in Dungaress, Population 5,602 — and two ten-passenger motor coaches to move everybody around wherever they were to high-class restaurants, stores, et cetera.

In exchange for throwing all this business at the airlines, hotels, high-class restaurants, stores, et cetera, two "travel professionals" would be permitted to get the same services at no charge, plus a finder's fee of ten percent of the purchase price on whatever the shoppers bought. This is what the Plus-Two meant.

Mary-Louise and Amos Frathingham were going to join the jaunt out of the goodness of their hearts, and at no cost to themselves.

II
ACTIVITY BEFORE THE TRIP

[One]

102 Country Club Road
Foggy Point Country Club
Foggy Point, Mississippi
9:30 a.m. Sunday, September 7, 1975

Phil Williams — who was forty-five years old, weighed 185 pounds, was not quite six feet tall, and was a victim of early-stage male pattern baldness — was sitting at his computer with a six-inch-long light brown cigar clamped in his teeth when the telephone on the credenza behind his desk rang.

Phil said, "Oh, shit!" and reached for the receiver.

Williams was an author — the difference between a writer and an author is that the former is just about anyone with a typewriter and the latter someone who not only has actually published a book, or books, but manages to support himself with the proceeds therefrom — and really disliked being distracted when he was plying his trade.

Telephone calls are well-known for their ability to distract. Knowing this, Williams had two telephone lines installed in his domicile at 102 Country Club Road. One had five extensions scattered around his three-bedroom, four-bath, pool-with-pool-house, three-car-garage, 3,100-square-foot home, and the second was installed only in his home office.

Moreover, the number of the instrument in his office was not only not published in the telephone book but was known to only a very few people. They included his son, Philip Wallingford Williams IV, known as "Little Phil," who was, incredible as it might sound, the food critic for *The Dallas Afternoon Gazette,* the largest newspaper in Texas, and the fifth largest in the nation; Phil III's editor, Chauncey S. "Steel" Hymen, vice president, publisher, and editor in chief of J. K. Perkins & Brothers, Publishers since 1812; his literary legal counsel, the legendary Gustave "Rabbi" Warblerman; his literary agent Jennifer "Big Bad Jennie" Waldron; and a very few friends and acquaintances, including Bobby "Fender" Bender, proprietor of Foggy Point Garage & Good As New Used Parts, who maintained Phil's twenty-year-old Jaguar.

"What?" Phil snapped into the telephone.

"Why don't we go to Scotland for ten days and shoot some pheasants with Bertie?" his caller responded.

Phil recognized his caller to be Randolph "Randy" Bruce, as much from the question as the sound of his voice.

Among things said about Mr. Bruce was that he owned half of downtown Muddiebay and that if one of God's creatures had fur or feathers, and wasn't a dog or a milk cow, ol' Randy hungered to shoot it. Muddiebay (population 260,000) was twenty miles distant across Muddiebay Bay from Foggy Point.

"When?"

"A week from tomorrow."

Phil considered the proposal for ten seconds, and then said, "I'll have to ask the Angry Austrian."

The Angry Austrian was Mrs. Brunhilde W. Williams, a native of Vienna, Austria, who had been Phil's wife for almost twenty-six years, which sometimes seemed longer. Much, much longer.

"So ask her."

"I am never so foolish as to awaken the AA," Phil replied. "When she does so herself, I will ask and get back to you."

"Come by the house at one-thirty. Our plane leaves Muddiebay International at quarter to three," Randy ordered, and hung up.

Randy was prone to give orders and to rudeness, both of which Phil understood and to a degree tolerated. Randy was not the first rich socialite he had known. There had been a plethora of them in his youth at the seven boarding schools Phil had attended, and then been sent home from.

[Two]

Shortly after ten, Phil thought that by now his wife would have arisen and be in the kitchen having her breakfast. He went there to see if that was the case.

It was.

Brunhilde was sitting at the kitchen table with "Miss Grace," full name Mrs. Grace Hail, the septuagenarian African-American woman who had been in their employ since they had come to Foggy Point twenty-odd years before.

They had not lived on the grounds of the Foggy Point Country Club then, but in a nice, much simpler home in the adjacent town of Goodhope, Mississippi, to which they had moved when Phil had been discharged from the United States Army

Advanced Marksmanship Unit at Fort Benning, Georgia.

That house, on Creek Drive in Goodhope, had been purchased on a No Money Down thirty-year mortgage guaranteed by the Veterans Administration. It had three bedrooms, two baths, a one-car garage, and in the backyard, instead of a swimming pool, a shallow stream that flowed eventually into Muddiebay Bay, and thus the source of the street name.

"Good morning," Phil said, when he walked into the kitchen of 102 Country Club Road, the French doors of which opened upon the swimming pool, the pool house, and the gazebo that sheltered the gas-flamed barbecue grill, and the fairways beyond of the Foggy Point Country Club.

"Good morning," Miss Grace replied. "Can I fetch you a cup of coffee?"

Brunhilde said nothing.

Brunhilde was blond, five feet six, weighed 135 pounds, and was nine months older than her husband. There was a dancer's grace about her, which was not surprising, as she had begun the study of ballet when she was six years old, and given up the art only when she became pregnant with their first child, also named Brunhilde.

"No, thanks, Grace," Phil said. "I'm

36

already coffee'd-up."

Phil looked at his wife.

She looked away.

"Randy wants me to go to Scotland for ten days with him next week to shoot pheasants with Bertie," Phil said. "Is that all right with you?"

"I don't give a good EXPLETIVE DELETED!! where you go," Brunhilde said.

"You ought to be ashamed of yourself, talking to Mr. Phil like that," Miss Grace said.

"EXPLETIVE DELETED!! him," Brunhilde said.

"I'll take that to mean I can go," Phil said.

Brunhilde snorted.

Phil walked out of the kitchen.

Brunhilde had become increasingly difficult over the last several years or so, something Phil attributed primarily to two things. First, she had entered "the change of life." As one of the corollaries of that, she had put on some weight, and that to a ballet dancer is akin to having leprosy.

Second, Brunhilde was suffering from Nearly Empty Nest Syndrome.

Brunhilde Williams, their oldest child, had eloped two years before to marry Robert Brown, whom she had met when he was the editor of *Mississippi Traveler,* the university newspaper, the day after he graduated.

"Brownie," as he was called, had accepted a job as a reporter on the Jackson *Afternoon Gazette* and Brunhilde, who could not bear the thought of being separated from him, had married Brownie, even though she knew this would probably drive both of her parents up the wall.

Although the marriage seemed to be working well — Brownie had become assistant state editor, and Brunhilde was now assistant society editor — Brunhilde remained terribly unhappy about her daughter.

Little Phil was of course now in Dallas.

And only Franz Josef — named after Brunhilde's late father and also after the former head of the Austro-Hungarian Empire — remained at home. "Franzel," as Brunhilde called her baby, spent just about all of his time, depending on the season, on the tennis courts or at the swimming pool of Foggy Point's Grand Hotel.

One of Phil's unlikely friends was Professor James K. Strongmensch, who, although he had never graduated from college, had twenty-seven honorary doctorates. Strongmensch had published forty-odd books (the titles of most of which Phil didn't understand) and was simultaneously both professor of philosophy and professor of psychiatry at Tulane University in New Orleans.

Jim was aware of Brunhilde's problems, and had told Phil there wasn't much that could be done for her except to wait for nature to take its course. The alternative was for Brunhilde to take mind-altering drugs, which (a) probably wouldn't work and (b) were liable to be addictive.

So Phil waited for nature to take its course.

[Three]

Phil went from the kitchen to his office, and there photocopied what he had written so far on his current book in progress.

Twice before when he had been out of town, Brunhilde had, in innocent curiosity, turned on his Dictaphone to find out about his latest work and in the process had somehow erased it. Phil believed this was done innocently, of course, just as be believed in the good fairy and that the earth was flat, but he was determined it would not happen again.

He put one of the copies into his briefcase and took the other with him to the gun room, a concrete block structure with a steel door that he had built in the rear of the garage when he bought the house. Sometime after Brunhilde had begun to act strangely, he had replaced the original door to the gun room with one that was both stronger and had a combination lock.

Phil didn't think that Brunhilde really would carry through with her threat to go into the gun room, get one of his EXPLETIVE DELETED!! guns and use it to blow the EXPLETIVE DELETED!! off the next EXPLETIVE DELETED!! golfer whose EXPLETIVE DELETED!! ball crashed into the EXPLETIVE DELETED!! windows of the EXPLETIVE DELETED!! pool house.

But, as they say, better safe than sorry.

Professor Strongmensch had described the gun room as a "miniature arsenal" and his description was accurate. It was full of weapons. One wall held the "long guns," mostly shotguns, but also a dozen rifles of different calibers. Another held more than twenty-five pistols of all shapes and sizes. Sturdy wooden worktables held rows of shotgun shell reloading machines, and across the room from them were the presses, tools, scales, and other equipment necessary to "reload the brass" of all the calibers of the rifles and handguns hanging on the walls.

This might suggest to some, especially readers of romance novels, such as this, that

Phil was something of a "gun nut" who drooled and breathed deeply as he fondled his instruments of death, or that he was one of those rural boobs "who cling to their guns" for no good reason, to more or less quote a herein unnamed former instructor of constitutional law who later entered politics.

The truth is far less dramatic. His association with firearms began in his sixteenth year, on the day he was loaded aboard the New York City–bound train of the New York, New Haven & Hartford Railroad by the Reverend James Ferneyhough Fitzhugh, D.D., who had just expelled him from St. Malachi's School.

"Philip Wallingford Williams the Third," Dr. Fitzhugh had told him, "by stealing Miss Bridget O'Malley's intimate undergarments and then hoisting them to the top of our flagpole and then cutting the rope, you have brought shame upon Saint Malachi's School, the Protestant Episcopal Church, and the entire fraternity of Northeastern U.S. boarding schools named after saints. I am left with no alternative but to give you the boot."

On the train, Phil had naturally wondered where his life would now take him.

He considered several possibilities, of

course, but it never entered his mind that he would one day become a world-class rifle, pistol, and shotgun marksman. At sixteen, the only firearms he had ever fired in his life had been the .22 caliber rifles with which one could fire at movable little duck targets at Coney Island in the hope of shooting well enough to win a stuffed animal. (*Five shots for only a dollar!* the carnies barked.)

And, if this needs to be said, although even at that tender age he had quite an imagination, it never entered his mind that he would one day become a special agent of the U.S. Army Counterintelligence Corps, or marry a dancer of the Corps de Ballet of the Vienna State Opera, or become a *Wall Street Journal* and *New York Times* best-selling novelist.

What he did on the train to Manhattan that day was consider his options for the immediate future. He decided they did not include going home to face the tearful wrath of his mother in South Orange, New Jersey. He literally shuddered at the thought of what would follow once his mother stopped weeping and screaming long enough to solicit the support of her husband in dealing with him.

His mother was married to Keyes J. Michaels, M.D. Dr. Michaels was a psychiatrist she had met professionally when she was in the process of seeking a divorce from Phil's father, P. Wallingford Williams, Jr.

Once she had married Dr. Michaels, which she did two days after her divorce became final, she prevailed upon him to "help" Phil, who even then was having trouble accepting authority figures such as teachers, guidance counselors, and headmasters of schools named after saints.

Phil knew that if he went home to South Orange, he would shortly thereafter find himself prone on Dr. Michaels's couch, and the exchange between them would go something like this, as the good doctor sucked noisily on his pipe:

Dr. M: Well, *Slurp,* Philip, my boy, *Slurp,* why do you think *Slurp* you wanted to hoist *Slurp* Bridget O'Malley's intimate undergarments *Slurp* to the top of the flagpole? *Slurp.*

Phil (knowing that "It seemed like a good idea at the time" would not be a satisfactory answer): Doctor, I just don't know.

Dr. M: Tell me, Phil. *Slurp* Do you spend a lot of time thinking about *Slurp* panties,

43

Slurp brassieres, *Slurp* and other such things?

Phil (having decided either "Yes" or "No" in response to the question is going to further excite the doctor's curiosity, says nothing).

Dr. M: Phil, my boy. *Slurp* How can I *Slurp* help you if you *Slurp* refuse to help yourself? *Slurp* Why don't we start over? *Slurp.*

And from there it would go downhill.

Phil knew this because this would not be the first time his mother had asked the man she called "My Own Sigmund Freud" to help her only son.

He thought again about joining the Army, leaving his shame and the painful wrath of his family behind him for all time. He knew what was involved with that. He had thought of joining the Army twice before, first when he'd been booted from St. Charles's School (for smoking in his room) and again when he'd been sent home from St. Timothy's (for selling beer and cigarettes in his room during the poker game he was running).

He hadn't had to go through with signing up then — although the first time he'd gotten as far as changing the date on his birth certificate to make him a year older than was the case — because other schools had given him a second chance. But he'd run out of schools willing to give him a second chance.

This time it was the Army!

When he got off the train in New York, he caught another to Newark, New Jersey. He went from Pennsylvania Station to the Public Service Building. That was sort of a misnomer for the latter. The Public Service Company was a for-profit business enterprise that did very well, indeed, selling electricity, gas, and bus and trolley service to the public of New Jersey. They had a monopoly on all four services.

He knew this because his mother's father was vice president, legal, of the Public Service Company. He also knew that in his grandfather's secretary's desk was an embossing device that punched the fact that she was a Notary Public of the State of New Jersey into sheets of paper.

Phil "borrowed" the Notary Public stamping tool and a dozen or so sheets of paper and returned to Manhattan. He went to his father's apartment at 590 Park Avenue, got the doorman to admit him, and once inside wrote two letters on his father's typewriter.

One was to his father, in which he said he

45

realized he had shamed the family more than enough, and was going to join the Army to spare the family any further pain. The second was To Whom This May Concern.

The second said the undersigned had no objection to the enlistment of his son Philip W. Williams III in the Army. He signed the letter P. Wallingford Williams, Jr., and Marjorie B. Alexander, Notary Public of the State of New Jersey, and applied the stamp to it.

It took him three tries to get it right, but finally it looked legitimate.

He took the letter and the previously altered birth certificate from where he'd hidden it in a copy of *War and Peace* on his father's bookshelves, and went back to Newark, this time to the Recruiting Office in the Post Office Building.

He didn't get to join the Army that day. But the Army put him up overnight, and the next morning, after a physical examination, swore him in and put him on a bus for Fort Dix, New Jersey.

It wasn't until his father returned to Manhattan three days later that his family learned what he had done. A family conference was held on how to get him out of the Army — "My God, he's only sixteen!" —

as the Army says that, twenty fifty-five hours.

At that hour, Sergeant Andrew Jackson McCullhay, one of Phil's instructors, walked down the barracks aisle en route to the switch that would turn off the lights at twenty-one hundred.

As he passed the bunk to which PVT WILLIAMS P had been assigned, he saw something that both surprised and distressed him. PVT WILLIAMS P had somehow managed to completely disassemble his U.S. Rifle, Cal. 30, M-1 Garand. All of its many parts were spread out over his bunk.

In the gentle, paternal tone of voice for which Basic Training Instructors are so well known, Sergeant McCullhay inquired "EX-PLETIVE DELETED!! head, what the EXPLE-TIVE DELETED!! have you done to your EXPLETIVE DELETED!! rifle?"

"Sergeant, sir," PVT WILLIAMS P replied, "I have disassembled it."

"So I see," Sergeant McCullhay replied. "Now show me, EXPLETIVE DELETED!! head, how you're going to get your EXPLE-TIVE DELETED!! Garand back together before I turn the EXPLETIVE DELETED!! lights off in four minutes and fifteen EXPLE-TIVE DELETED!! seconds."

"Yes, sir, Sergeant," PVT WILLIAMS P

51

replied, and proceeded to do so with two minutes and five seconds to spare.

"I'll be a EXPLETIVE DELETED!!," Sergeant McCullhay said. "EXPLETIVE DELETED!! head, you're a EXPLETIVE DELETED!! genius!"

"Yes, sir, Sergeant," PVT WILLIAMS P said.

He had already learned the most important rule of all in the Army: *Never Argue with a Sergeant.*

Sergeant McCullhay was genuinely impressed with the speed with which PVT WILLIAMS P had reassembled his stripped Garand, especially after he timed himself at the task. When, that same night, he told his buddies at the sergeants' club what he had seen, they didn't believe him.

One of his fellow noncommissioned officers made a challenge: "I've got ten EXPLETIVE DELETED!! dollars that says your kid can't completely disassemble and reassemble a EXPLETIVE DELETED!! Garand in less than five minutes."

As a result of this challenge — it was a challenge, not a "bet" or a "wager," as betting and wagering are violations of Army Regulations and those who do so are subject to court-martial — PVT WILLIAMS P was awakened after midnight by Sergeant Mc-

Cullhay.

He and the Garand rifle with which he had been sleeping were taken to McCullhay's room in the barracks, where five noncommissioned officers were waiting to challenge Sergeant McCullhay's assertions *vis-à-vis* the speed with which PVT WILLIAMS P could dis- and re-assemble a Garand.

After PVT WILLIAMS P had done so, which made Sergeant McCullhay fifty dollars richer than he had been earlier in the evening, the sergeant was in a very good mood.

"You can get in your bunk now, EXPLETIVE DELETED!! head," he said. "And you can skip the Zero Five Hundred Roll Call and Physical Training. I wouldn't want you to hurt your beautiful EXPLETIVE DELETED!! hands doing EXPLETIVE DELETED!! push-ups."

[Five]

U.S. Army Reception Center
Fort Dix, New Jersey
Monday, November 18, 1946

During the next five weeks, whenever and wherever Sergeant McCullhay could find gullible souls wishing to challenge what he claimed for PVT WILLIAMS P's dis- and re-assemble times for the Garand, PVT WILLIAMS P did so.

On the side of three different roads during fifteen-mile hikes. Half a dozen times in the Regimental Mess Hall. Once in the back of the Regimental Chapel while the chaplain was warning the trainees about loose women. And once while wearing a gas mask in the tear gas chamber.

But then it was actually time for the trainees to fire the U.S. Rifle, Cal. 30, M-1 Garand.

This took place on one of the one-hundred-yard KD ranges. Some weeks later, PVT WILLIAMS P learned that KD stood for "Known Distance."

There were twenty firing positions on the range and, one hundred yards distant from them, twenty bull's-eye targets. The targets were on frames that rose and fell on command from behind an earthen berm.

The procedure was explained in detail before the trainees were issued the one round of ammunition, *Cartridge, Rifle, Cal. .30, AntiPersonnel, w/168 grain projectile,* with which they would fire their first shot.

Once twenty shooters were in the prone position, with a *Strap, Leather, Rifle* attaching them firmly to their rifles, and had a cadre-man lying beside them, the range officer would issue over a loudspeaker several commands:

"The flag is up!"

Whereupon a red flag in the target area would be hauled to the top of a flagpole.

"The flag is waving!"

Whereupon another flag, this one checkered, would be waved in the target pit, and the bull's-eye targets would be raised.

"The flag is down! Commence firing!"

Whereupon the checkered flag would drop out of sight and the shooters were free to fire.

This required that the cadre-man hand his shooter the one cartridge he was trusted to have, and for the shooter to then insert the cartridge into the chamber of his Garand, and then to close the action of the Garand, which would make the Garand ready to fire once the safety on the front of the trigger guard was pushed out of the way.

The trick here was to get one's thumb out of the way after depressing the magazine guide in the open action of the Garand before the bolt slammed closed.

PVT WILLIAMS P had no problem with this, but eleven of the twenty shooters on the line already had what was known as "M-1 Thumb," a physical injury, the symptoms of which were a black (or missing) thumbnail, and smashed tissue in the thumbnail area.

After the cartridge was chambered, the shooter was to disengage the safety by pushing it forward in the trigger guard. Then he was to align his sights on the bull's-eye, take a deep breath, exhale half, check his sight alignment, and then slowly, gently squeeze the trigger until the weapon fired. He then, after inspecting the now-open chamber of his rifle to make sure it was indeed open, would lay his weapon down and wait for further instructions.

When the sixty seconds allotted for the firing of the trainees' first shots had expired, the range officer would announce, repeating the command twice, to make sure everyone heard him: "The flag is down! Cease firing!"

Whereupon the red flag would come down from its pole, and the targets disappear downward into the berm, where they would be marked.

If the bullet had struck any part of the target at all, including the frame, a "peg" would be inserted in the bullet hole. This was a ten-inch black dot exactly the size of the bull's-eye in the center of the target. When the target was raised, the shooter could see where his bullet had hit.

In case the target pullers could find no bullet hole anywhere, they would raise and wave a red flag, called "Maggie's Drawers," to tell the shooter he had completely missed the target.

When the range officer completed the series of commands ending with "Commence firing," the cadre-man next to PVT WILLIAMS P handed him the cartridge he was to fire with a little paternal, or perhaps brotherly, advice: "EXPLETIVE DELETED!! head, if you EXPLETIVE DELETED!! up your EXPLETIVE DELETED!! thumb loading this, I will kick your EXPLETIVE DELETED!! from here to EXPLETIVE DELETED!! Trenton."

Sergeant Andrew Jackson McCullhay feared that "M-1 Thumb" would keep PVT WILLIAMS P from being able to manipulate M-1 parts with the extraordinary facility that was making him so much money.

PVT WILLIAMS P loaded his rifle without harm to his thumb, lined up the sights, and squeezed the trigger. The recoil, while not pleasant, was not nearly as bone-shattering as Sergeant McCullhay had led him to believe it would be. He checked to see that the action was indeed open, and then laid the rifle down.

The sixty-second firing period expired.

The range officer proclaimed the flag to be down, and ordered "Cease firing!"

The targets dropped down behind the berm.

One by one, they rose again.

The first several to rise had pegs on them, which showed where the bullet had stuck. Some were actually within a foot or so of the bull's-eye, but most were scattered all over the target. Two marksmen had shot the frame.

PVT WILLIAMS P's target rose, but he could see no peg on it, and he braced for the shaming Maggie's Drawers, which would soon flutter to announce his lousy marksmanship to the world.

No Maggie's Drawers fluttered before his target, although they proclaimed the shame of seven other marksmen.

"What the EXPLETIVE DELETED!!?" Sergeant McCullhay asked rhetorically, and then raised his voice. "Tell the EXPLETIVE DELETED!! in the pit to mark EXPLETIVE DELETED!! Number Seven."

A minute or so later, the range officer appeared at Firing Point Number Seven.

"The pit reports Number Seven is in the X Ring," he reported. "Obviously a fluke. Have your shooter fire again."

This time PVT WILLIAMS P had the

entire flag-is-up-and-down procedure all to himself. He was given a cartridge, loaded it without damage to his thumb, lined up the sights, et cetera, et cetera, and in military parlance, "squeezed off another round."

This time the pit again reported "In the X Ring."

PVT WILLIAMS P had no idea what the X Ring was, but he was shortly to learn that it was sort of a bull's-eye within the bull's-eye, a three-inch circle in the center of the ten-inch bull's-eye.

"I'll be a EXPLETIVE DELETED!!," Sergeant McCullhay exclaimed.

"Very possibly, Sergeant," the range officer said. "But let us not jump to a hasty conclusion. One in the X Ring may be a fluke. Two in the X Ring may indeed be an extraordinary coincidence. But we should investigate further. Give your shooter another round, Sergeant. No! Give him a clip."

"Yes, sir," Sergeant McCullhay said, and handed PVT WILLIAMS P a metal clip holding eight cartridges.

PVT WILLIAMS P loaded the clip into his Garand and squeezed off eight rounds.

"I don't EXPLETIVE DELETED!! believe this," the range officer said, when the pit crew had marked PVT WILLIAMS P's target and reported what they had found.

59

"Bring the target to the line."

The target was removed from the frame and brought to the line. It showed beyond any question that PVT WILLIAMS P had fired a total of ten shots. All of them had gone into the bull's-eye. Six of them had gone into the X Ring.

"Son," the range officer said, "I predict a brilliant career for you as an Army Marksman."

[Six]

1000 Scharwath Road
South Orange, New Jersey
Friday, December 13, 1946

During the sixth week of his Basic Training, Phil turned, depending on which birth certificate one looked at, either eighteen or seventeen.

And eight weeks and five days after getting the boot from St. Malachi's School, Phil finally made it home to South Orange.

On his sleeves were the single stripes of a private first class, to which rank he had been advanced the previous day after being adjudged the "Distinguished Graduate" of his Basic Training Company.

And on his chest was a silver medal, looking not unlike the Iron Cross of Germany.

It was the Expert Marksman Badge. Hanging from it were three small pendants, one reading Rifle, a second SubMachine Gun, and the third Pistol.

He saw his mother on that Saturday. On Sunday, he went to New York to see his father. His father took him to lunch at his favorite watering hole, which was on West Fifty-second Street not far from Radio City Music Hall.

Jack, one of the two proprietors of the establishment, on seeing the marksmanship medals on Phil's chest, said, "I wish you'd seen me before you enlisted, Phil. I'd have steered you to the Corps. They really appreciate good shots."

It was well-known that the proprietors of what the cognoscenti called "Jack and Charley's" bar had served in the Marine Corps and had never quite gotten over it.

Phil didn't argue with Mr. Jack, as he had been taught to call him, but he thought he was better off where he was. From what he'd heard of Marine Corps recruit training, he didn't want anything to do with it.

After lunch, he went to Pennsylvania Station and took the train to Trenton, where he caught the bus to Fort Dix.

The next Monday morning, Phil learned

that rather than being shipped off to a remote corner of the world to fill an empty slot in the manning tables of an infantry regiment, he would be retained at Fort Dix as cadre.

He was just the man, Training Division officers decided, to teach the dis- and re-assembly of the U.S. Rifle, Cal. 30, M-1 Garand, to the stream of recruits that flowed incessantly through the battalions and regiments of the division.

This training was conducted in three two-hour periods over as many days. On Monday mornings, Phil would go to the Basic Training Company where this training was scheduled, do his two-hour bit, and then have the rest of the day off. He would do this for the next two days, and then have the rest of the week off.

During the week, Phil spent most of his off-duty time on the KD ranges. It was like Coney Island for free. He didn't get to win any stuffed animals, of course, but on the other hand the Garand was a much nicer weapon than the Winchester pump-guns firing .22 shorts at Coney Island, and instead of five shots for a dollar, he had all the ammunition he wanted at no charge at all.

His weekends were free. He spent most of them in Manhattan, in a relentless but ultimately failing attempt to get a tall, thin, blond seventeen-year-old named Alexandra Black, who lived in the apartment directly above his father's, to part with her pearl of great price.

Close, but no brass ring, so to speak, which caused Phil to suspect that he and Alexandra were the only seventeen-year-old virgins in the world.

On the Thursday of his fifth week as the dis- and re-assembly cadre instructor, one of the officers, Captain Barson Michaels, head of the Fort Dix Skeet and Trap Shooting Club, needed someone to operate for him the "trap" at the Post skeet range while he practiced, and his eye fell upon PFC Williams.

The "trap," Phil learned, was an electro-mechanical device that, when triggered, would throw a frangible clay disc into the air at great speed. Captain Michaels showed Phil how to load stacks of the discs, which were called "birds," into the trap, and handed him the trigger.

"When I call 'pull,' Hotshot," Captain Michaels ordered, "you push the button, which is the trigger, whereupon the trap will fire, the bird will fly, and I will shoot at it. Got it?"

"Yes, sir, Captain Michaels, sir."

Perhaps forty-five minutes later, during which time PFC Williams had flawlessly carried out his orders, and most of the carton of birds had flown, Captain Michaels, perhaps because he had heard a probably EXPLETIVE DELETED!! story that the kid was some sort of Annie EXPLETIVE DELETED!! Oakley in pants with an M-1, decided he could afford to be a nice guy.

"You ever fire a shotgun, PFC Hotshot?"

"No, sir."

"Let me show you how it's done, and then you can have a try at it."

"Yes, sir."

Captain Michaels then handed Phil a shotgun. It was the first shotgun he had ever had in his hands. He later learned that it was a Remington Model 11, but at the time all he knew about it was that it was a semiautomatic weapon into which one fed — through the side, not the top — shotgun shells.

He was given a sixty-second course in its operation — *Drop the shell in, push that little button, and you're ready to go.*

Captain Michaels put Phil in position.

"Anytime you're ready, son."

Phil called "pull."

Captain Michaels pushed the trap's trigger. The bird flew. Phil fired. The unscathed bird kept flying.

Captain Michaels then imparted to PFC Williams the First and Great Commandment of Skeet and Trap Shooting, to wit: *Shoot where it's going to be, Hotshot, not where it's at.*

"Yes, sir."

The second bird at which Phil fired disappeared in a cloud of dust.

And the third and the fifth — not the fourth — and the sixth, and the seventh, *und so weiter,* until the twenty-second, which he also missed, and then the twenty-third, -fourth, and -fifth, which were also reduced to puffs of dust.

"You sure you never did this before, Hotshot?"

"No, sir. I mean, yes, sir, I'm sure I never did this before."

"I'll be a EXPLETIVE DELETED!!," Captain Michaels said, his mind full of images of the greenbacks he was going to take from his pals at the next skeet shoot after betting this innocent young enlisted man could beat them.

"Get another box of shells, my boy, and we'll have another go at it."

"Yes, sir."

Phil went "straight" — that is, broke all of

the twenty-five birds — in his second "round" of twenty-five birds.

Phil repeated the feat the next Saturday morning — in fact went fifty-two straight — at the weekly competition of the Fort Dix Skeet and Trap Shooting Club, following which Captain Michaels handed him two twenty-dollar bills with the explanation he'd made a small bet for him. As PFC Williams was being paid fifty-eight dollars a month at the time, this was a small fortune.

Phil blew just about all the forty bucks that same night on Alexandra Black in Manhattan. But to no avail. Worse, that night as she gave him a friendly kiss on the cheek good night, Alexandra told him that she had met a very nice boy from Yale and didn't think she and Phil should see each other anymore.

Even worse, the next Monday morning, Phil was summoned by his first sergeant.

"How come you know General Schwarzkopf, PFC EXPLETIVE DELETED!! head?"

General H. Norman Schwarzkopf, Sr., who invented the New Jersey State Police and later returned to the Army for service in World War II, was a pinochle-playing crony of Phil's grandfather, the corporate counsel for the Public Service Company of New Jersey. The other General H. Norman Schwarzkopf, his son, the one who would win the first Desert War, was at about this time a second lieutenant.

"First Sergeant, sir, he's a family friend."

"Well, he got you a Top Secret security clearance. I never saw one of the EXPLETIVE DELETED!! come through so EXPLETIVE DELETED!! quick."

Why in the world, Phil wondered, *would General Schwarzkopf get me a Top Secret security clearance?*

And then he remembered that early in his military career he had opted for the Army Security Agency to avoid going to West Point, and that he had been then required to fill out a multi-page form wanting to know every detail of his life. The form had asked for references, and as he was hard-pressed to think of any, he had given General Schwarzkopf as one of these.

"Just as soon as you pass the Morse Test, PFC EXPLETIVE DELETED!! head, you will pack your duffel bag and head for Fort Monmouth, New Jersey, for Army Security Agency training," the first sergeant said.

"The what test, First Sergeant, sir?"

"There are three requirements to get into the ASA, PFC EXPLETIVE DELETED!!

Head," his first sergeant explained. "You have to type thirty EXPLETIVE DELETED!! words a minute, hold a Top EXPLETIVE DELETED!! Secret clearance, and pass the EXPLETIVE DELETED!! Morse Test. You know, Dit EXPLETIVE DELETED!! Dot EXPLETIVE DELETED!! Dit?"

"Yes, sir, First Sergeant."

"You got two out of EXPLETIVE DELETED!! three, and as soon as you take the Morse Test, you'll have all EXPLETIVE DELETED!! three. And then sayonara, PFC EXPLETIVE DELETED!! Head, don't let the doorknob hit you in the EXPLETIVE DELETED!! EXPLETIVE DELETED!! on your way out."

Phil saw a problem concerning a military career as an Intercept Operator in the ASA. He had learned that while such personnel did in fact perform their duties indoors sitting out of the sun, snow, and rain, they did so while wearing earphones for eight hours at a stretch, day after day.

That didn't seem like much fun compared to working three half days a week and spending the rest of his duty time on the KD and skeet and trap ranges. Besides, there was a possibility, however slim, that Alexandra might become disillusioned with the nice boy from Yale she had met.

Before the EXPLETIVE DELETED!! Yalie had appeared on the scene, Phil had been tantalizingly close to achieving what was the greatest ambition of his entire seventeen years.

"First Sergeant, do I have a choice in this?"

"Indeed you do, PFC EXPLETIVE DELETED!! Head. You can get the EXPLETIVE DELETED!! out of my sight now, or delay doing so for thirty EXPLETIVE DELETED!! seconds, after which I will shove my boot so far up your EXPLETIVE DELETED!! that you'll have EXPLETIVE DELETED!! shoelaces coming out of your EXPLETIVE DELETED!! nose."

After giving the subject a great deal of thought, Phil purposefully failed the Morse Test. Failed it twice, as the tester suspected he wasn't really trying on his first try. And then a third time when his failure came to the attention of various officers in the chain of command.

Phil saw for the first time in his life the unexpected ramifications that can occur when there is a bureaucratic misstep. This took place immediately after he failed the Morse Test for the third time.

Captain Barson Michaels, who looked

kindly on Phil as a result of their time together on the skeet and trap ranges, turned to him and said, not unkindly, "What the hell are we going to do with you now, Phil?"

"Make him take the EXPLETIVE DELETED!! Morse Test once an hour until he passes the EXPLETIVE DELETED!! thing," another officer in the room suggested.

"There has to be another option," Captain Michaels said. "I know this young soldier, Lieutenant. He's given the test his best shot, so to speak."

He winked at Phil, which suggested to Phil that Captain Michaels understood and sympathized with Phil's reluctance to become an ASA Intercept Operator.

"The regulation is clear," the lieutenant argued. "Complete background investigations, which cost a EXPLETIVE DELETED!! arm and a leg, are not to be initiated until all testing has been satisfactorily completed. It's the same with the CIC. No background investigation until the soldier passes the tests. Do you want to tell the Inspector General who EXPLETIVE DELETED!! that up here?"

Phil had never heard of the CIC.

"What are the tests required for the CIC?" Captain Michaels inquired.

"Two years of college. PFC Williams has two years and two months of high school. I thought of the CIC, Captain," the lieutenant said.

"The U.S. Army moves on a trail of paper, Lieutenant," Captain Michaels said. "You may wish to write that down. That suggests to me that the CIC may have clerk-typists to care for its special agents."

"They call them CIC administrators."

"And what does the CIC demand, education wise, of potential CIC administrators?"

The appropriate regulations were consulted. Nothing was mentioned at all about minimum educational standards for potential CIC administrators.

"Permit me, PFC Williams, to wish you all the best in your CIC career," Captain Michaels said.

"Yes, sir. Thank you, sir. Sir, what's the CIC?"

[Seven]

The CIC Center and School
Fort Holabird
1019 Dundalk Avenue
Baltimore, Maryland
0845 Monday, February 3, 1947
PFC Williams stood at the position known

71

as Parade Rest — feet spread, hands locked behind his back — before the desk of the company commander of Company B.

The company commander, a captain who had been sitting behind the desk when Phil had first been taken into the office by Company B's first sergeant, was now standing against the wall next to the first sergeant.

The captain had given up his chair to the major who, after the first sergeant had brought the problem at hand to the captain's attention, had brought it to the major's attention, whereupon the major had announced, "I'll be right there."

The problem was that there was indeed a minimum educational requirement for CIC administrators, although it had not reached Fort Dix. It clearly stated that high school graduation was a prerequisite. And, as first the first sergeant and then the captain had learned — and the major was now learning — from the classified *SECRET Final Report, Williams, Philip Walling ford III, Complete Background Investigation of* — Phil's formal education had ended after two years and some months of secondary school.

"That's as far as you got in school, son, is it?" the major asked. "Got kicked out again, did you? And ran off and joined the Army? With a forged birth certificate?"

"Yes, sir," Phil confessed.

He had visions of himself blindfolded and tied to a stake, as he waited for the firing squad to do its duty.

"We'll have to send him back, of course, sir," the captain said to the major. "But I thought I'd better check with you first, sir."

The major ignored him.

"Tell me, son, did you get the boot from Saint Malachi's School for academic deficiency? Or was it something else?"

"Sir, it was something else."

"What else? Every detail of what else."

Phil confessed to stealing the intimate undergarments of Miss Bridget O'Malley, a student of Miss Bailey's School who was visiting St. Malachi's as captain of Miss Bailey's School's Debating Team, from where they had been hung out to dry, and then hoisting them up St. Malachi's flagpole. And then cutting the rope.

"I see," the major said. "And tell me, son, where did you get that Expert Marksman's Badge pinned to your tunic? You bought it at an Army-Navy store, to impress the girls, right?"

"No, sir. I got it from the Army."

"You expect me to believe that in your brief military career, you have become an expert with the rifle, the pistol, and the

73

submachine gun?"

"Yes, sir, and also the shotgun."

The major then rummaged through Phil's records.

"I'll be a EXPLETIVE DELETED!!," he said softly. "Very interesting," he went on. "First Sergeant, take PFC Williams to the Education Center and see that he is administered the GED test. When it has been graded, bring him and it to my office."

"Yes, sir."

Phil had no idea what the GED test was. On the way to the Education Center, the first sergeant told him. GED stood for General Educational Development. It had been developed to see if an individual's life experiences had given him knowledge equivalent to that of someone who had actually finished high school or gone to college for two years. If one passed the test, the Army considered that the same thing as actually having graduated from high school, or having been exposed to two years of college instruction.

Phil took the test, spending about an hour and a half with it.

"You're quitting?" the test administrator, a captain, said. "Give it another shot. You have three hours to take it. Don't give up!"

"Sir, I finished the test."

The test administrator graded Phil's GED test.

When he had finished doing so, he said, "I'll be a EXPLETIVE DELETED!!" and then said, "Congratulations, PFC Williams, you have scored in the ninety-fifth percentile."

Phil didn't know what that meant and confessed his ignorance.

"That means you have scored better that ninety-four percent of all others who have taken the test."

I'll be damned, Phil thought.

I am now the legal equivalent of a high school graduate!

He was wrong.

This was brought to everyone's attention ten minutes later when Phil was again standing at Parade Rest before a desk, this time the major's. The major barely had time to open the envelope containing the Certificate of GED Test Results when the administrator sought and was granted access to the major's office.

"What?" the major inquired.

"Sir, there's been a little mix-up," the administrator said. "We gave PFC Williams the wrong test."

"How wrong?"

"We gave him the college-level GED test,

sir. Not the high school level."

"According to this, he scored in the ninety-fifth percentile."

"Yes, sir. He did. But he wasn't supposed to take that test. He'll have to be retested."

"He scored in the ninety-fifth percentile on the college test and you want him to take the high school test? What the EXPLETIVE DELETED!! is wrong with you? Dismissed!"

The major then turned to PFC Williams.

"Welcome to the Counterintelligence Corps, son," he said.

So that's what CIC stands for!

"Thank you, sir."

"I think you'll like Fort Holabird," the major went on. "There's all sorts of things to do here. We even have a skeet team which competes against other governmental investigative agencies in the Baltimore-Washington area. The first sergeant will show you where the skeet range is on Saturday morning."

"Sir," the first sergeant protested, "on Saturday morning, CIC administrators in training have a barracks inspection."

"Not if they're on the Fort Holabird Skeet Team, they don't," the major said. "I intend to kick the EXPLETIVE DELETED!! out of the EXPLETIVE DELETED!! Naval Intelligence Team at the Sunday shoot, and I want PFC Williams to get all the practice he can. Have him there at oh-eight-hundred."

[Eight]

Phil did like Fort Holabird.

He learned a great deal in the CIC Administrator School, including how much of a threat the Soviet Union posed to the world in general and the United States specifically, and how they did so — subjects that previously had escaped his attention.

He learned what the Counterintelligence Corps did, and, presuming he completed the training, how he would fit into the Corps.

Put simply, there were three kinds of laborers in the CIC's fields. At the very bottom of the totem pole were CIC administrators, and their major contribution was to prepare the final reports of CIC special agents and CIC analysts.

His instructors impressed upon him the cardinal rules for preparing reports: One, there were to be no strikeovers, misspellings, and grammatical errors, and, most important, reports could contain absolutely no ambiguities.

If something can be interpreted in more than one way, it will be.

He learned there were two kinds of people senior to ordinary CIC special agents. One of these categories was supervisory special agents, and the other was CIC analysts. It got a little confusing here, as analysts could be pure analysts (that is, neither CIC agents nor supervisory special agents) or they could not.

Analysts analyzed what the agents had discovered in the course of their investigations, and reported their analysis to their superiors, aided and abetted by CIC administrators who prepared — not just typed — such analytical reports.

This was an important distinction.

Any Quartermaster Corps clerk-typist could type a report, many of them without a single strikeover, but a CIC administrator was expected not only to type a report without a single strikeover, but was also expected to inspect it for ambiguities and grammatical errors and then to seek out the author of the report and get him (or her) to fix the ambiguities and errors.

Phil suspected this might cause problems when he "got into the field" over what was and what was not really an ambiguity.

He also learned that the CIC — in addition to denying the Russians and the Cubans and a long list of other "un-friendlies"

78

access to the secrets of the U.S. Army — had two other roles.

One of these was investigating the misbehavior — usually the sexual misbehavior — of field rank and above officers and their dependents. That meant majors through generals and their dependents. Sexual shenanigans of captains, lieutenants, and noncommissioned officers and their dependents were dealt with by the Criminal Investigation Division of the Corps of Military Police.

Phil thought preparing the special agents' reports of the sexual shenanigans of majors and up — and their dependents, which he had learned meant their wives and offspring — might be very interesting and quietly hoped he would be assigned to a CIC detachment in some hotbed of forbidden sexual activity.

But he thought of himself as a realist, and the reality was that he was probably not going to wind up assigned anywhere interesting, but instead wind up in someplace like Sunny Lakes, Wisconsin, preparing the reports of CIC special agents who spent their days working on complete background investigations.

This was known somewhat disparagingly in the counterintelligence community as "ringing doorbells" because the CIC special agents conducted these investigations by going to the neighbors of those being investigated, ringing their doorbells, and then when the door was opened making a presentation from a script they had memorized along these lines:

Good afternoon (or morning), ma'am (or sir). I am Special Agent (Insert Name) of the U.S. Army Counterintelligence Corps. (Show CIC credentials folder.)

Your neighbor, John (or Mary) (Insert Last Name), who is now a PFC (or second lieutenant) in the U.S. Army, is being considered for assignment to duties which will give him (or her) access to classified information.

The U.S. Army would be very grateful for your opinion of John (or Mary) and whether or not you think it would be safe for us to entrust him (or her) with the nation's secrets.

We are especially interested in what you may have heard (or suspect) about John's (or Mary's) character flaws, such as, but not limited to, tendencies to write "Insufficient Funds" checks, imbibe intoxicants to an excessive degree, or engage in abnormal sexual activity either within or without the bonds of matrimony.

Your answers will of course be held strictly confidential.

Phil, who had by then accepted the CIC premise that the worst scenario of any situation was nine times out of ten the one right on the money, saw himself spending the foreseeable future in Sunny Lakes, Wisconsin, or some similar bucolic metropolis in the middle of the corn belt, preparing the reports of CIC agents who had spent their days ringing doorbells.

He was wrong.

When graduation day from CIC Administrator School came, and with it both his promotion to corporal and his assignment orders, the latter read:

```
17.  CPL Williams, Philip W.,
142-22-0136 detchd Co B CICC&S
trf in gr wp XXXIII CIC Det APO
09237. Tvl by CIV AT in CIV
clothing dir. 10 DDERL Auth. PP
Auth. CIV Clothing Allow of $350
auth.  Approp.  99-99999999903
(Secret).
```

Because he had paid attention while a CIC administrator in training, Phil had no difficulty at all in deciphering his orders. He was a bit surprised to see that Sunny Lakes, Wisconsin, or whatever bucolic village in the Great American Midwest he was to be banished to had its own Army Post Office (APO) number, but the rest of his orders he understood.

He was being detached from Company B, CIC Center & School, and transferred in grade and would proceed to the 33rd CIC Detachment (for reasons never explained, the CIC used Roman, rather than Arabic, numbers on its CIC detachments). Travel by civilian air transportation in civilian clothing was directed. Ten days of delay-en-route leave were authorized, and so were a passport and a $350 allowance to buy the civilian clothing. The money was to come from Congressional Appropriation 99-99999999903, which was classified Secret because Congress didn't want the Russians and the other un-friendlies to know how much they were willing to pay to keep the U.S. Army's secrets secret.

As soon as he could, Phil found the book listing all APO numbers and the physical locations thereof. With a feeling of great foreboding, he ran his finger down the list of numbers until he came to 09237.

When he found it, he exclaimed, "I'll be a

EXPLETIVE DELETED!! I'm not going to EX-PLETIVE DELETED!! Sunny Lakes, or any other EXPLETIVE DELETED!! place in the EXPLETIVE DELETED!! Midwest! I'm going to Berlin! Berlin, *Germany*! Not the Berlin in EXPLETIVE DELETED!! New Hampshire!"

"Watch your mouth, Corporal!" a stern voice chided him.

Phil turned to see that he was being addressed by a second lieutenant who was wearing the identification badge of a CIC agent in training.

"You're in the CIC now," the second lieutenant went on. "We of the CIC do not use obscene language such as 'EXPLETIVE DELETED!! New Hampshire,' which is one of the United States we are sworn to defend from undue Soviet and other unfriendly curiosity."

"Yes, sir. Sorry, sir. I will endeavor to remember that."

"See that you do!"

Over the next few days, as he waited for the administrative wheels of the CIC Center to slowly turn, Phil wondered if his assignment to Berlin was possibly a *sub-rosa* award for his having been a member of the Fort Holabird Skeet Team, which not only had kicked the EXPLETIVE DELETED!! out of the

Navy Intelligence Skeet Team the very week he had joined it, but on other occasions during his time as a student had inflicted similar defeats upon the skeet teams of the National Park Service and the Pentagon Police Force in Washington, D.C., and the security forces of the National Center for the Control of Venereal Diseases in Baltimore.

In the end, he decided it was just a coincidence, as he had been told again and again there was no room for personal favoritism in the CIC.

As soon as he got the $350 check to buy civilian clothes, his new passport — which identified him as an employee of the U.S. Government — and his airline tickets, Phil started to faithfully execute the orders laid out in Par. 17 above.

Well, maybe not faithfully.

If he executed them absolutely faithfully, he would have gone on leave — he was headed for New York — at his own expense.

Ten days later — if he faithfully followed his orders — he would have taken the train back from New York, again at his own expense, and upon his arrival in Baltimore gone to Baltimore-Washington Airport and taken an Eastern Airlines flight to Newark using the Army-provided ticket. From Newark he would have taken the shuttle bus (ticket provided) to Idlewild Airport, where he would board the Pan American flight to Frankfurt.

He decided it would make more sense to skip the Go Back To Baltimore *et seq* elements of this agenda, and instead take a cab to JFK from his father's apartment in Manhattan when his leave was over.

In the club car of the train carrying him to New York City, to which, having no civilian attire, he was traveling in uniform, he picked up a discarded copy of the Sunday edition of *The New York Times.*

In it was a society section story informing the world that Mr. and Mrs. T. Jennings Black III of New York City and Rowayton, Connecticut, announced the marriage of their daughter Alexandra to Mr. Hobart J. Crawley IV, son of Mr. and Mrs. H. J. Crawley III of New York City and East Hampton. The story went on to relate that the ceremony had taken place in the Yale Club of New York City, with the Reverend K. Lamar Dudley, D.D., of St. Bartholomew's Episcopal Church, presiding, and that the groom was at Yale University, New Haven, Connecticut, where the couple would reside following their return from their wedding trip to Bar Harbor, Maine.

Phil was understandably distraught.

Alexandra had married another.

After all of my efforts, she married a EXPLE-TIVE DELETED!! Yalie!

And that EXPLETIVE DELETED!! Yalie was going to get — by now probably had gotten — her EXPLETIVE DELETED!! pearl of great price.

Which leaves me not only desolate but the last EXPLETIVE DELETED!! seventeen-year-old EXPLETIVE DELETED!! virgin in the world.

He decided he would drown his sorrows.

He caught the waiter's eye.

"Bring me a double Famous Pheasant, no ice, please."

The waiter leaned close to him.

"No EXPLETIVE DELETED!! way," the waiter said softly, so that no one else would hear him. "How old are you, boy? Eighteen?"

Following the theory that when all else fails, tell the truth, Phil shrugged his shoulders and confessed, "Seventeen," and then blurted, "The love of my life has married a Yalie."

He held up *The New York Times* as proof.

"Well, that would tend to make a man turn to drink," the waiter said. "But this is the Pennsylvania Railroad and you have to be old enough to vote to buy a drink in a

PRR club car. Which you ain't. Sorry."

"I understand," Phil said.

The waiter left only to return several minutes later with a teapot and cup.

"Drink this, boy. It'll make you feel better."

"Thank you kindly, sir, but I don't drink tea."

"This is special tea. They make it in Dungaress, Scotland. I understand Her Majesty the Queen herself really likes to sip it. Try a little sip, why don't you? See for yourself if you think it's worth the ten dollars a cup market forces require me to charge for it."

By the time the train reached Manhattan's Pennsylvania Station, Phil wasn't feeling much of the pain he had been feeling since learning of Alexandra's nuptials. Or much pain at all.

When he entered his father's apartment, his sire was there.

"I would say 'welcome home,' " his father greeted him, "except it's Wednesday, and my own military experience has taught me that privates are rarely, if ever, given time off in the middle of the week. Which makes me suspect that you have experienced more of the rigors of military life than you like, and have, as we old soldiers say, 'gone over

87

the hill.' "

P. Wallingford Williams, Jr., having taken ROTC at Harvard College, had entered military service as a second lieutenant of artillery and gone to Fort Sill, Oklahoma, where in the sixth week of the Basic Artillery Officer's Course he had dropped the trail of a 105mm howitzer on his left foot while attempting to set the cannon up for firing. Army surgeons saved the foot, except for the big toe, the loss of which caused Lieutenant Williams to be medically retired from the service with a five percent disability pension. He later became quite active in several disabled veterans organizations.

"Actually, Pop, I'm on my way to Berlin."

"I have to tell you, son, that it won't do you any good to go to New Hampshire. The military police will run you to earth no matter where you try to hide. My advice is that you go to Penn Station, or Grand Central, whichever you prefer, and surrender yourself to the military police who patrol there. Perhaps, considering your youth, the courts-martial will temper your sentence with compassion."

"I'm not AWOL, Pop. I'm en route to the Berlin in Germany."

"And why are you wearing corporal's

chevrons? In my day in uniform, impersonation of a noncommissioned officer was nearly as serious an offense as impersonating a commissioned officer. You're never going to get out of Leavenworth."

"I'm wearing corporal's chevrons, Pop, because I am a corporal. Here, have a look at my orders."

On doing so, Second Lieutenant P. Wallingford Williams, Jr., Artillery, Medically Retired, announced, "I can't make heads or tails of that gibberish. Why don't we start over?"

"Sir?"

"Hello, Philip. What brings you home, wearing corporal's chevrons, in the middle of the week?"

Phil told him.

"Obviously, I owe you my profound apologies," his father said when he had finished. "I can only offer in extenuation that on the last seven occasions on which you appeared unexpectedly at my door in the middle of the week, it was because you had been booted from the finest boarding schools on the East Coast. And each time that happened, it cost me an arm and a leg — I shudder to remember what it cost me to get you into Saint Malachi's — to get you into another one."

"I understand, Pop. No apology is necessary."

"But I must tell you, Philip, that even when I so unthinkingly thought, 'My God! Now he's Gone Over The Hill,' I also thought, *Well, at least he didn't do to me what Hobo Crawley's boy did to ol' Hobo.*"

"Pop, are you talking about Hobart J. Crawley the Fourth?"

"Indeed I am. The son of Hobart J. Crawley the Third."

"And what was that, sir?"

"I ran into ol' Hobo at the bar at the New York Athletic Club. Actually, I picked him up off the floor of the bar at the Athletic Club, where he was curled in a fetal position and weeping piteously. When I got him into an armchair in the lounge and got about a quart of black coffee into him, he confided in me his shame."

"And what was that, Pop?"

"That idiot son of his, the one they call 'Little Hobo,' couldn't keep his You Know What in his pocket and instead used it to get another mental deficient in the family way. You may have seen her around. They live in this building. Tall blonde with a vapid face and no bosom worth mentioning. Anyway, these two are now going to contribute to the further degeneration of the gene

90

pool, and poor ol' Hobo's stuck for the tab for the whole operation for the foreseeable future. Little Hobo is now on his third try to get out of the freshman class at Yale. I thank you from the bottom of my heart, son, for not doing anything like that to me."

"You're welcome, Pop."

"I do have one question, Philip, about your orders."

"Sir?"

"That three-hundred-and-fifty-dollar clothing allowance. What's that all about?"

Phil told him.

"And how long are you going to be in Berlin?"

"I enlisted for two years. I've got about seventeen months left to go."

"That's outrageous!" the elder Williams said indignantly. "How the hell does the Army expect you to spend seventeen months in Berlin with only a sports jacket and a pair of slacks — well, maybe two pair, one wool, one khaki — to wear?"

"I thought I would go to Brooks Brothers in the morning, Pop, to see what they might have on sale."

"Tomorrow, my boy, we will go to J. Press — I thought you understood, God knows I've told you this often enough, that J. Press serves gentlemen and Brooks Brothers the less fortunate others — we will go to J. Press and get you enough clothing to spend seventeen months in Berlin."

"Yes, sir."

"On my nickel, of course, in the hope that you will find it in your heart to forgive me for what I thought — *My God, what's it going to cost me to keep him out of Leavenworth?* — when you came home just now."

On the tenth day of his son's delay-en-route-leave, P. Wallingford Williams, Jr., loaded CPL Williams Philip W. III — and the three leather suitcases containing the corporal's new wardrobe — into a taxicab on Park Avenue and waved goodbye as Phil headed for Idlewild and the Pan American Flight to Frankfurt.

III
OL' PHIL'S FIRST GRAND EUROPEAN TOUR

[One]

22-26 Beerenstrasse
Zehlendorf, Berlin, Germany
Monday, May 5, 1947

The black Volkswagen Beetle drove through Zehlendorf, which looked to Phil very much like South Orange, New Jersey — that is to say, the part of South Orange where his mother lived with lots of big houses with lawns, not downtown South Orange by the Delaware, Lackawanna & Western railroad commuter station, which was sort of lower-middle-class in ambience — and then through a set of twelve-foot-high cast-iron gates that opened at their approach.

Inside, Phil saw a rather large three-story building before which were parked seven Volkswagens essentially identical to the one in which he was riding. Phil, who had paid attention during the classes in Techniques

93

of Observation he had been subjected to at Fort Holabird while in training, quickly saw that, while on casual observation the Volkswagens were essentially identical, upon closer examination the eye trained to be alert for details could see that they were not.

One of the VWs was painted olive-drab green all over, including the bumpers, and on the bumpers had been stenciled some numbers and letters, including the legend *U.S. Army.* The others were of various colors, including one that was startlingly purple.

And they had different license plates. Two had large, egg-shaped plates with black numbers and letters on a white background. Both plates had the letter *B* followed by numbers on them. Phil thought the *B* might have something to do with Berlin. One of them, which was dark blue in color, had an American-shaped white license plate with the legend *US GOVT* above its numbers. The remaining four Beetles also had white plates and numbers, but their legend read *US of AMERICA.*

"Here we are," the driver of the Volkswagen said, as he pulled to a stop beside its cousins.

The driver, a large young man in civilian

attire — a corduroy jacket and khaki pants — was not very loquacious.

When Phil had been claiming his luggage at the airfield, which was called Tempelhof, the driver had walked up to him and inquired, "Williams, P.?"

When Phil had replied in the affirmative, the driver had picked up one of Phil's suitcases, announced, "I've got the EXPLETIVE DELETED!! driver duty," and motioned for Phil to follow him.

The driver assisted Phil with his luggage, carrying his suitcases into the foyer of the building. Once there, he pointed to a door, put the suitcase on the floor, and walked back outside.

Phil went to the door and knocked.

"Come."

Phil went inside.

A heavyset man in his early thirties in a gray flannel suit rose to his feet from behind a desk.

"Williams, P.?" the man inquired.

"Yes, sir."

The man examined him carefully.

"You have made a good first impression, Williams. The last three replacements Holabird sent us were sartorial disasters. One of them was actually wearing cowboy boots and blue jeans, and another a baseball cap with the brim turned sideways."

"Yes, sir. Thank you, sir."

"I'm the first sergeant, Williams. As I'm sure you know, first sergeants are not addressed as 'sir.' I am also a CIC special agent. You may therefore call me, at your option, either 'Special Agent Dumbrowski' or 'Mr. Dumbrowski.' "

"Yes, Mr. Dumbrowski."

"I am now going to send you in to meet Supervisory Special Agent O'Reilly, who commands the Thirty-third CIC Detachment. He likes to become personally acquainted with all newcomers.

"But before I actually do that, CIC Administrator Williams, there are certain things I wish to bring to your attention. First, Supervisory Special Agent William O'Reilly is a lieutenant colonel of Infantry, pay grade O-5. He is also a graduate of the United States Military Academy at West Point. With me so far?"

"Yes, Mr. Dumbrowski."

"Now, I am sure in your previous uniformed service you were trained in, and, it is to be hoped, became proficient in practicing the protocol one follows when first meeting one's new commanding officer, to wit: The newcomer marches into the commander's office, stops four feet — no more,

96

no less — from the commanding officer's desk, where he comes to attention, salutes, and says, 'Sir, STATE NAME AND RANK reporting to the commanding officer for duty, sir.' You are familiar with this protocol?"

"Yes, Mr. Dumbrowski."

"Good. Now we are not required here in the Thirty-third to follow this protocol, because we are in civilian attire, and one does not salute when so attired. Nor are we required to use the term 'sir' when addressing another member of the CIC family, even if we are aware that the individual is a commissioned officer.

"Having said that, CIC Administrator Williams, I suggest that when Supervisory Special Agent O'Reilly gives you permission to enter his office, you march into his office, stop four feet — no more, no less — from his desk, come to attention, and without saluting, repeat, without saluting, say, 'Sir, CIC Administrator Williams reporting to the supervisory special agent in charge for duty, sir.' Can you remember that?"

"I thought you said we're not supposed to say 'sir.' "

"If memory serves, and mine invariably does, the word I used was 'required.' Supervisory Special Agent O'Reilly has told me on several occasions that rather than taking offense as he does when one of his peers refers to him as 'Bill,' when someone calls him 'sir,' it warms the cockles of his Irish heart as it reminds him of his happy days as an upperclassman in the West Point Corps of Cadets tormenting plebes." He paused, then added, "Clear?"

"Yes, Mr. Dumbrowski."

Dumbrowski walked to an interior door, knocked on it, opened it a crack, and announced, "Mr. O'Reilly, sir, newly arrived CIC Administrator Williams is here and requests audience."

"Send him in."

Phil entered the office, went through the routine previously described, and found himself looking at Lieutenant Colonel William O'Reilly, who wore a red crew cut above a freckled face. He was about five feet four in height and appeared to weigh somewhere in the 125- to 135-pound body weight range.

"You may relax," the colonel, who was in civilian attire, said.

Phil decided this was the CIC version of At Ease and relaxed.

The colonel stared at him intently.

"I have been going over the final report of

your complete background investigation, Williams. It has been my experience that when one wishes to learn all there is to know about an individual, one is wise to do so. Reading yours makes me suspect that whoever assigned you here is either grossly incompetent or had been drinking.

"According to your FRCBI, your secondary education ended with your expulsion from Saint Malachi's School, at which time you had completed two years and some months of your secondary education. Is this true?"

"Yes, sir."

"Phrased another way, you do not have a high school diploma?"

"Yes, sir. Correct."

"The FRCBI also states that you were expelled from Saint Malachi's School for moral turpitude, but does not go into the details of such turpitude. Would you care to share them with me?"

"No, sir."

"Do it anyway."

Phil related his transgression with regard to the intimate undergarments of Miss Bridget O'Malley.

"I have to tell you, Williams, that even having the acquaintance of another former student of Saint Malachi's School and

99

knowing the depths of depravity to which he frequently sinks, I consider the humiliation of a nice Irish Catholic girl by a teen-aged Protestant sexual deviate, such as you obviously are, absolutely indefensible. And I warn you sternly herewith that if you pull anything like that while assigned to the Thirty-third CIC, you will rue the day you did."

"Yes, sir."

"Dismissed."

Phil went through the protocol of leaving an officer's presence when dismissed — except for the rendering of the hand salute — and left Lieutenant Colonel William "Don't Call Me Bill" O'Reilly's office.

"What happens now?" he asked Special Agent/First Sergeant Dumbrowski.

"Well, once we get you settled in your room, you will commence ROTPIP."

What the EXPLETIVE DELETED!! *is rot pip? Sounds painful.*

"Rot pip, Mr. Dumbrowski?"

Dumbrowski nodded.

"Required Orientation Training Program for Incoming Personnel. On your completion of that you will be assigned to CIC administrator duties. Any other questions?"

"I couldn't help but notice that," Phil said, pointing to a wall-mounted cabinet that held a dozen Thompson submachine guns. "What are they for?"

"This will be covered in some detail during your ROTPIP, Williams, but briefly, those are Caliber .45 M1A1 Thompson submachine guns. They are used to shoot people. I'm surprised you didn't know that."

"I meant, what are they used for here?"

"That will also be covered during your ROTPIP, but to satisfy your frankly unwelcome premature curiosity, I will tell you that certain highly trained members of the Thirty-third are sometimes called upon to carry such weapons during the exchange of spies — the EXPLETIVE DELETED!! Russians return to us the innocent Americans the EXPLETIVE DELETED!! East Germans have arrested on absolutely unfounded accusations that they are spies and we return to them the EXPLETIVE DELETED!! Russian spies we have bagged.

"In this connection, not for dissemination, of course, most of the EXPLETIVE DELETED!! Russian spies we have bagged have been bagged by our own — the Thirty-third's own — Supervisory Special Agent Jonathan Caldwell the Third, who is, again not for dissemination, one EXPLETIVE DELETED!!, not only *vis-à-vis* the EXPLETIVE DELETED!! Russians but also with regard to his fellows in the Thirty-third who do not measure up to his high standards.

"But I digress. The exchange of spies takes place in the center of the Glienicke Bridge, which spans the Havel River, which is the border between the West — specifically the Wannsee district of Berlin — and the East — specifically the city of Potsdam, which is the capital of Brandenburg. Six or more men of the Thirty-third go to the bridge armed with, and carrying spare fifty-round magazines for, the Thompsons on my wall to ensure that the EXPLETIVE DELETED!! Russians don't do anything they are not supposed to during the exchange procedure.

"But I wouldn't bother your innocent seventeen-year-old head with this, Administrator Williams, as it will be a long, long time before you are allowed anywhere near Supervisory Special Agent Caldwell, who handles the spy exchange, the Glienicke Bridge, or a Caliber .45 M1A1 Thompson submachine gun.

"Perhaps especially the latter. I myself, as difficult as it may be for you to believe, had a great deal of difficulty qualifying with the Thompson. Despite the apparent ease with which the gangsters and heroes wield the weapon in the movies, in real life the Thompson is a EXPLETIVE DELETED!!. It kicks like a EXPLETIVE DELETED!! mule, for one thing, and, unless one tightly buttons one's shirt, has a nasty habit of ejecting hot brass cartridge casings into open necks, whereupon they burn one's chest and tummy as they drop to one's testicles. I speak from painful experience when I say that having one's jockey shorts filled with a dozen or so just-ejected .45 cartridge cases causes unbelievable EXPLETIVE DELETED!! discomfort."

Phil took a deep breath and decided that honesty required him to go on.

"First Sergeant, what would you say if I told you I'm an Expert Marksman with the Caliber .45 M1A1 Thompson submachine gun?"

Dumbrowski considered his reply before giving it.

"I would say," he said finally, "that you have been smoking funny cigarettes, because even as dumb as you look, I don't think you'd be dumb enough, unless flying high on the fumes of a controlled substance, to try to lay such incredible EXPLETIVE DE-LETED!! on your first sergeant."

"It's in my service record, First Sergeant."

First Sergeant Dumbrowski checked Phil's service record. After doing so, he said, "First of all, Administrator Williams, please accept my apologies for my having questioned your claim of marksmanship excellence, and in suggesting you were a grass head.

"Second, please accept this advice in the spirit in which it is offered. Keep this remarkable talent of yours to yourself. It may turn out to be a very useful arrow in your quiver of self-defense arrows in the future. And you may well need a full quiver of such arrows. I could not help but over-hear Colonel O'Reilly refer to you as a teen-aged Protestant sexual deviate. His detrac-tors don't call him 'Bad Bill O'Reilly' without cause. Enough said?"

"Yes, First Sergeant. Thank you."

"Come with me, Williams. I'll show you to your room, and then we'll get you started on your ROTPIP."

[Two]

Over the next two weeks, both through the ROTPIP program and simply by living in what the Army called his barracks, Phil learned a great deal about Berlin generally, and the XXXIIIrd CIC Detachment specifi-cally.

For one thing, the barracks was like no other Phil had lived in elsewhere in the Army.

At Fort Dix, he lived in a two-story

wooden barracks that had been constructed in 1940 with an expected life of three years. There, each "squad bay" — one on each floor — had accommodated thirty double-decker bunks. At one end of the barracks was the room with toilets and showers, which the Army called the "latrine."

Phil, having studied Latin for three years at six different schools, knew the term "latrine" was derived from the Latin word *latrina,* a contraction of *lavatrina,* from *lavare,* which meant to wash. But no one else in his basic training company had ever heard the word before donning a uniform.

Although the Fort Dix latrine had indeed offered facilities to wash — eight shower heads mounted eighteen inches apart on one wall and eight sinks on the other, it also had offered facilities for the 120 men it served as a disposal point for the fluids and solids for which the soldier's bodies had no further use. This was accomplished through eight water closets placed so close together that defecators had no trouble sharing a copy of a magazine during the 180 seconds allotted to them twice a day to do their business.

The barracks and latrines at Fort Holabird had similarly been constructed to last only three years — and this was long before any of the current inhabitants had been born. The differences then were that the bunks on each floor were single bunks, which meant that only sixty men were competing for occupancy of the water closets, rather than 120, which further meant that the occupancy time allotted could be, and had been, upped to 240 seconds, or four minutes, twice daily.

The floors of the Holabird barracks and latrine were not nearly as sparkling as those at Dix. Not that they were dirty, but nothing can make a floor sparkle more than 120 men attacking it with toothbrushes and lye soap on a twice daily basis, as was the practice at Fort Dix.

The room to which he had been assigned on his first day in Berlin was larger than his room in his mother's house, larger than any room to which he ever had been assigned in any boarding school, and about twice the size of the closet his father insisted on calling "Phil's Room" in the Williams apartment at 590 Park Avenue.

It had a bath with a tub, a stall shower, a double-sink, an enclosed water closet, and next to the water closet another porcelain device through which water flowed in all directions, including straight up into the air, the purpose of which Phil could not imagine.

Inasmuch as he was a junior administrator — in point of fact, *the* junior administrator — he was no doubt going to be forced to share the bath with another junior administrator. Only the more senior administrators (and of course CIC special agents) were given private accommodations.

He met the other junior administrator that same day. He came into Phil's room from their shared bathroom.

He was a slight young man — even smaller than Colonel O'Reilly — whose skin was reddish brown in color. He was wearing horn-rimmed glasses and tennis whites.

"Gott im Himmel!" the young man proclaimed. "EXPLETIVE DELETED!! Holden EXPLETIVE DELETED!! Caulfield in the EXPLETIVE DELETED!! flesh!"

"Excuse me?"

"You're unfamiliar with the protagonist of J. D. Salinger's opus *Catcher in the Rye?*"

He spoke with what Phil thought sounded like a Harvard accent, that is, as if through his nose with his teeth clenched.

"I've read it. What's that got to do with me?"

"Let me put it to you this way, Holden. If I were producing a motion picture of Mr. Salinger's novel, and had asked one of the better casting agencies to send me someone for the lead role, and they sent me you, I would think the Lord God himself was beaming on my project."

The young man put out his hand.

"I am Administrator G. Lincoln Rutherford, Holden. In addition to having to share the bathroom with you for God only knows how EXPLETIVE DELETED!! long, I will be your guide through the ROTPIP program. You may call me 'G. Lincoln' and you already know what I'm going to call you."

"I don't think I like the idea of being called 'Holden.' My name is Phil."

"Well, as we sergeants are permitted to say to corporals, too EXPLETIVE DELETED!! bad. That's the way your EXPLETIVE DELETED!! ball has bounced."

"I understand."

"Good. Now give me a few minutes to shower, Holden, and to dress, and we will begin your ROTPIP training by dining, at your expense . . . You have some money, presumably?"

Phil nodded.

". . . At the agency mess. They do a very nice steak tartare."

"What's the agency?"

"Holden, the depth of your ignorance is amazing," G. Lincoln said, and went back into their shared bath.

[Three]

Fifteen minutes later, G. Lincoln reappeared dressed much like Phil, in a white button-down-collar shirt, a striped necktie, a tweed jacket, gray trousers, and loafers. Phil's father had an identical necktie, which identified him to other alumni of Harvard College, and Phil wondered again if G. Lincoln was similarly connected with Harvard College.

G. Lincoln loaded him into one of the Volkswagens — this one pale green and carrying a license plate with the *US of AMER-ICA* legend — and drove him out of the compound onto Beerenstrasse.

After winding their way through the streets of Zehlendorf for perhaps ten minutes, they turned off the street and were stopped by a policeman at a striped pole barrier. Phil saw a sign:

German-American Gospel Tract Foundation

Bringing in the Sheep

Praise the Lord!

What the hell? Phil wondered, and then corrected himself: *What the heck?*

The striped pole barrier was raised and

G. Lincoln drove past it. They came to a large two-story building before which were parked a number of automobiles on which were mounted the same variety of license plates there had been on the fleet of Volkswagens at the CIC barracks.

But only one of the automobiles parked there before a sign reading Automobiles Only! was a Volkswagen. The other vehicles were BMWs (two), Mercedes-Benzes (four), Chevrolet Suburban Carryalls (two), and a Fiat, a Buick, and a Harley-Davidson motorcycle with sidecar.

Phil wondered if the latter could be properly classified as an automobile, but then from his studies of Latin, recalled the word came from the ancient Greek word *autós,* meaning self, and the Latin *mobilis,* meaning movable, and thus meant a vehicle that moves itself. A motorcycle, Phil decided, thus did qualify as an automobile.

"Let's go, Holden," G. Lincoln said, "and, once inside, speak only when spoken to and don't ask any questions."

Then he took Phil's arm and led him into the building, down a corridor therein, and ultimately through a door.

Phil found himself in a room that anywhere but in a building dedicated to the purposes of a Gospel Tract Foundation

110

would have been called a "bar" or "saloon." There was a wooden bar behind which was arrayed an impressive selection of bottled intoxicants, and in front of it a half-dozen very attractive females on stools showed a good bit of upper thigh as they sipped what in Jack & Charley's establishment at 21 West Fifty-second Street would be called martinis. There were eight or so men at the bar, all wearing suits and ties, most of them ogling the lady drinkers.

Phil and G. Lincoln took seats at the bar. G. Lincoln was kind enough to order for the both of them. "A double Famous Pheasant, two ice cubes, water on the side, and a Coca-Cola. Run a tab."

Before the drinks could be served they were joined by an Asian gentleman who looked like a midget sumo wrestler in a suit.

"How goes it, Geronimo?" he asked. "How's everything in the ol' teepee?"

"EXPLETIVE DELETED!! you, Fu Manchu," G. Lincoln replied.

"Who is this boy?" the minuscule Asian gentleman asked, pointing to Phil. "And more to the point, what's he doing in here with the adults?"

When he pointed, his suit jacket opened to the point where Phil could see something he recognized as the butt of a 1911A1 Colt

111

semiautomatic pistol. He naturally wondered what a man so armed was doing in the German-American Gospel Tract Foundation building.

"He is a newcomer, freshly arrived to labor beside us doing the Lord's work."

"Praise God! As He knows, we need all the help we can get. Unless, of course, you are pulling my leg, as you have a lamentable EXPLETIVE DELETED!! tendency to try to do."

"I am not. With the Almighty as my witness, this is CIC Administrator Philip Wallingford Williams the Third . . ."

At least he didn't call me Holden!

". . . who prefers to be called Holden," G. Lincoln concluded.

"Well, I'll be a EXPLETIVE DELETED!! monkey's EXPLETIVE DELETED!! uncle!" the Asian gentleman declared. "Looking at you, I never would have guessed you might be one of us. How old are you, Holden?"

"Seventeen, sir."

"Well, my boy, don't let anyone look down on you because you are young. That's First Timothy, Chapter four, Verse twelve, so you can take it to the bank. But on the other hand, I can't help but wonder how ol' J.C. Three is going to react when he sees who has been sent to assist us."

"I suspect the PL is going to keep Holden hidden from ol' J.C. Three as much as possible," G. Lincoln said.

"One never really knows what the PL will do, does one?" the diminutive Asian gentleman observed. "Especially if he's had a couple of belts of Old Bushmills."

Curiosity overwhelmed Phil, and he disobeyed G. Lincoln's order not to ask questions.

"What are you talking about?" he asked.

"Ah, the innocence of youth!" the Asian gentleman said. "Old Bushmills, my son, is the modern version of what Saint Patrick and his fellow monks called *aqua vitae,* which means —"

"Water of Life," Phil interrupted. "I know my Latin. What I want to know is who is the PL and who is ol' J.C. Three?"

"Geronimo, when had you planned to bring Holden up to speed on those matters?"

"Now is as good a time as any, I suppose," G. Lincoln said. "But why don't we let Holden buy us a libation before we get started?"

"Every once in a great while, Geronimo, you do make a good suggestion."

The waiter was summoned. G. Lincoln ordered "another just like this" and after being advised what that meant, the over-weight Asian said, "That will do nicely for me, too."

Whereupon the waiter turned to Phil and asked, "And for you, sir?"

"Holden," the midget sumo wrestler then quoted, " 'My son, if sinners entice you, do not give in to them.' Proverbs one:ten."

"I'll bear that in mind," Phil replied. "I will have the same, please, bartender. By the same I mean a double Famous Pheasant, two ice cubes, water on the side."

"Didn't you hear the scripture Fu Manchu just quoted?" G. Lincoln demanded indignantly.

"I did, and the next time someone I'm given proof is a sinner tries to entice me, I'll have another Coca-Cola. Got it, Geronimo?"

" 'Whoever keeps his mouth and his tongue keeps himself out of trouble,' " Fu Manchu quoted, "Proverbs —"

"Twenty-one, Verse twenty-three," Phil interrupted.

"You know Holy Scripture?" Fu Manchu asked incredulously.

"Wouldn't you say that's self-evident, Fu Manchu?" Phil countered.

It was in fact the only scripture that Phil had ever committed to memory. It had been burned indelibly therein as a result of his having written Proverbs 21:23 fifteen hundred times on a blackboard as punishment for his having suggested to a fifteen-year-old upperclassman at the Bordentown Military Academy that he "go EXPLETIVE DELETED!! himself" when the latter told him to "Give me another fifty," by which he meant that Phil should perform fifty additional repetitions of the push-up exercise in addition to the fifty repetitions Phil had just finished.

"Holden, I may be forced to reassess my initial assessment of you, which frankly isn't very flattering," Fu Manchu said.

The bartender delivered the drinks.

"Bottoms up!" Fu Manchu cried, and downed his.

When G. Lincoln tossed his drink down, Phil decided he had no choice but to do the same.

The next morning, Phil was forced to conclude that tossing down a drink had not been wise, as from that point onward, he could remember only bits and smidgens of what happened later.

He remembered Fu Manchu saying, "Barman, inasmuch as Confucius has taught us that 'Flight on one wing is difficult if not entirely impossible,' you'd better do that again."

And after Phil had downed a third double Famous Pheasant, two ice cubes, water on the side, without touching the water, Phil remembered, if not very clearly, the following exchange:

"I've decided there is a place for you, Holden, my boy, laboring beside Geronimo and myself in the Lord's vineyards," the diminutive Asian had said. "And as proof of my sincerity, you may now address me as 'Angus.'"

"Why should I call you Angus?"

"Because you will be speaking to me, and my Christian name is Angus. My surname is McTavish. Is that so difficult for you to comprehend, Newfound Friend Holden?"

"My name is not Holden. It's Philip. Philip Wallingford Williams the Third."

"You won't mind if I call you Phil, I hope, as your entire moniker is a bit of a mouthful. I suspect that is the reason Geronimo has dubbed you Holden."

"And while we're at it, why do you call him Geronimo?"

"Because that is my name," Geronimo said. "Geronimo Lincoln Rutherford."

"I can tell from the look of utter bafflement on ol' Phil's face that he is somewhat confused by all this. Inasmuch as it has a bearing on his future labors at our side doing the Lord's work, I suggest we clarify the matter for him."

"You first, Angus."

"If you insist. Phil, my grandfather, Fergus McTavish, was known professionally as Fearless Fergus. 'Fearless Fergus and His Savage Beasts' was what was known as the center ring attraction of the Smith, Barney & Sons Three Ring Circus and Freak Show.

"Attired in riding britches and boots, a white polo shirt, and with a pith helmet on his head and holding a 1917 Colt revolver loaded with blank cartridges, he entered a cage and caused lions and tigers to jump through hoops, et cetera.

"One day, he looked out of the lion's cage to the attraction in the ring to his right. And then quickly looked away as he wasn't at all interested in vertically challenged Japanese jugglers or oversized sumo wrestlers.

"Then Grandpapa Fergus, as he often related, looked at the attraction ring to his left, in which a troupe of Chinese acrobats was doing their thing. His eye fell upon one of the latter, a young woman, and after she finished doing a dozen backward somersaults over Shetland ponies and two men on miniature motorcycles and had regained her feet, their eyes met and locked.

"Grandmama Chu-hua — 'Chrysanthemum' in English — as we called her, said she knew it was love at first sight, and this made her sad, as she knew her family would never give their permission for her to wed a Scots-American, as they regarded all white men as crude savages and Scots-Americans as the worst of that entire ethnic subdivision.

"Grandpapa Fergus overcame Chu-hua's father's objections by taking his friend Oscar with him when he called on Chu-hua's father to ask for her hand in marriage. Permission came quickly when Oscar started to drag Chu-hua's brother, Desheng — that means Virtuous — out of the tent. At that point, Grandmama's father decided he'd rather feed a daughter to a Scots-American savage than a son to Grandpapa's Bengal tiger, Oscar.

"The couple was shortly afterward united in holy matrimony in the center ring while the Smith, Barney & Sons Three Ring Circus and Freak Show was playing Irvington, New Jersey.

"As the Irvington theological establishment refused to have anything to do with the circus — they objected strenuously to the bare-breasted Hawaiian hula dancers in the Freak Show — the ceremony was performed by the Reverend Wilson Graham, the circus chaplain.

"Brother Billy, as he liked to be called, had just started his evangelical career by talking John Smith — the Smith in Smith, Barney — into permitting him to set up a small tent on the circus grounds into which he attempted to lure sinners as they left the Freak Show.

"Grandpapa Fergus was surprised when the Japanese — both the vertically challenged and the sumo wrestlers — showed up for the wedding because he knew the Japanese and the Chinese were always saying unkind things about one another.

"Only much later did he learn that all Chinese did not dislike all Japanese and vice versa, and that this was especially true under the Big Top. He did not realize how much they liked one another until I was born, and by then the die had been cast, so to speak."

Phil remembered, somewhat vaguely, confessing he didn't understand.

Angus McTavish answered: "My father, an only child, was perfectly normal, physically speaking, except that he suffered terribly from ailurophobia and was thus unable to follow in Grandpapa's footsteps into the lion's cage. But the circus was in Daddy's blood, and he remained with Smith, Barney, first playing the double bell euphonium in the circus band, then becoming ringmaster at a very young age, and ultimately becoming, following the deaths of first Barney and then Smith, chief executive of the circus, making him the Big Shot of the Big Top, as it were.

"My mother similarly was of perfectly normal height and weight, of good solid Midwest Polish-German stock. My father met her when she had run away to join the circus, and he had given her employment as a bare-breasted Hawaiian hula dancer in the Freak Show.

"When I was five years old I was considerably shorter than other five-year-olds, and conspicuously heavier in weight than my peers, and was putting away a quart of *chankonabe* at both lunch and dinner . . ."

The next morning, Phil remembered that he had confessed his ignorance *vis-à-vis chankonabe,* and that Angus McTavish had explained it was a stew made from a variety of meats, fish, and vegetables all cooked in a broth and served with numerous side dishes.

And that Angus had gone on: "Where was I? Oh, yes. At that point, aware as he was of the genetic teachings of Augustinian Friar Gregor Johann Mendel, my father began to suspect that unbeknownst to Grandmama Chu-hua, certain of her female antecedents had been a lot cozier with the Japanese jugglers and sumo wrestlers, with whom they shared the Big Top, than anyone had suspected at the time. He didn't know who, of course, but he did know that the genes causing vertical insufficiency and gross obesity in his first — and as it turned out only — son had not come from his side of the family."

At that point, they had another round, and that was the last thing Phil could remember the next morning when he was rudely awakened by Geronimo pouring cold water from a small wastebasket onto him.

"Rise and shine, Holden, it's zero-eight-hundred and zero-eight-hundred means ROTPIP time."

"Why did you pour cold water on me?"

"It was the only thing I could think of after pushing, shouting, and twisting your big toe failed to call you from slumber. How's your head?"

"Excuse me?"

"I was afraid you might have hurt it when you fell off the Clydesdale at the Pferd und Frauen."

Holden had no idea what he was talking about, but could not ask as he had a sudden urgent need of the sanitary facilities in their shared bathroom.

[Four]

About an hour later, as they drove down Karl-Marx-Strasse in the Spandau district, Phil asked, "May I ask where we are going?"

"Back to Block One, 'Familiarization with Berlin,' of your ROTPIP."

"I don't understand."

"As Angus explained to you last night, you will almost certainly be assigned duties as a courier, in addition to your other duties, whatever they may turn out to be. Couriers take things from one place to another. And if you think about it, Holden, you can't take something somewhere if you don't know where somewhere is, can you?"

"I guess not."

At about this time, Phil solemnly vowed that as long as he lived to *Never again consume more than four Famous Pheasant doubles, two ice cubes, water on the side — or equivalent — in a twenty-four-hour period, So Help Me, God.*

(Truth being stranger than fiction, Phil has lived up to his vow — with a few rare

122

exceptions — to this day.)

It was not only Phil's four-star hangover that caused him to swear partial abstention in perpetuity but also that he had blacked out, was confused, and had hallucinated.

While he was sure that he had indeed had drinks and dinner, and then "gone on the town" with G. Lincoln and a diminutive Asian gentleman named Angus McTavish, and that Angus did indeed look like a miniature sumo wrestler, Phil had no idea whether Angus was pulling his leg with the explanation he offered or whether Angus was in fact the grandson of a lion tamer named Fergus who had married a Chinese acrobat whose grandmother had fooled around with both Japanese sumo wrestlers and dwarf jugglers.

That was a bit hard to believe, but not in the same league, incredibility-wise, as a clear memory he had of having been taken from the German-American Gospel Tract Foundation by Angus and G. Lincoln and driven to a bar just off the Kurfürsten-damm.

The establishment — in what Phil decided was not a simple memory, but a memory of an alcohol-induced hallucination — was called Pferd und Frauen. In it, six white Clydesdale horses marched proudly around in a circle to the music from the beginning of Act III of the opera *Die Walküre,* which is often called *The Ride of the Valkyries.*

On the Clydesdales were six blond Valkyries wearing nothing but derby hats and patent leather knee-high riding boots. In his hallucination, Phil remembered having nimbly leapt up onto one of the Clydesdales and wrapping his arms around the *Walküre* already sitting there.

Phil remembered G. Lincoln, shortly after he'd poured the ice water on him, having said something about his having fallen from a horse.

"G. Lincoln, you said something earlier about my having fallen from a horse?"

"Right. One moment there you were in Pferd und Frauen, up on the Clydesdale, hanging on to the Valkyrie's boobs, and yelling 'Hi-Yo, Silver! Away!" Everybody cheered, and the next moment you were passed out in the sawdust. Angus picked you up and we brought you home."

"I guess I embarrassed you and Angus, as well as disgraced myself, and my CIC career is about to end in shame and dismissal?"

"Not at all. You made a very good impression on Angus last night. He thought your imbibing was in keeping — especially when you started drinking what you called

Spritzers . . ."

"Spritzers?"

"You showed us how to make them. Two three-ounce hookers of Slivovitz added to a liter of beer, along with a *soupçon* of Pernod. Quite tasty. But I digress. Angus said your imbibing, and your capacity, was in keeping with the highest traditions of the agency."

Holden then and there made another solemn vow, this one to never imbibe a Spritzer again in his lifetime.

"By the agency, I gather you mean the Central Intelligence Agency?"

"Bite your tongue, Holden! We of the agency never say that out loud!"

"Sorry."

"Perhaps I should have said 'the highest traditions of the German-American Gospel Tract Foundation,' which is what we call 'the beard' for that organization the name of which is never supposed to pass our lips. But I digress yet again.

"Angus said that I should make every effort to hasten your passage through your ROTPIP. The sooner you do, the quicker you can start assisting in the saving of souls."

"I don't know what that means," Phil confessed.

"In layman's parlance, it means causing some EXPLETIVE DELETED!! Russian to change sides. Ol' J.C. Three is the master of that —"

"Last night, I asked you who ol' J.C. Three is," Phil interrupted.

"And I told you four times that he is Supervisory Special Agent Jonathan Fitzwater Caldwell the Third, who is also a lieutenant colonel of cavalry, pay grade O-5, both identities being the beard for his being presiding pastor of the German-American Gospel Tract Foundation, which itself is the beard for his being the Berlin station chief of that organization whose name is never supposed to pass our lips."

"It must have slipped my mind."

"I'm not surprised. You were pretty well occupied most of the evening trying to have bareback carnal congress with the Valkyrie."

Oh, my God! Phil suddenly thought. *What if I succeeded?*

Is it possible that I finally lost my status as the world's only seventeen-year-old virgin yet can't remember even one lousy lewd and lascivious detail of doing so?

And I can't ask, obviously, for clarification.

If one passes a milestone of life like that, one is expected to remember it!

I may have to give up all intoxicants of any kind!!!

"And who is PL?" Phil asked. "Did you tell me that, too?"

"Four times. PL, which stands for Pugnacious Leprechaun, is Lieutenant Colonel William 'Don't Call Me Bill' O'Reilly. That's not a beard for anything. He's pugnacious, and looks like a leprechaun. *Ergo sum* it fits."

"I think you meant to say, '*Id est,* it fits,' " Phil said. "*Ergo sum* is two-thirds of the Latin phrase *cogito, ergo sum,* which means 'I think, therefore I am.' "

"I think I am going to regret you coming into my life, Holden. One thing I can't stand is a smart-ass who talks Latin."

IV
PHIL MEETS THE WRATH OF GOD

Berlin, Germany
Monday, May 19, 1947

While Phil was having breakfast alone the following Monday morning, First Sergeant/Special Agent Dumbrowski stopped at his table and inquired, "Where is your accomplice in absolutely disgusting public behavior to the detriment of good military order and discipline, Administrator Williams?"

"I beg your pardon?"

"Specifically, where is Administrator Rutherford?"

"I don't know specifically where he is, First Sergeant, but he left a note for me, written in soap, on our communal bathroom mirror saying there would be no ROTPIP for me today as he would be busy."

"Busy doing what?"

"He didn't say, First Sergeant, but I would

hazard the guess that he is about the Lord's work."

"I would hazard the guess that the EXPLETIVE DELETED!! bribed my EXPLETIVE DELETED!! company clerk to keep him abreast of any developments in my office that might affect him, and that my EXPLETIVE DELETED!! company clerk tipped him to the fact that Supervisory Special Agent O'Reilly is in possession of a photograph of you in *Berlin am Nacht* — which means *Berlin at Night* — magazine, said photograph showing you in your EXPLETIVE DELETED!! birthday suit fondling the bosom of a naked blonde while the both of you are on the back of a EXPLETIVE DELETED!! horse."

Phil's stomach suddenly ached as it had the morning after the incident First Sergeant Dumbrowski was apparently describing, although since then absolutely nothing stronger than Listerine mouthwash had passed his lips.

"And I would hazard the further guess that once he was so tipped, he found something to do that would keep him from having to discuss what the caption on the aforementioned photograph describes as 'Horny Horseplay in the Pferd und Frauen,' " Dumbrowski went on. "That guess ring any bells, Lone Ranger?"

"I really don't know where he is, First Sergeant."

"Then you will have to face Supervisory Special Agent O'Reilly on your lonesome, Administrator Williams, which you will do now. And may God have mercy on your soul."

"Yes, First Sergeant."

"If I had my druthers, Administrator Williams," Supervisory Special Agent William "Don't Call Me Bill" O'Reilly began a few minutes later, "I would immediately ship you, you miserable Protestant sexual deviate EXPLETIVE DELETED!!, on the next plane to Fort Benning, Georgia — after I busted your miserable EXPLETIVE DELETED!! to Recruit, of course — in the perhaps wishful-thinking hope that the rigorous training and disciplinary measures available at the U.S. School of Infantry Excellence might turn you into a soldier."

"Yes, sir."

"Don't interrupt me while I'm chewing your EXPLETIVE DELETED!!, Williams!"

"Yes, sir. I mean, no, sir."

"Unfortunately, there is a protocol in place here in the Thirty-third which I must follow. This misguided document requires that when drastic disciplinary action is

proposed for a miserable EXPLETIVE DE-
LETED!! such as yourself, it must be reviewed — a last court of appeal, so to speak
— by Supervisory Special Agent Jonathan
Fitzwater Caldwell the Third.

"Don't get your hopes up, you oversexed
underage deviate, that when he is apprised
of your outrageous behavior, Supervisory
Special Agent Caldwell . . . Did I mention
he is a lieutenant of cavalry, pay grade O-5?"

"No, sir. You didn't mention that."

"Where was I? Oh. Don't get your hopes
up that Colonel Caldwell will temper the
action I am proposing with mercy. He is
deeply offended by sexual misbehavior of
any kind, and they don't call him 'The
Wrath of God' for nothing.

"So, what's going to happen now is that
you will be taken to Supervisory Special
Agent Caldwell the Third's office for the
pro forma review I have mentioned, following which you will be returned here to pack
your duffel bag and get on the plane to Fort
Benning.

"Be prepared to say *Auf Wiedersehen, Berlin,* you miserable Protestant sexual degener-
ate."

"Yes, sir."

Phil was driven to Colonel Caldwell's office

in an olive-drab Volkswagen by the field first sergeant, a huge bull of a man who was not known for his intellectual ability.

He guided Phil with a massive hand on his arm into a building in the *kaserne* housing the Office of the Chief, Military Government, and then into an office with a sign identifying it as the Office of Liaison Coordination, and finally into an office with a sign identifying it as the Office of the Deputy Liaison Coordination Coordinator.

It was empty.

The "field first," as he was known to his underlings, sat Phil down in a straight-backed chair beside a desk with a sign that identified it as that of Captain J. K. Brewster, Cavalry.

"Stay there, EXPLETIVE DELETED!! head. Somebody will come and get you."

"Yes, Field First."

After several minutes, Phil's eye naturally wandered.

It fell upon the "Out" basket on Captain Brewster's desk. He quickly averted his glance as a document in the "Out" basket was stamped Top Secret and it seemed pretty clear to Phil that the loss of his Top Secret clearance was looming, if it had not already been jerked.

A minute or so later, reasoning he didn't

know that his Top Secret clearance had been jerked, only that it seemed entirely likely, he had another look in the "Out" basket. On the document's cover sheet was a red-lead pencil. Phil picked it up to get it out of the way and then lifted the cover sheet.

His eyes widened as he read what was typed on the sheet under the cover sheet:

TOP SECRET

From: J. F. Caldwell III, Station Chief, Berlin
To: (EYES ONLY)
Hon. Ralph Peters
Deputy Director for Soviet Affairs
Central Intelligence Agency
Langley, Virginia
Via: By Hand of Armed Officer Courier
Subject: Report of Successful Recruitment of NKGB Colonel Vladimir Polshov

TOP SECRET

I really shouldn't be reading this, Phil thought, *whether or not my Top Secret clearance has been jerked.*

But on the other hand, it can't be the real thing.

The real thing wouldn't be lying around in an "Out" basket in an empty office.

Probably it's only a sample, an example of how this sort of thing should be done.

And this is as close as I'm ever going to get in my life to even an example of how a real one should be done.

He took the document from the "Out" basket and put it in his lap, and then, without thinking about it, picked up the red pencil. Then he began to slowly examine the document.

He was so engaged ten minutes later when someone came into the office.

"Well, I must say this, young fellow," the newcomer, a pleasant-looking gentleman in his late thirties, said, "I like your taste in sports jackets."

Phil was momentarily confused until he realized that both he and the man were wearing identical sports jackets, light brown herringbone tweed with brown calf leather sewn into the seams. Phil recalled the J. Press salesman having told him it was — they were — called the "Skull and Bones Two Button with Leather."

"And I admire yours, sir."

"What are you doing in here, son?" the

man asked. "And what is that in your lap?"

Phil held it up and showed him.

The man snatched it from his hands.

"Where did you get this?"

"It was in the 'Out' basket, sir."

"And what are you doing with it?" the man asked, and before Phil could reply, asked, as if of himself, "And what are these notations in red pencil?"

"Sir, they indicate the six ambiguities and four grammatical errors I found. I didn't have time to get all the way through it, of course."

"Why were you looking for ambiguities and grammatical errors?"

"Sir, I was trained as a CIC administrator. That's what CIC administrators do."

"Son, I'm going to ask you a couple of questions. They may strike you as a bit odd, especially considering your youth, but please answer them as best you can."

"Yes, sir."

"Tell me, my boy, as incredible as this might sound, have you ever gone horseback riding with a naked lady?"

"Yes, sir. I'm afraid I have."

"And are you familiar with an officer by the name of O'Reilly? Lieutenant Colonel William 'Don't Call Me Bill' O'Reilly?"

"Yes, sir, I am."

"And when did you last see Colonel O'Reilly?"

"Earlier this morning, sir. Just before he sent me over here."

"In connection with your equestrian escapade in the Pferd und Frauen?"

"Yes, sir."

"And one last question. If you have been here less than two weeks, I wonder how you managed to find your way to the Pferd und Frauen?"

"Sir, I was taken there by two friends."

"One of them about so high?" the man asked, holding his hand about four feet off the ground. "And the other, by chance, called Geronimo?"

"Yes, sir."

"And one final thing. Would you be good enough to point out to me the six ambiguities and four grammatical errors you say you found in this document?"

"Yes, sir," Phil said, and proceeded to so.

"I'll be a EXPLETIVE DELETED!!," the man said.

It was the first time he had used an expletive. But that would soon change.

"Come with me, son," the man said. "And bring that report with you."

"Yes, sir."

The man led Phil out of the office and

down the corridor, and finally into another office. Two officers, a major and a captain, jumped to their feet when they saw the man.

"Good morning, Colonel, sir," they said in chorus.

"In no EXPLETIVE DELETED!! way can this be judged a good EXPLETIVE DELETED!! morning," the man replied. "Where's that EXPLETIVE DELETED!! idiot Captain Brewster?"

"Sir, I believe the captain is checking on the arrangements for the regular Monday West Point Alumni luncheon," the major replied.

"Major, you get your EXPLETIVE DELETED!! over there and drag the EXPLETIVE DELETED!! back by his EXPLETIVE DELETED!! testicles," the man ordered. "When you get him here, find a EXPLETIVE DELETED!! blackboard and some EXPLETIVE DELETED!! chalk and have the incompetent EXPLETIVE DELETED!! write 'I will not leave documents classified Top Secret unattended in my Out box.' Have the stupid EXPLETIVE DELETED!! write that fifteen hundred EXPLETIVE DELETED!! times. Clear?"

"Yes, sir, Colonel, sir," the major said.

"And you, Captain, will get your EXPLETIVE DELETED!! out of that EXPLETIVE DELETED!! chair and go find EXPLETIVE DE-

LETED!! Angus McTavish and EXPLETIVE DELETED!! G. Lincoln Rutherford, wherever the little EXPLETIVE DELETED!! may be hiding. Drag them back here by their you-know-whats. Get two more EXPLETIVE DELETED!! blackboards and more EXPLETIVE DELETED!! chalk, and have them write 'For the wages of sin is death. Romans 6:23' fifteen hundred EXPLETIVE DELETED!! times."

"Yes, sir, Colonel, sir," the captain said.

"And while you are so occupied, I'm going to take this splendid young man — who kept me from sending Deputy Director Ralph Peters in Langley a report containing six ambiguities and four grammatical errors — home with me for coffee and croissants. While we are there, I will prevail upon him to finish his examination of said report to see how EXPLETIVE DELETED!! many more EXPLETIVE DELETED!! ambiguities and/or grammatical errors that EXPLETIVE DELETED!! moron Brewster missed."

V
PREPARING FOR THE HUNTING TRIP (PART 2)

Executive Apartment One

The Warren

2700 Muddiebay International Airport
   Boulevard

Muddiebay, Mississippi

1430 Monday, September 1, 1975

"Soon, my precious," Mrs. Homer C. (Carol-Anne) Crandall said to Mr. Randolph C. Bruce, as she hoisted her panty hose up and around her derriere, "we will have hours and hours — even days — to do the sort of thing we've just been doing instead of the thirty-eight minutes we have just had."

"You're the one who insisted on having a quickie before your husband came home from the bank," Randy replied.

"And it was wonderful, my precious."

"Yeah," Randy agreed without much enthusiasm. He had just noticed that the

139

derriere up and around which she had just tugged her panty hose seemed to be sagging a bit more than it seemed to be sagging the last time he looked.

"I have to worry about him," Carol-Anne said, a bit petulantly. "You don't have to worry about the ladies."

She was referring to the ladies with whom Randy lived — his grandmother, Mrs. Jefferson Davis (Abigail) Bruce, who was ninety-two and known as "Auntie Abby," and her sister, Miss Penelope Warwick, who was ninety and known as "Auntie Penny."

Randy had lived with them since he was twenty, when he was summoned home from Ole Miss and told by the two of them, in tearful chorus, that his "Mommy and Daddy had been called home to the Lord."

He was later to learn that the call had come after his mother — not satisfied with his father's explanation of why he was taking a nap with a nude statuesque nineteen-year-old African-American upstairs maid named "Boopsie" — had opened fire with his James Purdey & Sons Best Grade 12-bore shotgun, causing two 1 1/4 ounce loads of #6 lead birdshot to enter his chest.

His mother, later that day, had been called home to the Lord after she put the 28-inch barrels of her own James Purdey & Sons

Best Grade .410-gauge shotgun in her mouth and pulled the trigger, thus delivering 3/4 ounce of #9 lead birdshot into her cranium.

She had been simply unable to face the prospect of being hauled off in handcuffs and shame to the Muddiebay County Jail as the sheriff said he was going to have to do, inasmuch as she had earlier that day attended the regular meeting of The Tuesday Luncheon Club and there had announced to the full membership her intention to "go home now and blow that EXPLETIVE DELETED!! philandering EXPLETIVE DELETED!! husband of mine into EXPLETIVE DELETED!! Louisiana."

Considering that, the sheriff said, he was sorry but her explanation that she didn't know her late husband's Purdey was loaded was not going to wash away what had happened.

Randy still had both shotguns. "Daddy's Purdey" was one hell of a gun for pheasant and other large wildfowl, and "Mommy's Four-Ten" was just about perfect to deal with the EXPLETIVE DELETED!! starlings that were always eating the expensive grass seed sown upon the lawn of "Our Tara," the antebellum mansion that the Trust Fund owned and in which Auntie Abby and

Auntie Penny lived.

When informed of the untimely passing of his Daddy and Mommy, Randy had been assured that he had nothing to worry about. He would now live with "Auntie Abby" and "Auntie Penny." He was also told that his parents had left their only son all their worldly possessions, and that said worldly possessions had been left to him in the Randolph C. Bruce Trust, which would be administered by Auntie Abby.

A certain portion of the trust — actually a hell of a lot of money, but only a small fraction of the trust — would come to him on his twenty-first birthday, presuming he had by then graduated from Ole Miss. If he had not so graduated, the "On Majority & Graduation Bequest" would not be granted until he did. If ten years passed and he still hadn't graduated, the Trust Fund would be cashed out, and the cash given to Beauvoir, the Jefferson Davis Home and Presidential Museum in Biloxi.

In the three years that followed — of the total of eight years he spent at Ole Miss — Randy learned many things. First and most difficult to live with was that Auntie Abby — in a noble effort to teach her only grandson that following in the philandering, gambling, and over-imbibing footsteps of

his father, her only son, was a no-no —
would shut off his allowance if she learned
he was so engaged.

At this point, he came across an old Army
adage, to wit: *If indiscretions you must have,
keep them one hundred miles from the flagpole.*

Reasoning that his flagpole might well be
the one in front of "Our Tara" in Muddiebay, or one of the two from which the flags
of the Confederacy and the United States
fluttered on the lawn of the president of Ole
Miss in Oxford (whom he suspected was
reporting on him to Auntie Abby), he
thereafter did his philandering, gambling,
and over-imbibing at least a hundred miles
distant from both locations.

This proved to have two beneficial results.
The amount of his allowance was quite
generous, as Randy's father, who himself
claimed Ole Miss as his alma mater, understood the cost of philandering, gambling,
and over-imbibing at the institution.

Because Randy now rarely had the chance
to travel one hundred miles in search of sin
— he was really cracking the books — he
wound up with an astonishing amount of
cash. He had never before really understood
how expensive philandering, gambling, and
over-imbibing were.

He was cracking the books, of course, so he could get what he now thought of as the EXPLETIVE DELETED!! degree and thus come into the Majority & Graduation Bequest. And in so doing, to his surprise, he found several books in his Business Administration course to be absolutely fascinating.

Among them were *Brilliant Swindles, How Charley Ponzi Almost Got Away with It, What Exactly Is Usury?, Greed Pays,* and perhaps most important, *Why You Should Seek Legal Counsel Before You're Caught.*

The latter caused him to establish a much closer relationship with another student, a fellow native of Muddiebay, than had existed before Mommy and Daddy were called home to the Lord and he had to start thinking about his future.

Moses Lipshutz, who had been at Ole Miss for just over two years, was about to graduate and enter the Ole Miss School of Law.

"Moses, old buddy," Randy said, "is there anything I can do for you here at Ole Miss?"

"Not unless you can get me into your fraternity . . ."

"Why the hell would you want to do that? My brothers in Kappa Omega Delta are, to put it bluntly, the dumbest EXPLETIVE

DELETED!! EXPLETIVE DELETED!! kickers in the South. The only reason I joined was to get in their high-stakes poker games, which I milk regularly twice a month."

"When I commence my practice, Randolph —"

"Call me 'Randy,' Moses," Randy interrupted.

"Why?"

"We might become friends."

"Huh!" Moses snorted. "Fat EXPLETIVE DELETED!! chance of that."

"You were telling me why you want to join the EXPLETIVE DELETED!! kickers in Kappa Omega Delta."

"It would look good on my résumé when I begin my practice of law. The Ol' Miss Good Ol' Boy network, so to speak."

"Okay. Anything else?"

"Indulging your fantasy, Randolph, my beloved Rachel, to whom I am betrothed, would like to be Ole Miss Homecoming Queen."

"I can handle you getting into Kappa Omega Delta, Moses, buddy, but I don't know about the Homecoming Queen."

"In case this has somehow escaped your attention, Randolph —"

"Please call me Randy."

"I only address my friends by their infor-

145

mal names."

"Sorry."

"As I was saying, Mr. Bruce, in case this has escaped your attention, I am, and my beloved Rachel also is, of the Hebrew persuasion. There has never been a Hebrew in Kappa Omega Delta. And it should go without saying there never has been a Jewish Princess who metamorphosed into an Ole Miss Homecoming Queen. How are you going to handle that, Mr. Bruce?"

"I hold about fifteen thousand in markers acquired in friendly play with my Kappa Omega Delta brothers. I could get you in if you were a Ubangi in a grass skirt."

"Randy, ol' hometown buddy, I think I have underestimated you. You get me into Kappa Omega Delta, and I'll get those EX-PLETIVE DELETED!! kickers — you did say Fifteen Large in markers, didn't you, old pal?"

"That's what I said."

"Randy, my pal, you get me in EXPLETIVE DELETED!! KOD and turn those markers over to me, I'll have those EXPLETIVE DE-LETED!! kickers and their EXPLETIVE DE-LETED!! girlfriends standing in line to elect my Rachel to be Homecoming Queen, or to any other position her adorable little heart desires."

Randy did, and Moses did, and that was the beginning of their lifelong acquaintanceship.

They graduated from Ole Miss together, Randy with a bachelor of fine arts degree in Southern culture after eight years of study, and Moses, after just over five years of study, with a bachelor of science (banking), a master's degree in business administration, and a doctoral degree in law. In other words, entitled to append to his name the letters B.S., M.B.A., L.L.D.

With graduation, Randy came into his Majority & Graduation Bequest. Accompanied by Auntie Abby and Auntie Penny, he went to the law offices of Tancey, Castleberry & Porter, where they took turns over three hours explaining precisely what the bequest was, what it meant to him, and why the sensible thing for Randy to do, now that he had come into all that money, was to let Tancey, Castleberry & Porter continue to handle things for him.

"There it is, Randy," Burton Castleberry concluded. "Do you have any questions?"

"Just one, Mr. Castleberry."

"And that is?"

"Can you get all the documents involved in my bequest over to the chambers of Dr.

Lipshutz this afternoon, or will it take longer?"

"Why would we want to do that?"

"Because Dr. Lipshutz is my legal counsel."

"Randolph," Auntie Abby said, "I don't think that's wise."

"Have you been at the bourbon again?" Auntie Penny had inquired.

"Randy, my boy. Not that I am in any way prejudiced," Burton Castleberry said, "but you are aware that Moses Lipshutz is a Jew?"

"Oh, yes. That's why I want him to represent me legally. He marches in the sacred footsteps of Judah Benjamin, reverently remembered as 'the Confederate Kissinger,' who was also a Jew. According to all accounts, he had a brilliant law practice in New Orleans before the War for Southern Independence, during which he served as, successively, attorney general, secretary of war, and secretary of state in the Confederate Cabinet, and was President Jefferson Davis's closest and most trusted adviser."

"I never knew he was Jewish," Auntie Penny said.

"And following the war," Randy went on, "after having narrowly escaped the clutches of the infernal Yankees the day they arrested

Jefferson Davis, he made his way to England, where he became legal counsel to Her Majesty the Queen."

"Well, if a Jew named Judah Benjamin was good enough for Her Majesty," Auntie Abby, who was a great admirer of the late Queen Victoria, said, "then a Jew named Moses Lipshutz is good enough for my Randy. Do what he says, Burton."

The documents to which Randy referred were moved to Dr. Lipshutz's chambers that very afternoon. That very night, Tancey, Castleberry & Porter had a partners' meeting, during which it was decided to offer one Moses Lipshutz, L.L.D., a partnership in the firm.

"If he's under the roof, so to speak, we can at least keep our eye on him," Burton Castleberry had argued.

On Moses's acceptance the next morning, the firm was renamed Tancey, Castleberry, Porter & Lipshutz, and Randy's documents returned to where they had previously been.

Although he now had his hands on some real money, which he and Moses could — and did — immediately put to work making more real money, Randy believed that they could make even more money if they could tap into the Randolph C. Bruce Trust.

He realized that this was going to be difficult if not impossible. He knew that Auntie Abby devoutly believed in the words of Benjamin Franklin — specifically *A penny saved is a penny earned* and *Neither a borrower nor a lender be* — even though she regarded the kite-flying founder of the U.S. Postal Service as "a shameful libertine who cavorted with Parisian ladies of the evening young enough to be his granddaughters and should have been castrated."

Worse, Randy knew that tapping his trust would be absolutely out of the question if either Auntie Abby or Auntie Penny caught him at any philandering, gambling, and over-imbibing whatsoever. She could no longer withhold his allowance, but she could, and would, keep him from borrowing any of his own money.

So he decided he had to follow the old military adage *vis-à-vis* sin and the flagpole, and keep his philandering, gambling, and over-imbibing one hundred miles from the flagpole on the lawn in front of "Our Tara."

He never got even close to dipping into the money in the trust. But once, when he and Moses were discussing a cash flow problem — Moses had dropped a large bundle at the baccarat table in Biloxi's famed Hotel Beau Rivage Casino and Randy had had to settle a lawsuit with a

EXPLETIVE DELETED!! outrageous sum of money after a boat owner during duck-hunting season innocently sailed into the tidewaters near the MSB&DD&CSR&FC, Inc., facility and, he alleged, had been brought under gunfire that reminded him of his service at the Inchon Landing in Korea — Randy did happen to mention to Moses that his grandmother was getting on in years, and there was a family tradition of accidental death by firearm.

"Forget it, Randy," Moses wisely counseled. "No one's going to believe that an eighty-four-year-old in a wheelchair took out her eighty-six-year-old sister by accident while cleaning her shotgun."

But as the years passed — and especially since the formation of MSB&DD& CSR&FC, Inc., which had brought both Señor Pancho Gonzales and Executive Apartment One in The Warren into the equation — Randy began to wonder if it was really necessary for him to keep religiously following the One Hundred Mile Rule.

For one thing, the ladies didn't seem to notice — Auntie Abby's sight wasn't what it used to be, and Auntie Penny was of course confined to her wheelchair — that he on occasion was already violating both the no-imbibing and no-gambling tenets.

They believed, for example, that when he went to Executive Apartment Three with Moses Lipshutz and other gentlemen, it really was to discuss business in a private social atmosphere, not that they were playing No Limit Texas Hold 'Em.

Neither did either of the ladies seem to find anything out of the ordinary when he took tea with them each Thursday afternoon at five that his tea came in an oversized cup with ice cubes and a glass of water on the side.

He hadn't violated the third no-no, the one dealing with philandering, until two months ago, and then Demon Rum, so to speak, was involved.

Feeling a strong urge to bust some birds, and fearing that if he telephoned his shooting crony Phil Williams to ask if he felt similarly inclined, Phil would say, "Sorry, working," and hang up, Randy elected instead to drive to Mr. Williams's residence to ask him face-to-face.

So he got in his Lamborghini and drove the forty-odd miles from "Our Tara" to Foggy Point.

At first, things seemed to be going his way. As he turned off Scenic U.S. Highway 98 onto the grounds of the Foggy Point Country Club, a fire-engine-red Mercedes-Benz convertible coupe — making perhaps thirty-five miles per hour over the posted twenty-five-mile speed limit — caused Randy to drive into a ditch to avoid a collision.

Wonderful! Randy thought, having recognized the driver as Mrs. Philip W. (Brunhilde) Williams. *The AA won't be home.*

"The AA," which was the acronym for Angry Austrian, was not one of Randy's admirers.

And when he turned into the drive of 102 Country Club Road, he saw a twenty-year-old Jaguar in the process of being hauled away by a wrecker bearing the corporate logo of Foggy Point Garage & Good As New Used Parts.

Wonderful! Randy thought again. *Ol' Phil will be home, since the Jag apparently once again needs a little attention.*

Mr. Williams answered the ring of his doorbell — actually a chime, which played the first twenty bars of "Wiener Blut" — after the third repetition of said theme caused by Randy holding his finger steadily on the button.

"Hey, Randy," he greeted him cheerfully. "What's up?"

Wonderful! Randy thought a third time. *The absence of the AA has understandably put ol' Phil in a good mood.*

"How would you like to bust some birds?"

"I'd love to . . ."

"Wonderful!"

". . . but . . ."

Oh, shit!

"But what?"

"I called out to the range to make a reservation, and they told me the traps are undergoing semiannual overhaul and that the range is closed."

"All the traps?"

"That's what they told me."

"Every EXPLETIVE DELETED!! trap on every EXPLETIVE DELETED!! range?"

"That's what they said," Phil said. "Give me a call in a couple of days and we'll have another shot at it."

"Well, then, let's go out to the clubhouse and have a couple of tastes."

"Sorry, but when the AA flew off on her broom, and knowing that busting birds was off the agenda, I started to work," Phil said. "And that's what I'm going to do."

He closed the door.

Randy went to the clubhouse of the Foggy Point Country Club and into its bar even though a sign in the lobby proclaimed that it was Ladies' Day and the last thing he needed was a barroom full of Foggy Point

154

and Muddiebay females in their forties and up.

He was on his third double Famous Pheasant, two ice cubes, water on the side, when he simultaneously smelled some interesting perfume and felt a hand on his shoulder.

"Well, whatever are you doing here, Randy, on Ladies' Day?"

He turned to see Mrs. Carol-Anne Crandall, wife to Homer C. Crandall, president of the First National Bank of Muddiebay.

Resisting the very strong temptation to reply by asking, *What does it look like I'm doing, you dumb broad? Calisthenics?* he instead said, "Hey, Carol-Anne."

"Yes, thank you, don't mind if I do," Carol-Anne replied. "Barman!"

Carol-Anne drank her first — of three — double Famous Pheasant, two ice cubes, water on the side, while standing. When she was halfway through number two, the seat beside Randy became vacant, and as she moved to slide onto it she lost her balance and seemed to be about to fall down.

Randy had a good deal of experience in keeping his male drinking buddies from falling, and his reaction to Carol-Anne's predicament was Pavlovian. He grabbed what on a male drinking buddy would have been the seat of his pants and hoisted Carol-Anne onto the empty stool.

My God, what have I done? he wondered.

At that point, Carol-Anne leaned close to him, stuck her tongue in his ear, and whispered, "You naughty, naughty boy! If you're planning on doing that again, we'd better find a nicer place to do it."

She thereupon finished her second drink and signaled for a refill.

My God, Randy wondered, *what am I going to do now?*

I can't screw the wife of Homer C. Crandall, president of the First National Bank of Muddiebay.

He took a pull at his third Famous Pheasant.

On the other hand, why not?

Every time I have to borrow money from that usurious EXPLETIVE DELETED!! he screws me.

Turnabout is fair play!

"Carol-Anne," he said, "have you ever seen the sun set over the waters of beautiful Muddiebay Bay?"

"Now that you mention it, no. Why do you ask?"

"I have a little *pied-à-terre* that nobody knows about, from the windows of which one can see the sun set over the waters of beautiful Muddiebay Bay. Does that answer your description of a nicer place to do again

156

what I did before?"

"Oh, you naughty boy," she said, as she again lasciviously teased the external and middle sections of his auditory organ with the extraordinarily long external portion of her tongue. "I don't give a darn about the sun setting, and, anyway, I will have to be at home waiting for Homer to come home from the bank before it does."

"I understand," Randy said.

I have just been saved from a potential disaster!

"But I'm sure we can find something interesting for you to do to me, and vice versa, in your little *pied-à-terre* that nobody knows about in the little time we have between now and when I will have to leave in order to be home when Homer gets home from First National. Presuming we leave right now."

She raised her glass.

"Bottoms up, Randy!"

In the days and weeks that followed, Randy had tried hard, but utterly failed, to put his relationship with Carol-Anne into some sort of perspective.

For example, after they had frolicked — her term — the first time, she had shyly confessed that it was her first time with someone besides ol' Homer.

He had serious reservations about the veracity of this claim, inasmuch as he was perfectly willing to admit that despite his extensive experience in this area, he had never met someone as eager to explore the many possibilities of physical union as Carol-Anne.

After a couple of weeks, she shyly admitted that she had not been fully entitled to the white dress she had worn down the aisle the day she became Mrs. Homer C. Crandall, as she had had "some little naughty schoolgirl experiences" at Ole Miss.

Randy had no trouble with imagining what these might have been. Before Mommy and Daddy had been called home to the Lord, and Miss Abby was in a position to shut off his allowance if she caught him philandering, he had worked his way through at least half of the sorority sisters at Ole Miss, including most of those in Kappa Omega Delta, to which sisterhood Carol-Anne belonged.

But months passed before Randy concluded he had the real answer to what caused Carol-Anne's now unleashed passion. It was a combination of the fact that ol' Homer was getting a little long in the tooth with a concomitant decline in libido;

that Carol-Anne, on the other hand, having gone through the change of life, had emerged on the other side with a newfound freedom to enjoy herself without the black cloud of conception hovering over her; and finally that Carol-Anne had bought a book in a yard sale.

It was leather bound with gold leaf decoration, and she thought it would look very nice in the living room on the coffee table beside her leather-bound copy of *The Memoirs of General J. Bonaparte Robertson, CSA*. On the cover of the book she bought at the yard sale was the legend *The Kama Sutra. Translated from Hindi by Sir Richard Burton.*

Once she'd read the title, Carol-Anne had no interest in the book beyond its attractive leather binding. She had never liked cookbooks to begin with, and she was really not interested in anything Sir Richard Burton translated from any language, especially after the despicable way he had treated poor Elizabeth Taylor.

But one day — two weeks before she bumped into Randy at the bar of the Foggy Point Country Club clubhouse — she had accidentally dropped the book to the floor while dusting the table on which it had rested unopened for about five years. The impact caused it to open.

At first she was absolutely shocked at what she saw. It was really wicked, even for Richard Burton — and the whole world knew what a s*x maniac he was.

But then she remembered that every picture she had ever seen of Elizabeth Taylor had shown her smiling . . . as if she was satisfied about something.

At that point, she had another look at the *Kama Sutra.*

And another.

And another.

After about two weeks, she concluded there was a price for everything, and the price she was paying for her good life in Muddiebay was that there were no oversexed, wholly amoral men like Sir Richard Burton around who were going to carry her off and work their wicked way on her body following the illustrated "How to Do It" instructions in the *Kama Sutra.*

That very afternoon, she happened to bump into Randolph C. Bruce in the bar of the clubhouse of the Foggy Point Country Club. She had no way of knowing if he was oversexed or not, but if one believed only half the things they said about ol' Randy, there was no question that he was wholly amoral.

So, taking a deep breath and tossing down

what was left of her drink, she walked over to him and laid her hand on his shoulder.

There were other problems with their illicit relationship, of course, but the main sources of annoyance from the beginning had been the lack of someplace other than Executive Apartment One to do what they were doing, and the limited time to do what they wanted to do once they'd made it into what Carol-Anne called "Our Little Naughty Love Nest."

It was obvious that the lovebirds had to find a place where they could be alone for more than forty-five minutes at a time. But where?

Ordinarily, when Randy had a problem, he would discuss it with his two best friends — Moses Lipshutz, B.S., M.B.A., L.L.D., and Philip W. Williams, 2yrCollege GED Test — because between them they had a wealth of experience, and, although Randy really hated to admit it, both were smarter than he.

But he could not do so here. For reasons Randy didn't pretend to understand, both Moses and ol' Phil were faithful husbands. They didn't fool around even a little on business trips or hunting trips or anywhere else, even when there was zilch chance of getting caught. And they even frowned upon people who availed themselves of the opportunities presented when there was zilch chance of getting caught.

Randy had, of course, asked them why they both were behaving so oddly, and they had both offered explanations, neither of which Randy entirely believed. Both had a connection with the male organ.

Phil said that shortly after he had married Brunhilde, she had told him that if he ever "stuck that thing" in another female, she would blow it off with one of his *gottverdammt* shotguns, and that he believed her.

Moses said that, although it was not common knowledge, Abraham Cohen, his beloved Rachel's father and proprietor of Cohen's Kosher Meats & Delicatessen in Biloxi — the only establishment of its kind in the state — was also a *mohel,* an observant Jew trained in Jewish Law and the techniques of *Brit Milah,* which was ritual circumcision.

Rachel was not only familiar with the procedure, Moses told Randy, but had her own *izmel,* the razor-sharp scalpel-like knife used in the ceremony. She promised to use this on Moses if he ever did what he was commanded not to do in Exodus 21:14 — i.e., *Thou shalt not commit adultery.*

162

And after her performance of the *Brit Mi-lah* procedure, Rachel had further explained, Moses would not only be incapable, in a penile sense, of again violating the Seventh Commandment that his namesake had brought down from Mount Sinai, but for the rest of his life would have to sit down to take a leak.

And, Moses said, Rachel never makes idle threats.

After a good deal of thought and some preliminary consultations with Señor Pancho Gonzales — who was always looking for a chance to escape for a week or two from the demands of his family, which consisted of a wife, seven children, his mother, his wife's mother, and others — Randy came up with what seemed to him, in all modesty, to be an absolutely brilliant plan.

Carol-Anne would get one of the dimmer bulbs in The Tuesday Luncheon Club chandelier to propose that the ladies propose to their husbands that everybody go to London, England, and then to Dungaress, Scotland. The ladies would get a chance to shop in London, and the men to shoot grouse and other wildfowl in Scotland.

Because Homer C. Crandall was not at all

interested in shooting anything except bank robbers, he would not be going. And because Mrs. Homer C. Crandall, as president of The Tuesday Luncheon Club, whose idea the excursion was, had the moral duty to accompany the girls, she would.

In addition to the husbands of the Ladies of The Tuesday Luncheon Club who would be going, so would Señor Pancho Gonzales, president of MSB&DD&CSR&FC, Inc., who would probably be accompanied by a niece.

Mr. Philip W. Williams III would also be going along, with a mission in the plot that Randy decided he needed to hear only when it was necessary for ol' Phil to perform it.

The shooting in Scotland would be done on the grounds of Abercrombie Castle near Dungaress, Scotland. The father of the present earl, who was also of course the Earl of Abercrombie, who was the Rt. Honorable Charles William George Michael Bertram and known to his friends as "Bertie," had years previous graciously struck a deal with Amos T. Bruce, Jr., of Muddiebay, Mississippi, who was Randolph C. Bruce's father, which opened the ancestral lands to pheasant shooters for a financial consideration.

It was not the first deal the Abercrombies had struck with the Bruces. The first was in

1920, with Amos T. Bruce, Sr., Randy's grandfather, from whom, it was generally acknowledged, ol' Randy had inherited his business acumen. Old Amos, as he was called with varying degrees of affection, immediately saw, with the passage of the XVIIIth Amendment to the U.S. Constitution, a chance to turn a dollar.

Old Amos knew the tipplers of America, and maybe especially the tipplers of Mississippi and New Orleans, Louisiana, were not going to happily switch to Coca-Cola or Welch's grape juice simply because it was now against the law of the land to imbibe anything stronger. And he knew that his still (est. 1805) in a wooded area on the grounds of "Our Tara" was already at maximum production, and he was having a hard time meeting local Baptist and Methodist demand for "Mississippi's Best" white lightning. Unless Old Amos found an alternate supply of hooch, he was going to miss out on all the money that could be earned supplying the tipplers in New Orleans.

And, although Old Amos personally thought Scotch whisky tasted like horse piss, he knew that there were a lot of people in New Orleans who actually liked it. A lot.

Thus, he knew what he had to do — catch the next steamer from Charleston, South

Carolina, to Glasgow, Scotland — and he did it.

Three weeks after landing in Glasgow, and after sampling all the Scots whisky he could lay his hands on, he had found the one that was the least worst. It was called "Old Pheasant" and it came from a distillery in Dungaress. He went there and sought out the chief distiller.

This turned out to be a gaunt six-footer his own age by the odd name of Myelord, who wore a plaid skirt and had a woman's purse hanging from his belt over his crotch.

Telling himself that he should know that the booze business caused strange bedfellows, Old Amos introduced himself to Myelord as a brother distiller from the New World and offered as proof a taste of Mississippi's Best. Myelord liked it, and by the time the first Mason jar was empty, Myelord and Old Amos were pals. At that time, Old Amos asked Myelord who owned the Old Pheasant distillery.

"Actually, Amos, my newfound fellow distiller chum, I own it."

"In that case, Myelord, old buddy, I have a business proposition for you."

By the time Old Amos and Myelord had emptied a second quart-sized Mason jar of Mississippi's Best, not only had a deal been struck, but Myelord, after asking if Amos liked to shoot birds, invited him up to the castle for dinner, and to spend the night, and in the morning to have a go at popping a few pheasants.

Amos, never having seen a pheasant before, happily agreed.

The deal struck was that the Old Pheasant distillery would sell to Amos all of its output, relabeled "Famous Pheasant" and packed in wooden cases marked "Scottish Tweed," and arrange for its shipment by sea to Muddiebay Bay, where it would be off loaded in the dead of night for further shipment to New Orleans's "speakeasies" and "gentleman's clubs."

The change of name was necessary, Amos explained, because the tipplers in New Orleans never having seen a pheasant would be happier with "Famous" than they would be with "Old," the latter which would suggest to them something like an ancient chicken — in other words, tough, stringy, and smelling like a chicken coop.

Sometime during that night, Amos learned that Myelord was not his new business partner's real name, and that he was actually Bertram William Louis Oswald Harold James, Earl of Abercrombie, and that the building in which they were emptying yet another Mason jar of Mississippi's Best was not, as he had first thought, the Scottish National Museum, but rather what ol' Bertie thought of as Home Sweet Home.

Popping a few pheasants the next morning was equally an eye-opener for Amos. Not only was it almost as much fun as popping duck in the tidewater around the MSB&DDC, Inc., facility back home in Muddiebay, but ol' Bertie said, "The bloody birds are a real pest. The more of them you shoot, the more of them there are."

That could not be said about mallards in the Mississippi Flyway.

Amos decided that he'd have to give that some thought. But for the time being he did only what was incumbent upon him as a Southern Gentleman. He invited ol' Bertie to visit him and pop some mallards over Muddiebay Bay. Bertie didn't seem enthusiastic until Amos told him Muddiebay was not far from New Orleans and its famed cuisine and gentleman's clubs.

Thus began their lifelong friendship and business relationship. The latter turned out to be far more successful than Old Amos had ever dreamed it would. Attempting to satisfy the unquenchable thirst of New Orleanians with Famous Pheasant was futile, but on the other hand quite profitable.

In time, Old Amos took Young Amos to Dungaress and introduced him to Scottish country life. And during this period, earning them the lasting gratitude of the Earl of Abercrombie, and later his son, the Earl of Abercrombie, they came up with an idea — actually two ideas — on how to convert the pheasants of Castle Abercrombie from pests into a cash crop.

The first idea was simplicity itself. Old Amos and Young Amos knew very well how many shooters were willing to pay through the nose for the privilege of getting a few shots at mallards, and it followed that they would be willing to pay as much for the privilege of getting a few shots at Scottish pheasants.

Old Amos said that when he floated the idea, he was confident the would-be shooters would line up like politicians at the public trough — that is, drooling and with a wide-eyed look of happy anticipation on their faces.

Ol' Bertie said that was fine, but they would have to factor in the cost of getting rid of the pheasants once they had been blasted from the Scottish skies, probably by dumping them into a ditch dug for that purpose, which, considering the price of petrol and wear and tear on the tractor that

169

would dig said ditch, et cetera, would cost a pretty penny, indeed.

"Why would you want to bury the pheasants?" Young Amos asked.

"Well, what we have been doing for the past century or so, after shooting the bloody pests, is to send them to the Royal Dungaress Orphans Home, and its sister charity, the Royal Dungaress Home for Unwed Mothers-to-Be. But they can swallow only so many of the buggers — nobody, including orphans and unwed mothers-to-be, can be expected to eat pheasant day after bloody day — and you're going to cause a great deal more than so many."

"Let me think about it, Bertie," Old Amos said.

And he did.

But it was Young Amos who came up with the solution, which everyone agreed was brilliant. He had spent enough of his time in New Orleans, which of course is known for its *ambience Français,* to learn something of the French mind. He suspected, and was later proven right, that *les chefs Français* in the five-star restaurants of Paris would like nothing better than to be able to add to their menus "Fresh Scottish Pheasant, flown from Scotland Directly to Our Kitchen," and be prepared to pay through their *nez Français* for the privilege.

A deal was struck with TWA, which had two flights a day from Glasgow's Abbotsinch to Paris's Charles de Gaulle to do the actual flying, and then the money began to roll in.

The "guest gentleman shooters" would appear at Abercrombie Castle, where they would be welcomed by the Earl and Countess of Abercrombie. The earl — or sometimes Lady Margaret, who was known to her friends as "Maggie" — would then explain the traditions of the hunt and the costs thereof. These were ten dollars per pheasant downed and one dollar for each shot shell provided to accomplish the former.

The earl, who was wearing the kilt of Clan Abercrombie, would further explain that gentleman shooters were expected to make a small gift — twenty dollars was acceptable, but greater generosity would not be rejected — to the "gillies" who would accompany them to the stands from which they would down their game.

The gillies had several functions. The first of these was to point the gentleman shooters away from other gentleman shooters. Next, they would keep careful count of the number of shells they issued to the gentleman shooters, and finally they would keep careful count of how many pheasants "their" gentleman shooter downed at ten dollars per downing.

Gillies, who were paid five dollars a day, plus twenty percent of the amount their shooters paid at ten dollars per bird for each shot down, quickly learned that most gentleman shooters were so thrilled to have the gillie enthusiastically cry, "Jolly good shot, sir!" that they never challenged the call even when they told themselves they "didn't come within fifty EXPLETIVE DELETED!! feet of the EXPLETIVE DELETED!! bird."

When all the birds had been driven past the stands by the "beaters" — children from the Royal Dungaress Orphans Home — the gentlemen were taken by their gillies to sort of a picnic lunch, where cucumber sandwiches and other victuals were available at nominal prices.

Meanwhile, assisted by a fifty-strong herd of Labrador retrievers, the more mobile of the expectant ladies at the Royal Dungaress Home for Unwed Mothers-to-Be swept through the killing fields picking up the downed pheasants and moving them to an out-of-sight shed where they were quickly gutted by the less mobile of the ladies-in-waiting, so to speak. Next they were loaded into coolers, covered with ice, and then driven to Abbotsinch for their final flight to Charles de Gaulle and ultimately into the ovens of the Frog chefs.

The system thus devised outlasted both Old Amos and Young Amos, which left ol' Randy as the last of the Bruce line; and it outlasted the Earl of Abercrombie, which left Captain Charles William George Michael Bertram of Her Majesty's Own Scottish Light Lancers, who had become, of course, Captain Charles William George Michael Bertram the Earl of Abercrombie on the death of his father, as the last of his line.

The two got along well even after the earl reluctantly hung up his uniform to assume his earl-y responsibilities, which included administration of the Castle Abercrombie estates and the siring of an heir to keep the ball rolling, so to speak.

Randy didn't even think of this burden upon Bertie until he showed up at the castle one day and found Bertie in the company of a petite, fair-skinned young woman.

"Randy, old boy, this is my Maggie, who has just agreed to become the Countess of Abercrombie."

"Nice to meet you, Maggie," Randy had replied, offering the young woman his hand.

"Randy, old boy," Bertie said, "I hate to

appear stuffy, but there are traditions to be upheld, you know. Among them is that commoners like you are required to address my darling Maggie as either 'My Lady' or 'Lady Margaret.' And commoners do not attempt to touch members of the nobility, such as my Maggie, the Honorable Margaret Patricia Alice McNess, third daughter of the Earl of Ipswich, is."

"And I will call you 'Randy,' " Lady Margaret said. "As I not only have a soft spot in my heart for commoners, I have a small favor I — the earl and I — would like to ask of you."

"I'm at your service, My Lady," Randy had replied. He had quickly decided that if the price he had to pay to continue shooting at Castle Abercrombie was putting up with all this nobility EXPLETIVE DELETED!! and Bertie's EXPLETIVE DELETED!! newfound love, then so be it.

"Bertie and I would like you to be Bertie's Best Man when we are united in Holy Matrimony at the High Kirk of Glasgow, sometimes called Saint Kentigern's, on Tuesday next. I suppose it's too much to ask that you have morning clothes?"

Randy had been running around with Bertie long enough to have learned that, in Scotland, morning clothes were different from the mourning clothes — dark suit, black tie, and absolutely no white socks — one wore to a funeral in Mississippi. In Scotland, morning clothes were a pastel version of the long-tailed black "Fish and Soup Monkey Suits" the social elite of Muddiebay wore to Mardi Gras balls. In Scotland, morning clothes were what one wore at a morning social event, such as a wedding at St. Kentigern's in Glasgow.

"Why me, My Lady?" Randy asked.

"Because having a commoner such as yourself will spare Bertie and myself from the tiring business of having to choose between the thirty or forty members of the nobility who will think they are entitled to that honor."

So Randy was best man at the nuptials of the Earl and Lady Margaret.

As time passed, to his genuine surprise, Randy came to really like Lady Margaret. She was one hell of a shot, for one thing, and when she was not in the family way, she liked a little nip.

One day, when they were having a couple of the latter in the Minor Dining Hall of Castle Abercrombie, the countess said, out of the blue, "Bertie tells me you are acquainted with Philip Williams, the author.

Is this so?"

"Actually, I know him rather well. Actually, one might say, My Lady, that I am as close to him as a Southern gentleman, such as myself, ever gets to what we Southern gentlemen think of as EXPLETIVE DELETED!! Yankees. Once a Yankee, we say, always a Yankee."

"I'd like to meet him," Lady Margaret said.

"Oh, I don't think so, Lady Margaret."

"Randy, I thought I told you Maggie doesn't care what you think," Lord Bertie said. "Produce this chap so that my Maggie can meet him!"

Getting ol' Phil to Castle Abercrombie was easier ordered than accomplished. In addition to his usual suspicion of anything Randy proposed, Phil said from what he had heard it was always raining in Scotland, and that the high point of Scottish cuisine was a dish called haggis, which was made of the heart, liver, and lungs of a sheep or lamb stuffed into the stomach of one or the other of said creatures.

And, as a final argument, although he had as a young man known a skirt-wearing Scot who was perfectly normal, sexual preference wise, he was leery of going anywhere skirt-wearing by men was considered normal behavior.

But eventually Randy prevailed, and one day, Bertie having sent it to the airport to meet them, the ducal Rolls-Royce deposited them before the main door to Castle Abercrombie, where the earl and countess awaited them.

Randy said, "For God's sake, try to forget you're a EXPLETIVE DELETED!! Yankee and behave," and got out of the car.

Phil followed him.

"Your Lordship, Lady Margaret, may I present my friend —"

"I'll be a EXPLETIVE DELETED!!" Phil cried cheerfully. "Tally EXPLETIVE DELETED!! ho, Bertie!"

"Hi-Yo, EXPLETIVE DELETED!! Silver! Away yourself, old chap!" the earl replied.

"Who's the bimbo, Lone Ranger?" Phil inquired. "That can't be Tonto! Not with a set of knockers like that."

They then embraced.

"I gather that you have met?" Randy and Lady Margaret asked, in chorus.

They had, but relating the details of that here would be getting ahead of the story. That sometimes happens to less skilled writers of romance novels. As the astute reader of same may have noticed, the male and female protagonists therein are often depicted in loving, or lascivious, embrace before any justification for their behavior is offered.

Suffice it to say here that ol' Phil became very close friends of the Earl and Countess of Abercrombie, which had a bearing on how Randy planned to get some time alone with Carol-Anne in Merry England, to wit:

Once everybody got to Dungaress, after they had spent two days in London — or until the ladies had reached their credit card limit, whichever came first — Pancho Gonzales's beloved niece would fall ill. Her loving Uncle Pancho would charter a private jet with a capacity for no more than five passengers to fly her to the famed doctors whose offices line London's Harley Street.

Out of the goodness of her heart, Carol-Anne would volunteer to go along, so that Poor Pancho's Poor Sick Niece would have some female companionship. Randy, who would blame the Poor Sick Niece's illness on the haggis she had eaten before he had Done His Duty to warn her not to do so, would, stricken by guilt, consider it his duty as a Southern Gentleman to go with them to London.

They would go directly from Heathrow to Claridge's Hotel, where Randy had reserved suitable accommodations.

And for the next week, ol' Phil would take care of the hunters, and Lady Margaret, because ol' Phil would ask her to, and they were buddies, would take care of the ladies.

Everybody would be happy. Showtime!

The only thing that remained to be done was to telephone Pancho, to make sure everything was going as planned with him. Pancho and his niece were critical components of the plot.

He did so immediately after Carol-Anne had hoisted her panty hose up and around what Randy now recognized to be her deteriorating derriere and left so as to be home before her husband came home from the bank.

"Pancho, buddy! How's every little thing?" he greeted his Miami-Cuban coconspirator.

"I told you I'd meet you in the General's Club in the Atlanta airport tomorrow. So why are you calling me?"

"Just checking, amigo. I suppose Consuelo's all excited about going to London?"

"Actually, Randy, Consuelo's not going."

"What do mean, Consuelo's not going?"

"I mean, she ran off with that jai-alai player she was always eyeing, the one they call Pedro the Perfect because of his body."

"That's awful."

"Not to worry. I'm bringing Ginger Gallagher instead."

"Correct me if I'm wrong, but isn't Ginger Gallagher that pale-skinned long-legged blonde, the one whose hair hangs down to her waist? The tall one? The one you were chasing around the American Virgin Islands with your tongue hanging out?"

"You got it, Randy. I have always been attracted to gorgeous twenty-five-year-old blondes whose Daddy left them just over half a billion dollars."

"Pancho, you dumb EXPLETIVE DELETED!! fried banana eater — which, come to think of it, is what Ginger called you — no one is going to think that Ginger Gallagher is your niece!"

"You're right. I guess I just glossed over that possibility. So, what do we do?"

"You're not trying to tell me you talked Glamorous Ginger into going to Europe to fool around with you?"

"What happened, Randy, is that I happened to mention the hunting trip and that Phil Williams is going along. Then she sort of invited herself. She confessed to me that she has a thing about balding middle-aged intellectuals who smoke cigars and know so much about women and life."

"You're suggesting that she wants to fool around with Phil?"

"That's the impression she left me with."

"And what's going to happen when she finds out that Phil never fools around?"

"She knows of his reputation in that regard, and obviously considers it a challenge."

"My question was, what are you going to do when she finds out that what they say about Phil is true?"

"Then perhaps, I was thinking, she might find room in her heart for a Miami-Cuban who would console her when she learned the truth about Phil."

"Forgive me for saying this, Pancho, but that's what I would call the dumbest EXPLETIVE DELETED!! thing I've ever heard you say, and I've heard you say a lot of really dumb things."

"Hope springs eternal, Randy, in the heart of we Miami-Cubans."

"Pancho, it's too EXPLETIVE DELETED!! late to call this off. You better come up with a niece who's going to get sick in Scotland!"

"Maybe I can meet somebody on the plane. I'm flying to Atlanta on Guatemalan Air, and I know a couple of their stews."

"I remember Marcella," Randy said. "Spectacular boobs."

"No. That was Pilar. Marcella was the one with spectacular legs and the gold diamond-studded teeth."

"It doesn't matter. We've reached the point of no return on this operation. Tomorrow, you bring either Marcella or Pilar to Atlanta. Leave Ginger in Miami. Take whoever's going to be your niece to the General's Club. Get your niece whatever she wants to drink and sit her down on one side of the room and tell her not to try to pick anybody up. Then you go sit on the other side of the General's Club. I'll meet you there and we'll figure this thing out."

"I won't be able to leave Ginger in Miami. She said she'll fly there in her private jet, as she has no intention of getting on the same plane with me and having people think we might be traveling companions."

"Pancho, listen carefully. I have no intention of letting Glamorous Ginger EXPLETIVE DELETED!! up my carefully laid romantic plans. Deal with it!" Randy said, and hung up.

VI
PHIL LEARNS FROM THE WRATH OF GOD

[One]

Berlin, Germany
Monday, May 19, 1947

As Supervisory Special Agent Jonathan Fitzwater Caldwell III drove Administrator Philip Wallingford Williams III down Onkel Tom Allee toward his Zehlendorf home in what looked like a brand-new Cadillac, Williams said, "This is a very nice car, sir."

"It's a piece of EXPLETIVE DELETED!!," SSA Caldwell replied. "But since those EXPLETIVE DELETED!! idiots at Packard drove the company into bankruptcy, and since Henry the Second has never forgiven me for knocking him on his EXPLETIVE DELETED!! at Groton, and won't come up with a Lincoln Continental, it's either a EXPLETIVE DELETED!! Cadillac or a EXPLETIVE DELETED!! Chrysler. Nobody in his right mind drives a EXPLETIVE DELETED!! Chrysler, and actually buying a car myself is obviously out of the EXPLETIVE DELETED!! question."

"Yes, sir."

"It's a tax thing, son," Caldwell explained after he saw on Phil's face that Phil didn't entirely understand what he was talking about. "The company chalks it up to Research and Development. What you and I are doing is testing to see how well Fitzwater Cold Tanned Leather seats will hold up in the car of an officer on foreign service. You understand?"

"Yes, sir," Phil lied, and then to quickly change the subject, asked, "Did I understand you to say, sir, that you were at Groton?"

"I did say that. Why am I not surprised to learn you know what Groton is? But how is it that you do?"

"My father is a Groton graduate, sir."

"And you didn't go there? Why not?"

Well, as soon as he gets a look at my final report of complete background investigation, he'll know, so I might as well get it out of the way now.

"I did, sir," Phil said, "for a while. Before the Reverend Doctor Peabody decided that I would, and Groton would, be happier if I

finished my secondary education elsewhere."

"Amazing! Those are the exact words Old
Endicott P. used on me when he gave me
the boot after I knocked two teeth out of
Henry the Second and set him on his EX-
PLETIVE DELETED!!. I wound up in Saint
Malachi's. You're familiar with Saint Mala-
chi's?"

"I was at Saint Malachi's, sir."

"What an amazing coincidence!" SSA
Caldwell said. "But I gather you didn't finish?"

"No, sir, I did not."

"So Colonel 'Don't call me Bill' O'Reilly
said. He mentioned something *en passant . . .*"

"What happened, sir . . ." Phil began, and
then related what he had done with Bridget
O'Malley's intimate undergarments.

"Well, I can see how that might trigger
the disapproval of Reverend James Ferneyhough Fitzhugh, D.D. He always was a bit
of a prude. Papa always said he thought Old
Ferney was a Methodist who didn't have
the balls to come out of the closet."

"Yes, sir."

"I just thought of something else Papa was
always telling me," SSA Caldwell went on.
" 'Anyone who fools around with Irish girls

185

or buys his clothes at Brooks Brothers is asking for trouble.' I suggest you keep that in mind."

"Yes, sir, I will."

"Ah, here we are," SSA Caldwell said, as he stopped the car before his home.

Once inside, he introduced Phil to his wife. She was a tall, slim woman who reminded Phil of his Aunt Grace, his father's sister. In other words, the lady came across as an icy-blooded Back Bay Bostonian who looked askance at anyone who could not prove they were directly descended from a passenger who had traveled in first class on the *Mayflower.*

"Victoria, this is Philip Williams," SSA Caldwell said. "We were at both Groton and Saint Malachi's together."

"How is that possible, Jonathan? He looks like he's nineteen years old."

"Actually he's seventeen. I didn't mean we were at Groton and Saint Malachi's during the same time period. What I had hoped to convey is that he's one of us, and that hereafter you can no longer complain that you have absolutely no one of our kind, save me, of course, here in Berlin, with whom to converse."

"In that case, how do you do, Philip?"

186

"Have Frau Whatsername bring some croissants and coffee into the library," SSA Caldwell ordered. "Phil's going to have another shot at examining something that idiot Brewster was supposed to examine but failed miserably to do so adequately."

"Well, Jonathan, you know what you're always saying."

"Specifically, what am I always saying?"

"About West Pointers. That when dealing with them one must remember where they came from, and the heavy baggage that forces them to carry through life."

"When Phil and I have finished, you two can chat."

A half hour later, Phil had detected another seven ambiguities, thirteen grammatical errors, and six strikeovers, in the *Report of Successful Recruitment of NKGB Colonel Vladimir Polshov* that Captain Brewster had presented to SAA Caldwell as perfect in every respect and ready to be taken By Hand of Armed Officer Courier to the Hon. Ralph Peters, Deputy Director for Soviet Affairs, Central Intelligence Agency, in Langley, Virginia.

"*Entre nous,* Phil, what I would really like to do to that West Point EXPLETIVE DELETED!! is shove that EXPLETIVE DELETED!!

West Point ring he's always knocking so far up his EXPLETIVE DELETED!! that the phony ruby in it would pop out of his left EXPLETIVE DELETED!! nostril. But, lamentably, I cannot do so."

"Yes, sir."

"It wasn't this way in the Office of Strategic Services, Phil, as I'm sure you understand . . . No. On reflection, I'm sure you don't understand — you're not old enough to understand. So you'll just have to take my word as a fellow Saint Malachi's Old Boy that it wasn't this way in the good ol' OSS. The OSS was staffed with our kind, Phil, gentlemen who knew what an ambiguity was when they saw one and rarely made a mistake in grammar.

"God, during the war we used to have Hasty Pudding Club soirees once a week in Claridge's Hotel in London. They said OSS stood for Oh, So Social, and by God it did!

"But that's all gone, Phil. At the risk of sounding self-pitying, I find myself all alone here in Berlin battling the Red Menace."

"Yes, sir."

"Let me tell you how it was, Phil. One day I was sitting in the Harvard Club on West Forty-fourth Street wondering how I could serve my country in the war to end all wars without having to associate myself with riffraff when I bumped into a chap I knew from the Hasty Pudding Club. I asked him how he planned to solve that conundrum and he said he already had — he had gone into the OSS.

"I didn't even know what the OSS was. He replied that OSS was the acronym for something that had slipped his mind, but everybody called it the Oh, So Social, and what they were going to do was make life unpleasant for Herr Hitler. That sounded like what I was looking for, so I asked him how one might associate oneself with the OSS.

"He replied that he had been recruited for the OSS several weeks before while having a little taste of Famous Pheasant and a dozen oysters on the half-shell in the Oak Room bar of the Plaza Hotel . . . You know whereof I speak, I presume, Phil?"

"Yes, sir, my father used to take me there after sailing my sailboat in Central Park. It's not far from my father's apartment, and he used to say my sailing my sailboat exhausted him to the point where he needed sustenance before going farther downtown to Jack & Charley's on West Fifty-second for more recuperative sustenance."

SAA Caldwell nodded. "Well, anyway, my chum said he'd been in the Oak Room and this chap, a complete stranger, approached him and asked if perhaps the phrase *So then we'll conquer all old Eli's men* had any meaning for him.

"Of course it did. It was the fourth line, first verse, of 'Ten Thousand Men of Harvard.' So, my chum told me, he told this chap of course he well knew the fight song and why. Then this chap asked my chum if he had any interest in serving his country in a manner appropriate for a Harvard man. When my chum replied in the affirmative, this chap told him about the OSS, and one thing led to another, and soon, my chum told me, he was in the OSS.

"So I got in a cab and went up to the Plaza and into the Oak Room, hoping to encounter the chap my chum had told me about. To no avail. I had to go back to the Oak Room three times, the last time wearing a crimson Harvard sweatshirt, before I was approached.

"But once I established contact, things moved very swiftly. A week later, I was at the Congressional Country Club outside Washington, D.C., serving our country. There was a training program. This included training in marksmanship. Once it became apparent this would be a waste of my time and theirs . . ."

"Excuse me?"

"Phil, you would be astonished, as I was, to learn how few people in the OSS, including Harvard men, could tell a howitzer from, say, a Browning Diamond Grade Superposed 12-bore with a gold trigger and selective ejectors. The training program began with we students being handed single-shot Sears, Roebuck Economy Model 12-bores, which we were to fire at a barn door to give us confidence.

"While I was waiting for my turn at the barn door, a murder of crows flew over, and in a Pavlovian reflex I dropped four of them with the Economy Model single shot they had given me. Actually, I got four of the vexatious buggers with three shots. I was then told I could go to the Congressional links and play some golf for exercise until my classmates caught up with me, marksmanship wise.

"The Congressional links weren't Winged Foot or Baltusrol, of course, but it wasn't as completely plebian as I thought it might be . . .

"I digress. Cutting to the chase: Shortly thereafter, I found myself in London, in a small but adequate suite in Claridge's Hotel, and shortly after that in Scotland, at Castle Jedburgh, where some characters released from prison for the purpose — Irish Republican Army terrorists and English safe crackers — taught us how to blow things up and crack safes, and then I traveled back to London and Claridge's.

"There I met a chap, Bill Colby, who was a gentleman even though he'd gone to Dartmouth. One night at the bar, ol' Bill told me that he was going to France in the morning and asked if I'd like to tag along.

"The next afternoon I dropped my first bridge into a river with seven pounds of an absolutely marvelous explosive called C-4, and the day after that, I got my first locomotive, which was really great fun, lots of noise and huge clouds of steam. And three days after that, we were back in Claridge's.

"And so my war went. Three weeks in London chasing the girls — this was before Victoria, of course — then a week in France — once two weeks in Albania — blowing things up and then back to London for what the OSS called R&R, for Rest and Recuperation, and what we in Hasty Pudding called I&I, for Intercourse and Intoxication. And then back to the Continent for another week of great fun blowing things up. What more could a real man ask? Am I shocking you with this, Phil?"

"No, sir."

"But all good things come to an end, and so inevitably did World War Two. So there I was, a changed man — I was by then a major — knowing I really did not want to spend the rest of my life in automobile upholstery . . ."

"Excuse me, sir? 'In automobile upholstery'?"

"I thought I explained that to you while I was explaining why I am driving that piece of EXPLETIVE DELETED!! Cadillac. You're going to have to learn to listen carefully to me, son, while I'm talking."

"Yes, sir. I'll try."

"All right then, one more time. No. I'll go back to the beginning. Perhaps if I do that, I won't have to go through everything again in the future."

"Yes, sir."

"Around the turn of the century a man appeared at the offices of the Caldwell Fabric Manufactory in Boston. Somehow, he got into the offices of my great-grandfather, whose son was the first Jonathan Fitzwater Caldwell.

"The man said that he was a bicycle repairman from Detroit and that he intended to transform the world by mass-producing horseless carriages.

"Family legend holds that my great-grandfather had just returned from a rather liquid luncheon, but whether or not that's true, my great-grandfather decided, what the hell, I'll hear this chap out.

"The fellow said that he had already made a half-dozen such vehicles and was ready to really start rolling them out the door 'by the dozens, or maybe even the hundreds.'

" 'If you're trying to sell me one of your infernal machines, forget it,' Great-grandfather said. 'The only person I'd like to see get in one is my mother-in-law sixty seconds before it becomes enveloped in flame.'

"The man told him that what he was really after was a large quantity of fabric, preferably but not absolutely necessarily black in color, with which to upholster the seats of his horseless carriages, which would be called 'Lizzies' after the daughter of a neighbor, Miss Elizabeth Firestone. He said Mr. Firestone had loaned him enough money to put tires on the first Lizzies.

"The man said that what was absolutely necessary *vis-à-vis* the fabric he sought was that it be made available on credit to be paid for after he had produced enough Lizzies to put the nation on wheels.

"Ordinarily, asking for credit would have been enough to see this chap thrown out the window for effrontery, but this was different for a number of reasons. One was that my great-grandfather had in the warehouses eleven thousand yards of sturdy, black woolen fabric he had ordered loomed for the Roman Catholic Church, who would use it as suiting for their clergy.

"That deal had fallen through when the cardinal archbishop of Boston demanded a substantial discount after the two monsignors, six priests, and two friars who had been issued trial suits for testing all complained that the material was so stiff that they had trouble getting down to their knees to pray and then found it almost impossible to get off their knees when they were finished asking the Good Lord for whatever it was they were asking of Him.

"Great-grandfather knew unloading the eleven thousand yards elsewhere was going to be difficult if not impossible. The material was not up to the sartorial standards of the Episcopals, far above Methodist sartorial standards, and the Lutherans simply didn't have any money and ritually dressed their clergy in Episcopal discards.

"Other reasons may have included that Great-grandfather rather liked the image of my great-great-grandmother being toasted in a flaming Lizzie. And, of course, he had been drinking.

"Whatever the reasons, history tells us that a historic deal was struck that day. The bicycle mechanic from Detroit was given all the sturdy black fabric he needed to upholster his Lizzies at a fair price — cost of manufacture plus ten percent — with payment to be made after Lizzies had 'rolled off the line' and, it was to be hoped, been purchased. In return, Henry, the bicycle mechanic, signed a contract perpetuating the cost-of-manufacture-plus-ten-percent deal in perpetuity for all the seating material for the Lizzies that Henry could make and foist off on the public.

"About nine months later, Henry reappeared at my great-grandfather's office. Great-grandfather feared he was coming in an attempt to get out of the deal, but that was not the case.

" 'Mr. Caldwell,' Henry said, handing Great-grandfather a check. 'The line's been running a little faster than I thought it would. Here's a check for the nine thousand yards of your Clerical Black fabric that is already cushioning the bottoms of Lizzie owners, which means the line's supply is down to about two thousand yards. So I urgently need more. How soon can you get another five thousand yards of Clerical

Black out to Detroit?'

" 'Henry, two thousand yards will be on this afternoon's Detroit Flyer, with more to follow in the immediate future,' " Great-grandfather said. 'And I think the time has come that I may permit you to call me Abner.' "

"That, sir," Phil said, "if I may be permitted to say so, is a fascinating bit of unknown Americana."

"Why not? Well, where was I? Aha!

"So there I was, son, fresh from saving the world for democracy and having a hell of a good time doing it, and there's my father telling me what he thinks I should do is enroll in MIT and get a Ph.D. in Polymer Science and Textile Technology so that I would be prepared to take over the business knowing a little something about fabric.

"I had no choice of course. I had to do what Daddy said, or go get a job like ordinary people, which of course was absolutely out of the EXPLETIVE DELETED!! question. So I went to MIT and got my doctorate in Polymer Science and Textile Technology.

"I never use the title, of course, out of modesty, except when I call my doctor's office. I had quickly learned if I said, 'Dr. Caldwell is calling Dr. Chancremechanic' or whatever, they would put me right through to the EXPLETIVE DELETED!! pill-pusher. Otherwise they would put me on hold. Now when I need a doctor, I have that EXPLETIVE DELETED!! idiot Brewster, or another member of the West Point Ring Knockers Association who works for me, call up and order one to report to me.

"Where was I? Oh. Then Daddy put me in charge of the Detroit office. The only good thing I can say about that is that I met Victoria there at the Grosse Pointe Country Club.

"When people like you and I, Phil, look up 'Hell on Earth' in *Compton's Pictured Encyclopedia* or a similar reference work, what we get is a picture of either the Detroit Auto Club or the Grosse Pointe Country Club. The Detroit Auto Club has nothing to do with coming to help when your battery is dead or you have a flat tire. The Detroit Auto Club is full of men who work in the automobile business, and hang out there to talk about Guess What, and the Grosse Pointe Country Club is where their wives go to pick up a little romance.

"I forget why I went to the EXPLETIVE DELETED!! GPCC that day, as significant a day as it proved to be in my life, but I did. And I came across Victoria near the ninth tee, quietly weeping as she dabbed at her eyes with a lace hankie.

"As strange as I knew the customs of the people out there seem to people like us, Phil, I didn't think any of their women looking for a little romance were so weird as to believe a good way to pick up a man while looking for romance was to stare coldly at him from bloodshot eyes while noisily blowing their nose.

"I took the chance. I tend to take chances where good-looking women are concerned.

" 'May I be of assistance?' I inquired.

"Victoria replied: 'I wouldn't reply if I didn't hear Harvard in your somewhat nasal voice. Please tell me it's so.'

" 'It is. And please tell me that's Wellesley I hear in yours.'

" 'It is. Until just now, I didn't think there was anyone in Detroit who could distinguish between a Wellesley accent and Adamawa, which is what the poor Ubangi speak. Whatever are you doing in this terrible place?'

"I told her, and she told me, when I posed a counterquestion. Her father was a lawyer involved in the legal problems of failing automobile manufacturers. It was a lucrative practice, as they were falling like pins in a bowling alley, and as her PopPop, as Victoria calls him, naturally was following the lawyer's creed of never getting far from the business entity or person which, or whom, a good barrister can easily shove into bankruptcy, and then onto the street, here she was surrounded by the GPCC and DAC barbarians.

"It was love at first sight, and I said, 'My dear, let me take you somewhere away from all this.'

"What I had in mind was my suite in the Book Cadillac Hotel, and she came with me, but only as far as the Motor Bar Restaurant & Bar on the ground floor. She said she had a strict rule to never go above the ground floor on a first date.

"The way it turned out, what she meant was that she was going to hold off on getting onto the Book Cadillac elevator until I had, with appropriate ceremony, slipped both a diamond engagement ring — an emerald cut of at least five carats — and a matching wedding ring onto the somewhat bony third finger of her left hand.

"Cutting to the chase again, Victoria and I tied the knot at a small ceremony at the Cathedral of Saint John the Divine in Manhattan, presided over by the presiding bishop of the Protestant Episcopal Church in the USA. The Philadelphia Orchestra played appropriate music, and the Metropolitan Opera sent over a massively bosomed mezzo soprano who sang 'I Love You Truly.'

"As we came, now Dr. and Mrs. Jonathan Fitzwater Caldwell the Third, down the aisle to the strains of Felix Mendelssohn's 'Wedding March,' I thought I was hallucinating, for I saw a face from my past among the Standing Room Only guests near the door.

"Because there was no question in my mind that the face belonged to a comrade-in-arms who was now looking up at the grass from an unmarked grave somewhere in what had been Nazi-occupied France, I attributed the hallucination to the several healthy belts of Famous Pheasant I had taken to give me the courage to go through the nuptials ceremony, and put it from my mind.

"A month later, shortly after returning from our honeymoon to what had been the Dodge Brothers Suite in the Book Cadillac but was now, having been so re-dubbed by Victoria 'Our Passion Pit,' I received a rather eerie telephone call.

" 'Fitzy, this is Dartmouth Billy,' my caller said.

" 'Bill Colby?' I asked incredulously. 'It can't be. You're dead!'

" 'Yes, I am. What I want you to do now is tell those thugs guarding your elevator to pass a man named Ralph Peters and his two thugs.'

" 'Who the hell is Ralph Peters?'

" 'I can't tell you that over a nonsecure line. And tell your thugs that if they even look like they're even thinking about patting down me or my thugs looking for weapons, I'll have to kill them. Acknowledge.'

" 'Fitzy acknowledges last Billy. Fitzy out,' I said.

"The phrase brought back many warm memories of World War Two.

"Then I hung up and gave instructions to our security people, and finally turned to Victoria, who was standing there wearing a look that suggested bafflement and absolutely nothing else.

" 'Victoria, my precious,' I said, 'as much as I hate to say this, you're going to have to put your clothes back on. We are about to receive our first guest. And two of his thugs.'

"Two minutes later, the door opened and two men burst in, weapons drawn, and moved quickly through the apartment.

" 'Clear!' one of them called loudly. 'Nobody else in here but a skinny bimbo pulling on her panty hose.'

"And then ol' Bill came into the apart-ment.

" 'Fitzy,' he said. 'It's been a long time.'

" 'No, it hasn't, Bill. Not if that was you standing with the Standing Room Only people in Saint John's.'

" 'That was me. But don't call me Bill. Bill's dead. Or at least we want people to think I am.'

" 'Well, whoever the hell you are, I'm delighted to see that you're alive.'

" 'So delighted that you might have, after all these years, finally forgiven me?'

" 'Forgiven you for what?' Victoria asked, as she swept into the room in her dressing gown. 'More to the point, how dare you burst into the home of a just-returned-from-their-honeymoon couple?'

" 'My dear lady,' ol' Bill said. 'Unfortu-nately, I was forced to conclude that asking your husband to answer again the trumpet's call to duty and mount up and ride to the sound of AK-47 and other musketry in the bloodstained hands of the Red Menace had a greater priority than any middle-of-the-afternoon lascivious plans you might have had for him.'

" 'Huh!' Victoria snorted, and then said, 'When you speak, sir, you sound like my cousin LeRoy, who, when bounced from

Harvard finished up at Dartmouth. How close does that arrow strike?'

" 'Bull's-eye, my dear lady.'

" 'What did you say your name was?'

" 'They call me Ralph Peters. The Honorable Ralph Peters.'

" 'Then why did my precious Fitzy call you Bill when you came in? And, more important, what was it you did to him that you entertain the hope that he will, after all these years, forgive you for doing?'

" 'Why don't you tell her, Fitzy?'

" 'If you like, Ralph.'

" 'You can continue, of course, Fitzy, to call me Bill, as our wartime service taught me that most of the time you can be trusted to keep secret our beloved nation's most secret secrets. But when others . . . Got it?'

" 'Got it, Bill. And what would you like my beloved bride to call you? Bill or Ralph?'

" 'The former. Surprising me no end, you seem to have married well.'

" 'Well, my precious, what Bill here did, years ago, that did annoy me a little —'

" 'A little?' Bill said. "What I recall was that when you finally sobered up and learned that I had gone to Norway without you, you stormed into David Bruce's office and declared . . . What exactly did he say, Mulligan?"

"The larger of the thugs took a notebook and an S&W Detective Special Model .38 Special revolver from his briefcase. While dangling the revolver by his index finger in the trigger guard, he went through the notebook, then handed it to Peters.

" 'Here it is, Mr. Deputy Director, sir, on page nine of the things you said you might want to review on the Learjet.'

"Peters read it, as the man tried, and failed, to slip the revolver into the holster on his ankle.

Chief of London Station David Bruce: Caldwell, what brings you staggering into my office looking like death warmed over and smelling like a Scottish distillery?

Captain Caldwell: Is it true that EXPLE-TIVE DELETED!! Dartmouthian EXPLETIVE DELETED!! went to Norway without me to do all those things we discussed?

Bruce: Yes, it is. He put it to me that you were in no condition to go parachute jumping, much less skiing, and one look at you convinced me he was right. When I looked in on you in Claridge's Hotel, you were in the bathtub with a rubber duck in one hand, a bottle of Famous Pheasant in the other, and singing "When the roll is called up yonder, I'll be there" at the top of your lungs.

Caldwell: Be that as it may, I wanted to go, and he knew it. And now he's having all the fun. So, be advised, sir, that if that EXPLETIVE DELETED!! Methodist Dartmouthian manages to get back alive from Norway, I'm going to turn him into a EXPLETIVE DELETED!! soprano with a dull EXPLETIVE DELETED!! bayonet before I kill him.

" 'May I have a peek at that, Bill?' Victoria asked.

" 'I'd like nothing more than to show it to you, Victoria, but I'm afraid it contains some naughty words. Soldier talk, so to speak.'

" 'I'm a married woman now, Bill. And since our nuptials Fitzy has brought me up to speed on those few profanities, obscenities, and vulgarisms I somehow missed learning at Wellesley.'

"She put out her hand and Bill put the notebook in it. She read it. Then looked back at Bill.

" 'Well, my beloved Fitzy was really pissed off, wasn't he? In addition to being simply pissed in his bathtub, I mean. What was that all about, my darling?'

" 'If you think I was angry when I had that little chat with ol' Dave Bruce, my little dumpling, you should have seen me when I heard what Bill actually did when he went to Norway, leaving me behind.'

" 'And that was?'

" 'After skiing all over Norway's absolutely wonderful slopes for a week, popping Krauts as he went, he ended up at a Kraut heavy water plant with a rucksack full of an explosive we called C-4. When Bill blew it up, there was what we in the profession call a secondary explosion. The next time the world heard an explosion and saw a mushroom cloud like that was when we vaporized Nagasaki, Japan, later in the war.'

" 'Well, I can certainly understand why you were a little miffed at being excluded from something like that, but as Alexander Pope has taught us, 'to err is human, to forgive divine.'

" 'Frankly, Scarlett, I don't give a damn what the Pope says,' I said.

" 'Not *the* Pope, Precious. Alexander Pope.'

" 'Oh.'

" 'What I want to know is why Bill is here in Detroit,' she said.

" 'And I want to know why his thug, who can't even get his .38 in his ankle holster, called him "Mr. Deputy Director." Deputy director of what?'

" 'The questions are interrelated,' Bill said. 'But I can't answer either until I get an answer to a question of my own. Fitzy, are you prepared to answer again the trumpet's call to duty and mount up and ride to the sound of musketry, the musketry this time being AK-47s, et cetera, in the bloodstained hands of the Red Menace, not Mausers and Schmeissers in the bloodstained hands of the Nazis, as was the previous case?'

" 'Didn't you ask me that before?'

" 'Yes, I did, and you didn't reply, so far as I can remember.'

" 'Bill, how far from Detroit is this place you're asking Fitzy to ride off to?' Victoria asked.

" 'A great distance, I'm afraid, Victoria. At this stage of the recruitment interview, I can only give you a hint. Across a wide, wide ocean.'

" 'We enlist,' Victoria said. 'I can only hope you are referring to the Pacific Ocean, which is wider than the Atlantic.'

" 'In that case, welcome to the CIA, of which I am the deputy director for Soviet Affairs.'

" 'The what?' I said.

" 'The CIA. It is the successor organization to our beloved Oh, So Social. It stands
for Central Intelligence Agency. Surely
you've heard of it.'

" 'Now that you mention it.'

" 'And what did you say Fitzy and I will
be doing for the CPA?'

" 'That's CIA, Victoria. *I* not *P.*'

" 'Whatever. What will my precious Fitzy
be doing for the CIA once he rides off to
wherever he'll be doing it, and where precisely will that be?'

" 'What he will be doing, Victoria, with
your assistance, is causing senior Russian,
Hungarian, and other Eastern Bloc officers
to realize the error of their ways and change
sides.'

" 'I don't have a clue how I could do that,
and I don't think Fitzy does, either.'

" 'I'm afraid you underestimate your soul
mate, Victoria.'

" 'I don't think that's possible, but I'm
willing to be corrected.'

" 'I have seen his mind at work.'

" 'Give me an example.'

" 'Well, there are so many examples to
choose between it's hard . . . Well, I suppose Cannes is as good as any.'

" 'As in Cannes, France?' she asked.

" 'That one. Try to picture this, Victoria. A bright early spring day in 1944. A month or so before D-Day. Fitzy and I are sitting in the sidewalk café of the Carlton in Cannes.'

" 'The one at 58 La Croisette in Cannes?' Victoria asked.

" 'That one. We are sipping at a very nice Sauvignon Saint-Bris, '38 if memory serves, our little gift to ourselves for just having blown a tunnel on the Paris-Cannes lines of Chemins de fer Français as a train containing three sleeping cars full of senior German officers and their mistresses was passing through it.

" 'Two SS officers — you know, the ones who wore black uniforms and riding boots and carried riding crops although few of them had ever been near a horse — come to the table and with that exaggerated courtesy they thought was so clever say, 'Good afternoon, gentlemen. Perhaps you would be kind enough to explain what you are doing here wearing U.S. Army Paratrooper boots and carrying a bag full of what looks to me like Composition C-4.'

" 'What you have your dirty fingers in, Señor," Fitzy replies, off the top of his head, "is the Buenos Aires empanada dough my wife prepared as a small gift to Herr Himmler, whom she calls Heinie Baby, and who really appreciates a good empanada. What my friend Señor Gonzalo and I have on our feet is what all we Argentine gauchos wear on the pampas. Is there anything else you'd like to know?"

" 'No, sir, I don't think so. Thank you very much, and pardon the interruption. If there is anything the SS can ever do for you, all you have to do is ask.'"

" 'Your Fitzy, Victoria, was on a roll,' Bill said. 'Fitzy went on: "*Hauptstandartenführer,* actually there is something you can do for me. Take that bag of empanada dough and have one of your underlings deliver it to Heinie Baby . . . Herr Himmler . . . in Berlin, thus sparing Señor Gonzalo and myself that boring train ride.'"

" 'An hour later, still chuckling about what was going to happen in Berlin when Frau Himmler tried to bake, or fry, anything at all with the empanada dough — C-4 goes boom at 325 Fahrenheit — we were in the speedboat and on our way back, via Gibraltar, to Claridge's Hotel in London.'

" 'Good times,' I said. 'I remember ol' Sterling . . . Whatsisname? The actor? Great big guy.'

" 'It's on the tip of my tongue, but . . .'

" 'Anyway,' I went on, 'ol' Sterling was

driving the speedboat that day. As I was saying, Bill, good times.'

" 'Yes, they were. But as I was saying, Victoria, I remembered Cannes and some other places where Fitzy had manifested his amazing talent to lie so convincingly off the top of his head and decided all he could do was say no if I tried to enlist him for duty again. And here I am.'

"And Victoria said, 'When would you like us to leave Detroit for wherever Fitzy will serve his country? And where, exactly, is that?'

" 'It's Berlin, actually. And as soon as possible. How soon do you think you can work leaving Detroit into your schedule, Victoria?'

" 'How does thirty minutes fit into your schedule, Bill?' "

"And that's how Victoria and I came to Berlin, Phil," SSA Caldwell said.

"Fascinating story, sir. May I ask a question?"

"Certainly."

"How do you get those senior Russian, Hungarian, and other Eastern Bloc officers you mentioned to realize the error of their ways and change sides?"

"In due time, I will tell you, of course, but right now what I want to do is get that

EXPLETIVE DELETED!! idiot Brewster out here to retype the *Report of Successful Recruitment of NKGB Colonel Vladimir Polshov* now that you have uncovered the . . . how many was it?"

"If you're asking about ambiguities and grammatical errors, sir, I found a total of thirteen of the former and seventeen of the latter, plus six strikeovers."

"Each EXPLETIVE DELETED!! one of all those EXPLETIVE DELETED!! errors which would have made me look like a horse's ass to ol' Bill, now Ralph, of course, had that report landed on his desk. It is painful for a Harvard man, you will understand, to have ambiguities and grammatical errors pointed out to him by a EXPLETIVE DELETED!! Dartmouthian, even if they are old comrades-in-arms."

"Yes, sir. But, sir, I am a CIC administrator who is supposed to do the typing of reports prepared by people like Special Agent Captain Brewster."

"Not anymore, Phil. A new day has dawned on the German-American Gospel Tract Foundation. In this bright new world, you will find the errors, and Brewster and his EXPLETIVE DELETED!! ring-knocking buddies will do the typing."

"Sir, if I may say so, I don't think Captain

Brewster and his fellow West Point alumni are going to like that."

"Good!" SSA Caldwell said.

[Two]

Over the next several days and weeks, Phil learned SSA Caldwell's *modus operandi* — which he knew from his Latin studies meant "mode of operation" — *vis-à-vis* getting senior Russian and other Eastern Bloc officers to change sides.

As he learned this, he also learned that in the smoke-and-mirrors world of intelligence, things were often not what they appeared to be, including CIC administrators Angus McTavish and G. Lincoln Rutherford.

"What I did, Phil," SSA Caldwell explained, "when ol' Bill, who was now Ralph Peters, laid the heavy burden on my broad shoulders of getting these Commie chaps to change sides was do what Caldwell Automobile Fabrics International, Inc., calls Market Research.

"Between you and me, CAFI, Inc., actually did a good deal of the research for me, as I knew all those overpaid EXPLETIVE DELETED!! were doing was hanging around the Detroit Automobile Club soaking up booze on their expense accounts and had the time.

"Anyway, they did it. And giving credit where credit is due, they did a pretty good job. A good bit of what they learned was eye-opening. I confess that I had been taken in by the propaganda that what the Soviet and Eastern Bloc NKGB big shots did for relaxation from their labors in trying to enslave the world was go to the Bolshoi and other places where ballet was offered for cultural enrichment.

"They did — and do — spend a lot of time watching ballet, to be sure, but not for cultural enrichment, unless one considers ogling young women bounding around the stage in very brief costumes culturally enriching.

"Where the NKGB chaps actually went to relax was to the circus. This was true all over the Soviet Union but especially in Hungary. At first we had no explanation for this except to suspect they may have gone to the circus hoping to witness a lion tamer being eaten alive by his lions, or one or more of the high wire trapeze artists falling to their deaths, but whatever the reason, they went to the circus.

"The other interesting fact about these NKGB chaps that the CAFI, Inc., market researchers turned up was that most of them were married to Russian women, and we already knew that with very few exceptions Russian women tended to be built like Green Bay Packer tackles and had one or more stainless steel teeth.

"The exceptions to this rule, we came to conclude, were those attractive daughters of Mother Russia who were ballet dancers and high wire trapeze artists, who both performed their art wearing the very brief costumes I mentioned earlier.

"Once we'd gotten our thinking caps into the problem thus far, especially my thinking cap, things began to take shape.

"Why had previous attempts to get these fellows to change sides by appealing to their senses of decency, and when that failed, offering them lots of money, failed miserably? My predecessors had nabbed the odd NKGB captain, and once a major, but no colonels and no generals.

"Well, the answers seemed to me self-evident. They had no senses of decency, for one thing, and they weren't very much interested in money. So what were they interested in? Watching lion tamers being mauled and eaten? Was that why they were so circus-oriented? Or was it something else, and if so, what?

"Perhaps, I asked myself, they are interested in the high wire performers, the *female* high wire trapeze artists, in their abbreviated costumes. And if they were interested in young women in revealing costumes, that would explain their fascination with the ballet.

"That raised the question of how we might get the ballet dancers and the high wire trapeze artists on our side, and the answer to that was simple. They were female. Females will do anything for money; it's the nature of the beast.

"Instead of offering NKGB colonels, et cetera, money to change sides, I decided it would make much more sense to give ballerinas and high wire artists money to change sides. And once they were this side of Check Point Charlie, that we should offer them even more money to induce the NKGB colonels they had left back in Moscow, or Budapest, or Sofia, to change sides.

"Because I was obviously both too busy and too important to go behind the Iron Curtain myself, I asked Bill/Ralph for some skilled contractor people to help me. You can imagine what would have happened if I sent that EXPLETIVE DELETED!! idiot Brewster to sweet-talk some Bolshoi ballerina into changing sides. The next thing you know he'd be seen on NBC television pirouetting around the Bolshoi stage singing 'Army Blue' and wearing nothing but a jockstrap stuffed with handkerchiefs to keep his inadequacy in that area a secret.

"So Bill sent me two contractors, one released from Leavenworth and the other from Saint Elizabeth's."

"Sir, I'm sorry, I don't fully understand. What's a contractor? And isn't Leavenworth a federal prison?"

"While the standards aren't as high in the CIA as they were in the OSS, we still try to keep out as many felons as possible, instead putting them under contract to do the dirty work necessary. Hence, contractors. And yes, Leavenworth is a federal prison. Saint Elizabeth's is a federal institution for the criminally insane. Rutherford was paroled to me from the latter, and McTavish from the former."

"Sir, are you referring to CIC Administrator Angus McTavish and CIC Administrator G. Lincoln Rutherford?"

"Yes, of course I am."

"Sir, you're not suggesting that they were incarcerated at those places you mentioned, are you?"

"I'm not suggesting anything of the sort, son. I'm *telling* you. Angus McTavish was doing fifteen to twenty-five in Leavenworth for having sold three elephants, a giraffe, a rhinoceros, a Perdido Key beach mouse, and a San Francisco garter snake that he didn't own to the Bronx Zoological Gardens. The judge, who was a tree-hugger, really socked it to him because the beach mouse and the garter snake were on the protected species list."

"And CIC Administrator Rutherford, sir? In a mental hospital for the criminally insane? He's insane, sir?"

"That's what he was trying to convince them of when ol' Bill got him out so that he could help me stem the tide of the Red Menace. In an attempt to avoid life behind bars as a recidivist offender, Geronimo was trying to sell the shrinks on the notion that only a crazy person would do what he did, and thus he should be adjudged innocent by reason of insanity. He said a sane person, especially one who was half Native American and had had the honor of being social secretary of the Harvard Law School Alumni Association, Inc., would not have done what he was accused of doing."

"Which was, sir?"

"Embezzle four point three million dollars from the Chiricahua Apache Tribe's Geronimo Resort and Casino, Inc., in Arizona and another million and a quarter from the

Apache Widows & Orphans Relief Trust, both of which he was serving, *pro bono,* as legal counsel."

"But they're CIC administrators, just like me!"

"Son, now that you have entered the smoke-and-mirrors world of intelligence, you're going to have to learn to think things through before you open your mouth."

"I'm not sure what you mean, sir."

"How does one get into the CIC, Phil?"

"Well, first you have to be in the Army."

"Right. And how tall do you have to be to get in the Army? And how tall is Angus McTavish? See where we're headed?"

"Mr. McTavish could not be in the Army because he's about four feet ten inches tall . . ."

"And a bit overweight, wouldn't you say?"

"Yes, sir. But how about Mr. Rutherford? He's of normal height and weight."

"How do you think he could undergo a complete background investigation without it being discovered that he is a criminal recidivist, sometimes known as a Three Strikes, You're Out Loser?"

"I take your point, sir."

"They are beards, son."

"Beards, sir?"

"There had to be some reason for me having those two around the German-American Gospel Tract Foundation besides the real one."

"What is the real one, sir?"

"I break that down into Sales and Logistics, Phil."

"Yes, sir?"

"Sales is the part where Geronimo Rutherford goes behind the Iron Curtain and seeks out two kinds of people. First are ballet dancers and high wire trapeze artists. Attractive ones. Sweet ones. Gentle ones. Geronimo then sells these young women on the many advantages of immigrating to the West, in other words, how much we're willing to pay for their services. If you're ever called upon, Phil, to talk attractive, sweet, gentle young women into swapping their virtue for cold cash, get a Harvard-trained lawyer to do your talking for you."

"Yes, sir, I'll make a note of that."

"The second ethnic group Geronimo seeks out behind the Iron Curtain contains the senior Soviet and Soviet Bloc NKGB officers we're trying to turn. He arranges to get himself seated beside one of the latter at the Bolshoi or a circus. Then when some attractive blonde is pirouetting around the stage in *Swan Lake,* or hanging from her knees on a trapeze, he says something like,

'Boy, I'd really like to hide the old salami in something like that. How about you?'

"One time in three point six times, he gets an affirmative reply. Once that happens, we have our defector. If you ever need to talk some respectable senior officer into betraying everything he holds dear, get yourself a Harvard-trained lawyer to do your talking for you."

"Yes, sir. I'll make a note of that."

"That's Sales. Logistics is getting the girls and the NKGB this side of Check Point Charley. That's where Angus McTavish's circus heritage comes in. Throughout history, Phil, as I'm sure you know, circuses — or is that circi? — have continuously moved across the European Continent much as the Bedouins move across the shifting sands of the Sahara on their camels. That is, without paying any attention at all to international borders and that sort of thing. To put a point on it, to circus people making their historic rounds, the barbed wire, ferocious German shepherds, land mines, et cetera, which close the Iron Curtain to ordinary people, are nothing but a minor bump in the road.

"What many people don't ask themselves, as they should, when visiting a circus is, 'Where does the circus get their elephants, hippopotami, and other pachydermi and their tigers, lions, and other panthera?'

"The answer is obvious, unless of course you're a Socialist and believe the government should have its nose in everything, including providing circuses with their wild animals. There are businesses serving that need. Wild animals are bought, sold, and traded much as used cars are by businessmen hoping to turn an honest, or mostly honest, dollar doing so.

"Putting all these factors together, what I then had ol' Bill, now Ralph, do was buy a couple of wild-animal cages, a selection of tigers, lions, and other savage animals, and two elephants which were surplus to the needs of Ringling Brothers, Barnum & Bailey. He then prevailed upon the Air Force to airlift them into Berlin. Once they were here, I had the cages modified to suit our needs and repainted appropriately. I was then ready to hook the elephants up to tow the animal cages and send A. McTavish Used Wild Animal Dealer into the sphere of Soviet influence.

"And I did so.

"Soon, Angus was able not only to reestablish relationships with other members of his circus family in circuses all over Eastern Europe and in Russia itself but able to cross back and forth over the border with no more effort and just about as much speed as a Ping-Pong ball being whacked by a Japanese Olympic Ping-Pong Team champion.

"The way it works is that the elephants tow Angus and the cages full of young, healthy savage beasts behind the Iron Curtain. He sells the beasts to circus proprietors, taking as partial payment their savage beasts that are getting a bit long in the tooth. Then the elephants tow Angus and the trade-in savage beasts in their cages back across the border. We then donate these decrepit wild beasts to Kiss A Tiger, Inc., Rhinoceri Are Beautiful, Inc., and other such lunatic do-gooder organizations, and begin looking for younger ones available at a good price.

"So far, the NKGB has not figured out what has happened to all the senior NKGB officers, ballet dancers, and high wire trapeze artists who have gone missing, and as far as we know they don't have a clue that they have departed Holy Mother Russia, or the Hungarian Republic, et cetera, in elephant-drawn wild-animal cages, comfortably ensconced behind cupboard doors reading, 'Caution, Wild Animals DO NOT ENTER!' "

"That's very clever, sir," Phil said.

"I like to think so," SSA Caldwell said. "I've often been told I'm clever. But right now, I face a conundrum that baffles me."

"What might that be, sir?"

"Well, because I absolutely need you to find the ambiguities, et cetera, in the reports my semi-literate CIC agents prepare for my signature, you and I are going to be spending a good deal of time together."

"Yes, sir?"

"Please don't take this the wrong way, son. But when a man my age, and a man — really, boy — your age spend a lot of time together, a lot of people begin to wonder, often aloud, if there isn't something a bit odd about the relationship. If you take my meaning?"

"I'm afraid I do, sir."

"I thought of one beard we could put on you. But, on reflection, it wouldn't work as no one in his right mind would allow someone of your tender years near a loaded pistol."

"Excuse me, sir?"

"Well, if you had, which I am quite sure you couldn't possibly have, qualified with the ol' .45 in Basic Training . . ."

"Yes, sir?"

". . . the beard we could put on you would

225

be that of my bodyguard. I don't have one now, although ol' Bill, now Ralph, says I really should, as after I saw my EXPLETIVE DELETED!! phalanx of EXPLETIVE DELETED!! West Pointers trying, and failing miserably, to qualify with Ol' Reliable on the range, I vowed never again to be within a thousand yards of a EXPLETIVE DELETED!! West Pointer with a loaded modern-day equalizer in his hand."

"I don't think I follow you, sir."

"Bodyguards have to carry guns, Phil. That's not just in Regulations, if you think about it, it actually makes sense."

"Sir, are you, when you say 'ol' .45' and 'ol' Reliable' and 'modern-day equalizer' perchance referring to the U.S. Pistol, Caliber .45 ACP M1911A1?"

"You've heard of it, have you, son? They showed you — but didn't permit you to actually hold — one in Basic Training?"

"With which weapon, sir . . . perhaps you had better sit down . . . I qualified as High Expert on the seven- and twenty-five-yard KD ranges, and on the Pistol Simulated Combat Range. In rapid-fire mode on the latter, I put six of the seven rounds of my magazine into the life-sized human silhouette target's left eye at fifty yards, sir. I flinched, and one shot went in the target's nose."

SSA Caldwell didn't reply for a long moment, during which he stared intently at Phil.

Finally, he said, "I am ashamed for doubting you as I did, even if only for a long moment until I realized that Saint Malachi Old Boys, even young Old Boys, such as you, never tell whoppers like that one to other Saint Malachi Old Boys unless they're true."

He put out his hand, and then went on, "Phil, my bodyguard, from this moment, my life is in your capable hands. Let's go find you a gun."

VII
PREPARING FOR THE HUNTING TRIP (PART 3)

[One]

Muddiebay, Mississippi
Wednesday, September 10, 1975

With the exception of Carol-Anne Crandall, the individual looking most eagerly forward to hanky-panky during what had formally become "The Tuesday Luncheon Club's European Excursion" was Mary-Louise Frathingham, co-proprietor — with her husband, Amos — of Muddiebay Exotic & Exciting Vacations Travel, Inc.

Although they presented to the world a picture of a loving, long-married couple who shared not only a business relationship but a trusting and faithful personal one, the latter was not exactly true.

Both did indeed see in "The Excursion" both a cornucopia of kickbacks from all the providers of services to the Excursion-ees plus the chance to direct to ME&EVT, Inc., a great deal of business they didn't presently have. The latter would come primarily, presuming things were handled properly, from Mr. Randolph C. Bruce, his business associate Señor Pancho Gonzales, and Cadwallader Howard III, president of the Muddiebay Mercantile Company.

Mary-Louise had told Amos of her intention to get close to Randy Bruce during The Excursion for that purpose. Not knowing how really close Mary-Louise intended to get, Amos said he thought it was a splendid idea. He said if she worked on Randy Bruce, he would work on getting close to Cadwallader Howard III to the same end. After thinking about it for a moment, Mary-Louise decided Amos meant with regard to getting more business for ME&EVT, Inc., and nothing else. For one thing, Amos wasn't inclined that way, and for another the EXPLETIVE DELETED!! had his lecherous eye on Bobbie-Sue Smith, the stockbroker's wife.

Mary-Louise had started to think about getting close to Randy Bruce while attending a Special Ladies Only Matinee showing of an old motion picture starring Errol Flynn at the Muddiebay Palace Theatre, Bowling Alleys & Flea Circus.

While it was true that she'd had a couple

of beers in the bowling area bar before perusing the flea circus offerings, and had smuggled a third can into the theater concealed in a Jumbo Cola insulated cup, when she thought about it later, it was not alcohol but rather a mental glitch that caused her to envision what she had envisioned.

In the film, Errol Flynn, playing a nobleman turned pirate, had given up his life of high seas criminal to come to the aid of Queen Bess, a/k/a "The Virgin Queen," when the Spanish Armada was approaching the White Cliffs of Dover with evil intent.

There was a scene in which Flynn, attired in what on a female would have been white panty hose, knelt before Her Majesty. She laid a sword on his shoulder and ordered, "Go and save the British Isles from the Spanish monsters!"

To which Errol Flynn replied, "I hear and obey, Your Virgin Majesty!"

Her Majesty then tapped him on both shoulders and proclaimed, "Rise, Sir Richard!"

He did so, and looked soulfully into the Virgin Queen's eyes.

At that point, Mary-Louise had two thoughts, one being that Mr. Flynn's costume in the groin area was much too small for him. The second thought inexplicably called the diminutive of "Richard" to her mind.

Several scenes later, Mr. Flynn appeared again. He was bare-chested and carrying a sword as he swung on a rope from his ship onto the deck of one of the Spanish ships.

Moments later, as he began to behead Evil Spaniards with his sword, Mary-Louise noticed he was attired only in a leather loincloth, and again for some reason Mary-Louise inexplicably recalled the diminutive of "Richard."

"Death to those dirty Spaniards who would despoil my Virgin Queen!" Errol Flynn/Sir Richard declared as he lopped the head off another would-be despoiler.

What apparently had happened then was that Mary-Louise's mind had put that information together with some that was already stored. Among that information, especially, was an idle comment made by one of Amos's cronies at their regular Wednesday Evening Fifty Cent Limit poker game. Mary-Louise had been innocently eavesdropping on the poker game in the hope that she would hear Amos boast to the boys about his relationship with Bobbie-Sue Smith. All she knew for sure about that was that whenever the EXPLETIVE DE-LETED!! was within fifty feet of Bobbie-Sue, he started breathing heavily and began to stroke his pencil-line mustache with his pinkie finger.

Bobbie-Sue did not come up in the gentlemen's conversation. Randolph C. Bruce did, to wit: "I'm not surprised that EXPLETIVE DELETED!! Randy Bruce gets so much EXPLETIVE DELETED!!. I saw the EXPLETIVE DELETED!! in the shower at the Muddiebay Country Club. The EXPLETIVE DELETED!! is hung like a EXPLETIVE DELETED!! horse."

The synapses in Mary-Louise's brain coordinated this data and the images and then flashed a combined image, a collage, so to speak, to Mary-Louise's visual senses, her theater of the mind, so to speak. That imagery caused her to spill most of the EXPLETIVE DELETED!! beer in the EXPLETIVE DELETED!! Jumbo Cola insulated cup into her EXPLETIVE DELETED!! lap.

The image was of Sir Randy Bruce, in white panty hose, one hand wielding his sword to behead Spaniards, and the other trying to stuff his you-know-what back into the panty hose from which it had burst free.

From that moment, she had trouble keeping the image from her mind. This was true even while she was making other arrangements for The Excursion. While she was anxious of course to recruit others for The Excursion, to fill up the Twenty-Plus-Two, she was careful not to make the pitch to any of The Tuesday Luncheon Club girls in whom Randy, even in his cups, would be at all interested.

Mary-Louise was now determined to have Randy, whom she now thought of as "Sir Randy," all to herself at least once or twice for at least an hour of illicit union. She thought this might be possible in London, but it wouldn't be easy.

She had quickly come to a Twenty-Plus-Two arrangement with Claridge's Hotel, and they had been very obliging insofar as room assignment was concerned. She and Amos would be at the center of their rooms on the third floor of the famed London hotel, so to speak. Sir Randy would be on one side of the Frathingham room and Señor Gonzales and his niece on the other. The other ladies and their husbands would be housed across the corridor according to seniority, with the ugliest and oldest females closest, and the youngest and better-looking farther away.

Bobbie-Sue would find herself at the end of the corridor. Mary-Louise was a little worried about Bobbie-Sue. Ferdinand Smith was a stockbroker, and a stockbroker would stop at nothing to pick up a new gambler in capitalism. That certainly included telling his wife to be very nice to someone who could put a lot of chips into the pot of Wall Street, like Randolph C. Bruce.

Neither could Mary-Louise dismiss the possibility that Bobbie-Sue had also heard that Randy had been very generously treated in the package department.

The first priority of almost all the girls who weren't thinking about hanky-panky on foreign shores was, of course, shopping, and Mary-Louise had spent long hours contacting retail merchandising establishments in London. Most of them, including Harrods, Marks & Spencer, and Selfridges, had been very obliging with regard to the ten percent "steerer's fee" Mary-Louise had asked for.

The second priority of almost all the girls was visiting Buckingham Palace. Mary-Louise understood this interest, which would allow them, once they returned to Muddiebay, to casually drop into their conversations with the less privileged that they had done so, e.g., *The last time I was at Buckingham Palace, I learned that tea, Earl Grey, of course, is even better when brewed without those lower class toilet tissue bags one sees here, and is instead brewed au naturel and then poured through a sterling silver strainer into one's cup.*

Or, *The last time I was at Buckingham Palace, or "Buck House" as we frequent visitors call it, I learned that H.M.'s Little Darlings, by which I mean Her Majesty's Corgis, really like to snack on bangers, which is what we Buck House frequenters call hot dogs and not what it sounds like.*

Et cetera.

Here Mary-Louise ran into a problem that she had not yet resolved.

After two letters to Buckingham Palace to ensure she would get her standard ten percent finder's fee had gone unanswered, she had gotten on the phone. She was put through to the Palace, but when she asked to speak to the person in charge, and the person on the line asked "in regard to what?" and she told him, he laughed, said, "Bugger off, Yank, and sober up!" and then hung up.

After this happened three times, Mary-Louise decided it was a problem she would deal with once they got to Old Blighty, even if that meant slipping a few bucks into the hands of the guys with the funny hats who guarded the portals, and that in the meantime she would extol the virtues of Abercrombie Castle to the ladies. The pictures of the castle that came up in her research showed that it was just about as large as Buckingham Palace, and when she showed them to the ladies, they were delighted.

Getting the ladies in there, Mary-Louise decided, would be a snap. Randy had told her the pheasant and grouse shooting would take place on the grounds of the palace and that she didn't have to trouble herself with the financial arrangements as he would handle that himself as "Bertie and Maggie, the gamekeepers," were old friends of his. All she would have to do, Randy said, was collect the thousand-dollars-per-shooter fee from the Excursion-ees, give it to him, and he would handle getting the money to the gamekeepers.

All she was going to have to do, Mary-Louise decided, once she had lured Randy into her bed, was get him to ask his friend the chief gamekeeper to let the ladies into the castle. She thought that if she could get Randy into a good mood — and she certainly intended to try — he might even reconsider his blunt refusal to even consider giving Mary-Louise her standard ten percent finder's fee.

[Two]

In sunny Miami, Señor Pancho Gonzales had had time to consider his last conversation with Randy, during which Randy had pointed out that no one was going to believe that Ginger Gallagher was his niece and that he had announced he had no intention of letting Ginger EXPLETIVE DELETED!! up his romantic plans.

He gave the problem more thought. Even if he took Ginger to Scotland, and ol' Phil was there, there was no way Ginger was going to feign a mysterious illness treatable only by Harley Street medical professionals and allow herself to be flown to London for treatment.

If ol' Phil was in Scotland, that's where Glamorous Ginger was going to be. If she couldn't get ol' Phil in the sack, it would be her first failed seduction in her entire twenty-five years, and she had her reputation to uphold.

He concluded that, for once, Randy was right about something: Ginger could not go to Scotland, or even to Atlanta or London as waypoints on the way to Scotland. Ginger was going to have to stay in Miami.

Pancho bit the bullet, so to speak, and called Ginger in her penthouse apartment, which overlooked Biscayne Bay. He told her that on reflection he had come to conclude that her going to England and Scotland was not such a good idea.

"I must beg to disagree," Ginger said. "First, Pancho, I should tell you that I have just finished reading Dear Phil's latest book, *Love and Lust in the Kremlin Necropolis,* which confirmed yet again my belief that Tolstoy, Dickens, Hemingway, and Pat O'Malley are vastly overrated.

"My dream now is to sit at the master's feet, or perhaps in his lap, and absorb through osmosis, or, preferably some other more intimate contact, some of his saintly genius.

"Since Master Philip is going to be in Scotland, perhaps researching a book on the subject of Zen and pheasant shooting, I am going to be in Scotland, and you, you EXPLETIVE DELETED!! fried banana eater, are going to take me to him, or you will wish that you had fallen off of that EXPLETIVE DELETED!! shrimp boat on which you escaped from EXPLETIVE DELETED!! Cuba with five EXPLETIVE DELETED!! dollars and the shirt on your EXPLETIVE DELETED!! back and EXPLETIVE DELETED!! drowned. Please tell me that we understand each other, Pancho, baby."

After that conversation, Pancho had realized that unless he took some other action, Ginger and ol' Phil were going to be in Scotland and he was going to be all alone in London except for Randy and his new bimbo.

So he called Guatemalan Air, got Pilar on the line, and asked her how she would like to go to London and Scotland.

Once everybody was in Atlanta, he reasoned, they could sort things out.

VIII
PHIL VERSUS THE RED MENACE

[One]

Berlin, Germany
Saturday, August 9, 1947

While it could not be truthfully said that Phil was ever in any real danger of being named an Honorary Member of the Berlin Garrison Chapter of the West Point Protective Association, it is true that he soon worked out a harmonious relationship with those members associated with the German-American Gospel Tract Foundation.

For one thing, he used the respectful term "sir" a good deal when conversing with them and, for another, when he came to work in the morning, he fell into the habit of taking his U.S. Pistol, Cal. .45 ACP Model 1911A1, from his shoulder holster and laying it on his desk for all to see.

Within a very short time, most, if not all, of the West Pointers realized that it was really better to hand their reports of investigations and other activities over to the man they described — behind his back, of course — as "a EXPLETIVE DELETED!! enlisted man who didn't even finish EXPLETIVE DELETED!! high school" for his red pencil, than the alternative, which was to send them directly to SSA Caldwell, with the inevitable result there, presuming undetected ambiguities and errors of grammar would surface, as they inevitably would, of having a new anal orifice reamed by SSA Caldwell, who could and did ream such orifices as only a lieutenant colonel of cavalry, pay grade O-5, can ream them.

And then firearms, in particular smooth bore shoulder arms, often called "shotguns," entered the picture.

On a Saturday morning about three months after Administrator Williams had assumed his duties as chief, Literary Division, German-American Gospel Tract Foundation and as bodyguard to the pastor-in-charge, Phil went to his office after driving Pastor-in-Charge and Mrs. Caldwell in their Cadillac to Tempelhof Airfield, where they caught the 10:20 a.m. Pan American flight to Frankfurt am Main.

They were headed for the Frankfurt International Book Fair, which was to be the beard for a meeting between Pastor Caldwell and the Reverend Phineas Logan, which was the beard ol' Bill Colby, now Ralph Peters, was using for the moment.

After making a quick stop to examine the religious tomes on display at the book fair, they were going to Baden-Baden, in the Black Forest, where they would discuss Intelligence Business, and then put to the test on the *vingt-et-un* tables of the Baden-Baden Casino a new theory of mathematical probability ol' Bill had developed.

On the way from the Caldwell residence to the airfield, they had made a quick stop at an apartment on Onkel Tom Allee the German-American Gospel Tract Foundation maintained to house very senior NKGB officers, or very senior officers of other Eastern Bloc nations, and/or their families, following their defection until they could be moved to Palm Beach, Florida, or Palm Springs, California, or wherever they would begin their new lives in the United States.

"Be a dear, Philip," Mrs. Caldwell said, "and pop in there for me. The countess is going to loan me her Persian lamb to wear in Baden-Baden. She knows you're coming."

Phil understood that Mrs. Caldwell meant Persian lamb *fur coat,* not a live animal, as his mother had a Persian lamb fur coat. And he looked forward to popping in and getting the coat from the countess, a/k/a Magda, Countess of Kocian, who was a redheaded older Hungarian woman — probably twenty-eight, maybe even twenty-nine — but remarkably well preserved, especially in the bosom department.

Angus McTavish had spirited the countess across the border hidden in a cage with an aging gorilla and an about-to-expire python. She had brought with her only the clothes on her back and a small pigskin suitcase holding the Kocian family jewels, mostly diamonds but with a sprinkling of rubies and pearls.

The countess had left her husband, a colonel in the Hungarian Secret Police, behind in Budapest. She would wait in Berlin for him to join her.

The countess had met the pastor's wife, and soon they were chums, spending long hours together comparing the socio-sexual foibles of the Hungarian aristocracy with those of the aristocracies of Detroit, Michigan, and Boston, Massachusetts, while sipping at Slivovitz, a Hungarian plum brandy with which the pastor's wife had previously not been familiar, but had quickly come to really appreciate.

Phil had overheard the pastor's wife confide in her husband, "Don't push that EXPLETIVE DELETED!! dwarf of yours, McTavish, too hard about getting Magda's husband out. For one thing, I'm going to miss the countess terribly when she's gone to Palm Springs, or wherever, and for another Magda has confided in me that their marriage was one of convenience. The EXPLETIVE DELETED!! Reds had taken over her castle and it was either marry him or move out. And the only reason he married her was that his hanky-panky with barely pubescent girls of the Magyar Állami Operaház Corps de Ballet was getting to be too much of an embarrassment for even the EXPLETIVE DELETED!! Hungarian Secret Police to keep overlooking and he needed a beard."

The countess answered Phil's buzz at her door with both her flaming red hair, which reached her waist, and her dressing gown askew. Before she pulled her neckline together, he inadvertently happened to notice perhaps eighty percent of the left of her bosom.

"Good morning, Countess. I'm here to pick up the Persian lamb."

"Nem vagyok grófné, az én kis szilva cukor,"

the countess replied, taking her hand from where it was holding her gown closed and using it to pinch his cheek.

Phil now had what was known to intelligence professionals as a *one hundred percent clear with zero obstructions visual* of both of the countess's mammary glands.

His heart jumped. When he could find his voice, he confessed, "Countess, I'm afraid I don't speak Hungarian."

"What I said, my little dumpling," she said in English, "was that you don't have to call me countess."

"Yes, ma'am."

"You may — when the pastor and his wife are not around, of course — call me Magda."

"That's very kind of you, Magda."

"And what are your plans for this Saturday, after the pastor and his wife fly off to Frankfurt, dumpling?"

"Actually, I have none, Magda, so if you would like me to drive you anywhere at all you'd like in the pastor's Cadillac, I would be happy to oblige."

"Well, maybe that, too, but what I was thinking was that since you don't speak Hungarian, I would like to teach you a little Hungarian. And some other things, which your innocent face, my little dumpling, tells me you have yet to learn. Would you like that?"

"That would be very kind of you, Magda."

"I'll get the coat."

When she handed him the coat, she said, "I wouldn't mention our conversation to the pastor. I'm afraid he would understand."

"Yes, ma'am . . . I mean, Magda."

After dropping Pastor-in-Chief and Mrs. Caldwell at Tempelhof, Phil drove to his office. He realized that he needed time to think things through and that was the place to do it, as no one else in the German-American Gospel Tract Foundation worked on Saturday but him.

Logic told him, of course, that it would be illogical to think that a startlingly beautiful redheaded, magnificently bosomed older woman of at least twenty-eight could possibly be interested in an administrator who was the world's last known living seventeen-year-old virgin.

On the other hand, she had pinched his cheek, and called him her little dumpling. And, having already acquired the cynicism that is the hallmark of those who labor in the intelligence fields, he wasn't absolutely sure that her bosom exposure had been entirely accidental and thus innocent on her part.

And he was having trouble thinking clearly, as the visual of Magda's bosom kept interrupting his chain of thought. And then his thought chain was again interrupted when there came a knock at his office door.

He ran to open it, throwing caution to the wind, and just knowing it was Magda come to teach him Hungarian and whatever else she had in mind.

[Two]

It wasn't.

It was a delegation of members of the Berlin Garrison Chapter of the West Point Protective Association.

"How may I help you, sirs?" Phil politely inquired.

"We're hoping you might find time in your schedule, Administrator Williams, to discuss with you a problem we're facing."

"Sirs, my time is your time. Please come in, sirs, and have seats."

The delegation — consisting of Captain J. K. Brewster, cavalry, pay grade O-3, and two of his underlings — entered the office and sat down.

"We are hoping, Administrator Williams, that you will keep this conversation to yourself," Captain Brewster began.

"Sir, you have my word that what's said in this room will stay in this room."

"We are aware, Administrator Williams, that in order to better serve him, the pastor-in-charge has moved you out of the barracks housing the Thirty-third CIC detachment's enlisted men and into the field grade bachelor officers' hotel."

"Yes, sir. The pastor-in-charge did so in order that his Cadillac, in which I often drive the pastor-in-charge's wife to the PX, the Senior Officers' Club, and similar destinations, and in which I have just now driven the both of them to Tempelhof Field to catch the Frankfurt flight, can be parked out of the sun and rain, and also to separate me from certain members of the Thirty-third CIC he felt were trying to corrupt me."

"Despite this, we are hoping that you still remember Lieutenant Colonel O'Reilly from your days in the Thirty-third's barracks."

"Yes, sir, I do."

"And we hope you also remember that despite your civilian clothing status and residence in the field grade bachelor officers' hotel, you are still, *de jure,* so to speak, a corporal, pay grade E-3, and carried on the Morning Report of the Thirty-third as such."

"Sir, I am also fully aware of that."

"*Entre nous,* Administrator Williams, Lieutenant Colonel William 'Don't Call Me Bill' O'Reilly is what we call a 'ticket puncher.' Behind his back, of course."

"Sir, I have heard that allegation, but I'm afraid I don't know precisely what that means."

"Let me put it to you this way, Administrator Williams. A ticket puncher is an officer who believes the way to higher command lies in getting his ticket punched as many times as possible, whatever the cost. Understand?"

"No, sir."

"Well, let's try this. Word comes from Berlin Brigade that the commanding general hopes that the brigade will support the Red Cross Drive. The response of normal officers, such as myself and these gentlemen, to the general's hopes would range from the verbal — 'Yeah, us too' — to a decision to actually drop a dollar in the Red Cross's bucket if one is presented to us. Understand?"

"Yes, sir."

"On the other hand, a ticket puncher such as Lieutenant Colonel William 'Don't Call

Me Bill' O'Reilly, on learning of the general's hopes *vis-à-vis* the Red Cross, will regard it as a clarion call from on high to see that every last member of his organization contributes a dollar to the Red Cross Drive. Understand?"

Phil said, "Yes, sir," and handed Captain Brewster a dollar.

"I'm always willing, sir, to do my part."

"Jesus H. EXPLETIVE DELETED!! Christ!" Captain Brewster exclaimed.

He then got control of himself and continued, "We seem to have gotten a few paces off my intended path, Administrator Williams. Pray let me attempt to get us back on course."

"Yes, sir."

"Now, presuming that Lieutenant Colonel William 'Don't Call Me Bill' O'Reilly succeeds, by fair means or foul, to have every member of the Thirty-third contribute a dollar to the Red Cross, he will then make every effort to make sure the general learns of this. When the general does, and then says, 'Good job, Bill, *vis-à-vis* the Red Cross,' or words to that effect, Colonel O'Reilly will consider that to mean his ticket has been punched. Get it?"

"Yes, sir."

"Now, as a practical matter, rather than

see us having to harass every last mother's son in the Thirty-third for a buck for the Red Cross, what the Berlin Garrison Chapter of the West Point Protective Association does is call in Special Agent Dumbrowski, who is also actually First Sergeant Dumbrowski, and demand from him the total number of personnel, enlisted and commissioned, on that morning's Morning Report. When he furnishes that number, we then take up a collection amongst ourselves to match that number at one dollar per name. We then hand Dumbrowski the money, and wink at him, and say, 'Happy Red Cross Donation Day.'

"He takes the money and passes it upward in the chain of command. He and we are happy because we don't have to harass people to give a buck to the EXPLETIVE DELETED!! Red Cross. Lieutenant Colonel William 'Don't Call Me Bill' O'Reilly is happy to be able to report to the general that one hundred percent of the Thirty-third, under his inspired leadership, has contributed to the EXPLETIVE DELETED!! Red Cross, and when the general says, 'Good job, Bill, *vis-à-vis* the Red Cross,' the colonel assumes he's had his EXPLETIVE DELETED!! ticket punched. Clear now?"

"Yes, sir."

"The problem we are facing now, Administrator Williams, is akin to, but not identical to, the problem we face each year *vis-à-vis* the EXPLETIVE DELETED!! Red Cross. This time the Berlin Brigade's commanding general has expressed the hope that all U.S. Army organizations in Berlin, which includes organizations like the Thirty-third that are physically in Berlin but not subordinate to the Berlin Brigade, will participate in the First Annual Berlin Brigade Brandenburg Gate Skeet Shoot. You do know what a skeet shoot is, don't you, Administrator Williams?"

"Yes, sir. I do."

"Well, let me give you the skinny on this one. It is sponsored by the Browning Arms Company of Arnold, Missouri, and Liège, Belgium. What they are hoping to do is incite the interest of members of the U.S. Army in the sport of skeet shooting. The reason they want to do this is because such new skeet shooters will be in the market for a shotgun, and that's what Browning makes a lot of.

"In golf, as you may or may not know, there is a devout belief that the more expensive the golf clubs in the hands of the golfer, the lower his score, which is good. In skeet shooting, low is not good, insofar as scoring is concerned. High is good, so what the Browning people are trying to do is adopt the golf philosophy to skeet, in other words to convince people that the more they pay for their shotgun the higher their skeet scores will be. Understand?"

"Yes, sir."

"To get this idea across, what the Browning people are going to do is dangle a carrot before the noses of skeet shooters. Specifically, they are going to award to a skeet shooter who does well — very well — a top-grade Browning — specifically a Diamond Grade 12-bore Over and Under with full factory engraving, a gold trigger, and selective ejectors — whatever the hell that means —"

"It means, sir," Phil interrupted, and furnished helpfully, "that the weapon will eject, when the action is opened, only the shot shell which has been fired, leaving the unfired shot shell in the chamber. If neither barrel has been fired, no shot shells will be ejected, and if both barrels have been fired, both shot shell casings will be kicked out."

"So Dumbrowski was right. You do have some elementary knowledge of shotguns."

"Yes, sir. I do."

"The commanding general of Berlin Brigade has heard of the Browning company's generous offer and inasmuch as he has always believed the more shooting a soldier does the better the soldier, he has strongly encouraged the participation of as many soldiers as possible in the First Annual Berlin Brigade Brandenburg Gate Skeet Shoot. He himself will participate to show the strength of his support, and possibly also because he was overheard remarking to his aide-de-camp that since he knows he is the best skeet shot in Berlin, and quite possibly in the European Command, the Diamond Grade Browning being offered 'is in the bag.'

"I think it safe to presume that what the general meant to say was that the Diamond Grade prize is safely in his bag, and by that he meant to say the alligator-hide gun case which comes with the prize. With me so far, Administrator Williams?"

"Yes, sir."

"Lieutenant Colonel William 'Don't Call Me Bill' O'Reilly is determined that the Thirty-third CIC Detachment will enter a team in the First Annual Berlin Brigade Brandenburg Gate Skeet Shoot. He knows that after the general walks home from the shoot with an alligator-hide gun case containing the Diamond Grade Browning he won, the general will certainly be so happy as to again punch Colonel O'Reilly's ticket and may indeed punch it two or more times."

"I understand, sir."

"Now, there are strict rules under which the First Annual Berlin Brigade Brandenburg Gate Skeet Shoot will be conducted. One of these is that each unit team will consist of both officers and enlisted men, two of each. So far as the officers are concerned, these two" — he pointed to the officers with him — "will constitute the commissioned element of the team and First Sergeant Dumbrowski half of the enlisted element of the team. I will be the coach. Which brings us to you."

"Sir?"

"First Sergeant Dumbrowski reports that a diligent search of the records of the Thirty-third CIC Detachment has revealed that only two enlisted members of the detachment can be trusted with a loaded shotgun. Dumbrowski himself and Guess Who?"

"Sir, with all possible respect, if you're suggesting that I participate in the First Annual Berlin Brigade Brandenburg Gate Skeet Shoot, I'm afraid I could not do so without the express permission of Pastor Caldwell."

"Why not?"

"Pastor Caldwell said that I must ever be mindful that as a member of the German-American Gospel Tract Foundation, it is my duty to avoid sin wherever possible and never to call attention to myself or the German-American Gospel Tract Foundation itself. I respectfully suggest, sir, that by appearing in a sports competition at the Brandenburg Gate open to the public, I would be calling attention to myself."

"Three things, Administrator Caldwell. First of all, I'm sure you noticed that we didn't come here until after Pastor Caldwell and his wife were well on their way to Frankfurt, meaning Lieutenant Colonel William 'Don't Call Me Bill' O'Reilly is in charge in his absence, and he wants to field a team. Second, you will be wearing your U.S. Army uniform, not the Brooks Brothers banker's gray three-button suit in which you are now attired . . ."

"Actually, sir, it's from J. Press," Phil said.

". . . and you should have learned by now that no one pays attention to a lowly corporal, and, finally, I would like to know what sin could possibly be connected with a skeet shoot."

"I can't think of one myself, sir, now that you mention it," Phil said.

That was a lie.

The sin of greed or lust, or both, had popped into his mind the moment he heard that a Diamond Grade Browning with full factory engraving, a gold trigger, and selective ejectors was going to be passed out by the Browning people.

"Well, Corporal Williams," Captain Brewster said, "now that we understand one another, why don't you put on your uniform and we'll saddle up and mosey on over to the Brandenburg Gate?"

[Three]

Phil saw that there was only one skeet field. A low row of bleachers had been set up facing away from the Brandenburg Gate and the Soviet Zone of Berlin beyond. The skeet course consisted of seven shooting stations spaced equidistant in a semicircle, with an eighth midway between the High House, which was to the left of, and just over 120 feet distant from, the Low House to the right.

There was an opening ceremony, most of it dedicated to the exhibition of the Diamond Grade *und so weiter* that was to be awarded, and the circumstances under which it would be.

These were fairly simple: The first shooter

to "go one hundred straight" — break one hundred clay targets in a row — got the gun.

A Browning spokesman said that today, and in the years to follow, the Browning Diamond *und so weiter* would serve as a symbol of fine marksmanship and dedication to the art of skeet shooting. He went on to say that when someone, perhaps within the next five years, shot that magical "hundred straight," Browning would replace the Diamond Grade that that marvelous marksman would take home with another, and thus preserve what they hoped would be an annual ritual approaching the holy.

On the way to the Brandenburg Gate, Phil's mind had been filled with the sins of greed and lust. Should he, or should he not, try to take the Diamond Grade *und so weiter* back to his room in the field grade bachelor officers' hotel?

If he did, Pastor/SSA/Lieutenant Colonel Caldwell would learn how he had come into possession of the gun. Or he would see the story in *Stars and Stripes,* the Army's daily newspaper, or *Berlin Weekly,* the brigade's weekly newspaper, or the advertisements of the Browning people. Photographers and reporters and copywriters from all of these entities were all over the place.

He knew that he could not blame his presence here on Captain Brewster. Every time Pastor Caldwell mentioned Captain Brewster, usually referring to him as one incredibly stupid EXPLETIVE DELETED!! EXPLETIVE DELETED!!, he would ask Phil if Phil agreed, and Phil had always answered in the affirmative.

"Phil," he could hear the pastor saying, "since we have always agreed that Brewster is an incredibly stupid EXPLETIVE DELETED!! EXPLETIVE DELETED!!, what was in your mind when he asked you to violate my orders *vis-à-vis* never calling attention to yourself or the EXPLETIVE DELETED!! German-American Gospel Tract Foundation?"

Phil had just about concluded that the smart thing for him to do when he got into the firing position was step over the white line and disqualify himself, and then get the hell away from the whole skeet shooting contest as quickly as possible.

And then greed and lust were replaced with simple lust.

He saw Magda the Countess Kocian in the crowd of spectators.

As he wondered what she was doing there, he could not help but be reminded that he was the last living seventeen-year-old virgin in the world, and when she smiled at him and waved, which action caused more of her bosom to be displayed than was displayed when she was just standing there, his mind was filled with erotic images of him leaping onto her prone body as she encouraged him on.

Later, he was not able to decide whether it was the mental images of Magda the Countess Kocian *au naturel,* so to speak, in his mind or Captain Brewster's last-minute coaching in his ear — "Do your best, Corporal Williams, break as many as ten or twelve; we don't want anyone to think we're throwing the game" — that caused him to do what he did on the firing position, although he did have a faint recollection of remembering the phrase "Faint heart never won a splendidly bosomed red-haired Hungarian old woman of twenty-eight or twenty-nine."

And then he dropped a Winchester AA shot shell loaded with 1 1/8-ounce #9 lead shot into the breech of the Remington 1100 self-loader they had handed him with a warning to be careful, punched off the safety, and called, "Pull!"

The clay disc flew, and immediately the bird, surprising him not at all, disappeared in a puff of smoke.

As did the next ninety-nine birds, which,

in due course over the next hour, whenever it was his turn to call "Pull!" were thrown for him to shoot at.

Pandemonium not unlike that which occurs in Las Vegas when some lucky lever puller hits the jackpot ensued.

"We have a winner!" the shoot manager shouted.

The senior representative of the Browning company wept with joy, or, more likely, shock, as he handed Phil the Browning Diamond Grade *und so weiter.*

The general who had so enthusiastically supported the shoot said a lot of colorful words and then grabbed his personally owned Remington 1100 Skeet Special by the barrel and began to hammer a handy fire hydrant on Pariser Platz into the ground.

Magda Kocian worked her way through the crowd of photographers, et cetera, and kissed Phil wetly on the forehead.

"*Gyere fel hozzám valamikor,* my cupcake!"

Phil had no idea what she was saying, but he liked the sound of it.

All the while, of course, flashbulbs were going off.

And then suddenly someone screamed, "*Ach, mein Gott, ein bengalischer Tiger!*"

Whereupon the crowd parted as the Red

Sea is rather reliably reported to have parted.

Then G. Lincoln Rutherford appeared, followed by Angus McTavish, who had a Bengal tiger on a leash. G. Lincoln, moving with great speed, grabbed a photographer's camera, ripped the film from it, knocked the photographer off his feet, and turned to the other photographers with the obvious intention of doing the same to them.

G. Rutherford was shouting, "If I've told you EXPLETIVE DELETED!! press people once, I've told you a hundred EXPLETIVE DELETED!! times. You EXPLETIVE DELETED!! do not take EXPLETIVE DELETED!! pictures of members of the EXPLETIVE DELETED!! German-American EXPLETIVE DELETED!! Gospel Tract EXPLETIVE DELETED!! Foundation."

Then, with one hand on Phil's arm and the other holding the leash of the Bengal tiger, Angus McTavish led Phil through the retreating, somewhat hysterical, spectators who were leaving the area, and loaded him — and of course the Browning Diamond Grade *und so weiter* in its alligator-hide case with combination lock — into a Volkswagen that then roared off across Pariser Platz to safety.

Phil looked for Magda, but didn't see her.

[Four]

Angus drove Phil to Magda's apartment building on Onkel Tom Allee, where she was waiting for them, which explained why Phil hadn't seen her as they had raced across Pariser Platz.

"Ah," she greeted them. *"Itt, az én drága litte gombóc."*

"Excuse me, Countess?" Phil inquired politely.

"She said," Angus, who of course spoke Hungarian, translated, " 'Ah. Here you are, my precious little dumpling.' And I don't think she was talking to me."

"It's nice to see you again, too, Magda," Phil said.

"While I can barely wait to wrap you in my arms, Phil, my precious little dumpling, that will have to wait until I deal with the dwarf here."

"Is there anything else I can do for you, Countess, anything at all?" Angus asked politely.

"Let's go over what's already on the schedule," Magda said.

"Yes, ma'am," Angus said.

"Starting with what you're going to do in Budapest."

"Right. Trust me, Countess, to handle that. When the Moral Righteousness Sub-

Committee of the Central Committee of the Hungarian Communist Party sees the pictures of the colonel whooping it up with those thirteen- and fourteen-year-old ballerinas, the colonel will be on the next prison train to Yeniseysk, Siberia."

"Possibly. But I've heard disgusting things about the comrades on the Moral Righteousness Sub-Committee, things I wouldn't want repeated in the hearing of my *Drága és futkároznak mindenféle messze mén* . . ."

"That means 'my precious and so far unridden stallion,' " Angus, glancing at Phil, furnished helpfully.

". . . that make it equally possible that those degenerates will develop a sudden interest in the ballet," Magda went on. "Well, we'll just have to see how that turns out and then decide how to handle it. Now, what are you going to do for me here in Berlin?"

"Well," Angus said, "make absolutely sure that Pastor General Caldwell doesn't get a whiff of what's going on with you two."

"And what else?"

"Make sure that none of the amoral women in Berlin, of whatever nationality, get within fifteen feet of Phil here."

"If my *Drága és futkároznak mindenféle*

messze mén is to be sullied, I will do the sullying," the countess said. "And what's going to happen to you, Angus, if I hear that my *vanília fagylalt tölcsér . . .*"

"Your what?" Phil asked.

"Vanilla ice cream cone," Angus furnished.

". . . has been anywhere near naked women and horses in any combination, not only in the Pferd und Frauen but any-where?"

"You have made me fully aware of the dire consequences to myself and G. Lincoln Rutherford if something like that happens, Countess."

"Hell hath no fury like a pissed-off Hun-garian redhead, Angus. You might wish to write that down. You may go."

"Yes, ma'am, thank you, ma'am," Angus said, and left.

"Well, my *vanília fagylalt tölcsér,*" Magda said to Phil. "Do you have any questions?"

"I have many questions, Magda, but the one that interests me the most is why are you so peeved at the husband you left be-hind?"

"Well, since I certainly don't want to discourage your curiosity *vis-à-vis* the intimate details of either my persona or my body, my *vanília fagylalt tölcsér,* I will tell you.

"The deal I struck with that *a kurvapecér* — that means son of a bitch — was that I would come out with Angus, bringing half of the family jewels, and that he would follow later, bringing the other half with him. Then we would go to Palm Beach, I would set him up in the automobile business — he was a used-car salesman before he joined the secret police — and then we would divorce and I would then go to Palm Springs.

"I found out yesterday — I didn't tell the pastor so as not to ruin their weekend at the tables in Baden-Baden — that the *a kurvapecér* never had any intention of holding up his end of the bargain. He's got word to me that he prefers ballerinas half my age —"

"How old are you, Magda?"

"Almost twenty-eight. As I was saying, he said he prefers fourteen-year-old ballerinas to middle-aged women, and to afford them he needs to keep the other half of my family jewels. 'So have a good time in Palm Springs, and *auf Wiedersehen!*' "

"So you'll be leaving Berlin?"

"Tuesday morning, my *vanília fagylalt tölcsér,* so we don't have time to waste standing around talking. I'll bet you two dollars I can get my clothes off faster than you can get yours off. And then we'll play ice cream cone to get things rolling. How does that sound?"

And here the author must draw the curtain of modesty across the stage of this romance novel, except to say that when Phil left Magda — whom he had learned to call his *Forró magyar Nyalókát,* which means Hot Hungarian Lollipop — at Tempelhof Field the next Tuesday morning, he was twenty pounds lighter in weight than he had been when he went one hundred straight and won the Browning Diamond Grade *und so weiter* and was no longer able to claim that he was the last living seventeen-year-old virgin in the world.

IX
PHIL'S LIFE TAKES A NEW PATH (PART 1)

[One]

Berlin, Germany
Monday, August 11, 1947

Pastor Caldwell of course learned of Phil's triumph at the First Annual Berlin Brigade Brandenburg Gate Skeet Shoot just about as soon as he and the missus returned from Baden-Baden. He was, after all, the CIA's Berlin station chief and expected to know everything that happened on that Island of Freedom in the Red Sea, so to speak.

The first intel he received was from a man he had working undercover as a photographer at the *Berliner Tageblatt* newspaper. The photographer had managed somehow to elude G. Lincoln Rutherford at the Brandenburg Gate and was thus able to give Pastor Caldwell a stack of 8 × 10-inch photographs he had taken during the event.

They provided proof positive that Phil had

not only been a participant, wearing his corporal's uniform, despite his orders not to draw attention to himself, and thus the German-American Gospel Tract Foundation, but also that he had compounded this sin by winning the Grand Prize, a Browning Diamond Grade *und so weiter* shotgun.

The photos also showed a man clearly recognizable as the Berlin Brigade's commanding general trying to hammer a fire hydrant into the Pariser Platz with his personal Remington 1100 Skeet Special shotgun.

Pastor Caldwell got another version of what had transpired from Lieutenant Colonel William "Don't Call Me Bill" O'Reilly, who had tears in his eyes when he reported what the commanding general of the Berlin Brigade had said to him *vis-à-vis* his — O'Reilly's — role in the competition.

Summarized here because there is not enough space to chronicle *verbatim* what the general said in his fifteen-minute speech, O'Reilly said the general said that he was shocked that a fellow West Pointer would be complicit in sending in a "ringer" disguised as a simple corporal into the skeet competition, thus depriving a "sportsman" skeet shooter, such as himself, of the opportunity to bask in the glory of winning the contest, and the Browning Superposed *und so weiter* that went with it, and that if Colonel O'Reilly thought the general would ever again punch Colonel O'Reilly's ticket for any reason whatsoever he probably believed in forgiveness of the unforgivable and in the Tooth Fairy.

There were other reports of what happened, but the one in which the pastor placed the most faith was the one he got from Magda, the Countess Kocian. Poor Dear Magda, as the pastor thought of her after learning what her EXPLETIVE DELETED!! husband had done to her, said that she knew how lonely Phil would be with the Caldwells out of town.

With that in mind, Magda said, she had walked all the way from her Onkel Tom Allee apartment to the pastor's office, where she suspected Phil might be. What she had in mind, Magda said, was taking "the poor boy" to the movies.

She said that as she approached the office, she saw three of the pastor's officers enter it, including Captain Brewster, whom she knew the pastor thought of as the dumbest EXPLETIVE DELETED!! West Pointer he had ever met.

She was naturally worried, she said, that they were intent, as Angus McTavish and

G. Lincoln Rutherford had been, on taking advantage of Phil's innocence for their amusement, as Angus and Geronimo had when they had taken the boy to Pferd und Frauen and caused him to go steeplechasing with a naked woman on a Clydesdale.

Eavesdropping at the door, Magda said, she had learned that was indeed their purpose, except that it had something to do with a German experimental theatrical performance at the Brandenburg Gate and not a naked woman on a Clydesdale. But inasmuch as she knew experimental actresses could be inclined to loose morals, Magda said that she knew she had to do something to save Phil from the evil intentions of the dumbest EXPLETIVE DELETED!! West Pointer the pastor had ever met.

So, reasoning that if they could get "Poor Philip" into trouble so easily, they could probably keep him out of trouble with equal facility, she had called Angus McTavish and G. Lincoln Rutherford and told them (a) it was clearly their Christian duty to rescue Philip, and (b) that if they did so and she told the pastor, which she promised to do, that would more than likely get them off the pastor's EXPLETIVE DELETED!! list.

"And then," Magda finished, "I went to my apartment and prayed that they were going to be successful."

"Magda, my dear," the pastor gently intoned, "what was going on at the Brandenburg Gate wasn't a theatrical performance —"

"But there were all those pictures in the papers of that bald, fat man destroying something by beating it against a fire hydrant while screaming foul obscenities at the top of his lungs. What else could that be but an experimental theatrical performance?"

"That wasn't just 'something,' Magda, dear. It was a Remington 1100 Skeet Special."

"A what?"

"It's not important, Magda, dear. Pray continue."

"My prayers were answered," Magda said. "Angus delivered Phil to my apartment door."

She thought: *At least that much is absolutely true.*

"So if you can find forgiveness for Angus and Geronimo in your heart, Dear Pastor?"

"I'll take that under advisement. So, what happened next?"

"Poor Philip was terribly shaken up. It was all I could do to resist my female urge to hold him against my breast to comfort him.

But I did."

At least until I got rid of the dwarf.

"And then what happened?"

"I finally got him calmed down."

I am not going to tell you how I did that.

"Good for you. And then?"

"The poor exhausted — physically and emotionally — boy dozed off."

That must have been three hours later.

My, how time did fly!

"And?"

"I draped something . . ."

Actually that was me.

". . . over him and let him sleep."

Probably for at least thirty minutes.

"And then?"

"I didn't have the heart to send him to his cold and lonely room in the field grade bachelor officers' hotel, so I arranged for him to spend the night . . ."

In lewd and lascivious behavior with me.

". . . in my apartment."

"How arranged?"

"You know, simple things. Putting a mattress on the floor . . ."

With incense candles burning all around the mattress, teaching him what a Forró magyar Nyalókát *was and how to do the Hot Hungarian Lollipop.*

Boy, was he a quick learner!

"That was very kind of you, Magda."

"Not at all. Then on Sunday, we had a late breakfast . . ."

Steak Tartare, and raw eggs, to give him back his vigor, washed down with a medicinal bottle of Egri Bikavér — *"Bull's Blood" — which I thought might — and indeed did — live up to its reputation for restoring exhausted vigor.*

". . . and then I consoled him for the rest of Sunday. Which, as I'm sure you know, Pastor, the Scripture refers to as a 'day of rest' and which I interpreted to mean that I should encourage the dear exhausted boy to spend the day in bed. Which he did, until duty called and he had to go to Tempelhof to meet you on your return from Baden-Baden."

"Rest assured, Dear Magda, you will get your reward in heaven," Pastor Caldwell said.

"I hope you can find it in your heart, Pastor, in Christian compassion, to forgive him for not following to the letter your instructions."

"Forgive him? Don't be absurd! After he made a jackass out of the Berlin Brigade commander — I have never liked that EX- PLETIVE DELETED!! ring-knocking West Pointer EXPLETIVE DELETED!! — I'm going to promote him to sergeant!"

"He'll be so pleased! You are a good man, Pastor Caldwell."

"So I keep hearing. Is there anything else I can do for you, Dear Magda, before you fly off to your new life in America tomorrow morning?"

"Do you suppose it would be possible for you to send Philip by my apartment? — before he picks me up to take me to Tempelhof, I mean. I could use a little help packing, and I'd like to give him a little something to remember me by."

"I'll have him there by the time you get there. And you may tell Phil, Dear Magda, that he may consider any request from you to do anything — anything at all — that you would like him to do as a direct order from me to do it."

[Two]

Sergeant Philip W. Williams realized, as he drove away from Tempelhof Airfield and seeing Magda fly off to her new life in Palm Beach, that his life had really changed as a result of what had happened in the previous thirty-six hours.

He knew he would have to give the matter a good deal of thought, but realized it would be better to wait until he had a couple of hours' sleep before he started thinking about anything.

His cheerful, willing obedience to Lieutenant Colonel Caldwell's order to do anything at all Magda wanted him to do had taken a good deal of doing, and since his enthusiastic compliance with that order had lasted until five minutes before it was time to drive her to Tempelhof, he was a little tired.

But despite what he had presumed would happen now that he was no longer the world's only seventeen-year-old virgin, *id est* that he would henceforth be spending his spare time in joyful lewd and lascivious activities with an unlimited number of members of the opposite gender, that simply didn't happen.

Truth being stranger than fiction, in the months that followed he was as chaste *post* his instructive weekend with the countess as he had been *ante.*

There were several reasons for this. Not among them was what Angus McTavish and G. Lincoln Rutherford believed to be the reason behind Phil's chastity, which was that they had spread the word among Berlin's ladies of the evening that Phil had at least two venereal diseases that were absolutely immune to the curative effects of penicillin.

The truth, however, was elsewhere.

Phil had gone hunting, so to speak, just about as soon as his depleted stock of hormones had returned to normal, *post* Magda. But when he started to reply in kind to the smiles, or winks, of the ladies of the evening who had heard what Angus and Geronimo had said about him and decided it was bull EXPLETIVE DELETED!!, he remembered that Magda had taught him *vanília fagylalt tölcsér,* how to play ice cream cone, and realized he didn't want to become quite that cozy with any of the ladies winking at him.

And then he was very busy with his duties at the German-American Gospel Tract Foundation. Not only in an editorial sense, but in connection with his new additional duties as chief firearms instructor of the German-American Gospel Tract Foundation.

Lieutenant Colonel William "Don't Call Me Bill" O'Reilly had changed the protocol for the exchange of spies on the Glienicke Bridge.

What the protocol had called for *ante* the change was a detachment of eight enlisted men, each armed with a Caliber .45 ACP M1A1 Thompson submachine gun, under the command of a first lieutenant. *Post* the

O'Reilly change, the detail was of eight company grade officers, attired in the Class A — "pinks and greens" — uniform, with white accoutrements, under the command of a field grade senior officer.

It had come to Colonel O'Reilly's attention that the next spy exchange was not to be done in secrecy in the dead of night, as most of them were, but in broad daylight and in the glare of television floodlights. And this was to be done with the full co-operation of the Communist authorities.

The American spy the Russians had caught was forty-nine years old, and was using the name Boris Tolstoy. When the NKGB caught Boris, he had been moving stealthily around Moscow on a wagon pulled by a scraggly horse. The wagon had a sign reading "I buy empty vodka bottles" on its side. Some of the latter apparently hadn't been completely empty, as the American spy had been arrested for driving a junk wagon under the influence of alcohol. When Boris tried to claim his rights under the Fifth Amendment to the Constitution of the United States, his jig was of course up.

Boris getting bagged had quickly come to the attention of the Honorable Ralph Peters, deputy director for Soviet Affairs, Central Intelligence Agency, who was both professionally and personally distressed. In another life, Second Lieutenant Peter O'Shaughnessy, which was Boris's real name, had been a classmate of Second Lieutenant Peters (then known as Colby) in one of the first classes of the OSS at the Congressional Country Club outside Washington, D.C., and later at Jedburgh Castle in Scotland.

Peters was especially distressed to hear that his old pal had not been allowed to change clothes, bathe, or even shave since his arrest. In the Good Old Days, so to speak, at Claridge's Hotel in London, he had been known as "Smelly Peter" because of his fondness for scented bath soap and French cologne. A Russian spy would be needed to exchange for Boris, and he had just the one.

Peters sent the FBI to arrest the Russian spy — a thirty-two-year-old blonde known professionally as "Legs Benidik" — at her place of work, where she was posing for some disreputable photographs.

Peters knew a great deal about Miss Benidik, including that her real name was Natasha Grebenshchikov and that she was an NKGB major, and that prior to sneaking into New York to steal the secret formulas of the American cosmetic industry, she had been carrying on with Colonel Alexis Gorbachov of the NKGB.

Peters arranged a secret meeting with Sergei Petersovich — no relation — the attaché for religious affairs of the Russian Embassy in Washington. Over most of a bottle of Famous Pheasant Scotch whisky consumed in the Bird Cage Lounge of the famed Willard Hotel, the two struck a deal. If Legs Benidik confessed her role *vis-à-vis* stealing the secrets of the American cosmetic industry, Peters would be willing to exchange her for Boris Tolstoy.

Colonel Alexis Gorbachov immediately agreed to the deal. Ralph Peters sent the FBI to cuff Legs — Major Grebenshchikov — and she immediately confessed her NKGB affiliation, and told *The Washington Post* newspaper that she was doing so because she had been broken by the relentless demands of unscrupulous pornographers to do things a decent NKGB major just could not do, even in the furtherance of the peaceful espionage aims of Holy Mother Russia.

When Colonel O'Reilly heard that the exchange in the middle of the Glienicke Bridge would be televised all over the world, he decided it would be simply good public relations for him to happen to mention to the press that all those splendidly turned-out officers with the Thompson submachine guns were members of the Berlin Brigade Chapter of the West Point Protective Association.

And he also decided not to mention the changes he'd made to the exchange protocol to Pastor-in-Charge Caldwell, who would of course be very busy with the details of his end of the exchange.

Peter O'Shaughnessy was being held by the Russians in a disused stable in the former summer palace called Sans Souci, which means *Don't worry about it,* of Frederick the Great, King of Prussia, in Potsdam.

When the NKGB officers in the stables of Sans Souci had positive confirmation that Major Natasha Grebenshchikov had arrived in Berlin, they would drag the man they now knew to really be Lieutenant Colonel Peter O'Shaughnessy, pay grade O-5, from his stable, load him backwards onto a jackass, and take him to their end of the Bridge Over the River Havel.

Meanwhile, Major Grebenshchikov would come down the stair door of the personal plane of the Honorable Ralph Peters on which she had been flown from her place of confinement, the Harry Truman Suite of the Hay-Adams Hotel in Washington, and, with the Honorable Mr. Peters, enter the Cadillac of Pastor-in-Chief Caldwell. Then Administrator Williams, the pastor-in-chief's bodyguard, would drive the Cadillac to our — that is to say, the Free Western World's — side of the Bridge Over the River Havel.

When it appeared there, the 193rd U.S. Army Band would begin to play "The Washington Post March." Major Grebenshchikov would then exit the Cadillac and march toward the center of the bridge accompanied by the nattily turned-out members of the West Point Protective Association doing Honor Guard duty.

Simultaneously, Colonel Alexis Gorbachov would take the reins of the jackass with Colonel O'Shaughnessy on it, and march toward the center of the bridge, accompanied by six members of NKGB officers.

There the exchange would take place.

These well-laid plans went agley moments after Administrator Williams opened the door of the Cadillac. The Honorable Ralph Peters exited first, then turned to help Major Grebenshchikov from the vehicle.

She started to exit, which put a good deal of her left leg — actually that portion of her left leg between the knee and where the leg joined her torso — on display. This caused — Major Grebenshchikov was not known as "Legs" without reason — one of the members of the WPPA Honor Guard to tighten his grip on his Caliber .45 ACP M1A1 Thompson submachine gun.

Unfortunately, he had his finger on the trigger when he tightened his grip.

Fortunately, he remembered his instructions to keep the EXPLETIVE DELETED!! muzzle pointed at the ground unless he actually intended to shoot somebody. The rounds that burst from his muzzle didn't hit anyone, although they did puncture the bass drum and the horns of both tubas of the 193rd U.S. Army Band.

The three males in and around the Cadillac had, of course, heard the sound of bullets whizzing around in the air many times before, and their Pavlovian reactions to that kicked in.

Pastor-in-Chief Caldwell erupted from the front seat, U.S. Pistol Cal. 45 ACP Model 1911A1 in hand, and leaned across the hood looking for someone to shoot back at. The Honorable Ralph Peters did much the same thing except that he went behind the Cadillac and leaned over the rear fender searching for someone to shoot back at with his Uzi .45, which he preferred over the Colt semiautomatic as it fired more projectiles more quickly.

Sergeant/Administrator Williams had actually heard more shots fired — truth being stranger than fiction — than either Pastor Caldwell or the Honorable Peters because of his service on the KD and other ranges at Fort Dix, Fort Holabird, and elsewhere. There he had learned what to do when he heard a bang, or a series of bangs, and the whistles of projectiles, not preceded by the appropriate order, to wit: "The Flag is up, the flag is waving, commence fire!"

His Pavlovian reflexes kicked in, and he did what experience had taught him was the only intelligent thing to do in such circumstances. He dove for the ground.

When he did so, he encountered Major Grebenshchikov, with the result that he found himself lying atop the major on the ground.

Meanwhile, things were happening on the bridge.

The 193rd U.S. Army Band, with the exception of two flautists and one slide trombone player, had stopped playing. The jackass with Colonel O'Shaughnessy sitting backwards on it broke free of Colonel Gorbachov's hand on its bridle and galloped toward freedom across the bridge. Colonel Gorbachov and the NKGB chased after it.

And then Major Grebenshchikov kissed

Sergeant Williams on the mouth.

"You can get off me now, my hero, now that you have saved my life," she said.

Then she stood and shouted, as only majors of the NKGB can shout, "All is well, Alexis, my darling! This brave young American officer has saved my life by covering my body with his! Greater love hath no man than to lay down on a Russian NKGB officer to protect her!"

Phil regained his feet just as Colonel Alexis Gorbachov reached the Cadillac.

Colonel Gorbachov kissed Phil. Not on the mouth, of course, but on the forehead.

"You splendid *Amerikānskī,*" he proclaimed. "Not only have you saved the life of my beloved Natasha, but you have prevented World War Three."

Then he kissed Major Grebenshchikov with even more enthusiasm. He gathered her up in his arms and carried her back across the bridge.

By then the jackass with Colonel O'Shaughnessy on it had reached the Cadillac.

Pastor Caldwell stopped it, untied Colonel O'Shaughnessy, and hustled him into the Cadillac. The Honorable Ralph Peters got quickly in.

"Get us out of here, Phil!" Pastor Caldwell

ordered.

Phil backed quickly off the bridge, turned with a squealing of tires, and sped off.

"Open the power windows, young man," the Honorable Peters said. "Smells like we have a skunk back here. A long-dead skunk."

"Bill, I'm afraid that's me," Colonel O'Shaughnessy said. "Those EXPLETIVE DELETED!! Russians haven't even let me brush my teeth, much less wash or bathe, since they bagged me."

"Peter, old comrade-in-arms, I love you like a brother, but there's no way I will fly back across the Atlantic in the confines of my personal jet airplane with you smelling like that," the Honorable Peters said. "Jonathan, how about taking our old comrade-in-arms to your quarters so he can shower?"

" 'Smelly Peter' may bring back memories of rose petals, lavender cologne, et cetera, in the old days, Bill — sorry, Ralph — but the way he smells now, Victoria not only wouldn't let him in the house, she wouldn't even let me stand him against our garage wall and hose him down. Phil, take us to your quarters."

When he saw the sign — Field Grade Bachelor Officers' Hotel — on the building to which he was driven, Colonel

286

O'Shaughnessy first asked, "You live here?" and when Phil replied in the affirmative, then commented, "You certainly don't look like you're old enough to be a major."

"Sir, I'm not. I'm a sergeant, pay grade E-4."

The conversation was interrupted by the Honorable Peters, who said, "Let's not waste any time getting you into the shower, Peter. You're causing the paint on Caldwell's Cadillac to bubble."

It resumed tangentially thirty minutes later, immediately after Colonel O'Shaughnessy had failed his fifth sniff test and been ordered back into the shower, when the telephone rang.

The Honorable Ralph Peters answered it, listened for a long time, and finally said, " Я вернусь fo вы," which is Russian for "I'll get back to you," and hung up.

He turned to Pastor Caldwell and said, "That was General Smirnoff, chief of the Russian delegation over at the Allied Kommandantenhaus in East Berlin."

"Boris Smirnoff? Ol' Stainless Steel Teeth?"

"No. This was his brother Giorgi, the one they call 'Gorgeous George.' "

"What the hell did he want?"

"They're going to decorate 'the Officer

Hero of the Bridge Over the River Havel' with the order of Karl Marx, Second Class, which means it comes with pearls and rubies. He said Colonel Gorbachov tried to get the First Class, which comes with diamonds, pearls, and rubies, but the Kremlin wouldn't go along."

"Which Officer Hero of the Bridge Over the River Havel? You or me?" Pastor Caldwell asked.

"Actually, he was talking about the officer who put his body between that hail of bullets and Major Grebenshchikov's body."

"That was Phil, but, as splendid a young man as he is, he's not an officer."

"Commission him. The Russians are not going to give the Order of Karl Marx, Second Class, to a common enlisted man. You know as well as I do how class-conscious the Communists are."

"He's not old enough to be an officer."

"Well, what do you suggest?"

"What does ol' JFC suggest about what?" Colonel O'Shaughnessy asked, as he came into the room attired in a bath towel.

"Your turn to sniff him," ol' JFC said.

The Honorable Peters did so.

"Under the circumstances, I guess I can live with that level of olfactory offensiveness," he said. "What were you asking, Peter?"

"I was asking what does ol' JFC suggest about what?"

The problem was explained to him.

"Make him a CIC special agent. Then the Reds won't know he's a common enlisted man," O'Shaughnessy said.

"If memory serves, I think you have to be a staff sergeant to become a CIC special agent," Pastor Caldwell said.

"Then promote him and then give him the EXPLETIVE DELETED!! badge," the Honorable Peters said. "How long will that take?"

"Consider it done, Bill . . . Ralph," Pastor Caldwell said.

Thus it came to pass that Phil went through a remarkable metamorphosis that changed him in a very short time from being the only living seventeen-year-old virgin in the world into the only seventeen-year-old CIC special agent in the world.

Lieutenant Colonel William "Don't Call Me Bill" O'Reilly went through a similarly remarkable metamorphosis as a result of the events on the Bridge Over the River Havel.

One day he was commanding officer of the XXXIIIrd CIC Detachment in Berlin, and three days later he was deputy commanding officer of the Junior ROTC Training Detachment at the Joseph Smith, Jr., Junior High School for Girls, in Salt Lake City, Utah.

[Three]

Berlin, Germany
Monday, November 10, 1947

Several months later, depending on the birth certificate referenced, Phil turned either eighteen or nineteen. He spent the morning in his office searching for ambiguities and errors of grammar in agents' reports and the afternoon at the range teaching his regular Monday afternoon class in the care and handling of the Caliber .45 ACP M1A1 Thompson submachine gun to the Berlin Chapter of the West Point Protective Association.

When he returned to his quarters in the field grade bachelor officers' hotel, he found a sad-faced chaplain, a similarly sad-faced male Red Cross official, and a sad-faced but otherwise attractive Red Cross Girl — her bosom reminded him of the countess and her legs reminded him of Major Natasha Grebenshchikov's lower extremities — waiting for him.

Phil intuited that something was wrong.

"Be strong, my son," the chaplain said. "Your father is gone."

"Where did he go?"

"Decisions like that, my son, are made by Saint Peter, not by a humble clergyman of the Church of the Burning Bush now serving as a U.S. Army chaplain, such as myself. But I can tell you that he won't be coming back from wherever Saint Peter decided he should go."

"Oh," Phil said. "I see."

"Excuse me, Sergeant Williams," the Red Cross Girl said. "Is that a gun in a shoulder holster I see now that you've unbuttoned your jacket?"

"A U.S. Pistol, Caliber .45 ACP 1911A1, as a matter of fact."

"Why did you ask him such a question, Gwendolyn?" the chaplain said.

"Because when I was in Red Cross Girl School, they said it was very important to learn as much as possible about the poor enlisted men you might have to comfort in their hour of need before you actually start to comfort them," Gwendolyn replied.

"That's true, Brother Bobby," the Red Cross man said. "And if you think about it, it makes sense."

"Very well," the Reverend Brother Bobby

said, "ask away, Gwendolyn. That's what you're here to do, comfort this poor enlisted man in his sorrow."

"And since you're wearing that very nice tweed jacket with leather trimming and not an olive drab uniform, and living in the field grade bachelor officers' hotel, would I be out of line to suspect that you're not an ordinary, run-of-the-mill enlisted man?"

"Actually, Gwendolyn, I'm a special agent of the Counterintelligence Corps. That's how come I'm wearing civilian clothing, under which I'm carrying a .45, and living in the field grade bachelor officers' hotel."

"I saw the movie!" Gwendolyn cried excitedly. "Some actor — I can't remember who — played CIC Special Agent Trueheart, and he went through the halls of Congress shooting what he called nutty right-wing congressmen all over the place."

"I believe he was portraying a *rogue* CIC agent, Gwendolyn, in the motion picture to which you refer," Phil said. "In the real world, we CIC agents do not roam through the halls of Congress shooting anybody."

"Perhaps after these two leave, and I'm here comforting you, you can clear that up for me."

"Anything I can do to help, Gwendolyn," Phil said.

"Actually, my son," Lieutenant Colonel Robert R. Williams, Chaplains Corps, USA, a/k/a the Reverend Brother Bobby, said, "we're just about through here. I came to tell you your Daddy has joined the ranks of the Dear Departed, and I've done that, and Mr. Aristotle Jones here of the Red Cross has come to tell you why it will not be necessary for you to return to the United States for the internment of your departed loved one's remains."

"Why is that?"

"Well, primarily because not much remains of his remains. His remains were not found for six days after his demise and consequently were a little ripe when found. For that reason, the remains were quickly cremated and then spread around the Harvard Yard in Cambridge, Massachusetts."

"I see."

"Your late father's sister, your Aunt Grace, who was in charge of everything, has promised to write you and give you all the pertinent details. You should have that letter in a day or two, providing of course that Miss Williams puts an airmail stamp on the envelope. Otherwise it will take a little longer to reach you."

"I understand."

"We will leave now, leaving Gwendolyn to

comfort you."

They did and she did.

Gwendolyn said she was willing, so as to be better able to comfort him in his time of sorrow, to learn about his life, so he taught her what Magda Countess Kocian had taught him about *Forrós magyar Nyalókát,* and once he had turned her into his *Forró Sioux Falls, S.D., Nyalókát,* or Hot Sioux Falls, South Dakota Lollipop, she really couldn't get enough.

Finally, exhausted, he was able to talk Gwendolyn into going back to the Berlin Red Cross Club so that she could pass out comfort in the form of doughnuts and Coca-Cola to other enlisted men.

She gave him her telephone number — which was strictly against the rules, as Red Cross Girls are not permitted to socialize with enlisted men — and he promised to call her.

"Cross my heart and hope to die," he said, but he didn't mean it.

The letter from Aunt Grace came four days later.

MISS GRACE ALICE PATRICIA
HORTENSE WILLIAMS
MAYFLOWER-WILLIAMS HOUSE
BACK BAY, BOSTON, MASS.

Dear Nephew Philip:

By now I presume you have been apprised of the demise of my brother and your father, the late P. Wallingford Williams, Jr.

The cause of death was the rupture of an aortal aneurism. I have been assured that death came both quickly and painlessly, although with regard to the latter it was an unnecessary blessing as a blood test indicated the amount of alcohol in his system meant he had been incapable of feeling any pain for the four hours previous to his fall, apparently while trying to make his way from his bed to the water closet in his bathroom at approximately 3:25 a.m.

He was interred, so to speak, in the Harvard Yard in Cambridge, just as soon as the UPS-expedited special-delivery service could get his ashes from the Manhattan Crematorium to Boston. While the Harvard Men's Glee Club provided appropriate music by singing "When the Roll Is Called Up Yonder," a delegation of the Hasty Pudding Club scattered your Daddy's ashes across the yard.

I am sure you will be relieved to hear that I, to preserve the reputation of the

Williams name, have taken care of all of the debts your father left, of which there was a plethora, including a mind-boggling one from J. Press, where, at about the time you were sent to Germany, your father apparently went on a drunken clothes-buying spree.

As the figure is a five-digit negative there is no point in getting into the details of your inheritance here.

Which brings us to your future:

I have spoken to Dr. Peabody at Groton, and he has agreed, providing you can convince him you have learned your lesson in the Army, and intend to lead a decent and chaste life in the future, to let you back in on a probationary basis, which means that you will wait on tables during the week, and cut the campus grass, pick up leaves, or shovel snow, depending on the season, on afternoons and weekends.

I remain, faithfully yours,
Aunt Grace

A week after that, Phil received a letter from his mother:

Dear Philip:
Ever since I heard of the passing of

your late father from your late father's sister, your Aunt Grace, I have had several conversations with my husband, Keyes Michaels, M.D., who is now your stepfather, about your future.

"My own Sigmund Freud," as I so fondly call him, has willingly accepted his new responsibilities in your regard, to wit:

You may now call him "Daddy" or "Daddy Keyes." The choice is yours.

He is prepared to provide, pro bono, which means "for free," whatever psychiatric counseling you require to get you through both your grief and the trauma to your id caused by your service as a common enlisted man in the Army.

Additionally, and this is the really good news, your Daddy Keyes has arranged for your matriculation in St. Hippolytus's School for Troubled But Possibly Salvageable Through Tough Love Youth.

The school, in Pascagoula, Arkansas, is a joint venture of the Jesuit Order and the Brothers of St. Hippolytus. The former deals with academic matters, and the latter with disciplinary issues. Saint Hippolytus of Rome is the patron saint of jailers.

Please let me and Daddy Keyes know

as soon as you can when you will be paroled or otherwise let loose from the Army so we can get the ball rolling.

Love,
Mother

P.S. in re: Your late father's golf clubs.

Inasmuch as she doesn't play golf, your Aunt Grace, who didn't want them, sent them here via Recipient Pays Shipping Charges. And since you don't play golf, and your new stepfather does, I knew you would want Daddy Keyes to have them, so I gave them to him.

[Four]

Berlin, Germany
Wednesday, December 15, 1948

Just over a year later, a master sergeant wearing as many medals and ribbons as Phil had ever seen appeared at Phil's office door.

During that year, a good deal, good and bad, had happened.

For one thing, he got to go back to the Pferd und Frauen, something he had secretly hungered to do since his first visit. And he didn't have to sneak into it as he thought he might have to do. He was ordered to go there, by none less than Pastor-in-Chief Caldwell. And an order from Pastor-in-Chief Caldwell was like a deep voice from On High accompanied by the sound of celestial trumpets.

What happened was that Pastor-in-Chief Caldwell called him into the office and said that he had just had a call from the Honorable Ralph Peters telling him that the German-American Gospel Tract Foundation was about to be visited by Sir Oswald T. Cholmondeley, OBE, Knight Commander of the Garter, and DSO, who, using the beard "QT," headed the British MI-5, which was more or less the British equivalent of the CIA.

"Now, ol' Chummy isn't a problem. Ol' Ralph Peters, I, and ol' Chummy are old chums from the good old days of World War Two, and I don't mind at all showing him all the secrets of the German-American Gospel Tract Foundation. But he's bringing with him his aide-de-camp, Second Lieutenant Charles William George Michael Bertram of His Majesty's Own Scottish Light Lancers, who is the son of the Earl of Abercrombie."

"How is that a problem, sir?"

"Just because someone has four first names and lives in a castle, Phil, doesn't mean he gets to learn all the secrets of the

German-American Gospel Tract Foundation. I'm surprised I have to tell you that."

"I didn't think that through, sir. Sorry."

"So, what I want you to do, Phil, is entertain this Scotchman while he's here."

"Yes, sir. How should I do that?"

"Take him anyplace he wants to go, let him do whatever he wants to do."

"Sir, what if he wants to do something like go to the Pferd and Frauen?"

Pastor-in-Chief Caldwell, shaking his head, had looked at Phil for a long time. Finally, he said, "I knew from the moment I laid eyes on you, Phil, that you were one of us. I don't mean just socially. I mean one of us, intelligence-wise. I congratulate you for thinking of something I, as an intelligence officer of great experience, should have thought of myself.

"By all means, after laying on a photographer first, take ol' Four First Names to the Pferd und Frauen. It might be very useful in the future when dealing with my old chum Cholmondeley to have a picture — half a dozen pictures — in the files of his aide-de-camp cavorting with a naked woman on a Clydesdale. Phil — please don't let this go to your head — I think you have a great future in our chosen profession."

When Phil first met Second Lieutenant Charles William George Michael Bertram of His Majesty's Own Scottish Light Lancers, he wasn't at all sure Cholmondeley's aide-de-camp would be at all interested in cavorting with a naked woman on a Clydesdale, because the young Scot was wearing a skirt.

An hour or so and half a bottle of Famous Pheasant later, however, he was convinced that the young Scot was as heavy on his feet as he himself was, and half convinced that what the young man he was now calling "Bertie" had told him about "kilt" wearing being common in Scotland was true.

So they went to Pferd und Frauen, where the future Earl of Abercrombie, calling out, "Hi-Yo, Silver! Away!" took first place with the lady Valkyrie riding the Clydesdale with him in the 3 a.m. steeplechase competition.

And while the prize, a two-liter bottle of Slivovitz, was being awarded, Phil removed the film from the photographer's camera.

Other good things that happened included Phil's triumph at the Second Annual Berlin Brigade Brandenburg Gate Skeet Shoot. There he won "The Hundred Straight Grand Prize," which was another 12-bore Browning Diamond Grade *und so weiter*

301

shotgun. At the presentation ceremony, Phil dropped into the conversation that he already had an identical weapon.

"This one," Phil said, holding up the year-old 12-bore Browning Diamond Grade *und so weiter* shotgun he had won the previous year and which he had just used to go one hundred straight so that the press and Browning company photographers could get their own good "shots."

The man from Browning gritted his teeth and said the Browning company would be delighted to swap the second 12-bore Browning Diamond Grade *und so weiter* shotgun for a 16-bore version of the weapon, if that would make Staff Sergeant Williams happy, and providing he was willing to make a statement to the press, while holding one hand on a Bible, that he would have been unable to go one hundred straight without using a 12-bore Browning Diamond Grade *und so weiter* shotgun.

Phil agreed to do so, even though he knew it would almost certainly get him in trouble with his new boss, Pastor-in-Chief Peter O'Shaughnessy, who had replaced Pastor-in-Chief Jonathan Caldwell III. But that's getting ahead of the narrative of this romance novel.

Getting back to it:

Phil did make the sworn statement before the press, even knowing that he could have gone one hundred straight firing a Sears, Roebuck Single Shot Youth Special, which went for a relatively few dollars, as opposed to the EXPLETIVE DELETED!! incredible price Browning not only asked but got for their Diamond Grade *und so weiter* shotguns, and thus he was not being entirely truthful.

By then Phil had learned that in the intelligence profession, there is truth and then there is truth, and that the truth that matters is that truth which does one the most good at that moment. In this case, telling a little white lie seemed entirely justified since it resulted in his now having two Browning Diamond Grade *und so weiter* shotguns in alligator-hide cases.

Besides, it wasn't setting a precedent, as the Browning company announced that with deep regret they were canceling their sponsorship of the Annual Berlin Brigade Brandenburg Gate Skeet Shoots for financial reasons.

Having both Brownings on the wall of Phil's sitting room in his suite in the field grade bachelor officers' hotel helped toward assuaging the pain in Phil's heart caused by his loss of Gwendolyn's comforting, but did not completely do away with it.

As someone once observed, all good things must come to an end, and so it was with Phil's having his own personal Red Cross Comfort Girl.

What actually had done him in, he believed, was either one of two contributing factors, or both.

The first was a growing awareness on Gwendolyn's part that her comforting of Phil had gone beyond simple comforting and into something resembling a boyfriend/girlfriend relationship.

Such a relationship, of course, violated the XIth through XIIIth Commandments of Red Cross Girls, to wit:

XI — Thou shalt not allow enlisted men to get any closer to you than a ten-foot pole under any circumstances.

XII — Thou shalt have social relationships of any kind with only commissioned officers and gentlemen, preferably those who are graduates of the United States Military Academy at West Point or the U.S. Naval Academy at Annapolis.

XIII — (a) In the event that you find yourself bringing comfort to the enlisted men in a remote area where there are no USMA or USNA graduates with whom to socialize, you may have social relationships with commissioned officer graduates of lesser schools, such as the U.S. Air Force Academy and the U.S. Coast Guard Academy.

(b) If such 90 percent socially acceptable commissioned officers and gentlemen are not available, then, and only then, you may have social relations with commissioned officer graduates of such 50 percent socially acceptable schools as Norwich University, the Virginia Military Institute, the Citadel, and Texas A&M.

(c) For the purposes of this Commandment, except for commissioned officer graduates of Harvard, Princeton, Yale, and similar ivy-covered institutions, who are deemed 33 1/3 percent socially acceptable, all other commissioned officers no matter what their rank, or source of commission, are to be considered common enlisted men, and the ten-foot-pole rule of Commandment XI will apply.

The second factor that removed Gwendolyn and her comforting from Phil's life was

Second Lieutenant Oscar Hormell III, infantry, pay grade O-1, who the previous June had graduated from the USMA in the footsteps of his father, Major General Oscar "Hot Dog" Hormell, Jr., and his grandfather, Brigadier General Oscar Hormell, Sr.

Lieutenant Hormell had been assigned as the junior aide-de-camp to the Berlin Brigade's commanding general. This was a different Berlin Brigade commanding general than the one with whom Phil was familiar. That one had suffered a mental breakdown while watching Phil walk away from the Brandenburg Gate with his new 16-bore Browning Diamond Grade *und so weiter* shotgun and then had been reassigned to the War Plans Division in the Pentagon, where he had been given responsibility for launching missiles at the Russians should that, in his calm and rational judgment, be determined necessary.

As soon as Oscar went to his first meeting of the Berlin Brigade Chapter of the WPPA, his peers got him alone and — with the caveat "This is no bull EXPLETIVE DELETED!!, Oscar, this is the EXPLETIVE DELETED!! truth, the whole EXPLETIVE DELETED!! truth, and nothing but the EXPLETIVE DELETED!! truth" — began to fill him in on the EXPLETIVE DELETED!! staff sergeant who didn't even finish EXPLETIVE DELETED!! high school, who was not only living in the field grade bachelor officers' hotel but chauffeuring around town a Red Cross Girl named Gwendolyn — who had the most amazing EXPLETIVE DELETED!! teats and gluteus maxima — in his EXPLETIVE DELETED!! Cadillac.

"And not only that, the EXPLETIVE DELETED!! enlisted man cheated the previous commanding general of the Berlin Brigade, who was a USMA classmate of your father, which is why you're here in Berlin instead of learning how to dig foxholes at Fort Benning with the rest of your class, out of two — not just one — *two* EXPLETIVE DELETED!! Browning Diamond Grade *und so weiter* shotguns."

"How does he get away with all those gross infractions of Army Regulations? And how can a staff sergeant afford a Cadillac?"

"Well, the only thing I can say is that he goes around with a U.S. Pistol, Cal. 45 ACP Model 1911A1 in a shoulder holster and that when on rare occasions he wears his uniform, pinned to it are all his medals, of which he has two: The Army of Occupation Medal and The Order of Karl Marx, Second Class, with pearls and rubies."

"That sounds like it might be a Russian medal."

"You're a second lieutenant now, Oscar. Draw your own conclusions."

Lieutenant Hormell made a point of meeting the Red Cross Comfort Girl who the EXPLETIVE DELETED!! enlisted man was chauffeuring around Berlin in his Cadillac. He did so by waiting in the alley behind the Red Cross Doughnuts and Coca-Cola dispensary until her tour of duty was over.

For him, it was love at first sight. What he had been told about her physical attributes was right on the EXPLETIVE DELETED!! money.

"Excuse me, miss," he said. "If you are a Red Cross Comfort Girl, I would like to introduce myself."

"Why would you want to do that?"

"Just before I left the United States Military Academy at West Point to embark on my military career in the footsteps of my father, Major General Oscar Hormell, Junior, and my grandfather, Brigadier General Oscar Hormell, Senior, I was counseled to seek out, if possible, Red Cross Comfort Girls such as yourself. The guidance counselor said that your kind matches well with our kind, and are in fact the kind of young women a West Pointer should seek in case he is searching for a wife to march beside him in the Long Gray Line."

"You don't say?" Gwendolyn replied, pleased. She had joined the Red Cross hoping that she might bump into a young officer of good family. "My name is Gwendolyn. What did you say your name was, handsome?"

Oscar drove Gwendolyn from the alley to the Berlin Brigade officers' club in his Volkswagen. There, after he plied her with beer, he told her he could look into her eyes and know that the things he had heard about her — that she was socializing with a common enlisted man who was chauffeuring her around Berlin in his Cadillac — simply couldn't be true.

"I can't imagine where those scurrilous rumors got started," Gwendolyn replied.

The next day, she went to Phil's apartment in the field grade bachelor officers' hotel, handed him a chocolate-covered doughnut, a strawberry-stuffed doughnut, and an Economy Size 1.5-liter bottle of Coca-Cola to remember her by, and announced that it was all over between them.

[Five]

When the master sergeant, wearing as many medals and ribbons as Phil had ever seen, appeared at Phil's office door, as previously stated, a good deal of water had flowed under the Bridge over the River Havel during the previous year.

"What can I do for you, Master Sergeant?"

"If you are Staff Sergeant Williams, Philip W. Third, the question should be rather than 'What can you do for me? but 'What am I prepared to do for you?' "

"I am. So, what are you prepared to do for me?"

"I am Master Sergeant F. J. Lacitignola, known as 'Friendly Frank the Recruiter,' and I am here, Sergeant, to point out to you the manifold benefits of reenlistment in the U.S. Army."

"Why would you want to do that?"

"Because your enlistment is about over, and before you know it you're going to be out of the Army, living under a bridge somewhere, rooting through garbage cans for something to eat. Unless of course you have other alternatives in what we recruiters call the cold and cruel outside."

Phil was very much aware of his options on his discharge. He could either wait tables, et cetera, at Groton, or undergo what

310

horrors the Jesuits and the Brothers of St. Hippolytus had waiting for him in Pascagoula, Arkansas. After "Daddy Keyes" had counseled him at length, of course. None of which had much appeal.

He took a chance. Despite the reputation that recruiting sergeants have made for themselves, there was something about this one he liked. He suddenly understood why. Friendly Frank the Recruiter had big soft eyes like Pasquale of Pasquale's Pizzas and Subs in the Village of South Orange. And Pasquale had always slipped a couple of extra anchovies and/or slices of pepperoni onto Phil's pizzas without charge.

"Please tell me what you have to offer, Master Sergeant Lacitignola."

"Instead, Staff Sergeant Williams, tell me what you would want if you had your druthers."

"I would like to be an intelligence officer," Phil replied without hesitation.

"That we can do. You reenlist — and there is a five-hundred-dollar-per-year, up to six years, reenlistment bonus, plus a one-grade promotion, which I thought I should mention — and once you have that money in hand, and that extra stripe on your sleeves, you apply for West Point —"

"No."

"That AGCT score of yours makes you a shoo-in —"

"I said no."

"And then you go to the West Point Preparatory School."

"Not only no, but hell no."

"And on your graduation therefrom, you matriculate at West Point. On your graduation therefrom, which takes four years, you get your commission and then you apply for intelligence duties."

"Read my EXPLETIVE DELETED!! lips, Friendly Frank. I have no EXPLETIVE DELETED!! intention whatso EXPLETIVE DELETED!! ever of applying for EXPLETIVE DELETED!! West Point. The last thing I want to do with my life is to be identified as a EXPLETIVE DELETED!! West Pointer."

"Well, I can understand that. I don't like those EXPLETIVE DELETED!! ring-knockers much myself. Let me think."

He thought.

"You're nineteen, right?" he asked.

"I will be. Depending on which birth certificate we're looking at."

"Well, that knocks out Officer Candidate School as a possibility. You have to be twenty-one to get a commission from OCS. Let me think a little more."

Sixty seconds later, after having thought a

little more, he said, "Eureka, Staff Sergeant Williams! I have found it!"

"What?"

"As an enlisted intelligence man, I'm sure you're familiar with area intelligence specialist officers?"

"We have a couple — actually, three — of them around here."

"And you know what they do?"

"I don't have a clue. I have noticed that ours are always reading telephone books from cities behind the Iron Curtain."

"Well, let me fill you in. Imagine that the U.S. Army is going to invade someplace. Hungary, for example. It is obvious that the planners of such an operation need to know as much as possible about the target. Where is the police station in Budapest? For one example. What river flows between Buda and Pest? Where exactly is, and what is the phone number of, the brothel most popular with the Hungarian Officer Corps? That sort of intelligence. Can you see where I'm going with this?"

"I'm not sure."

"What the planners do when they need such intelligence to plan the invasion is to turn to the Army's corps of area intelligence specialist officers, whose area of specialty this is. These officers spend their careers learning everything there is to know about a potential target area so that it's at their fingertips when needed."

"Makes a lot of sense, now that I'm thinking about it for the first time. But what does that have to do with me?"

"Have you ever wondered where the Army gets its area intelligence specialist officers?"

"Frankly, Friendly Frank, I have not."

"Well, I can tell you they don't get them from West Point. Or ROTC. Or OCS. That give you a clue?"

"Doesn't help, I'm afraid."

"They get them, directly commission them as first lieutenants, from the Groves of Academe, specifically from the Groves of Academe in foreign countries. Like Venezuela and the Belgian Congo and, pertinent to this, Germany. I'm always on the lookout for such people, but believe you me, Staff Sergeant Williams, they're hard to come by."

"Why is that?"

"Well, to get a direct commission as a first lieutenant area intelligence specialist officer, you have to meet the following requirements. You have to be a U.S. citizen twenty-one years of age or older. You have to speak two — and three is better — foreign languages. And you have to have a Secret or higher security clearance. Now the potentials I've been dealing with pose no problems with regard to the first two criteria, but for them the third, the Secret security clearance, is a ball — I mean deal — breaker."

"Why is that?"

"Well, as I'm sure you're aware, the CIC will not grant a Secret security clearance to persons who sniff a certain white powder up their noses, or hypodermically inject controlled substances between their toes, or manifest a great interest in other persons of the same sex. Need I say more?"

"I take your point. I gather you mean to say that American students studying in foreign universities do have problems in those areas?"

"Phil, I could tell you stories that would curl your hair. But before we go any further, you do have a Secret security clearance, right?"

"Actually, I have a run-of-the-mill Top Secret security clearance. And also a Top Secret-Honorable Peters security clearance, so that I can deal with the CIA. And a Top Secret-Sexual security clearance, which is necessary for me so that I can deal with investigations — and I could tell you stories, Friendly Frank, if it wasn't against the law, that would curl your hair — of hanky-panky by senior officers and their dependents. I could write a book — more than one book — about such hanky-panky if it wasn't against U.S. Army Regulations for me to do so."

"I've heard those rumors," Friendly Frank said. "But let's deal with the situation at hand. You have two years before you're twenty-one and can take a commission. You have that college-level GED, which means you're only two years shy of the four years you need to get a college degree. How are you fixed for languages?"

"Well, I've become fluent in German since I've been here, and I had what I guess you could call a cram course in Hungarian pillow talk conversation."

"Well, here's what I suggest, Sergeant Williams. You reenlist for six years, which will get you a three-thousand-dollar reenlistment bonus. That bonus is nonreturnable if you are discharged for the convenience of the government to accept a commission as an officer and gentleman. Then you get yourself over to the Free University of Berlin and matriculate. It's not really free, but the Army will grab the tab. In your spare time, you take a heavy load of light courses — the theory and practice of volleyball, for example, or elementary basket weaving, things like that — and one more language. I suggest French. And as soon as you turn twenty-one, and have your degree, let me know, and I will be happy to have you commissioned as First Lieutenant Philip W. Williams the Third. How does that sound?"

"Where do I sign, Friendly Frank?"

X
PHIL'S *REALLY* NEW PATH OF LIFE

[One]

Berlin, Germany
Saturday, December 18, 1948

Phil intuited from the look on Pastor-in-Chief Peter O'Shaughnessy's freckled face that he was less than thrilled with Phil's announcement that Phil had just "shipped over" for an additional six years of military service, and his reasons for so doing.

Confirmation came almost immediately.

"Oh, EXPLETIVE DELETED!!," Colonel O'Shaughnessy said, and then asked rhetorically, "What in the names of all the EXPLETIVE DELETED!! saints am I going to do with you now?"

"I gather 'Congratulations and good luck' is not an option, sir?"

"Technical Sergeant Williams, let's try walking our way through the situation from the beginning."

318

"Yes, sir."

"That would be the incidents that occurred on the Glienicke Bridge, a/k/a the Bridge over the River Havel."

"Whatever you say, sir."

"I will never forget, Technical Sergeant Williams, that except for your selfless courage and dedication to duty, which caused you to shield the body of Major Natasha Grebenshchikov, NKGB, with your own, that her boyfriend, Colonel Alexis Gorbachov, NKGB, would have emptied the fifty-round magazine of his Kalashnikov NKGB Senior Officer's Special into me as the jackass on which I was mounted ass-backwards galloped toward freedom."

"I guess one might say that, sir."

"I'm saying that. So that's one point for you, Technical Sergeant Williams."

"Yes, sir. Thank you, sir."

"And you get another point for your selfless generosity in taking me into your apartment in the field grade bachelor officers' hotel despite knowing — having seen that my body odors were causing the paint on then Pastor-in-Charge Caldwell's Cadillac to blister — what damage I was likely to do, and indeed did, to the paint and varnish inside your apartment."

"It was the decent thing to do, sir."

319

"Nevertheless, it gets you another point. Which makes two."

"Yes, sir."

"I now realize, Sergeant Williams, that, in fairness, I have to go back to things which occurred before the incidents on the Bridge over the River Havel."

"Yes, sir?"

"Two come immediately to mind. One is your splendid work in reviewing agents' reports for ambiguities and grammatical errors. For that you get, as they say in the *las plazas de toros* in Spain and elsewhere known to bullfighting, both ears and the tail. Plus another point, for an interim total of three."

"Thank you, sir."

"And of course you certainly deserve a point for your contribution to intergovernmental cooperation in intelligence matters with a friendly ally."

"I don't understand that, sir."

"Pastor Caldwell told me that after you took care of Second Lieutenant Charles William George Michael Bertram of Her Majesty's Own Scottish Light Lancers, the son of the Earl of Abercrombie and aide-de-camp to QT, which is the beard Sir Oswald T. Cholmondeley, OBE, KCG, and DSO uses while running MI-5, relations with our brother intelligence service have never been better. Apparently the young officer you now call Bertie took QT riding at the Pferd und Frauen before they left Berlin and ol' QT had a jolly good time. How many points does that make?"

"I believe four, sir."

"Right. And then you get a fifth because of your relationship with Ralph Peters, formerly Lieutenant Colonel Caldwell, who became deputy director for Soviet Affairs of the Central Intelligence Agency when Bill Colby rose from the dead and became CIA director, thus vacating the deputy director for Soviet Affairs position."

"I don't think I understand, sir."

"Before Ralph Peters, who was then of course still Colonel Caldwell, left Berlin, which was the day after I arrived here to become pastor-in-charge, we had quite a chat about you. He said that he had come to look on you as the son he and Victoria never had. He said for that reason he had told the Cadillac Division of the General Motors Corporation that the vehicle they had provided to field-test Fitzwater Cold Tanned Leather seats in the car of an officer on foreign service had been worn out by the testing, and that he had sold it for one dollar to a deserving young person of his acquaintance, and therefore they should not expect to get it back.

"He then went on to say that his observation of you had convinced him that you possessed to an extraordinary degree the character traits an OSS, now CIA, officer should have. That is, you were a Saint Malachi's Old Boy, as he himself was, and also had demonstrated an unusual ability to lie convincingly and were not troubled by the prissy moral standards of the middle and lower classes when they got in the way of what your duty called upon you to do.

"He said that were it not for your youth, he would take you into the CIA the day after you got out of the Army. He said he asked Ralph Peters, who was of course by then Born Again Bill Colby, for a waiver of the rule which says CIA officers have to be old enough to vote, and that Born Again Bill turned him down.

"Ralph, the new Ralph, the former Colonel J. F. Caldwell, then said it was probably a good thing. Once you got out of the Army, you could spend the two years before you reached your majority by going to Harvard, into which institution, having passed the college-level GED test, you could matriculate as a junior. Then, upon reaching your majority, you could join the agency.

"He asked me to keep an eye on you after he went off to become Ralph Peters, until your enlistment was up and you could go to Cambridge. And I agreed to do so, even though, frankly, I thought that I was far more entitled to the worn-out Cadillac than you were, inasmuch as I had spent years driving a horse-drawn cart over the icy cobblestones of Moscow.

"But I digress. What was the point count, again?"

"Five, sir."

"Right. Well, you started off with five points, but you quickly began to burn them up. I hadn't been here three days before a delegation of officers resident in the field grade bachelor officers' hotel called on me, saying the presence of an EXPLETIVE DELETED!! enlisted man in their hotel was prejudicial to good military order and discipline, and asking what I planned to do about it.

"I told them you were there because of intelligence matters which I of course could not discuss with them, but not to worry because you would soon be leaving. What I had in mind, of course, was you going home and getting out of the Army."

"Yes, sir."

"And then the president of the Berlin

Chapter of the West Point Protective Association called on me with regard to what they called in a somewhat heated conversation 'that EXPLETIVE DELETED!! enlisted man of yours who hasn't even finished EXPLETIVE DELETED!! high school.' They were upset about you living in the hotel and also that the man we now call Ralph Peters had designated you as the marksmanship instructor which caused a number of their members to have to spend their Saturday mornings messing with dangerous submachine guns, which was detrimental to their self-images as well as their lives.

"I got rid of the delegation by telling them to be patient, that that situation was about to change. What I had in mind, of course, was you going home and getting out of the Army."

"Yes, sir."

"And then Gwyneth came up. That really tied a can to the old cat's tail."

"Gwyneth, sir? Who, or what, is Gwyneth?"

"Isn't that her name?"

"Whose name, sir?"

"The Red Cross Comfort Girl you've been chauffeuring around town in that Cadillac, which really should be mine."

"The name of the young lady to whom I

believe you refer, sir, is Gwendolyn. Gwendolyn Krauthammer."

"Well, let me tell you about Gwendolyn Krauthammer, Technical Sergeant Williams. The deputy chief of staff of Berlin Brigade came to see me and asked if he could talk to me man-to-man and out of school. To which I replied of course he could.

" 'Pete,' he said, 'I'm calling you Pete because this conversation is man-to-man and out of school. If I called you Lieutenant Colonel O'Shaughnessy then you would have to call me "sir" because I'm a chicken colonel and you're only a light bird. You understand?'

"So I said, 'Yes, sir,' and he went on, 'Do you have any idea what threat that EXPLETIVE DELETED!! staff sergeant of yours is posing to the rest of the life of one of our sweet and innocent Red Cross Comfort Girls?'

" 'No, sir,' I confessed, 'I don't.'

" 'Do you know what happens if a Red Cross Comfort Girl gets any closer, socially speaking, to an EXPLETIVE DELETED!! enlisted man than a ten-foot pole would permit?'

" 'No, sir,' I confessed, 'I don't.'

" 'Well, then,' the colonel said, 'I'll tell you. They have a ceremony in the Bingo &

Parcheesi Room of the Red Cross Comfort-the-Poor-Enlisted-Men Building. The Senior Red Cross Comfort Girl calls the other Comfort Girls to attention. Now, mano a mano, so to speak, I don't know how they get away with calling the Senior Red Cross Comfort Girl a girl. She's at least sixty, weighs about three hundred pounds, and generally gets around in a wheelchair, but they do.

" 'Anyway, she calls the girls to attention, and she-who-is-about-to-get-the-boot is dragged before the Senior Red Cross Comfort Girl —' "

"Sir, may I say something?"

"Not until I'm finished."

"Sorry, sir."

"Where was I? Oh. The deputy chief of staff of Berlin Brigade went on, 'and the charges of which she has been found guilty are read.' In your case, your Gwendolyn would have been found guilty not only of having been seen riding around Berlin in a Cadillac driven by an EXPLETIVE DELETED!! enlisted man, but also at the bar of the club of the German-American Gospel Tract Foundation in the company of said EXPLETIVE DELETED!! enlisted man drinking vodka martinis and exiting the field grade bachelor officers' hotel at oh-six-hundred hours, suggesting she had spent the night there in the room the EXPLETIVE DELETED!! enlisted man isn't even supposed to have —"

"Sir?"

"I told you once not to interrupt me until I'm finished. Don't make me have to tell you that again."

"Yes, sir. No, sir. Sorry, sir."

" 'All of the forgoing bringing shame upon the reputation of Red Cross Comfort Girls and justifying her discharge from said organization under dishonorable and shameful conditions.'

"Then the Senior Red Cross Comfort Girl would snatch the *Hello! My name is Gwendolyn. How may I comfort you?* sticky label from Gwendolyn's tunic lapel. Then she would cut all the Red Cross buttons from Gwendolyn's uniform tunic. Then, as the Red Cross Comfort Girls Jazz Quintet played 'The Rogue's March,' Gwendolyn would be marched out of the Bingo & Parcheesi Room onto the street and the door slammed after her. Her life, obviously, changed for the worse and forever."

"Now, sir?"

"Now you may speak, Technical Sergeant Williams."

"What you have just described, sir, just

would not happen."

"How so?"

"Because Gwendolyn, with one hand on the Bible, would swear on the heads of the children she hopes to have with Second Lieutenant Oscar Hormell the Third, to whom she is now affianced, that all of the charges are absolutely false and without basis in any facts whatsoever."

"Why would a sweet Red Cross Comfort Girl like Gwendolyn swear something false and blatantly dishonest like that?"

"Because if she admitted to them, the chances of her marching down the aisle with Second Lieutenant Oscar Hormell the Third would be reduced to zilch, if not lower. He's a West Pointer. They like to think their women are pure."

"But what if the Senior Red Cross Comfort Girl subpoenaed you before her bar of justice?"

"I would consider it my duty as a Saint Malachi's Old Boy to lie through my teeth about even knowing Gwendolyn. And, because I have what Ralph Peters described when he was Pastor-in-Charge Caldwell as the 'innocent face of a child,' I would be believed."

Colonel O'Shaughnessy looked thoughtfully at Phil for a long moment.

"I can see why Ralph Peters sees a future in the CIA for you, Williams. You're as devious and as amoral as any man I've ever known. So let's see how we can make that happen."

"Sir?"

"And at the same time get you out of my hair here, without giving Ralph Peters the idea that I haven't been looking after the young man he's come to look upon as the son he never had as he asked me to do."

"Yes, sir."

"You're to be relieved of your duties as editor in chief and chief firearms instructor of the German-American Gospel Tract Foundation and appointed chief of the armed enlisted courier section."

"Sir, I don't know what that means."

"You will be transporting classified documents between the German-American Gospel Tract Foundation and other CIA installations all over Europe. You will, for example, transport classified documents between Berlin and the Franco-American Wine Lovers Society, which is at 49 Rue Pierre Charron in Paris, France. This is in the Eighth Arrondissement, just a few steps from the Hotel George V, which is at 31 Avenue George V, which is where the CIA maintains a small, but rather nice, suite year-round in case Ralph Peters finds himself in Paris and needs a place to rest his weary head.

"I feel sure the Honorable Mr. Peters will have no objection to you, whom he regards as the son he never had, using the suite when he is not in Paris. Or even if he is, in which case you could sit around the La Galerie lounge together swilling champagne and swapping memories of Groton and Saint Malachi's.

"You will drive the Cadillac, which really should by all rights be mine, from Berlin to Paris, carrying with you whatever documents I decide to share with the Franco-American Wine Lovers Society. You will hand over the Cadillac to the valet parking service of the George V, telling them they can bury it in the garage as you won't be needing it for a while.

"You being in Paris with the Cadillac will serve the dual purpose of getting two thorns out from under the saddle of the Berlin Brigade, to wit: the Cadillac and you in the field grade bachelor officers' hotel.

"As you will be on temporary duty traveling away from your home station, you will be paid *per diem* in lieu of rations and quarters. And as you will be armed to protect the classified documents you will be

330

transporting, you will also be paid the additional *per diem* pay authorized for personnel performing hazardous duty while away from their home stations.

"Now, after you deliver the classified documents to the Franco-American Wine Lovers Society you will hold yourself in readiness to transport other classified documents the Franco-American Wine Lovers Society might wish to transfer to another CIA installation, such as the Anglo-American Fishing Foundation in London, England, or the Italian-American Opera Lovers Guild in Rome, Italy.

"Don't expect that call to duty to come quickly. It won't come for a month or six weeks, perhaps even a longer period. But when it does, you will saddle up and transport it. Say, to Rome. You will not, I repeat not, drive the Cadillac, but instead take the train. In Rome, you deliver the documents to the Italian-American Opera Lovers Guild and then rest from your travel for at least five days in the suite in the Hotel Majestic at Via Veneto 50 that the CIA rents on a year-round basis in case the Honorable Ralph Peters decides to call on His Holiness the Pope and needs someplace to stay before and after doing so.

"Then you will return to Paris and await

another call to duty. While you are waiting, you can continue your education. Because you will not be in Berlin, you obviously won't be able to do that at the Free University of Berlin, which isn't free anyway, in case you haven't heard. My suggestion is that you matriculate in the Off Campus Program of Troy State University, located in Troy, Alabama, which offers correspondence courses in the types of subjects — The Theory and Practice of Volleyball 101 and Cheerleading for Males 101, for but two examples — which practically eliminate the possibility of failure, in which you are, or should be, interested. Getting the picture, Technical Sergeant Williams?"

"I think so, sir."

"Now, if you can keep your nose to the grindstone, and don't do anything foolish, such as blowing your *per diem* in lieu of rations and quarters and your hazardous duty pay on Parisian hookers . . . Allow me to digress a moment."

"Yes, sir."

"If you have an overwhelming urge to deal with your raging teenage hormones, do not go to the Bois de Boulogne, despite its reputation for being an area where strikingly beautiful women gather hoping to find carnal congress with men."

"May I ask why not, sir?"

"I don't know how to put this to someone of your age, but I feel duty bound to try, and not only because the Honorable Ralph Peters would really put my ass in a sling if I didn't warn the young man he thinks of as the son he never had about the hazards the Bois de Boulogne poses for someone like you."

"What about the Bois de Boulogne, sir?"

"How do I put this delicately? Look at it this way, Technical Sergeant Williams. While the women in the Bois de Boulogne are without doubt as strikingly beautiful as women come, when it comes time to void their bladders, they do so as we do."

"I don't think I understand, sir."

"I was afraid I was going to have to draw you a verbal picture, and I was right. All right. What the strikingly beautiful women of the Bois de Boulogne do when they have to take a leak is stand up at a urinal, get a good grip on their EXPLETIVE DELETED!! tools, and aim them at the holes in the bottom of the urinal, meanwhile trying not to splash any of the You Know What on their shoes. You take my meaning?"

"Yes, sir. I think I do."

"Where was I? Oh. If you don't do anything foolish, like coming back to Berlin for any reason unless I summon you, when the next nearly two years are up, you will have a college degree, your majority, and your commission. Got it?"

"Yes, sir. Thank you, sir."

[Two]

Paris, France
Sunday, October 2, 1949

Not quite one year later, Phil walked out of the Hotel George V just before midnight and made his way to the Champs-Élysées, which is the wide street that runs down the hill from the Arc de Triomphe de L'Étoile traffic circle, which is where Napoleon is buried.

He was a changed man from the boy he'd been in Berlin. For one thing, he was almost an alumnus of Troy State University, of Troy, Alabama, which meant he was not far from being First Lieutenant Philip W. Williams, Military Intelligence Corps, U.S. Army, just as soon as he turned twenty-one.

The Troy State relationship had been a profitable one for him. They offered a plethora of courses that weren't all that difficult — he finished The Theory of Snooker Pool 202, for example, one afternoon while having his hair cut in the barbershop of the

Hesperia Emperatriz Hotel on López de Hoyos in Madrid, Spain.

And the Troy State Faculty Senate Board had just granted him credit for four years of physical education after he submitted his certificates of certification from the Royal Korean Archery & Taekkyeon Academy, located on Dried Fish Street in London, for their evaluation.

One certificate was for Dojunim and the other for Taekkyeon.

What had happened was that while wandering around London one day he happened across the RKA&TA, as it was known. Not having fired a bow and arrow since he was six years old, and having nothing better to do at the time, he figured what the hell, pass a little time, give it a shot.

Two hours and twenty pounds sterling later, he had learned that while shooting a Korean bow and arrow set was more physically tiring than pulling a trigger, it wasn't any harder for him to hit with an arrow what he was pointing it at than it was for him to go one hundred straight at skeet or trap.

This earned him a certificate, presented with many smiles and bows by pajama-clad Anglo-Koreans, saying he was now a 도주님 / 道主님, which is Korean for Dojunim, which means *Damn Good Shot with Bow and Arrow,* which he didn't pay much attention to at the time.

The next time he was in London, he went back to the RKA&TA to take a few more shots with a bow and arrow. This time there was a Korean in the RKA&TA who spoke English.

By then Phil had learned how to speak French and had greatly improved his Hungarian so that the next time — he prayed that there indeed would be a next time — he found himself sharing a pillow with Magda, Countess Kocian, they could chat more easily. But Phil didn't speak a word of Korean and the last time he'd been in the RKA&TA it had been all sign language, grimaces, and a lot of bowing.

This time a short gentleman, who when speaking sounded like the Queen, told him there was another Korean martial art called Taekkyeon, one that is characterized by fluid, dynamic footwork and utilizes a wide variety of kicks and fist and elbow strikes, as well as pressure point attacks, throws, and grapples.

He went on to say that as a result of Phil having been declared a 도주님 / 道主님 as a result of his remarkable bow-and-arrow marksmanship, the RKA&TA was willing to train him in this ancient art without any cost to him at all.

Phil, thinking that an intelligence officer as he was about to be might well find himself in a situation where he might have to defend himself, and that a knowledge of a wide variety of kicks and fist and elbow strikes, et cetera, might be useful in that regard, accepted.

It took him a half-dozen more visits to London before he was judged to be skillful enough kicking, striking, et cetera, to be a Taekkyeon Black Belt, but eventually it happened, and he saw himself enrolled in the leather-bound books of Taekkyeon as a Master (Beginner's Class) of the ancient art.

And then he just about forgot both certificates until he got a request for funds, described as "Alumni News," from Troy State University. He received similar alumni news publications from all but one of the boarding schools from which he had been booted at least once every two months.

Insofar as the boarding schools were concerned, they were quite willing to forget the circumstances of his having left the schools, and consider him an alumni, as long as he was prepared to cut a check.

The alumni news magazines showed pictures of all the good things that could be done on campi providing of course that the generous alumni cut a check.

The *Troy State Alumni News* showed a picture of a blonde in short shorts holding a bow and arrow, and said that if the generous alumni cut a generous check, the Troy State Archery Range could be doubled in size.

Phil certainly had no intention of cutting a check, generous or miserly, to Troy State as he had never been on the campus or for that matter knew where in the EXPLETIVE DELETED!! Alabama was and didn't much care. But there was something about the picture that held his attention besides the partially exposed buttocks of the blonde and he kept looking at it.

Then he knew.

If they have an archery range, he reasoned, archery is probably on the curriculum. When he checked the catalog, there it was. Not only was, but was sort of a big deal. In addition to Archery 101, there was Intermediate Archery 102, Advanced Archery 201, and Master Class Archery 202.

The problem was a line that read: Archery is On-Campus Study only.

He thought about that, and decided all they could say was "Hell no," and shipped

338

off his certificates from the RKA&TA and asked that they be evaluated for credit.

The faculty apparently knew all about 도주님 / 道主님 because their reply was quickly forthcoming. He would not only get credit for four years of regularly scheduled physical training, but inasmuch as they would love to have a bona fide 도주님 / 道主님 on the faculty, they were enclosing for his consideration an application for employment as a junior assistant athletic coach (Archery) on his graduation.

None of this was on Phil's mind as he walked out of the George V just before midnight and walked down Rue Pierre Charron to the Champs-Élysées. What he wanted to do was see if he could be of any service to fellow Americans, especially female Americans in their twenties.

He had learned that America's institutions of higher learning provided their female students "a year of study abroad" to widen their knowledge of the world by letting them spend a carefully chaperoned year in La Belle France.

More to the point, he had learned that many of these young ladies, after having spent the day examining the Eiffel Tower and the treasures of the Louvre, would escape their chaperones and head for the Champs-Élysées looking for a little of the romance they had heard was so common in the City of Lights but had not been on display at *La Tour Eiffel,* as it was known in Paris, or the Louvre.

When Phil encountered such young women, who usually traveled in pairs or trios, he would approach them — not getting too close — and smile and announce that he heard them talking, knew them to be Americans, and as an American himself who lived in Paris, wondered if he could be of any use whatever to them.

Once in two point three times, one of the young women would ask, usually dubiously, "You live in Paris?"

If that happened, Phil would reply, "Yes, *mam'selle,* I do."

Once in two times, that would trigger the response, "Student, are you? At the Sorbonne, or possibly the École Superior Polytechnique?"

Phil's study of the opposite gender had taught him that females took pleasure in demonstrating their knowledge even if they didn't have much knowledge. In this case, this meant that the female who asked if he were possibly a student at the École Superior Polytechnique almost certainly didn't have the faintest idea what that was, although she knew both how to pronounce it, and that there was an accent aigu over the *É* in École.

Phil, with a slight smirk on his face, would then reply, "No, *mam'selle,* I am not a student at either the Sorbonne or the École Superior Polytechnique."

If he got this far, the chances were 95 to 1 the next question to him would be, "Then what do you do here in Paris?"

To which he would reply, "I'm afraid, *mam'selle,* that I am not permitted to answer that question, even to patriotic fellow Americans, in public, but if you're really curious, there is a small café around the corner, Le Café Cricou, where I can show you something that may answer your understandable curiosity."

This was the critical point in the confrontation. There were two possible next moves by the female side. One was that Phil would be told "forget it" — unless the young ladies were students at one of the ivy-covered female institutions, such as Wellesley or Sarah Lawrence, in which case he would be told to go EXPLETIVE DELETED!! himself, and they would walk away.

If he got them into the Café Cricou, however, the battle was nearly over. The

341

female patrons of the Café Cricou were primarily practitioners of the oldest profession and they practiced it on the Champs-Élysées. Many of them were friends of Phil's. He had on many occasions, during his every-other-week exercise with the Cadillac to keep its tires from going flat on the bottom, filled the Cadillac with Cricou girls and driven them out to the Bois de Boulogne for a picnic.

The strikingly beautiful women of the Bois de Boulogne, who in fact stood in order to take a leak, deserted the Bois in daylight hours, leaving its tree-shaded grassy expanses free for picnics and other such innocent activities. Phil furnished the Cadillac and the occasional bottle of Cabernet Sauvignon and the Cricou girls furnished the Camembert, the baguettes, the oysters, the fried chicken, et cetera, and a good time was had by all.

The result of this was whenever Phil went into the Café Cricou, at least four, and often more, Cricou girls, who wore skirts slit nearly to their waists and ten-inch stiletto high heels, would walk over to his table and give him a little kiss.

Additionally, the Edith Piaf impersonator at the piano would, when she saw Phil come in, segue into her (actually Miss Piaf's) signature song, *"Je ne regrette rien"* which means, roughly, "I ain't sorry 'bout a EXPLETIVE DELETED!! thing," and blow him a little kiss.

All of this of course impressed the young American ladies Phil had talked into going with him into the Café Cricou. And then he topped this by showing them his CIC credentials and badge. This visibly dazzled them as, truth to tell, he knew damned well it would.

But at this point, instead of draping a friendly arm around one of their shoulders or under the table bumping his knee, or knees, against the knee, or knees, of one or more of them as all expected, some with happy expectations, him to do, he continued to ignore them as he had from the moment he had led them into the Café Cricou.

His extensive knowledge of women in sexual matters had taught him — or perhaps exposed to him — the greatest and most successful con job in recorded — and probably prerecorded as well — history.

He had come by this knowledge intellectually, as opposed to physically, as the number of his actual physical sexual encounters with the gentle sex could still be counted on his fingers and toes with both thumbs and a pinkie left over.

He had come by it professionally, that is to say when he had in his official capacity as editor in chief of the German-American Gospel Tract Foundation been charged with detecting ambiguities, grammatical errors, and strikeovers in reports filed by CIC agents regarding the alleged sexual misconduct of officers in the grade of major and above and their dependents.

He most often had to read these reports several times, for several reasons, including the fact that the CIC agents preparing these reports seemed to make about twice as many strikeovers, and make two or three times as many grammatical errors, and be as blind to that many ambiguities as they did when making a report on, say, a Bulgarian Plan to Blow Up the Statue of Liberty.

And then, when he had finally stripped the reports of all the strikeovers *und so weiter* and excess verbiage, he had to personally go through each and every one of them to extract what Pastor-in-Chief Caldwell referred to as the more pertinent passages.

He told Phil that Mrs. Caldwell had a natural interest in that sort of thing because she had taken Elementary Sexual Deviation 101 at Wellesley and wished to keep up to date on the subject.

"Now I understand this, Phil, but I don't think others — in particular those EXPLETIVE DELETED!! West Pointers we're surrounded by — would. So, to keep this between you, me, the lamp pole, and Victoria, what I want you to do is start a new file called 'Daily Notes of Administrator P. W. Williams.' In it you will record the more pertinent, in a lurid sense, of the sexual foibles of the majors and above and their dependents detected by the CIC agents investigating. Just the good stuff. Leave out kissing, public exposure, simple adultery, and that sort of thing. Think lurid. Got it, my boy?"

"I'll do my best, sir."

The Daily Notes of CIC Administrator P. W. Williams ultimately consisted of 722 single-spaced pages, which Phil mounted in three three-ring binders. He had kept them, as he thought Pastor-in-Chief Caldwell, now the Honorable Ralph Peters, might still be interested in them for historical, literary, or some other purpose, and ask for them.

After he moved into the George V, he read through the whole 722-page file again, this time very carefully. And it confirmed what he had first suspected in Berlin.

Women, not men, were the most deter-

345

mined sexual aggressors. Furthermore, they had managed to convince men of quite the opposite. Women encouraged men to think men were the pursuers of women, sexually speaking, when the reverse is true.

Women didn't ply men with flowers, champagne, diamonds, et cetera, to get them on the mattress for hanky-panky when they wanted a little, or a lot, of hanky-panky. They had learned that all they had to do was lower their eyes, blush, and show a little skin, and men would instantly start fighting with other men for the privilege of showering women with flowers, champagne, diamonds, et cetera, in the hope their philanthropy would entice the women to bestow upon them the hanky-panky the women wanted the men to provide in the first place.

Their skill in blushing, lowering their eyes, and showing a little skin had been polished to near perfection over the centuries as it was passed down from mother to daughter over countless generations. It was nearly irresistible.

Phil saw in "nearly irresistible" a potential chink in female armor. What would happen, he wondered, if instead of starting to pant and paw at the ground with his left foot when a member of the opposite sex batted her eyes at him, or showed him a little skin, he pretended not to be as interested in the woman doing that as he was in the woman sitting next to the woman, who was not batting her eyes and had her skirt in the modest place it was supposed to be?

He put his theory to the test in the Café Cricou, which he'd heard about but hadn't had the courage to enter, both because of its reputation and also because there was still burned in his memory the color motion pictures he had been shown at Fort Dix that showed what terrible things happened to one's male appendage if one was so foolish as to stick it in a loose woman.

After he had shown no interest in the first five of the Café Cricou girls who showed him a great deal of skin and batted their eyes with such skill that he was on the cusp of saying, "To hell with it! I'll worry about what happens to my you-know-what later. Come here, *ma chérie*!" the sixth approached him and asked if she could ask him a question.

He told her, "Certainly."

"If you're a *poofter, chéri,* why do you come in the Café Cricou?"

Phil knew what a *poofter* was, because Second Lieutenant Charles William George Michael Bertram of Her Majesty's Own Scottish Light Lancers had told him that what he was wearing was a kilt, not a skirt.

"*Poofters* wear skirts," Bertie had explained, "and Scots wear kilts."

Phil had taken Bertie's meaning.

"Let me think," Phil had said to the sixth Café Cricou girl.

"What's to think about, *chéri*? You're either a man who likes women or a *poofter* who doesn't. Simple question."

"Oh, I do like women," Phil hastily assured her. "I am in love with a redheaded Hungarian named Magda, and my Magda is across the ocean. I came in here because you beautiful Café Cricou girls remind me of my beautiful Magda across the ocean."

"And you're not fooling around because your Hungarian redhead is far away?"

"I couldn't do that to my beloved Magda," Phil lied. "Fooling around would constitute infidelity."

The Café Cricou girl then kissed him on the forehead.

"We don't get many decent men in here," she said. "The last one was six months ago, and he came in by mistake. So I'll tell you what, *chéri*. Me and my professional associates will provide you with chaste companionship and conversation while you're being faithful to your Hungarian. Please join us at the bar."

■ ■ ■ ■

So as Phil walked down Rue Pierre Charron to the Champs-Élysées, it was in anticipation of finding some nice American college girls thereon whom he could entice first
into the Café Cricou and ultimately into
the king-sized bed in his suite at the
George V.

That didn't happen.

As he crossed the Champs-Élysées and
then turned left toward the Arc de Triomphe traffic circle, a block down from
which was Rue Madeleine, on which the
Café Cricou was located, he saw a blond
young woman. While her skirt was not slit
to the waist, it was short enough to provide
a good view of her spectacular legs.

She had on a leash a dachshund — a
canine Phil thought looked like a hot dog
with legs — and was engaged in conversation with two men who looked like Frogs,
that is, looked like Frenchmen.

The first thing Phil thought was a little
unusual was that the blonde was doing what
she was doing where she was doing it. The
ladies of the Café Cricou regarded that area
as their place of business and theirs alone.

If that blonde with the spectacular legs isn't

careful, Phil thought, *those spectacular legs are going to be broken when the Café Cricou girls throw her under the next Arc de Triomphe–to–Place Vendôme bus that comes down the Champs-Élysées.*

The next thing he noticed was that the languages being spoken by the girl with the spectacular legs — and by now he could see that she had a bosom quite as attractive as her legs — were French and German, and that the Frogs apparently spoke no German and the girl with the nice knockers and spectacular legs apparently spoke no French.

"Verzeih mir, Fräulein," Phil said. *"Kann ich etwas Unterstützung?"*

Which means, "Excuse me, miss, may I be of some assistance?"

She looked at him, which caused their eyes to meet. His heart jumped.

"Ich bin Brunhilde Wienerwald, Tänzerin im Corps de Ballet von der Wiener Staatsoper," she said.

"How interesting," Phil replied, in German of course. "I've never actually met a ballet dancer before, although I have heard a good deal about the ballet dancers in Moscow and Budapest. And how may I assist you, Fräulein Wienerwald?"

Before she could reply, one of the Frogs

entered the conversation by saying, *"Esprit vous propre EXPLETIVE DELETED!! entreprise vous EXPLETIVE DELETED!! Nazi!"*

To which Phil replied, in French of course, "Please, *monsieur,* do not be so rude as to try to tell me what my EXPLETIVE DELETED!! business is. Or call me a EXPLETIVE DELETED!! Nazi."

To which the Frog replied by throwing a right hook in the direction of Phil's face.

Phil's response to this was Pavlovian. And he was of course a Master (Beginner Class) of Taekkyeon. One quick kick to the Frog's groin area and the Frog was on the ground, his hands on his crotch and moaning piteously.

On seeing his compatriot so distressed, the second Frog entered the fray. He produced a switchblade knife with a 28-centimeter (approx. 11-inch) blade sharpened on both sides and began to wave it around in a manner Phil considered menacing.

It took an array of elbow strikes, pressure point attacks, and grapples to do it, but shortly Frog Two was also on the ground moaning piteously. As Phil leaned over him to relieve him of the switchblade knife, the dachshund, whose name Phil was later to learn was Heisse Wurst, took advantage of the situation. Brunhilde had taken him for a walk in search of a Parisian version of a Vienna *Feuerhydrant* and they hadn't been able to find one. Since the Frogs on the ground smelled like a fire hydrant — as many Frogs do — Heisse Wurst decided he would have to go with what he had. And go he did.

Phil looked into Brunhilde's eyes again.

He said, *"Ich denke, wir sollten hier raus. Mein Hotel ist gleich um die Ecke."*

Which meant, "I think we should get out of here. My hotel is right around the corner."

In consideration of the fact that this is a romantic, as opposed to pornographic, novel, the author will draw a curtain of discretion and modesty across what happened in Phil's George V hotel suite that night, except to state that what happened that night began about thirty seconds after the door was closed and that it lasted until noon the next day.

At that point, Brunhilde said she had to put her clothing back on and get to the Place de l'Opéra as quickly as possible as she had a 1:30 p.m. performance in the Palais Garnier, as the opera house in Paris is known.

Because he was a St. Malachi's Old Boy and thus expected to be a gentleman, he had the Cadillac brought up from the garage and he drove her to the opera. There she said, "Thank you very much, and good-bye."

"You mean we're not going to see one another again?"

"I told you before that I am a dancer in the Corps de Ballet of the Vienna State Opera," Brunhilde said. "Although I am grateful for what you did for me on the Champs-Élysées last night, and to me later in the George V, the cold facts are that dancers of the Corps de Ballet of the Vienna State Opera, such as myself, simply do not become involved with unsophisticated . . . one might say *ohne kultur* barbarians . . . young Americans such as yourself. Think of what happened between us as two ships which have passed going in opposite directions in the middle of the night in the middle of the Atlantic Ocean, and *auf Wiedersehen!*"

And then she got out of the Cadillac and disappeared into the stage door of the Palais Garnier.

Truth to tell, Phil wasn't all that surprised or disappointed. For one thing, he had heard from both Angus McTavish and G. Lincoln Rutherford — and of course from Magda — what terrible people ballet dancers often were. For another, now that he was about to become First Lieutenant Williams, he really shouldn't be fooling around with ballet dancers, even ballet dancers like Brunhilde, who ranked as maybe a twelve or thirteen on the one-to-ten scale *vis-à-vis* the enthusiasm of sexual partners. And for a third reason, he was going to have to go on a delivering-classified-documents mission to Istanbul, Turkey, in the next day or two and had to pack.

He put Brunhilde Wienerwald out of his mind.

Just over five weeks later, Phil picked up the funny-looking telephone in his suite in the George V.

"Hello?" he said.

The calling party said, *"Könnten Sie mich an Herr Williams? Hier ist Brunhilde Wiener-wald von der Wiener Staatsoper."*

"Brunhilde, baby! How nice of you to call!"

"Where have you been? I've been trying to get you for days."

"Well, first I was in Istanbul, and then I went to Athens, and then to the Isle of Capri in the Tyrrhenian Sea. What's on your mind, Brunhilde, baby?"

" 'Baby' ist eine sehr unglückliche Wahl der Wörter."

"Why is 'baby' a really unfortunate choice of words, Brunhilde, baby?"

"Denn in nur acht Monaten ich werde noch eine sie EXPLETIVE DELETED!! EXPLETIVE DELETED!!."

"Did you just say you're going to have a baby in eight months, Brunhilde?"

"Sind Sie taub und mehr als in einen Ewigkeitszustand hinein Sie EXPLETIVE DELETED!! EXPLETIVE DELETED!!?"

"I am neither deaf nor oversexed, Brunhilde. And please try to remember that you're a lady, and ladies just don't call gentlemen EXPLETIVE DELETED!! EXPLETIVE DELETED!! as you just did."

"EXPLETIVE DELETED!! you, you EXPLETIVE DELETED!! ohne Kultur Amerikaner EXPLETIVE DELETED!!."

"To change the subject, Brunhilde. You are not implying that I have some connection with your upcoming blessed event?"

"You're EXPLETIVE DELETED!! right I am," Brunhilde replied in German. "I'll admit that I had a little to do with it. Being familiar with the statistic that conception occurs only once in 11,455 times when a virgin loses her pearl of great price, I took a chance in Paris with you. My EXPLETIVE DELETED!! mistake. On the other hand, you EXPLETIVE DELETED!!, you should not have taken advantage of my innocence and virginal state the way you did."

"Well, Brunhilde, what do you suggest we do about the problem we face?"

"I suggest you get in your EXPLETIVE DELETED!! Cadillac and get your EXPLETIVE DELETED!! to Vienna right EXPLETIVE DELETED!! now."

"Of course. And where will I find you in Vienna?"

"The EXPLETIVE DELETED!! opera house, where else? God, what a stupid EXPLETIVE DELETED!! question!"

Thinking that his status would change forever — as it did — when he married Fräulein Wienerwald, but knowing that as a St. Malachi's Old Boy, and thus a gentleman, he had no choice but to turn her into an honest woman by marrying her, he packed all of his personal belongings into the Cadillac before heading down French National Route 7 toward Vienna. All his personal belongings of course included the three three-ring binders containing The Daily Notes of CIC Administrator P. W. Williams.

[Three]

Vienna, Austria
Monday, November 14, 1949

Phil had no trouble finding the Vienna State Opera. It was right where the concierge of the George V told him it would be, i.e., in front of the Hotel Sacher and right across the street from the Hotel Bristol.

When he went to the stage door and identified himself and inquired of the stage doorman for Fräulein Wienerwald, the stage doorman replied, in Hungarian, which Phil now of course understood, "What I would really like to do is turn you into a EXPLETIVE DELETED!! soprano with a really dull saw, you EXPLETIVE DELETED!! EXPLETIVE DELETED!!. But I will get her, as what Brunhilde wants Brunhilde gets."

With a welcome like that from the stage doorman, Phil wondered, *what kind of a welcome will I get from Brunhilde?*

What he got from Brunhilde was not at all unpleasant.

Crying "Philip, my darling!" she threw herself into his arms and then cried, "Kiss me, my darling!" and pressed her lips against his.

Then she whispered in his ear: "Show some enthusiasm, you EXPLETIVE DE-

LETED!!. People are watching."

He complied by kissing her again, both because he liked it and because he was afraid of what she might do to him if he didn't show the proper enthusiasm.

After a minute or so, she let him loose, whispered, "Smile, you EXPLETIVE DE-LETED!!," and turned him to face the stage door.

There, a number of people were looking at them. Some with tears running down their cheeks and others with cold hate in their eyes.

"Friends, coworkers, fellow dancers, and childhood friend Waldo Pfefferkopf, this is my beloved Philip, who I am now going to take to the bar in the Hotel Sacher, where I will discuss the details of our upcoming nuptials with him."

She then picked up Heisse Wurst, who had been growling and gnawing at Phil's ankle during the passionate embrace, and then led Phil by the hand to the Hotel Sacher, which is right across the street from the stage door of the Vienna State Opera, and into the bar.

There she ordered a double Slivovitz, straight up, water on the side, and told the waiter to give Phil the same.

When the drinks were served, she tossed

hers down.

"Well, that's the last of those I get for a while," Brunhilde said. "Thanks to you and my stupidity."

"Excuse me?"

"Women in the family way should not imbibe intoxicants," Brunhilde said. "Why am I not surprised you don't know that?"

"I'll try to remember that in the future."

"Or smoke cigars," she added.

"You smoke cigars?" Phil blurted.

"Not any longer, I don't, thanks to you and my stupidity." She saw the look on his face, and explained:

"I did a six months' tour with the Royal Danish Opera Ballet Company. That's in Denmark. Danish women smoke cigars. Even in public. I tried it and liked it and kept doing it. Not in public, of course. But that simple pleasure is gone for the next eight months, too, as women in the family way are discouraged from smoking cigars."

"I see."

"Let me tell you what's going to happen," Brunhilde said. "I have a certain reputation here at the Vienna State Opera, where I have been dancing since I was six years old. I may be forced to leave the opera because I allowed my emotions to overcome my usual good sense in Paris.

"That I did so is understandable, of course. After you kicked that first EXPLETIVE DELETED!! Frenchman in his EXPLETIVE DELETED!! and then the second EXPLETIVE DELETED!! Frenchman in the ear and took that wicked knife away from him and then took me to your suite in the George V, I got a good look at you in the light and thought with a little training you might be able to become a premier danseur yourself —"

"You thought I might become a male ballet dancer?" Phil asked incredulously.

"Why not? They're not all *poofters,* you know. Half of the ones in the Corps de Ballet here have been trying — and failing — to get in my pants since I was twelve, which was when my bosom started to blossom."

"That's very interesting."

"If we are to be man and wife and march down life's path together, you're going to have to understand that you're not permitted to interrupt me when I'm talking. Got it?"

"Got it."

"As I was saying, it was understandable that I threw caution to the wind in the George V. My pearl of great price was going to have to go eventually, I knew, most probably to Waldo Pfefferkopf, my childhood

360

friend, who's been trying to get in my pants since I was six, so why not have a trial run, so to speak, with a decent-looking American rich enough to keep a suite in the George V . . ."

"Brunhilde, I'm not rich."

"What? *Mein Gott!* Just when you think things are as bad as they can get, they get worse!"

"Actually, I'm a technical sergeant in the U.S. Army."

"Ach du lieber Gott!"

"Who will, however, soon be a first lieutenant."

"Whoopee! I could tell you, but won't, how many lieutenant colonels and up of various armies have tried unsuccessfully to get in my pants."

"Thank you for not sharing that information with me."

"Shut up, my Philip, while I finish telling you what's going to happen and why."

"Yes, Brunhilde."

"I realized that my stupidity in allowing my lust to overwhelm my common sense was going to make me leave the Vienna Opera in shame and go God only knows where with a none-too-bright American, but then I thought there was a way around the shame part.

"I publicly admit that I threw myself into your arms — your arms, not your bed — because I had been struck with Cupid's arrow. They understand things like that in Vienna. There is a strong Hungarian ambience here, and God knows Hungarian women are always throwing themselves at some jackass because they think they're in love."

"I don't quite understand."

"Then shut up and I'll tell you. What I have told everybody, including my childhood friend Waldo Pfefferkopf, is that I have been struck by Cupid's arrow and am about to throw away everything I hold dear by marrying you, an American EXPLETIVE DELETED!! who hates opera, the ballet, and insists on taking me to Texas.

"They will — already do, as a matter of fact — hate you, but I will be able to leave behind the image of a poor girl who couldn't help herself, instead of the image of a stupid female who couldn't control her lust. Get it?"

"Got it."

"And since we'll be far away from my beloved Vienna when our child is born, and we're a little vague about exactly when that happened, no one will be able to count the months from the date of our marriage to the date of my delivery and conclude that I wasn't entitled to the virginal white wedding dress I will wear tomorrow. Got it?"

"Got it."

The result of this was the next day Brunhilde Wienerwald and Philip Wallingford Williams III were united in civil matrimony by the presiding justice of the Austrian Supreme Court in the Supreme Court Building in Vienna.

The bride, who wore a virginal white dress with matching veil, wept through most of the ceremony. The presiding justice glowered at Phil throughout the ceremony. The guests, including the bride's childhood friend Waldo Pfefferkopf, wept throughout the ceremony and between sobs glowered at Phil.

As Mr. and Mrs. P. W. Williams came down the wide marble steps to the Vienna Philharmonic Orchestra's rendition of "Treulich Geführt" — which means "Bridal Chorus," from *Lohengrin,* Richard Wagner's masterpiece 1850 opera — delicate, scented tiny grains of rice were tossed at Brunhilde.

Baseball-sized balls of frozen rice wrapped around rocks were thrown at Phil.

The couple drove from the Supreme Court

Building to the Bristol Hotel so the bride could change out of her wedding dress into something more suitable for their honeymoon wedding trip, which would be their drive to Berlin.

Once they were in their room, the groom went quickly into the bathroom where, standing, he dealt with the problem that had bugged him all though the wedding ceremony, while they were being showered with rice by the wedding guests, and on the drive to the Hotel Bristol.

This took a little time, and when he came out of the bathroom he expected to find Brunhilde already changed into the clothing she would wear as they drove to Berlin.

Instead, Brunhilde was lying on the bed, wearing only the most basic of black lace intimate undergarments and holding a rose from her wedding bouquet between her teeth.

He looked at her and she looked at him.

Finally, she took the rose out of her mouth.

"*Mein Gott,* didn't anyone ever tell you, *Dummkopf,* that a wedding isn't official until it's been consummated?"

Phil took her meaning, of course, but as he took off his clothing and joined her in bed he was sure, based on his bride's weeping throughout the ceremony, that the consummation would be brief and *pro forma.*

He was wrong.

They didn't get out of bed except twice to eat room service oysters and have a bottle of champagne until shortly after 1 p.m. the next day.

Only when their nuptial oaths had been truly consummated again and again did they check out of the Hotel Bristol, get in the Cadillac, and head for Berlin, where Phil looked eagerly forward to their becoming First Lieutenant and Mrs. P. W. Williams, MI, USA, which he was sure would occur as soon they got to Berlin.

Time would quickly prove he was wrong about that, too.

XI
PHIL RETURNS TO AMERICA

[One]

Berlin, Germany
Friday, November 18, 1949

"You did what?" Pastor-in-Chief Peter O'Shaughnessy asked incredulously when Phil informed him of his change in marital status.

Phil repeated that he was now man-and-wife with the former Brunhilde Wienerwald of the Vienna State Opera and was looking forward to his new life as a married man and commissioned officer and gentleman.

Colonel O'Shaughnessy momentarily forgot that commissioned officers and gentlemen are not supposed to use profane, vulgar, or indecent language when addressing subordinates who have in some way displeased them.

"You dumb EXPLETIVE DELETED!!, do you have any EXPLETIVE DELETED!! idea

366

what you've done?"

"Sir, I just told you what I've done."

"What I meant, you stupid EXPLETIVE DELETED!!, is do you know what that means?"

"Until just now, sir, I thought that Mrs. Williams and myself could move into company grade officers' quarters to await my new assignment and the birth of my first child."

"Oh, have I got news for you!"

"Yes, sir?"

"Well, for one thing, anyone who is dumb enough to marry a EXPLETIVE DELETED!! indigenous person can forget becoming a commissioned officer and gentleman."

"Why is that, sir?"

"Because commissioned officers and gentlemen are required — and it makes sense if you think about it — to have at least a Confidential security clearance. What security clearances did you say you had?"

"Sir, I have a run-of-the-mill Top Secret security clearance. And also a Top Secret-Honorable Peters security clearance, so that I can deal with the CIA. And a Top Secret-Sexual security clearance."

"The operative word there, you stupid EXPLETIVE DELETED!! is 'had,' meaning past tense. Which means you can say *auf*

Wiedersehen to your run-of-the-mill Top Secret security clearance and your Top Secret-Honorable Peters security clearance, and of course your Top Secret-Sexual security clearance."

"Yes, sir."

"And do you know what that means, about to be ex CIC Special Agent Williams, *vis-à-vis* your CIC career?"

"No, sir, I don't."

"You can kiss that goodbye, too. You were booted out of the CIC as of the moment you said, 'I do.' "

"I'm sorry to hear that, sir. What happens to me now?"

"First, give me your CIC credentials and badge and your U.S. Pistol, Cal. 45 ACP 1911A1. And the shoulder holster that goes with the latter."

"Yes, sir," Phil said, and laid everything on Colonel O'Shaughnessy's desk.

"Since you are now, at least for the moment, Technical Sergeant Williams, really out of uniform, since you are wearing civilian clothing, and are no longer a CIC special agent authorized to wear civilian clothing."

"I will change into my uniform just as soon as the opportunity to do so presents itself, sir."

"You will do so now," Colonel O'Shaughnessy said, "by going into the Enlisted Latrine, not the Officers' and Civilian Gentlemen's Restroom. Report back here to me when you have done so."

Phil changed in to his uniform and reported to Colonel O'Shaughnessy when he had done so.

"While you were gone, Technical Sergeant Williams," the colonel greeted him, "I had the opportunity to speak with the Honorable Ralph Peters on the secure radio telephone circuit about your unbelievable EXPLETIVE DELETED!! stupidity. He said to tell you that he is deeply disappointed in you. He said you should have learned what kind of lower-class amoral women ballet dancers are from your duties as editor in chief of the German-American Gospel Tract Foundation, and because you married a ballet dancer, he has been forced to revise his previously stated opinion *vis-à-vis* your future with the CIA.

"He said, and I quote, 'We have some really stupid people in the agency, but so far none of them has been so EXPLETIVE DELETED!! stupid as to marry a EXPLETIVE DELETED!! Viennese ballerina, and I am not going to be responsible for bringing the first one through those plate glass doors at the main entrance to Langley.' "

"Yes, sir," Phil said. "I am sorry to have disappointed Colonel Caldwell, excuse me, the Honorable Ralph Peters."

"And you should be. And he said for you to give me the keys to the Cadillac. He said he knew all along that he should have sold it to me for a dollar because he knew I wasn't the kind of person to be so EXPLETIVE DELETED!! stupid as to marry a EXPLETIVE DELETED!! ballet dancer and you had already shown a penchant for doing stupid things such as going steeplechase racing with a naked woman on a Clydesdale."

"Yes, sir," Phil said. "I understand the former pastor-in-charge's reasoning."

He handed Colonel O'Shaughnessy the keys to the Cadillac.

"You better fill it up as soon as you can, sir," Phil said. "It's almost on empty."

"I'll take that under advisement, even knowing that I shouldn't pay a whole lot of attention to any advice offered by someone who has displayed such monumental EXPLETIVE DELETED!! stupidity."

"Yes, sir. Just take it for what it's worth."

"Let me tell you what happens now, Technical Sergeant Williams. Your luggage and your Viennese ballet dancer will be unloaded from my Cadillac and into a truck, three-quarter-ton four-by-four, which Berlin Brigade has provided. Orders are in the process of being cut relieving you under dishonorable conditions from the Thirty-third CIC and assigning you to the Replacement Company of Berlin Brigade.

"On your arrival there — because we are Americans and believe that no one, not even a miserable EXPLETIVE DELETED!! like you, is guilty until proven guilty in a court-martial — you and your EXPLETIVE DE-LETED!! ballet dancer will be housed in transient noncommissioned officers' quarters.

"Don't make yourselves too comfy, because the first thing tomorrow morning a board of officers will convene to decide your fate. I wouldn't be at all surprised if by this time tomorrow you will be Recruit Williams, pay grade E-1, making little rocks out of big ones in the Berlin Brigade Stockade Wing of Spandau Prison."

"Yes, sir."

"You are dismissed, soon-to-be-ex-Technical Sergeant Williams."

Brunhilde surprised Phil — as much as she had surprised him by appearing in the bed, dressed as she was in the Hotel Bristol —

by refusing his offer of taking all the money he had and going back to Vienna.

"The wording was 'for better or worse,' " Brunhilde said. "Weren't you listening? The least I can do is stick around until they tell you how many years you'll be making little rocks out of big ones before I have to go back to Vienna and try to support myself while waiting for our child to be born in shame by standing in the rain in front of my beloved Wiener Staatsoper and selling pencils out of a tin cup."

She could not be dissuaded from her decision.

Phil was later to learn, over the many years of their marriage, that she rarely could be dissuaded from any decision she made.

The next morning, as Phil waited for whoever was going to drag him from the transient noncommissioned officers' quarters to wherever he was to be court-martialed, there came a knock at the door.

When he opened it, a second lieutenant of the Quartermaster Corps was standing there. Phil saw that he was wearing a ring identifying him as a graduate of the United States Military Academy.

He announced: "I am Second Lieutenant J. Thomas Smith, Junior, Technical

Sergeant Williams, and I have been appointed your defense counsel. We don't have time, as the court is on its way here, so very quickly, my legal advice is for you to plead guilty and throw yourself on the mercy of the court."

Phil opened his mouth to reply, but before he could say anything, the door burst open and a captain of infantry wearing the insignia of an aide-de-camp to a brigadier general burst into the room and called, "Atten-hut!"

Then a brigadier general entered the room, followed by a full colonel and a lieutenant colonel of the Judge Advocate General's Corps, a lieutenant colonel of the Quartermaster Corps, a lieutenant colonel of Military Police, a Corps lieutenant colonel of the Adjutant General's Corps, and half a dozen assorted field grade officers of various combat arms and technical services, half a dozen company grade officers of various combat arms and services, and four MPs, all enlisted men.

The company grade officers were immediately ordered from the room to find enough suitable furniture for a court-martial and enough chairs for everybody.

Finally, this was accomplished.

"If I may have your attention, gentlemen,"

the brigadier general said. "And yours, too, Technical Sergeant-for-the-moment Williams. This is my understanding of the situation. The senior Judge Advocate General's Corps officer, the colonel, will call the court to order. The next senior Judge Advocate General's Corps officer, the lieutenant colonel who will be serving as prosecutor, will read the charges. Technical Sergeant Williams will enter his plea of guilty or not guilty. The evidence will be heard. The board will debate. The board will then announce their decision of guilty as charged. The senior Judge Advocate General's Corps officer — the colonel — will pronounce the sentence, which I don't think should go so far as hanging but should be pretty stiff, considering what the accused has done.

"The MPs will then haul the prisoner off to Spandau, and you all can get back to your duties, and I can go meet my wife at the golf course. Any questions?"

No one had any questions.

"I will now leave the room and wait outside," the Berlin Brigade commanding general concluded, "as there are a bunch of EXPLETIVE DELETED!! pantywaists who would accuse me, if I stayed, of exercising undue command influence on this court-martial."

He then left.

The Proceedings proceeded to the part where the board president called upon the prosecutor to read the charges.

"May it please the court," the prosecutor said. "We have a small problem *vis-à-vis* reading the charges."

"Which is?"

"I can't find anything in the Uniform Code of Military Justice 1948 that makes getting married a violation of military law to the detriment of good military order and discipline and punishable by death or such other punishment as a court-martial may direct."

"Not only do I find that hard to believe," the JAGC colonel said, "but the general's not going to like it."

"Your Honor, I went over that EXPLETIVE DELETED!! UCMJ 1948 for hours. Until the wee hours, as a matter of fact. There's just nothing there."

"Perhaps you didn't know where to look. Somebody get me a copy of the UCMJ 1948."

This was done. The senior JAGC officer examined it very carefully. Twice.

"I'll be a EXPLETIVE DELETED!!, you're right. There's not a EXPLETIVE DELETED!!

thing in here that makes getting married to a EXPLETIVE DELETED!! ballet dancer a EXPLETIVE DELETED!! misdemeanor, much less a EXPLETIVE DELETED!! high crime, which is what we need here."

The senior JAGC officer then pointed at Second Lieutenant J. Thomas Smith, Jr., and said, "Go tell the general what you found in the UCMJ 1948 that will allow this court to send the accused you are defending to Spandau."

"Sir, there's nothing in the UCMJ 1948 that will allow us . . . you . . . to send Technical Sergeant Williams to Spandau."

"You tell the general that, Lieutenant. Perhaps because of your youth, he'll show you some compassion."

"So, what do we do with the EXPLETIVE DELETED!! now?" the commanding general of the Berlin Brigade asked, after he had himself perused the UCMJ 1948 and concluded it must have been written by the same EXPLETIVE DELETED!! pantywaists to whom he had previously alluded.

"General, we could take him to East Berlin, throw him out of the truck, and let the Russians deal with him," the Quartermaster Corps lieutenant colonel said. "Maybe they'd send him to Siberia."

"Frankly, that's the sort of stupid EXPLE-
TIVE DELETED!! suggestion I would expect
from a EXPLETIVE DELETED!! Quartermaster Corps officer," the general replied.

"May I ask why the general thinks my suggestion is stupid?"

"Because, stupid, if we turned the EXPLE-
TIVE DELETED!! over to the Russians, they'd
probably give the EXPLETIVE DELETED!!
another medal. Colonel O'Shaughnessy of
the German-American Gospel Tract Foundation told me they've already given the
traitorous EXPLETIVE DELETED!! the Order
of Karl Marx, Second Class, with pearls and
rubies."

"I take your point, sir."

"May I suggest, General," the Corps of
Military Police lieutenant colonel suggested,
"that we bust the EXPLETIVE DELETED!!
down to EXPLETIVE DELETED!! Recruit, pay
grade E-1, and then send him to the Quartermaster Corps, where he could stack one-
hundred-pound sacks of potatoes, or rice,
eight or more hours a day, to the point of
exhaustion, day after day in a dark ware-
house?"

"That's almost as stupid a suggestion as
the previous stupid suggestion," the general
replied. "May I tell you why?"

"Please do so, sir. I will take notes."

"For one thing, Colonel, the Quartermaster Corps has enough problems with its EXPLETIVE DELETED!! enlisted men as it is, and for another, since the EXPLETIVE DELETED!! UCMJ 1948 was written by EXPLETIVE DELETED!! pantywaists we can't bust the EXPLETIVE DELETED!! down to Recruit, pay grade E-1."

"Pardon the stupid suggestion, sir."

"Having said that," the general said, "there was something in your stupid suggestion that may offer some hope. I refer to what you said, I quote, 'eight or more hours a day, to the point of exhaustion, day after day, in the dark.' Surely there must be somewhere else in the U.S. Army where we could send this EXPLETIVE DELETED!! and cause that to happen to him."

"Sir, if I may make a suggestion?" Second Lieutenant J. Thomas Smith, Jr., Phil's defense counsel, asked.

"Why not?" the general replied.

"The U.S. Army School of Infantry Excellence at Fort Benning, Georgia."

"Huh!" the general exclaimed. "Go on, Lieutenant."

"If we sent the EXPLETIVE DELETED!! — I mean, my client, who would be the accused if it wasn't for the strictures of the UCMJ 1948 — there for infantry training, what would happen?"

"I have no EXPLETIVE DELETED!! idea," the general confessed.

"The United States Infantry Noncommissioned Officer Academy is a subordinate unit of the U.S. Army School of Infantry Excellence at Fort Benning, as is the U.S. Army School for those newly graduated from the U.S. Military Academy officers, of which I am a recent proud graduate."

"Bully for you, but so what?" the general asked.

"The Infantry Noncommissioned Officer Academy trains privates first class to be corporals, corporals to be sergeants, sergeants to be staff sergeants, and staff sergeants to be technical sergeants."

"Good for them," the general said. "So what?"

"Each course takes six months, during which the trainee, who is referred to as a candidate, undergoes five months of rigid physical training eight or more hours a day, to the point of exhaustion, day after day, in the dark. The other month is dedicated to shining the soles of their boots and learning how to shoot guns, and that sort of thing."

"How interesting. But what has that to do with our EXPLETIVE DELETED!!, who is already a technical sergeant, pay grade E-6,

because we can't bust his EXPLETIVE DE-
LETED!! down to Recruit, pay grade E-1?"

"Sir, my client, the EXPLETIVE DELETED!!,
is not an *infantry* technical sergeant. Which
means if we were to send him there, he
would have to start at the bottom, and take
the course prescribed for PFCs aspiring to
be corporals . . ."

"Goddamn it, you're a genius! Correct me
if I'm wrong, but what you're saying is that
if we send this EXPLETIVE DELETED!! to
Benning, he starts out taking the Corporal's
Course, which includes five months of rigid
physical training eight or more hours a day,
to the point of exhaustion, day after day, in
the dark. And when he finishes that, he
starts the Sergeant's Course . . ."

"Which includes five months of rigid
physical training eight or more hours a day,
to the point of exhaustion, day after day, in
the dark, yes, sir."

"Where's that EXPLETIVE DELETED!!
Adjutant General's Corps officer?" the
general snapped.

The officer in question popped to his feet,
stood at attention, and said, "Sir, I am here
awaiting to cheerfully and willingly obey any
orders the general might have for me."

"Immediately cut orders sending the EX-
PLETIVE DELETED!! to Fort Benning, Geor-

gia, for attendance at that school the lieutenant talked about."

14. TechSgt Williams, Philip W., 142-22-0136 NO SECURITY CLEARANCES OF ANY KIND detchd Berlin Brig APO 09237 trf in gr wp USASIE Ft Benning, Ga for purp of tng as Inf NCO. Tvl by Mil AT in unif dir. No DDERL Auth. Simul TVL of Dep Wife Brunhilde Wienerwald Williams INDIGENOUS BRIDE NO SECURITY CLEARANCES OF ANY KIND Auth. HG&PPL to follow when possible. Approp. 99-99999999911.

Phil explained to Brunhilde what his orders meant. He was detached from the Berlin Brigade and transferred to and would proceed to the U.S. Army School of Infantry Excellence at Fort Benning, Georgia, for the purpose of training as an Infantry Noncommissioned Officer. Travel by military air transportation in uniform was directed. No days of Delay En Route Leave were authorized. The simultaneous travel of his dependent wife, an indigenous bride who had no security clearances of any kind, was authorized. He confessed that he had no idea what HG&PPL meant.

[Two]

Fort Benning, Georgia
Monday, November 28, 1949

Their flight, aboard a USAF plane, had taken a long time. It first stopped in Giessen, Germany, where it took aboard a load of stoves, garbage cans, and other items being returned to what the Army called The Zone of the Interior for refurbishment. Then it flew to Naples, Italy, to pick up two one-hundred-pound bags of Strozzapreti — which means "priest-strangler" — a Tuscan pasta of which the wife of the assistant deputy chief of staff of the USAF was especially fond.

From there it had flown to Prestwick, Scotland, where it picked up in the duty-free store two cases of fourteen-year-old Famous Pheasant Scotch whisky, an intoxicant of which the second assistant deputy secretary of Defense was especially fond.

From Prestwick, the airplane flew across the wide, wide Atlantic Ocean at 275 knots per hour, landing in Goose Bay, Labrador. There it refueled before taking off for Washington, D.C., where it dropped off the Famous Pheasant and the Strozzapreti. Then it flew on to Fulton County Airport, near Atlanta, where the flight terminated.

The pilot announced that he would have preferred to terminate at Atlanta Airport, or at Lawson Army Airfield, which was on the Fort Benning reservation, but authorities there refused permission to do so as they classified the plane as an aerial disaster about to happen.

Fulton County Airport is near Fort McPherson, Georgia, which is built on the former site of the Atlanta Baptist Female Seminary and is named after Major General James Birdseye McPherson. Phil and Brunhilde took a taxicab to Fort McPherson, where he inquired about available transportation to his final destination.

"Yes, we do. Weekly service. Free. Unfortunately, this week's bus left ten minutes ago."

Earlier, while in the taxicab on the way to Fort McPherson, Phil had happened to notice that right outside the gate to Fort McPherson there was a business enterprise known as Kenny McLain's Previously Owned Motor Cars, and that a sign announced, "We Love Servicemen!!!"

Reasoning that if Mr. McLain was so stupid that he actually believed that any serviceman would believe Kenny McLain loved him, he could probably be talked out of a car at a price close to what it was actually worth. So he went there.

Thirty minutes later, Phil had negotiated the price of a ten-year-old Ford station wagon down to $900. At that point, Brunhilde asked if she might join the conversation. Ten minutes after that, after handing Mr. McLain $600, they drove off the lot in the ten-year-old Ford station wagon.

The Ford was of course not the Cadillac that Phil had grown accustomed to, but it did make it, forty-five minutes later, to their ultimate destination. He knew they were there, because behind an enormous, manicured lawn there was a sign:

WELCOME TO FORT BENNING, GEORGIA

HOME OF THE SCHOOL OF INFANTRY EXCELLENCE

ABANDON HOPE, ALL YE WHO ENTER HERE!

There was another much smaller sign on the enormous manicured lawn, stuck into the ground as "Keep Off the Grass!" signs are often stuck, that immediately caught Phil's attention:

SKEET TEAM TRYOUTS TODAY!!!!

SHOOT SOMETHING FOR YOUR COUNTRY!!

GIVE IT A SHOT!!

USAAMU 1002 FORT BENNING ROAD

Fifteen minutes after that, Phil was interviewed by an enormous fellow noncommissioned officer, a master sergeant, who had the friendly face of a constipated alligator, and was wearing a "shooter's vest."

Shooter's vests are sleeveless garments that shooters wear. They have two pockets, one on each side, capable of holding a box of twenty-five shotgun shells. There is enough room left over for the shooter to sew embroidered patches testifying to the shooter's marksmanship skills thereon.

To Master Sergeant Percy J. Quigley's vest were sewn embroidered patches identifying him as a shotgun instructor and as someone who had gone one hundred straight. There were two of these. The first, on the left, which apparently had been on Master Sergeant Quigley's vest for some time as it was frayed and faded, read, "1st Award — 100 Straight." The second patch, on the right, was essentially identical to the first, except it read "2nd Award — 100 Straight" and appeared to be almost brand-new. Phil decided this suggested Master Sergeant Quigley had first gone one hundred straight some time ago . . . say, five or six years ago . . . and had duplicated his superb marksmanship more recently, say, the day before yesterday.

"As I drove onto the post to report for duty to the Noncommissioned Officer Academy of the U.S. Army School of Infantry Excellence, I happened to notice your sign."

"Where are you reporting in from?" Master Sergeant Quigley said. "I ask because the minute I get a shooter trained, the EXPLETIVE DELETED!! Adjutant General's Corps sends the EXPLETIVE DELETED!! overseas, and I hate to waste my expert instructor's time on some EXPLETIVE DELETED!! who will be here at the USAAMU today and gone tomorrow."

"I was serving in Berlin, Master Sergeant."

"Doing what?"

"I was assigned to the German-American Gospel Tract Foundation."

"Chaplain's assistant, huh?"

"Something like that."

"And what makes you think you could

qualify for even the Junior Varsity of the USAAMU Skeet Team?"

"Frankly, I don't know if I could. But as a boy, I had a Sears, Roebuck single shot Economy Special that I loved dearly. I always thought that if I had some good instruction, I might learn how to really shoot."

"You ever see one of these before, Sergeant?" Master Sergeant Quigley inquired, holding up a Remington Model 1100 Skeet Special shotgun.

Phil of course knew the weapon. It was similar to the ordinary Model 1100 with which he had won the First Annual Berlin Brigade Brandenburg Gate Skeet Shoot, and identical to the one with which the Berlin Brigade commander had tried to hammer the fire hydrant on Pariser Platz into the cobblestones.

"Yes, I have."

"You ever fire one?"

"No, I haven't."

This was the truth. After he'd won the Diamond Grade Browning with full factory engraving, a gold trigger, and selective ejectors that had come with his winning of the First Annual Berlin Brigade Brandenburg Gate Skeet Shoot, there had been no reason to fire any kind of a Remington.

"Well, let me show you how it works," Master Sergeant Quigley said, and proceeded to do so.

Afterward he took Phil to the USAAMU Skeet Range. After learning from Master Sergeant Quigley that he would have to break at least seventeen "birds" to earn a place on the USAAMU Junior Varsity, Phil fired and broke sixteen.

"Well, I guess that blows my chances of winning a place on the USAAMU Junior Varsity Skeet Team," Phil said. "Thank you for allowing me to try."

"Actually, that wasn't at all bad for a beginner. Tell you what, Sergeant Williams. Consistency counts. So I'm going to let you have another shot. Shots. Twenty-five more shots. If you can break sixteen birds again twice in a row, you're on the USAAMU Junior Varsity."

Phil broke seventeen. Twice in a row.

"God EXPLETIVE DELETED!!" Master Sergeant Quigley exclaimed. "Am I a good judge of a potential good shot, or am I a good judge of a potential good shot? Let me see your orders, Sergeant, and tell me about the blonde in your beat-up old station wagon."

"That's my wife, the former Brunhilde Wienerwald."

"You got any rug rats?"

"No."

"I don't suppose she's knocked up? The reason I ask is that if you don't have any rug rats and your better half is not knocked up, what you'll get for quarters is a trailer. If, however —"

"My Brunhilde is in the condition you describe."

"Then you get a two-bedroom set of quarters in NCO Town, which is a good thing, because they come with a carport and I don't think that junk car of yours can stand many more nights out in the rain."

He then picked up a telephone, and Phil heard one side of the conversation that followed, to wit:

"Master Sergeant Quigley for Master Sergeant Richardson."

"How they hanging, you ol' EXPLETIVE DELETED!!?"

"And EXPLETIVE DELETED!! you, too, you EXPLETIVE DELETED!!. Let me tell you why I'm calling. I got a Tech Sergeant Williams here that just earned himself a spot on the USAAMU Junior Varsity."

Master Sergeant Quigley then covered the microphone with his hand and said, "He expected you last week, and wondered where the EXPLETIVE DELETED!! you were."

"We arrived at Fulton County Airport this morning at oh-seven-hundred and came directly here."

"On a plane?"

Phil nodded.

Quigley uncovered the microphone on his telephone.

"Sergeant Williams must have been on that USAF Round-the-World Garbage Pickup Flight. He got into Fulton County today at oh-seven-hundred . . .

"Anyway, Big Dick, he's here . . .

"Yeah, I've seen his orders and those no-security-clearance things. He was a EXPLETIVE DELETED!! chaplain's assistant for EXPLETIVE DELETED!! sake. If you're a EXPLETIVE DELETED!! chaplain's assistant, you don't need no EXPLETIVE DELETED!! security clearance . . .

"The reason you didn't think of that is because you've got EXPLETIVE DELETED!! for brains . . .

"You know as well as I do that that EXPLETIVE DELETED!! NCO academy has more EXPLETIVE DELETED!! instructors now than they know what to do with. They don't need one more, especially one who was a EXPLETIVE DELETED!! chaplain's assistant and I need him . . .

"Look, just cut some EXPLETIVE DE-

LETED!! orders assigning him to the USAAMU, and then get on the EXPLETIVE DELETED!! horn to base housing and get him a house in NCO Town. He doesn't have any rug rats, but his wife is expecting a blessed EXPLETIVE DELETED!! event . . .

"Okay. I owe you one. Don't take any wooden EXPLETIVE DELETED!! nickels," Master Sergeant Quigley said, hung up the phone, and turned to Phil. "Welcome to the Junior Varsity of the USAAMU, Sergeant Williams. Trust me. You pay attention to what I'm telling you, and in a year or two, you may get one of these for yourself."

He patted the one-hundred-straight patches on his shooter's vest.

[Three]

Quarters 103B
Bataan Death March Avenue
Fort Benning, Georgia
Tuesday, December 27, 1949

A month later a truck delivered to Quarters 103B on Bataan Death March Avenue in NCO Town, where Technical Sergeant and Mrs. P. W. Williams were now living, the HG&PPL mentioned in his orders.

HG, he came to understand, meant Household Goods. In this instance, this meant the shoeshine kit he had left in his suite in the field grade bachelor officers' hotel, as well as partially used tubes of toothpaste, bars of soap, and things of that nature, and the two alligator-skin cases containing his 12- and 16-bore Diamond Grade Brownings with full factory engraving, gold triggers, and selective ejectors.

As quickly as he could, he hid the shotguns under their mattress and told Brunhilde if she had any feelings for him at all, she would never tell anyone what he was hiding because if Master Sergeant Quigley ever learned about them he would be instantly sent over to the NCO Academy of the U.S. Army School of Infantry Excellence, where he would be subjected to rigid physical training eight or more hours a day, to the point of exhaustion, day after day, in the dark.

Brunhilde, surprising him, promised to keep her mouth shut.

And surprising him even more, she kept her promise.

PPL, he came to understand, meant Professional Papers Library. And in Phil's case, this meant the three volumes of The Daily Notes of CIC Administrator P. W. Williams.

These quickly joined the shotguns under the mattress.

[Four]

Over the next several months, things went well for Technical Sergeant and Mrs. Williams. Brunhilde complained every once in a while that she really missed her double Slivovitz with water on the side and her cigars, but understood that was the price she had to pay for having let her lust carry her away.

And she made some friends.

There were a number of other German-speaking women married to sergeants at Fort Benning and she had quickly met some of them. There were also a number of German-speaking women married to commissioned officers and gentlemen at Fort Benning, but they, of course, did not associate socially with their sisters unfortunate enough to be married to common enlisted men. The German-speaking women married to commissioned officers who belonged to the Fort Benning Chapter of the West Point Protective Association of course spoke only to each other.

Brunhilde's new German-speaking women friends quickly began to explain in detail what horrors she could expect when she got to the delivery room of the Fort Benning Hospital Maternity Ward, but she said that whatever these horrors would be, they were the price she would have to pay because she had been unable to control her lust.

On his part, Phil was learning that there were things associated with having one's wife in the family way that he had never previously considered. For one thing, now that she was eating for two, so to speak, her appetite doubled. And what she hungered for was filet mignon and fresh oysters, that sort of thing, as opposed to hamburgers and breaded fish sticks.

And she required additions to her wardrobe, as she was getting a little thick in the midsection and all of her shoes had apparently shrunk as she could no longer slip — or jam — her feet into them.

All of this cost money.

Phil had a nice little nest egg after two years on *per diem* in lieu of rations and quarters plus hazardous duty pay and especially after he had learned he could charge restaurant and room service charges to the CIA. But that nest egg was shrinking, if eggs can be said to shrink.

He was perfectly prepared to take a second job, so to speak, as many members of the USAAMU Varsity Team did, as bartenders in the many officers' clubs in which the Fort Benning Officer Corps slaked their thirsts.

The Varsity members could hold such

jobs, because they finished their shooting tours at about 1600, which gave them plenty of time to shower and put on their bartender's uniforms and get to the officers' clubs in time for the 1700 rush hour.

The Junior Varsity, on the other hand, was required, when the Varsity quit shooting at 1600, to "police the area for expended brass and hulls." This meant the spent casings of rifle and pistol cartridges and shotgun shells had to be picked up from the many ranges of the USAAMU, sorted by size, and then placed in boxes that then had to be loaded into Master Sergeant Quigley's Suburban.

Quigley generously took care of further disposal, which was whispered to be by selling them to the Columbus, Georgia, Reloader's Supply Company. Whether or not this was true, it was true that Master Sergeant Quigley had a Cadillac as well as the Suburban and had quite a reputation as a big spender at the Fort Benning NCO Club.

Policing the brass kept Phil at the USAAMU at least until 1730, which was too late to go to work at an officers' club bar, and almost too late to prepare whatever Brunhilde had found in the luxury foods section of the commissary for him to cook for her supper.

Phil was sorely tempted to get the hell off the Junior Varsity, which he could easily accomplish by going twenty-five straight, but feared that if he did so, Master Sergeant Percy J. Quigley would smell a rat about his suddenly improved marksmanship and ship him out to the NCO Academy of the U.S. Army School of Infantry Excellence, where he would undergo rigid physical training eight or more hours a day, to the point of exhaustion, day after day, in the dark.

So, as his nest egg shrunk by the day, he decided the best thing to do was stay with the Junior Varsity for a while.

[Five]

Quarters 103B
Bataan Death March Avenue
Fort Benning, Georgia
Thursday, March 9, 1950

A month after his HG&PPL arrived, so did his personal mail.

This consisted entirely of alumni news bulletins. Having nothing better to do at the time — Brunhilde was out with the girls learning more about what horrors she could expect to experience in the maternity ward — he read them.

The front page of one of them, the one from Groton, caught his eye. There was a photograph of a distinguished Groton alumni handing the Groton headmaster, the Reverend Peabody Jones, D.D., a check. Phil knew the chap to be Cumings Bradshaw IV because they had been at Groton together.

The accompanying story said that ol' Cumings was now editor in chief of the Old American Library, which was not surprising when Phil thought about it since ol' Cumings had been editor in chief of the *Monthly Grotonian* and had told Phil that when he finished at Groton and then at Harvard, he was going to ask his father to buy him a publishing company, as he didn't want to follow his father into the hedge fund trade because of its crass commercialism.

An idea popped into Phil's mind that at first seemed insane, but after some thought he decided might not to be so insane after all. He had said more than once that his perusal of CIC agent reports *vis-à-vis* the sexual hanky-panky of field grade officers and their dependents for strikeovers, grammatical errors, and ambiguities had given him enough knowledge of such hanky-panky to write a book.

What the hell? What have I got to lose? he

thought aloud, and reached for the telephone.

Ol' Cumings wasn't at the Harvard Club, but Phil ran him to earth at the 21 Club at 21 West Fifty-second Street.

Cumings came on the line: "Phil, old boy! How the hell are you? I've always wondered what happened to you after you got the boot from our beloved Groton."

"I went into the Army, Cumings, old chum, where I have had many experiences which I have been thinking of turning into a book. I wondered if you, as esteemed editor in chief of the Old American Library, might be interested in publishing it."

"There is always a market, old chum Phil, for books about our brave men in uniform, just so long as the patriotism, devotion to duty, courage, et cetera, is liberally laced with sex, the more perverted the better."

"Really?"

"I EXPLETIVE DELETED!! you not, old chum. So why don't you take a shot at it, so to speak, pop it into an envelope, and send it up here for me to peruse?"

Phil immediately, which means that very night, started work on what was to become his first published work, *Comfort Me With Love,* which is what a general's wife had ordered her husband's aide-de-camp to try to do.

The first passages of the work were written in pencil on a lined pad on the kitchen table of Quarters 103B on Bataan Death March Avenue in NCO Town, but the next day — and every day after that — Phil brought an Underwood typewriter home from the USAAMU and creatively wrote on that.

Brunhilde thought his creative writing was a *dumme EXPLETIVE DELETED!! Verschwendung von Zeit,* which means, "stupid EXPLETIVE DELETED!! waste of time," but he persevered, and a month later, when he had finished, he popped the pages into an envelope and sent them off to ol' Cumings for his perusal.

A week later, a letter arrived:

THE OLD AMERICAN LIBRARY
MADISON AVENUE AT 51ST STREET
NEW YORK CITY, NEW YORK

OFFICE OF THE EDITOR IN CHIEF

Dear Old Chum Phil —
I have now had the chance to peruse your manuscript, "Comfort Me With Love," and re-

grettably must inform you its 100 pages do not meet our minimum page count of 200.

On the other hand, it shows some promise, and I am enclosing herewith a contract for its publishing and a check for $500, which we in the publishing profession call an "on signing" payment. If you double the length of your literary work to 200 pages, and said doubling meets my approval, there will be another check for $500 which we in publishing call the "on acceptance" payment. Even further down the pike, there will be still another check for $500 when the book is published, which we plan to do so with a cover price of $ 0.25.

If I don't get the expanded manuscript within six months — and the more sex you can get into the expansion the better — you will have to return the "on signing" check for $500.

With best regards and fond memories of our days at dear

Old Groton, I am,

        Faithfully yours,

            Cumings

      Cumings Bradshaw IV

It took Phil — who had, the reader with even a half-decent memory will remember, literally years of experience removing excess verbiage from draft reports — about six days to put excess verbiage into his first draft of *Comfort Me With Love* and pop it into an envelope to send it to ol' Cumings for his perusal.

Ten days later, he got the $500 "on acceptance" check, and immediately began work on Opus #2, to which he gave the tentative title *Comfort Me with Cucumbers,* which was what a lieutenant colonel of the female persuasion had asked her lady friend, a captain, to do.

It is germane to note here that at this time Phil was being compensated for his labor at the USAAMU at a monthly rate of $367.70, and thus regarded each of the $500 checks as a EXPLETIVE DELETED!! fortune.

It is also germane to note here that Phil had learned that Brunhilde devoutly believed that money was made to be spent as quickly as possible and as he thought he should be establishing a little nest egg for his soon-to-be-born firstborn, he didn't tell her the truth, the whole truth, and nothing but the truth about his income from his creative writing. Specifically, he told her the total amount came to $500.

She was pleased to hear this, commenting that perhaps his idea to be a writer wasn't as much of a *dumme EXPLETIVE DELETED!! Verschwendung von Zeit* as she had previously thought.

The next step in Phil's new publishing career came with the arrival of the galley page proofs for *Comfort Me With Love*. When ol' Cumings had telephoned to announce, "I'm shipping you the galleys," Phil had a mental picture of two or more old-time nautical vessels with banks of oars protruding from their sides arriving at Quarters 103B on Bataan Death March Avenue on a flatbed eighteen-wheel truck.

The galleys turned out to be unbound pages of *Comfort Me With Love*. As soon as he made any corrections to them, the corrected pages would be sent to the printer for printing, binding, and ultimate release to the public.

Then Phil saw the title page: *A Novel by Philip W. Williams III.*

And he was as unexpectedly thrilled as he had been when he went in their bedroom at the Hotel Bristol and found Brunhilde lying on the bed in transparent intimate undergarments and with a rose in her teeth.

It was, like the sight of Brunhilde lying on the bed in transparent intimate undergarments and with a rose in her teeth the day of their marriage, something he would remember to his dying day.

But then a chill swept through his body.

He suddenly realized that with his name on the cover, the Army would quickly deduce that the literary lion writing in such detail about the hanky-panky of majors and up and their dependents was actually Technical Sergeant P. W. Williams of the USAAMU and then his EXPLETIVE DELETED!! or his EXPLETIVE DELETED!! — probably both — would really be in a crack.

What he needed was a *nom de plume,* which since he now spoke French, he knew meant pen name.

After many hours of deep thought and study of telephone books, he had narrowed the myriad name possibilities down to two. One was "Tom Clancy," which he thought had a really nice writer's ring to it, and the other was "Wallingford Philips," of which he one day could prove ownership if the need arose.

Unable to make an intellectual decision

between the two, he flipped a coin . . . and Tom Clancy lost.

[Six]

Fort Benning, Georgia
Monday, June 5, 1950

When the first ten free bound copies of *Comfort Me With Love* by Wallingford Philips arrived several months later, he looked at his first published work as awestruck as he would be at 0545 the next day when he looked for the first time at the somewhat ruddy wrinkled face of Brunhilde Williams.

Not his wife, but his firstborn.

The way that happened was that shortly after one a.m., he had been awakened by Brunhilde, who reeked of Slivovitz and had a cigar clenched between her teeth.

"Take me to the hospital!" she had ordered. "My day of reckoning for not being able to control my lust has arrived."

"I couldn't help but smell the Slivovitz and see the cigar," Phil said as he hastily dressed.

"I've been on the wagon for eight months," Brunhilde replied. "And suffered the pangs of unsatisfied nicotine addiction for a like period. That's over. It's been over since Mother Nature told me This Is The

404

Day, which occurred about a half hour ago. Got it?"

Approximately four hours later, he was allowed into Brunhilde's room, where Brunhilde was cradling an infant in her arms. The only reason Phil was allowed into the room at that time was that the chief of obstetrical services hoped that Brunhilde's husband could convince the new mother to give up her cigar, which he had been so far unable to do.

Finally, the chief of obstetrical services admitted defeat and left the new family alone.

"What are we going to call it?" Phil asked.

"It's a her, stupid," the new mother said.

"Well, what are we going to call her?"

"If she had been a he, what would you have suggested we call him?"

"I was thinking along the lines, should that have occurred, of Philip Wallingford Williams the Fourth. Sort of a familial tradition."

"I think it's a great familial tradition," Brunhilde said. "Say hello to your daughter Brunhilde, Daddy."

[Seven]

Fort Benning, Georgia
Friday, October 6, 1950

The next four months or so were a mixed bag for Phil.

On one hand, he realized that for the first time in his life, he was really in love.

With Brunhilde — the one in diapers, of course.

On those rare occasions when he was allowed to hold his firstborn in his arms, he made goo-goo eyes at her and made strange noises, to which she responded in kind.

He came to understand that Brunhilde was the only child he would ever have, as the day he brought Brunhilde and Brunhilde home from the hospital Brunhilde (the mother) moved him out of their bedroom and into the nursery, telling him that when the time came, she would move Brunhilde (the one in diapers) out of what had been their bedroom and back into the nursery and he could move back into Bedroom #1 with her.

From the way Brunhilde (the mother) was treating him — actually not treating him . . . it was as if he had suddenly become invisible — he thought that when the time came for him to move back into their bedroom, they would have to roll him in on a wheel-chair from where he would be living in the geriatric intensive care ward.

On the other hand, things at the USAAMU went well. He finally had enough of picking up brass and empty shot shells and "earned his way" off the Junior Varsity and into the big time, or Varsity.

What actually happened was that he had about six beers too many at lunch and forgot himself. What he did specifically was go ninety-eight straight — the first time he'd done that on a USAAMU range. Then, with two shells left, he compounded his sin by turning his back on the traps, bending over so that his head and the Remington Skeet Special were between his knees, and called for "doubles," which caused two birds to be thrown simultaneously from both the High House and the Low House. Both birds, which were of course #99 and #100 in his possible one hundred straight, disappeared in two puffs of black dust.

He waited for the ax to fall, but it didn't.

Master Sergeant Percy J. Quigley person-ally pinned his "1st Award — 100-Straight" embroidered patch to Phil's shooting vest at a specially called Retreat Parade, welcomed him to the Varsity Team, and told him to pack his bags, as the Varsity Team was going to Fort Dix, New Jersey, to compete against a team from the U.S. Coast Guard.

From the moment Phil had taken his head and the Model 1100 Skeet Special from between his knees, Phil had really expected that Master Sergeant Percy J. Quigley would personally take him over to the NCO Academy in handcuffs to begin the "eight or more hours a day, to the point of exhaustion, day after day, in the dark" regimen that would last until the day his enlistment was up.

The only things Phil could think of to explain Quigley's not having done so were that Quigley planned to arrange a fatal accident on the Fort Dix Skeet Range. Or that Quigley, himself a father, knew that new fathers often lost control, and took pity on him. Whatever the reason, Phil vowed it would be a cold day in hell before he would ever again be so foolish as to go one hundred straight again.

When he told Brunhilde that he was reluctantly going to have to leave her and Brunhilde alone for a few days, as the Army was sending him to Fort Dix, she replied, "I don't give a good EXPLETIVE DELETED!! where you go."

It was a reply Phil would grow very accustomed to as the years passed.

[Eight]

Fort Dix, New Jersey
Tuesday, October 10, 1950

They had no sooner gotten off the bus that delivered them to the Transient NCO Quarters at Fort Dix when Master Sergeant Percy J. Quigley took Technical Sergeant Williams's arm and said, "We have to talk!"

He led him to a small room and closed the door.

"Phil, did you see that EXPLETIVE DELETED!! sign?"

"Which EXPLETIVE DELETED!! sign was that, Master Sergeant Quigley?"

"The one that said 'Welcome USAAMU Skeet Team.' That EXPLETIVE DELETED!! sign."

"Yes, I did. I thought it was a nice gesture on the part of Fort Dix."

"Phil, the people we brought with us are not on the USAAMU Skeet Team. They are on the Fort Benning Skeet Team."

"I have no idea what you're talking about."

"We are going to compete against the U.S. Coast Guard Skeet Team. You know what that means, of course."

"I'm not sure."

"The EXPLETIVE DELETED!! Coast Guard has two hundred and thirty-five EXPLETIVE

409

DELETED!! installations around the world, each of which has a skeet field and a skeet team. They also have a bunch of EXPLETIVE DELETED!! boats from which they shoot at birds off the back."

"That's very interesting."

"The result of what I just told you is that the Coast Guard team against which what they think is the USAAMU team will compete consists of the best EXPLETIVE DELETED!! shooters in the entire EXPLETIVE DELETED!! U.S. Coast Guard. There is little question in my mind that the USAAMU Skeet Team could take them in fair conflict, but we don't have the USAAMU Skeet Team here with you and me. What we have is the Fort Benning Skeet Team, which is sort of the Junior Varsity to the USAAMU Skeet Team."

"You're suggesting there is a chance we could lose?"

"Indeed I am. And those EXPLETIVE DELETED!! sailors in the funny hats and the pants with thirteen buttons on the fly know that. The USAAMU Skeet Team is about to be grossly humiliated by the Junior Varsity of the U.S. Navy, a/k/a the EXPLETIVE DELETED!! U.S. EXPLETIVE DELETED!! Coast Guard. Unless . . ."

"Unless what, Master Sergeant Quigley?"

"Unless, against the odds, I manage to break my third one hundred straight."

"Good luck, Master Sergeant Quigley."

"And you, Technical Sergeant Williams, go three hundred straight."

"What makes you think I could accomplish such an amazing feat of marksmanship?"

"Because, Technical Sergeant Williams, the U.S. Army skeet world is a small world and I know who you are."

"Excuse me?"

"Where are you hiding those two Diamond Grade Brownings with full factory engraving, gold triggers, and selective ejectors, Williams, under your EXPLETIVE DELETED!! mattress?"

Phil blushed.

"Well, I guess my secret is no longer a secret. Why didn't you say anything?"

"Are you asking why didn't I drag your EXPLETIVE DELETED!! over to the NCO Academy and tell my friends there to really sock it to you, subjecting you to physical training 'eight or more hours a day, to the point of exhaustion, day after day, in the dark'?"

"I admit the thought may have crossed my mind, Master Sergeant Quigley."

"I was going to wait for you to humiliate

411

me with your superior marksmanship before our teammates *and then* I was going to drag your EXPLETIVE DELETED!! over to the NCO for *twelve* hours of physical training to the point of exhaustion, day after day, in the dark."

"I see."

"But you didn't do that. You were a team player. Not only did you keep your average well below mine, but you gave your teammates little pointers so they could up their averages."

"I thought that was the right thing for me to do."

"So the choice is yours, Technical Sergeant Williams. You can go three hundred straight tomorrow and save the USAAMU from humiliation at the hands of the EXPLETIVE DELETED!! U.S. Coast Guard, in which case all will be forgiven, I will name you deputy chief marksmanship instructor of the USAAMU and you can have just about anything else your little heart desires. Alternatively, if you do not go three hundred straight tomorrow, say hello to the NCO Academy of the U.S. Army School of Infantry Excellence and *twelve* hours of physical training to the point of exhaustion, day after day, in the dark, until your period of enlistment concludes."

"Would that anything else my little heart desires include a forty-eight-hour pass?"

"What an odd question."

"I have a friend in New York City, a chap I went to school with, who has been after me, if I had happened to be in the neighborhood, to drop in for a chat."

"You go three hundred straight tomorrow and you can have two weeks to go to New York to chat with your friend."

"Forty-eight hours will be more than enough, as I am anxious to return to Fort Benning and my darling Brunhilde, the one in diapers."

[Nine]

The Harvard Club
27 West 44th Street
New York City, New York
Thursday, October 12, 1950

Phil, two days later, at the noon hour, turned off West Forty-fourth Street and passed through the portals of the Harvard Club of New York, Inc., and told the man at the desk that he was to be the luncheon guest of Mr. Cumings Bradshaw.

"Would that be the Bradshaw Hedge Fund Cumings Bradshaw the Third, sir? Or the Old American Library Cumings Bradshaw the Fourth? Both gentlemen are honoring the Harvard Club with their patronage today."

"The latter."

"You'll find Bradshaw Four drinking his luncheon in the bar, sir."

"Long time no see, Phil, old boy," Cumings Bradshaw IV greeted Phil. "May I offer you a vodka martini, no vegetables, to cut the dust of the trail?"

"Don't mind if I do, Cumings, old chap."

The waiter appeared and took ol' Cumings's order, which he immediately modified: "You'd best make those libations doubles, as when this gentleman hears how shoddily this Groton Old Boy has treated him, another Groton Old Boy, he'll need it."

The waiter left, whereupon Mr. Bradshaw IV turned to Phil and said, "Our libations will go on my tab, that is to say the Old American Library's tab, old boy, inasmuch as I wish to make amends for the shoddy way in which I, as editor in chief of the ol' Old American, have been treating you."

"How shabby? You're going to publish four of my novels and have advanced me fifteen hundred dollars per book for the privilege of doing so. As we sergeants say, that ain't too shabby."

414

"Alas, it is. That fifteen hundred dollars per book is, I mean."

"Tell me more, Cumings, old boy."

The waiter delivered their double vodka martinis, no vegetables, and left.

"Mud in your eye, old boy," Cumings said, raising his glass.

"Up yours, Cumings," Phil responded. "Tell me how you've been treating me shabbily at fifteen hundred per book."

"Well, old boy, when Daddy bought me the Old American Library as a graduation present on my graduation from Fair Harvard, he offered me some professional advice based on his years as a hedge fund biggie.

" 'Cumings,' he said, 'the key to success in any business is to screw not your customers or your suppliers, but both.' He was speaking figuratively, of course, not physically.

"I of course took Daddy's advice to heart from the day the ol' Old American opened its doors for business. And I must say, with all modesty, we've been doing very well following that 'screw not your customers or your suppliers, but both' business philosophy."

"Why don't you get to the point, old boy?" Phil said evenly.

"Righto! You understand, of course, that as an author you fall into the 'supplier' category. If publishers didn't have a supply of manuscripts from authors, where would they be?"

"I see your point."

"Well, one day a couple of weeks ago, sitting at the bar at ol' Winged Foot, I had an epiphany, which I don't have to tell you, because you are an author who knows many big words, means a sudden realization: a sudden intuitive leap of understanding, especially through an ordinary but striking occurrence."

"I know the word."

"What I suddenly realized was that when I came across a first draft of a manuscript, yours, that showed great potential, I followed Daddy's advice to screw the supplier whenever possible and got you to sign a contract, actually contracts, plural, which screwed you royally."

"You're talking about the fifteen hundred?"

"That, too, but also with regard to other contractual details. For example, if *Comfort Me With Love* is sold to Hollywood for adaptation into a motion picture, the proceeds therefrom go five percent to you and ninety-five percent to the Old American

Library, which is to say, me."

"That sounds a bit unfair."

"Of course it is, but first-time novelists are so thrilled with getting a contract that they'll sign anything I send them."

"So that's what this is all about, Cumings, old boy, you want to tell me you're sorry you screwed me?"

"That, too, of course, but primarily to tell you what I've done to rectify the screwing I've given you."

"More money, perhaps?"

"That, too, of course, but primarily to tell you that I've talked the matter over with ol' Cushman Johns. You remember him, of course, from dear old Groton?"

Phil searched his memory. "Tall, thin drink of water, played the harmonica, looked like a skinny Abraham Lincoln?"

"Right. He was two years ahead of us at Groton, and then two years ahead of me at Harvard, because you never got to go to Harvard."

"What about him?"

"Well, ol' Cushman is now a literary agent, one of the better ones. So I popped the galleys of *Comfort Me With Love* over to ol' Cushie-Baby, as he's known in publishing, and asked him what he thought could be done with it. He promptly replied he was sure he could unload it onto J. K. Perkins & Brothers, Publishers since 1812, for a price in the five-figure range. That means a figure between $10,000.01 and $99,999.99. A penny more and it becomes six figures."

"You're kidding, right?"

"I EXPLETIVE DELETED!! you not, Philip, old chap. So I told Cushie-Baby to have a shot at seeing what he could work out. And he did. And as we speak he's on his way here, to speak with you, enormously relieved he's not going to have to go all the way to wherever the hell you live in the Deep South to do so."

Cushman Johns, of Cushman Johns & Associates, Authors' Representatives, came into the bar of the Harvard Club fifteen minutes later.

"I vaguely recognize the face," he said to Phil, "but can't put a name to it. I deduce further that since you're sitting here in the bar of the Harvard Club wearing a very nice J. Press tweed jacket, you're one of us. But what I'm here for is to deal with some sergeant ol' Cumings here has turned up who, truth being stranger than fiction, has come up with a manuscript that's going to make me some real money, so I don't have time to stroll down memory lane with you.

Perhaps some other time."

"Still wearing those really ugly blue suede shoes, I see, Cushman," Phil said.

"Then we do know one another? Harvard, perhaps?"

"Try Groton. My name is Philip Williams."

"Of course it is!" Cushman Johns said. "And I really would like to swap stories of dear Old Groton with you, Philip, old boy, but I can't, as I am here to deal with this Sergeant Wallingford Philips who ol' Cumings here has turned up."

"You're looking at him," Phil said.

"Let me give you," Cushman Johns counseled Phil ten minutes later, "the lay of the land over at J. K. Perkins & Brothers, Publishers since 1812, before we go to meet Chauncey S. 'Steel' Hymen, vice president, publisher, and editor in chief of J. K. Perkins & Brothers, and the other members of the triumvirate at the 21 Club."

"Why are we going there?" Phil asked.

"Because the Harvard Club now lamentably lets practically anyone in, which cannot be said of the 21 Club. If you take my point, I will proceed with giving you the lay of the J. K. Perkins business landscape."

"Please do."

"It is run by a triumvirate, anchored by 'Steel' Hymen. He is a great editor and publisher, but knows zilch about money. The money is handled by 'Two Gun' David Gobbet, so called because he is the current Fast Draw Champion of the Upper East Side of Manhattan Chapter of the Single Action Colt .45 Fast Draw Association.

"David knows zilch about literature or editing, but is a good man with a dollar. The third corner of the most successful management triangle in publishing is a woman whose name escapes me at the moment. Formidable female. She knows zilch about money or editing or publishing, but, being a woman — it's the nature of the beast — manages to take credit for all of the good work done by Steel and Two-Gun."

"I understand."

Readers of a romance novel such as this understandably would be bored with the details of what happened that afternoon in the 21 Club, so they will not be chronicled in detail here.

Suffice it to say that sitting at the bar right under the picture of the actor David Niven, who before he went on to cinematic glory sold intoxicants for the 21 Club and is fondly remembered by the proprietors, Phil signed a forty-eight-page new contract that among other things provided for the repurchase from the Old American Library of all the contracts for books save that of *Comfort Me With Love* and their resale to J. K. Perkins & Brothers, Publishers since 1812, for a price in the very, very high five-figure range. Each.

When Two-Gun Gobbet handed him all the checks with all those zeros on them, he asked if Phil, since he was around soldiers, and soldiers have guns, if Phil might be interested in becoming an out-of-town associate member of the Upper East Side of Manhattan Chapter of the Single Action Colt .45 Fast Draw Association.

Phil told him he would give the invitation serious consideration, as he didn't want to do anything at all to annoy "the Perkins money man" until he had deposited all the checks with all the zeros on them — and ensured that they indeed cleared — in the account he had maintained in the Park Avenue and Fifty-seventh Street branch of the First National City Bank of New York since he was six years old.

On the way back to Fort Benning, Phil decided he would have to tell Brunhilde (the one he was married to) about his good fortune. Then he decided that maybe telling her how much good fortune there was might be a mistake and decided instead to tell her they could now afford a slightly newer, say three-year-old, Ford station wagon to replace the one they had now and leave it at that.

She was delighted with that news, and that may — on the other hand, may not — have had something to do with the surprise she had in store for him.

That was that when he started to retire to his bed in the nursery, he heard a sharp piercing whistle, and when he went to investigate what his wife wanted, found Brunhilde in her bed wearing nothing but a rose between her teeth.

"Guess what your prize is if you can guess which baby has moved into the nursery and who gets to move back in here," Brunhilde said.

A second child was born to Technical Sergeant and Mrs. Williams nine months later.

He was named Philip Wallingford Williams IV.

XII
PHIL BECOMES
SECRETLY FAMOUS

[One]

After Phil's return to Fort Benning and the USAAMU from his meeting with ol' Cushman Johns and the star of the J. K. Perkins & Brothers, Publishers since 1812, Management Troika, Chauncey S. "Steel" Hymen, to find, so to speak, Brunhilde (the one he was married to) waiting for him with a rose in her teeth, a good deal happened. Including, of course, the birth of Philip Wallingford Williams.

Comfort Me With Love by Wallingford Philips had been published and found immediate success. It started out as #6 on *The New York Times* Cheap Paperbacks Best-Seller List, rose in three weeks to #1, and stayed there for three more weeks, when it moved to the *Times*'s General Paperback Best-Seller List at #2.

Suspecting this was going to happen, the Old American Library published the fifth *et seq* editions with a new cover price of $0.35 and a new cover. The latter was far less lurid than the original cover, which permitted sale of the book to the general public, rather than only in the Adult Toys & Naughty Books outlets that had previously been the only points of sale.

Then it set publishing history.

Chauncey S. "Steel" Hymen invited the publishing press (*The New York Times Book Review, Publishers Weekly,* et cetera, and book reviewers from major newspapers) to a luncheon at Sardi's in Manhattan.

There, to the popping of champagne corks, the vice president, publisher, and editor in chief of J. K. Perkins & Brothers, Publishers since 1812, announced that J. K. Perkins & Brothers, Publishers since 1812, had acquired the hardback rights to *Comfort Me With Love* from the Old American Library and would publish it with an embossed cover just as soon as it could be rolled off the presses of R.R. Donnelly & Company as a public service to those lovers of literature who wished to add it to their collections of great books in their personal libraries.

This was the first time in publishing memory that a hardcover book had been published as a result of the sales of a paperback work. Previously, it had always been the other way around, i.e., hardcover, then paperback.

On the one hand, these developments were naturally pleasing to Phil, because they meant there would be more checks with lots of zeros on them forthcoming. On the other hand, the concomitant publicity this generated *vis-à-vis* Wallingford Philips scared the living EXPLETIVE DELETED!! out of him.

To wit: What would happen if the Army found out that Wallingford Philips — who was writing all these terrible things about the hanky-panky their majors and up, and the dependents thereof, were in the practice of practicing during their off-duty hours — was really Technical Sergeant Philip W. Williams of the USAAMU?

The terrible and likely possibilities began with physical exercise twelve or more hours a day, to the point of exhaustion, day after day, in the dark, and got worse from there.

He confided his fears to his new author's representative, Cushman Johns, who agreed it was a problem inasmuch that if Phil were making little rocks out of big ones at the Army Prison at Fort Leavenworth, Kansas, twelve or more hours a day, to the point of exhaustion, day after day, in the dark, he would have precious little energy left to devote to his creative writing.

"I think what we should do, Phil, old chap, is call in the Rabbi. It will cost you a EXPLETIVE DELETED!! arm and a leg, but advice from the Rabbi is invariably worth every EXPLETIVE DELETED!! dime it costs."

"Who's the Rabbi?" Phil asked.

"You've never heard of the legendary Gustave Warblerman, L.L.D., literary legal counsel to the giants of literature?"

"Can't say that I have. And why do they call him 'the Rabbi'?"

"Because he has the soft eyes and benign ambience of a Jewish clergyman at one of the better temples. This masks of course his true persona. And right now, trust me, old chap, you need him."

On being apprised of the problem, "Rabbi" Warblerman said he was quite sympathetic as once, in his youth, he, too, had been a common enlisted man and thus knew to what depths those EXPLETIVE DELETED!! West Pointers would go to stick it to some poor EXPLETIVE DELETED!! enlisted man who dared question their claim to semi-divinity.

He recommended a program of disinformation.

"I'm in your capable hands, Rabbi," Phil

said. "Do whatever you think should be done."

"Only those whom I have skewered with my legal genius call me 'Rabbi,' Phil. My friends, and you may now include yourself in that select group, call me either 'Gus' or 'Your Honor.' "

"Gus, Your Honor, please do what you think should be done," Phil said.

He did.

Word was leaked to the publishing press that there was no such person as Wallingford Philips, and that Wallingford Philips was the *nom de plume* of Friar Aloysius of the Order of Cistercians of the Strict Observance, who resided at the Abbey of Gethsemane in Kentucky, and who did not give interviews to the press, because Trappist monks don't even talk to each other, much less to the press.

This worked, and the Army never found out that Phil was really Wallingford Philips or vice versa as long as he was in the Army. When they did find out his true identity, that is to say Wallingford Philips's true identity, Phil was out of the Army and it was too late for them to wreak vengeance upon him.

But this is getting a little ahead of the narrative of this romance novel, so back to it:

The other thing that bothered Phil was the necessity of concealing his newfound affluence from both the U.S. Army and from Brunhilde, the one he was married to. He had to conceal it from Brunhilde because he knew the moment she learned about it, the Brunhilde in diapers would find herself rolling around in a baby carriage manufactured by the Rolls-Royce Motor Car Company of Crewe, England, and the Army would wonder how the wife of Technical Sergeant Williams had come by the wherewithal to be so kind to her offspring.

He had told her that they could afford a newer Ford station wagon to replace the one he'd bought from Kenny McLain's Previously Owned Motor Cars outside Fort McPherson and which now, at almost fifteen years of age, was in terminal shape. So shortly thereafter they carefully drove it to the Columbus Ford and Jaguar Motor Company in Columbus, Georgia, and bought, on time, a five-year-old Ford station wagon in less terminal shape.

While Brunhilde was discussing the financial terms of the deal, Phil's eye fell upon something in the dealer's new-car showroom with which he immediately fell in love, specifically a British racing green Jaguar motor car with chromed wire spoke wheels like a bicycle.

He learned that day that the pain caused by not having the money to buy something every fiber in your body wants is nowhere near as painful as not being able to buy something every fiber in your body wants when you do have the money to buy it but can't because of other circumstances.

He managed to resist the temptation to buy the Jaguar that day — but it was a battle. He managed to resist it again six months later when their "new" Ford station wagon turned out to be more of a lemon than their old one, and they had to return to the Columbus Ford and Jaguar Motor Company for another one. The silver Jaguar then on display was even nicer than the first one he had seen, and he had been instantly enamored of it, as it had bloodred leather seats, chromed wire wheels, and, on its nose, the iconic hood ornament known to those in the know as the Jaguar Leaping Leaper.

He resisted the temptation to do something stupid like buy the silver Jaguar — which would really cause the Army to ask questions he didn't want to have to answer — despite many sleepless nights thinking about that adorable little chromed Jaguar on the hood, which was of course the bonnet, as Jaguars were of English manufacture, until after Philip Wallingford Williams IV was born into this vale of tears.

It was at this point that they again returned to the Columbus Ford and Jaguar Motor Company, this time to buy yet another Ford station wagon, replacing the three-year-old lemon with a new one. The occasion was Brunhilde-the-wife's announcement that she was again in the family way, having graciously moved him back into their bedroom as she had previously and with the same result.

Phil, without betraying the fact there was ample cash in the bank to pay cash, had told her that they had probably established enough credit for the Ford Motor Credit Company to loan them enough to buy a new vehicle, and she liked the idea, as in seven months they would have three little ones, not just two, to ferry from hither-to-yon.

While Brunhilde-the-wife was dealing with the salesman *vis-à-vis* the terms of the ten-year note Phil was later that day to sign, Phil sought out the proprietor of the Columbus Ford and Jaguar Motor Company and asked if he could have a quiet word with him.

"What would you say, sir," Phil said when

he had been led into a dark corner of the service department, "if I told you I am prepared to buy that silver car with the wire wheels and the chromed Jaguar on the bonnet on your showroom floor right now, providing that you let me keep it in your service department so that I can come here at night and on weekends and take my Jag for a little spin?"

"Let me get this straight. You want to buy the car and leave it here and then come and take it for a little spin every once in a while?"

"That is correct."

"Then I would say, Sergeant, although I can't smell anything, that you've been at the sauce and I will thank you not to waste any more of my valuable time. You know how much that Jaguar sells for?"

"To the EXPLETIVE DELETED!! penny," Phil replied, and then thrust a pigskin leather folder before the proprietor's eyes. "You know what that is?"

"I do indeed. I saw a story in *Forbes* magazine," the man said. "It's a City-Diamond pigskin leather checkbook holder, which the First National City Bank of New York issues to stinking rich people who maintain a minimum average balance of one million dollars in their City-Diamond checking accounts. I'm actually wondering where you found it, or more likely stole it."

"If you would be so kind, sir, as to call the number on the check and say 'Hotshot,' I feel my charge account executive at the First National City Bank, whose name is Ellward T. Fobby, will quickly assure you not only that this is my checkbook, but also that the funds in my account were acquired through absolutely legal means that he is not permitted to divulge."

"Let me get you a cup of coffee, Sergeant, while I get on the phone."

For the next seven months, Phil frequently visited the Columbus Ford and Jaguar Motor Company's garage late at night, or sometimes in the wee hours of the morning, to visit with the adorable chrome Leaping Leaper on the bonnet of his Jaguar, and to polish him and the rest of the car with loving swipes, and every once in a while to take quick trips up and down the Georgia back roads.

But — even after Franz Josef Williams was born, when he had been sorely tempted to drive his second son home from the hospital in the Jaguar — Phil never drove it in the daylight or told Brunhilde-his-wife what he had done.

[Two]

Foggy Point, Mississippi
Wednesday, December 15, 1954

Phil's enlistment was finally over. He was discharged under Honorable Conditions from the U.S. Army.

"Brunhilde," he said, when he returned for the last time to his — actually, their — quarters at 103B Bataan Death March Avenue in NCO Town, "before we go out to the USAAMU for the last time to say *auf Wiedersehen* to Master Sergeant Percy J. Quigley and the boys, we have to make a quick stop at the Columbus Ford and Jaguar Motor Company to pick up my Jaguar, which I have somehow neglected to mention to you previously."

"I knew the minute I laid eyes on you that you weren't to be trusted," Brunhilde replied. "But I am so happy to be able get the hell out of here that I will delay your punishment for the time being."

Two hours later, Brunhilde-the-wife, driving the Ford station wagon with "Little Phil," as he had come to be known, and Franz Josef aboard, and Phil, driving the Jaguar with "Little Brunhilde," as she had come to be known, and four cases of Winchester AA 12-gauge shotgun shells contain-

433

ing 1 1/8 ounces of #9 shot that had been Master Sergeant Quigley's farewell gift aboard, departed the gate of the U.S. Army School of Infantry Excellence for the last time.

They headed for Troy State University in Troy, Alabama, where Phil — presuming their offer to make him a junior assistant athletic coach (Archery) was still open — thought he might begin his new life as an academic until he could figure out how to disclose his undisclosed affluence to the woman with whom he and their three children were marching down the path of life.

Mrs. Brunhilde Williams took a good look at the campus of Troy State University and all the cultural and other advantages of the school and its campus, and announced that if Phil thought she would live here, he had best change his thinking, as rather than living here, she would rather spend the rest of her life at 103B Bataan Death March Avenue in NCO Town in Fort Benning.

"So, if you had another option, what would you like to do, Brunhilde?" Phil asked.

"As we came down that cow path — the one with potholes and signs that said U.S.

Highway 231 South and was lined with cheap motels — I noticed another sign that said, *Stay on US 231 South to the Sun-Drenched White Sandy Beaches of Gulf Shores, Alabama.* So get in that funny-looking car of yours and follow me. We're off to Gulf Shores!"

Perhaps predictably — Phil had learned that the mother of his children could, and often did, get lost in a closet — rather than ending their drive that day in Alabama, they wound up in Mississippi, in a bucolic burb called Goodhope.

There, when Phil asked a local if he could recommend a place where for a low price they might rest their weary heads overnight, the Goodhopian — who quietly hated all foreigners and, even more, all Yankees, and to his joy realized he had one of each at his mercy — directed them to the Grand Hotel, which he said was in Foggy Point, just a couple miles down Mississippi Scenic Highway 98.

Phil questioned the "low price" business as soon as they drove up to the magnificent front door of the Grand Hotel. Then he saw the cars parked there, the most shabby of these being an enormous two-year-old glistening black Mercedes-Benz. There were more Jaguars than Phil had ever seen in one place before.

"Speaking of Jaguars," Brunhilde said. "We're going to get something to eat and rest our weary heads in here if you have to sell yours to pay for it."

Brunhilde fell in love with the Grand Hotel the moment the tailcoat-attired *maître d' hotel* in the Grand Dining Room handed her a menu and then announced the special offering of the day was *Weiner Schnitzel Auf Weiner Art,* and the dessert of the day *Sachertorte mit importiert vom Ausland Schlagsahne,* which Phil knew, since he spoke German, meant a layer cake named after the hotel immediately behind the Vienna State Opera, and came topped with whipped cream imported from abroad.

Brunhilde told the headwaiter she was both thrilled and surprised that the menu featured such Viennese delicacies. He replied that this was because of Madame Violet Tenser-Schultz McNamara, who was a very good friend of Mrs. Gladys O'Hara, whose husband K.J. owned the Grand Hotel and just about all of the rest of Foggy Point, including the Foggy Point Country Club, and was — Madame Violet Tenser-Schultz McNamara was, or had in her bygone youth been — a Viennese.

436

When the headwaiter had left, Brunhilde said, "Say goodbye to your Jaguar, Phil. This is where we're going to stay until we run out of money, including the money we're going to get by selling that stupid Jaguar you never should have bought in the first place."

Phil of course wasn't worried about having to sell the Jaguar to pay the bill, because of the cash he had in his City-Diamond account. And anyway, the hotel cost was a deductible expense against his income tax. Rabbi Warblerman had told him that because of a decision of the U.S. Supreme Court (*The Internal Revenue Service v. William Bradford Huie*) all of his travel expenses, no matter where in the wide world he chose to go, or how much money he spent in so going, were deductible.

In what became known as "the Whorehouse Decision," Rabbi Warblerman had told Phil, the Supreme Court had unanimously come down on the side of the plaintiff, the journalist and author Mr. Huie, who claimed that all of the expenses he had incurred making trips to a Nevada brothel called The Fly Inn for Fun Inn, Inc., which had its own landing strip and into which he had flown in a Cessna 172 aircraft to stay ten days, were deductible as legitimate research expenses as he planned to pen a report on what life was like in The Fly Inn for Fun Inn, Inc., said report to be published in one or more magazines in which Mr. Huie had previously published reports of other notable topics he had investigated.

The steadfast position of the IRS, in brief, was that everybody already knew what goes on in a whorehouse, and that it was simply outrageous and possibly criminal for Mr. Huie to expect the American taxpayer to subsidize his amoral and prurient interest in what goes on in a whorehouse by claiming it as a deductible research expense.

Mr. Huie's law firm, which listed Mr. Warblerman as "of counsel" on its letterhead, countered that under Amendment I to the United States Constitution ("Freedom of the Press") the IRS had no more right to question what Mr. Huie thought he should investigate and write about than it did to question the veracity of all those congressmen who denied doing all the multifarious amoral and illegal things everybody knew they were doing.

The effect of the decision with regard to Phil was that he could deduct all his travel expenses because he was a bona fide author.

"Your Honor," as Phil was now permitted

to call Mr. Warblerman, said that Phil now qualified as a published writer because he had actually published and sold books, not just bought a typewriter and announced his intention to someday write one, as a whole lot of people had done once the Whorehouse Decision became public.

[Three]

On their fifth day in the Grand Hotel in Foggy Point, Brunhilde, as she had every day since they checked in, got in the Ford station wagon "to have a look around Goodhope."

While she looked around, Phil spent the days watching their children as they splashed around the hotel's enormous swimming pool, which was said to be the largest swimming pool east of the Mississippi and certainly looked like it.

Upon her return on the fifth day, there was a man in a suit and tie with her. He carried a briefcase, from which he took a six-inch-thick stack of legal forms that Brunhilde then laid before Phil, handed him a pen, and showed him where he was to make his mark.

"What am I signing?"

"We've bought a house," Brunhilde said. "Or will have bought a house just as soon as you sign these documents. You don't have to worry about how we're going to pay for it for two reasons. One, you're getting it on a Veterans Administration loan, which means no money down and $136.70 a month for the rest of your life. And, two, because after we sell your Jaguar, we'll have enough money to pay that $136.70 a month for a year, after which the Brunhilde Wienerwald School of Ballet should be up and running and in a position to pay the $136.70 every month *ad infinitum.* So sign it and shut up."

XIII
FAMILY WILLIAMS MOVES QUICKLY UPWARD SOCIALLY

[One]

Goodhope, Mississippi
Sunday, January 16, 1955

Phil liked the house Brunhilde had found for them on Creek Drive in Goodhope, which had three bedrooms, two baths, and a one-car garage. Creek Drive was thus called because it was on The Creek, which previously had been Fly Creek, and which in turn had previously been called Bayou Volante, which Phil, because he spoke French, knew meant "Flying Creek."

Investigation revealed that it had so been named by Jean-Baptiste Le Moyne, Sieur de Bienville (February 23, 1680–March 7, 1767), who had spent a few days in what was now Goodhope, Mississippi, en route to establish a city that would come to be known as New Orleans, Louisiana.

The Sieur had apparently been in what

441

was now Goodhope during a heavy rain, which had turned the gentle flow of the creek, or bayou, in what was now Phil's backyard, from a trickle into something stronger, which the Sieur decided justified deeming the creek Bayou Volante.

Brunhilde was very disappointed that what she thought of as her Ford station wagon would not fit into the garage. The Jaguar, however, not only did fit therein but left enough space, almost five feet over, so that Phil could build a shelf two and a half feet wide on which he put his "new" — actually used — $29.95 Underwood typewriter from Sears, Roebuck and Company. A "kitchen stool" ($6.50) from the same place fit in the remaining two and a half feet, and he now had an office in which to practice his creative writing.

In his own exploring of Goodhope, Phil found two things that interested him.

One was a small private school called the Organic School, which brought to Phil's mind the growing of tomatoes, for example, in water, but which he learned in fact made reference to the theories of the school's founder, Miss Marietta Fieldstone, who held that education was organic to life. But what really interested him about the school was that it didn't grade the students on how well they did on tests, but rather on how hard they tried.

Brunhilde, his daughter, was almost five, and soon she would be old enough for the pre-kindergarten class at the Organic School.

Phil was later to serve for decades on the Board of Directors of the Marietta Fieldstone School of Organic Education even though he had only a two-year College GED diploma and everybody else had either a Ph.D., an M.D., a D.D.S., or similar degree, or was, as the president of the board was, an Organic Old Boy in addition to being president of the First National Bank of Goodhope, which gave that gentleman a pass, educational degree–wise.

But that's me getting ahead of this romance novel narrative. Again.

The second thing Phil noticed while driving the Jaguar around Goodhope was the Goodhope Slightly Used Children's Clothing Discount Outlet.

He had already learned that as sure as the sun rises in the morning, two weeks after one buys one's children a pair of shoes, one's children have outgrown them.

So one day, he loaded Little Phil, who was now four, into the Jaguar and drove him to the Goodhope Slightly Used Children's

Clothing Discount Outlet. As he was trying slightly used shoes on Little Phil, he heard a woman's voice say, "What a darling little boy!"

He got to Little Phil in time to keep Little Phil from kicking the lady, who had a kind face and a motherly ambience.

"Thank you," Phil said.

"Can he swim?" the lady asked.

"No, but he splashes around wading pools very well."

"My God, if you don't teach that darling little boy to swim, he'll drown. Goodhope is, after all, on Muddiebay Bay, into which other navigable streams, such as The Creek, formerly Bayou Volante, flow. There's water all over the place."

"I take your point," Phil said.

"And I mean right now," the nice lady said. "Not when you get around to it in your own good time."

"I don't want to drown, Daddy!" Little Phil said, looking up at Big Phil and tugging at his hand. "I want to learn to swim so I won't drown and have to be buried where the worms will eat me up."

The nice lady nodded. "The thing for you to do, sir, if you don't mind a little advice, is take this darling little boy out to the Grand Hotel, this very afternoon, look up Woody Woodson, the Foggy Point Country Club's recreation director, and enroll this darling little boy in the swimming classes."

"Please, Daddy!" Little Phil said.

"I appreciate the suggestion, but I've been out there and I'm not sure I could afford that," Phil lied, and was immediately ashamed of himself, as this was not the truth and this was obviously a nice lady.

"Maybe, were it not for that overpriced Jaguar I saw you drive up in, you would have the money to buy swimming lessons for this darling little boy to keep him from drowning."

"I'm sorry I tried to kick you when you called me a 'darling little boy,'" Little Phil said.

"Two things," Phil replied. "Not only does a little more than eight years remain on the ten-year loan I used to purchase my Jaguar, but I have two more children in addition to this one, which is why I can't afford to take any of them out to the Grand Hotel and buy them swimming lessons."

The lies came quickly to his lips because of his experience in the intelligence business, where he had acquired the ability to lie automatically when the truth got in the way. Being a good liar was of course a hallmark of someone in the intelligence business.

But now he was ashamed of having lied to this nice lady. That had never happened before.

Is it conceivable, Phil wondered, *that I have been away from the German-American Gospel Tract Foundation long enough to have reacquired some shreds of decency?*

"I can understand that," the nice lady said, "as I have a son about your age who is always buying fancy cars he can't afford and otherwise squandering money. So, not because I like you, but because I don't want this darling little boy to drown, I'll tell you what I'm going to do."

"Yes, ma'am?"

She scrawled something on the back of a business card of the Goodhope Slightly Used Children's Clothing Discount Outlet and then handed it to him.

"Take this out to the Grand Hotel, ask for Mr. Woody Woodson, and give this to him. If you don't, and this darling little boy drowns in Muddiebay Bay because he can't swim, God will get you."

Phil read what the nice lady had written on the back of the card.

Woody, get this gentleman a Non-

"Please, Daddy, do what the nice lady says, so I can learn to swim and won't drown," Little Phil said.

"And please give some consideration *vis-à-vis* whether or not you need that expensive XJ6," the nice lady said. "Or whether that money could better be spent on this darling little boy."

She bent over and kissed Little Phil.

Really surprising Phil, Little Phil kissed her back. Usually when women tried to kiss him, he either kicked them or spit at them, or both.

[Two]

Woody Woodson turned out to be a bald, diminutive gentleman in his fifties with dark tanned leathery skin, the result of having spent most of his life in the fierce southern sun.

"Gladys gets what Gladys wants around here," Woody said when he had read the back of the card the nice lady had written on. "Consider it done. If you will give me your address, the post office will shortly deliver thereto your membership card in the Foggy Point Country Club, the keys to your

447

locker at the clubhouse, the keys to your personal golf cart, a sticker for that Jaguar you drove up in which will permit you to leave the grounds without having your Jaguar searched for items you might have purloined, and some other stuff. Welcome to the Foggy Point Country Club."

"I can't do it," Phil said.

"You understand that all of the above is free of charge because of Gladys's generosity?"

"That's the problem. She is being so generous because she doesn't think I have any money. Tell me, how much does it cost to join the Foggy Point Country Club?"

"More than you can afford."

"Tell me."

"Well, first you have to be recommended by two members, and three is better. Then you submit a cashier's check for five large —"

"As in five thousand?" Phil interrupted.

"Uh-huh, five large, which partially covers the cost of the Full Background Investigation. The results of the FBI, as we call it . . ."

"I know both what an FBI is and what the FBI is. Go on."

". . . the results are presented to the Membership Committee, which meets twice a year, for their review. One Proposee in three makes it through that review, as the Membership Committee loves to drop black balls in the box. Then, presuming the Proposee has gotten that far, his application is sent to Mr. K. J. O'Hara, Senior, who is president of the Foggy Point Country Club, because he owns it, for his review. One Proposee in four gets past Mr. K.J. Senior's review. If Mr. K.J. Senior does, the Proposee then is permitted to submit the cashier's checks."

"Checks plural? And what are those?"

"One is for fifty large and that pays for basic membership. Another five large is a deposit against towels, soap, and other incidentals at the clubhouse, and the third is also for five large, and is a deposit against the loss overboard of fishing rods, et cetera, when fishing off the club's fishing vessel, a seventy-two-foot Bertram called *The K.J.* And the fourth check is for just one large to cover the first month's dues."

"I see."

"And then the whole thing is laid on Gladys's desk for her approval. Nothing gets done around here unless Gladys approves."

"Just to satisfy my curiosity, what would happen if I were to write a check here and now for sixty-six thousand? Sixty-six large? Would that get me in?"

"You're kidding, right?"

Phil shook his head.

"No, I just can't bring myself to take advantage of Gladys's generosity because I lied to her about not having any money. I just can't take a free membership."

Woody Woodson considered that for a full thirty seconds.

"Well, like I said, what Gladys wants around here, Gladys gets. Most of that Membership Application Procedure is just EXPLETIVE DELETED!! anyway to keep the riffraff out. Gladys wants you in the Foggy Point Country Club, and I can't see where your being willing to pay for it is an insurmountable barrier in that regard. Write the check, and we'll see what happens."

[Three]

The next morning at about eight-thirty, Phil was hard at work writing creatively on his plywood desk in the garage when he heard the telephone ringing. When it stopped ringing, he decided that Brunhilde had either answered it or decided not to as she was busy setting up the advertisement she planned to run in *The Muddiebay Register-Press* newspaper announcing the establishment of the Brunhilde Wienerwald School of Classical Viennese Opera Ballet Dancing.

450

When the telephone rang again several minutes later, he decided much the same thing. But when it rang again several minutes after that, he said, "Oh, EXPLETIVE DELETED!!," and went into the house and answered it.

"Mr. Philip Williams, please," his caller said. "Mrs. Gladys O'Hara calling."

"This is he, ma'am."

"You lied to me yesterday, didn't you, Philip? The reason I know is because when I came to my office this morning I found a check drawn on your First National City Bank of New York City-Diamond checking account for sixty-six thousand dollars to pay for your membership in the Foggy Point Country Club."

"I'm not exactly broke, ma'am."

"Nobody with City-Diamond checking accounts is. I know that because I have one. Why did you intimate to me that you were broke, or nearly so?"

"I'm trying to keep my affluence under wraps, Mrs. O'Hara."

"I understand that. But surely your wife knows?"

"My wife, the former Vienna State Opera ballet dancer, known professionally as Brunhilde Wienerwald, is the primary person from whom I wish to hide my affluence and thus keep it under wraps."

"I understand that, too. One of my friends, Madame Violet Tenser-Schultz McNamara, is a former Vienna State Opera ballet dancer, and they apparently teach them from childhood that money is to be squandered as quickly as possible. But before we get into discussing Viennese State Opera ballet dancers, I'm curious about the source of your affluence, if I may ask."

"I'm trying to keep that under wraps, too, Mrs. O'Hara."

"I was afraid of that. I can say this to you, Philip, because I am old enough to be your mother: It is never too late to repent and start off on a new path of righteousness and legality. So tell me in what dishonest and amoral way you came by your affluence, and maybe I can help you avoid getting jailed."

"Actually, I'm a writer. An author."

"You're not going to lie to me again, I hope, as I know that only the masters of literature, such as Wallingford Philips, my favorite author, make enough money to qualify for First National City Bank of New York City-Diamond checking accounts."

"Guilty, ma'am."

"Now I know you're lying. Only someone like Friar Aloysius of the Order of Cistercians of the Strict Observance who obviously spent years listening to women confessing all in the confessional could have such intimate knowledge of women as the Friar, writing as Wallingford Philips, shows he has. All I can do when finishing one of the Wallingford Philips novels is to thank God those Trappist monks can't talk out loud to anybody and expose more of the secrets of the female heart than he already has."

"My real name, ma'am, is Philip Wallingford Williams the Third. Does that suggest anything to you?"

"What comes to mind is 'truth is stranger than fiction,' but what you've just said pushes that pretty close to the end of that envelope."

"Nevertheless, I am Wallingford Philips. Or Wallingford Philips is Phil Williams, whichever you prefer. Cross my heart and hope to die, Mrs. O'Hara. But please keep that under wraps."

"Well, I certainly can understand, presuming you're no longer lying through your teeth, why you would want to, as you say, keep that under wraps. Thousands, hundreds of thousands, of women would compete for the privilege of murdering you in the most painful way for exposing the secrets of their hearts to the men of the world."

"Are you in that number, Mrs. O'Hara?"

"No, I'm not. I decided early on in life that one has to play the cards one has been dealt. So when I married ol' K.J. I decided to play it straight with him, and it's worked out very well. I've spent a lot of time trying to talk my sisters in the gentle gender to play it straight with their husbands, but they just won't listen. I suppose it's the nature of the beast, as you've so often said in your novels."

"Yes, ma'am."

"Phil, why don't you call me Gladys? I think that we have a commonality of interests and may be useful to one another and that should put us on a first-name basis."

"How may I be useful to you, Gladys?"

"Let's talk about commonality of interests first. You said that you don't wish to share the full extent of your affluence with your wife. I understand that because I don't wish to share the full extent of my affluence with my husband."

"Why not? I thought he was loaded. I thought he owns the Grand Hotel, the Foggy Point Country Club . . ."

"And he and his lunatic brother also own a trucking company and have a lunatic idea

454

that they can take the wheels off an eighteen-wheeler's trailer and load what's left — they are calling the box a 'container' — onto ships and then put the wheels back on when the ship gets where it's going. They're going to call this lunatic idea The Land-To Sea-To-Land Company. But I digress."

"Yes, ma'am?"

"There is loaded, Phil, and then there is *loaded,* if you take my meaning."

"You mean you're more loaded than your husband?"

"Let me put it to you this way. Do you smoke, Phil?"

"Yes, ma'am. Excuse me, Gladys. I do. Cigars."

"Good for you. Cigarettes are really bad for you. But since you smoke, I presume you've heard of the American Tobacco Company?"

"Yes, I have."

"It was founded about the time of the American Revolution by a man named Heinrich Merican. Merican was my maiden name. I was born to Heinrich Merican the Fifth and his wife, Gertrude, as their only child, and later became their sole heir.

"When the first Heinrich Merican started selling Pocahontas cigars, he had the cigar bands and the labels on the box the cigars were going to go in printed by Benjamin Franklin in Philadelphia. Well, Ben was getting on in years, and as everybody knows he liked a little sip of Pennsylvania corn whisky every hour on the hour starting with his breakfast.

"Whatever the reason, what happened was a small printing error."

"I don't think I understand."

"The label on the cigar boxes and on the cigar bands was supposed to read 'Fine Pocahontas Cigars. A Merican Tobacco Company product.' Old Ben dropped the space between the *A* and the *M* in Merican. What the labels now read was 'Fine Pocahontas Cigars. AMerican Tobacco Company product.'

"Well, faced with having to peel all the labels off the cigar boxes and having to tear all the bands off the cigars and then glue the correct ones back on, ol' Heinrich said, 'To hell with it. Get the mislabeled cigars out to the public. Most of them can't read anyway.' "

"That makes sense," Phil said.

"And over the years the Merican Tobacco Company became the AMerican Tobacco Company."

"I see what you mean by 'there is loaded

and then there is *loaded.*' "

"If my husband, K.J. Senior, knew the full extent of my affluence, he would press upon me to financially support the idiot idea he and his idiot brother have about taking the wheels off perfectly good truck trailers, calling them containers, and then loading them on ships. Getting the picture?"

"Getting it. That's a dumb idea if I ever heard one," Phil said.

"We now turn to my eldest son, K. J. O'Hara, Junior, known as Junior, or Little K.J., who as I have previously mentioned is about your age, and whom I love dearly, much as you dearly love your Little Philip."

"What about him?"

"He needs some guidance, as I wish to dissuade him from his present lifestyle, which consists almost entirely of buying cars he can't afford even on the lavish allowance K.J. Senior insists on giving him, chasing airheaded blondes with large bosoms and tight little rear ends, and shooting at clay pigeons off our pier on Muddiebay Bay."

"He shoots at clay pigeons, you say?"

"He is the Browning Arms Company's most valued customer, as every time they change the location of a screw on their Diamond Grade Full Factory Engraved Over and Under shotguns with gold triggers and selective ejectors, he has to have it, as he believes it will make him a better marksman shooting at clay pigeons off our pier. So far he has bought nine such over-priced shotguns."

"That's what the Browning people are always telling people, in essence, 'Your scores will rise as does the price you paid for one of our better shotguns.' It is just not true."

"Try telling that to Little K.J.," Gladys said.

"I would be happy to, if you'd like."

"Why would he believe you?"

"At the risk of sounding immodest, once he sees me shooting doubles off your pier with my back facing the flight path with my head and my own Diamond Grade Full Factory Engraved Over and Under shotgun with gold trigger between my knees, he'll believe anything I tell him."

"I think that would do it," Gladys said. "Tell me about your wife, Philip. She obviously didn't marry you for your money, as you're keeping your affluence under wraps so as to conceal it from her. How would you describe her in one or two or perhaps as many as five words?"

Phil moved his lips as he counted to five on his fingers, and then said, "Decent, honorable, but often difficult."

"I understand, Phil, as that could be said about my friend Madame Violet Tenser-Schultz McNamara, who as I mentioned is — or was fifty years ago — also a Viennese ballet dancer. Phil, do you think it would be possible for you to point my jackass son away from airheaded blondes with tight rear ends and large bosoms and toward some females who are decent and honorable, if sometimes difficult? I would truly be grateful."

"Well, Gladys, I'm sure you know what they say about being able to lead jackasses to water, which in this case would be decent, honorable but often difficult females, but I'll have a shot at it, if you'd like."

"I'll think of some way to get you together."

"I'm at your service, Gladys. Is there anything else I can do for you?"

"Yes, there is. But I truly hesitate to ask."

"Feel free to ask away."

"I realize that it's asking a great deal, but do you think you could find it in your heart to autograph my personal first edition copy of *Comfort Me With Love*? The one that sold for a quarter and is now worth on the used-book market between three and five hundred dollars?"

"I would be happy to do so."

"Good. Thank you from the bottom of my heart. Just as soon as I get off the phone, I'll get it out of the safe and Rollo, the bell captain at the Grand, will get in the hotel's VIP Guest Rolls-Royce and bring it to you. Together with of course all the paraphernalia that comes to new members of the Foggy Point Country Club."

An hour later, Gladys called Phil.

"I am touched to tears by your inscription in *Comfort Me With Love,*" she said, her voice breaking with emotion.

"I thought you might be pleased," Phil said.

What he had written was:

To Gladys,
With fond wishes from her fond confidant, who trusts her with his secrets as she trusts him with hers.
Wally
(Wallingford Philips)

[Four]

Goodhope, Mississippi
Monday, March 7, 1955

Phil thought it almost inevitable that Brunhilde would eventually get to meet Madame Violet Tenser-Schultz McNamara, as they

460

shared a common background in that both had been dancers in the Corps de Ballet of the Vienna State Opera in Austria.

But he really could not have had any idea how soon that would happen, nor, in his wildest imagination, could not have guessed how it would change his and her social status in and around Muddiebay, Goodhope, and Foggy Point.

What happened was that three weeks after Phil and Gladys had become chums, Brunhilde saw an announcement in *The Muddiebay Register-Press* newspaper announcing a special, all–Johann Strauss program of Viennese music by the Muddiebay Symphonic Orchestra. It was going to be presented the following evening at the Muddiebay Symphony and Livestock Auction Hall in downtown Muddiebay.

Brunhilde thereupon announced that Phil was going to take her to this performance or could expect to sleep in the backseat of his Jaguar until death did them part.

Actually, Phil didn't mind all that much going. He liked Strauss and felt a little sorry for Brunhilde because, although her advertisement had been running every day in *The Muddiebay Register-Press* newspaper, there had been zero applications for matriculation in the Brunhilde Wienerwald School of

Classical Viennese Opera Ballet Dancing, which would be taught by a former dancer of the Corps de Ballet of the Vienna State Opera in Austria.

Brunhilde of course had the proper clothing to go to a symphony concert. Phil of course did not. But by then he had learned that the Goodhope Slightly Used Children's Clothing Discount Outlet had a sister — or perhaps brother — outlet, the Goodhope Slightly Used Gentlemen's Clothing Discount Outlet.

He went there and lucked out, and for $39.95 managed to deck himself out in white tie and tails. The collar was a little tight, and the tails a little long, but he thought he looked pretty spiffy when he loaded Brunhilde into the Jaguar for the thirty-odd-mile drive across the Muddiebay Causeway to the Muddiebay Symphony and Livestock Auction Hall in downtown Muddiebay.

When they entered the hall, a large and imposing septuagenarian woman — who was wearing about three pounds of pearls, a diamond tiara matching her dangling eight-inch diamond earrings, and an ankle-length mink coat — was standing in the middle of the entrance foyer.

"Mein Gott!" Brunhilde said. "Will you look

at that? She looks like a Hungarian madam who somehow got herself stuffed by a taxidermist."

Brunhilde spoke in German, because she knew her husband did, and she did not think it would be polite to share her little *bon mot* with the maybe three hundred other people in the entrance foyer who did not.

"Did I hear you speaking German in a gutter Viennese accent?" the septuagenarian asked, also in German.

"What's it to you, fat old Hungarian madam?" Brunhilde responded. "Who speaks lousy German in the patois of a Hungarian brothel madam."

"Well, if your name is Brunhilde Wienerwald, who is trying to pass herself off as a former member of the Corps de Ballet of the Vienna State Opera, I am here to expose you as a fraud before all these people."

"What makes you think Brunhilde Wienerwald isn't a former member of the Corps de Ballet of the Vienna State Opera, you overstuffed former brothel-keeper in your Shetland pony fur coat, glass fake diamonds, and pounds of phony pearls?"

"What would a former member of the Corps de Ballet of the Vienna State Opera be doing here in Muddiebay, Mississippi?"

"Well, off the top of my head, fat lady ex-madam, maybe she got carried away by lust and as a result had to marry a *gottverdammt* American who just moved here."

"Oddly enough, I've heard of that happening. As a matter of fact, fifty odd years ago, it happened to me, when I myself was a member of the Corps de Ballet of the Vienna State Opera."

"And why should you expect me to believe that *you* are a former member of the Corps de Ballet of the Vienna State Opera?"

"Because I know all the backstage secrets of my beloved Corps and I'll bet you don't."

"For example?"

"For example, how do members of the Corps de Ballet refer to the third stall in the ladies' restroom into which only lady members of the Corps de Ballet in the rank of dancer and above are permitted?"

"Ach, mein lieber Gott!" Brunhilde said. "If you know about that, then you must be bona fide and not a Hungarian whorehouse keeper."

"Answer the question."

"The Gusher," Brunhilde said. "Or Mount Vesuvius."

"And why do they call it that?"

"Because when you sit down on that thing, and do your business, and then yank on the chain, instead of the water going down, it erupts, or gushes, upward like Mount Vesuvius."

Madame Violet Tenser-Schultz McNamara reached for Brunhilde and gathered her to her breast.

"My dear sweet girl, I have misjudged you. Welcome, welcome, to Muddiebay, Mississippi!"

Then she turned and pointed to a septuagenarian gentleman in white tie and tails.

"That's my *gottverdammt* American," she said. "His name is Archie. Did you bring yours?"

Brunhilde pointed. "His name is Phil."

"Archie," Madame Violet ordered, "take this charming young woman and her *gottverdammt* American husband here to our box and give them a little champagne while I have a word with Whatsisname, the guy who owns the grocery stores, about a little announcement I want him to make before Maestro Whatsisname strikes up the band."

"Yes, dear," Archie said.

Five minutes later, a diminutive gentleman in white tie and tails and holding a baton allowing Phil to intuit he was Maestro Whatsisname, walked onto the stage to somewhat less than enthusiastic applause.

Then another gentleman walked onto the stage to somewhat greater applause, waited for it to die down, which didn't take long, and announced:

"I have an announcement, ladies and gentlemen, to make before the program begins. The Patroness of the Muddiebay Symphonic Orchestra, Madame Violet Tenser-Schultz McNamara, has told me that we have a distinguished guest in the audience tonight. She, like Madame Violet Tenser-Schultz McNamara, is a former dancer in the Corps de Ballet of the Vienna State Opera. Her name is Brunhilde Wienerwald and she's sitting up there beside Madame Violet in the Patroness's box. Why don't we give Madame Brunhilde a great big hand before the performance begins?"

They did, and the performance of the Muddiebay Symphonic Orchestra Viennese music began with "The Blue Danube," which is the name of the river, which is actually pretty muddy, rather than blue, that runs through the city of Vienna.

Phil was soon to learn the maestro's name was Stefan Woznitski and that he hated Viennese music.

The reason Phil learned this was because he had a visitor the very next day as he was writing creatively in his garage office on

Creek Drive. Phil had never met him before, but his face was familiar because he had been the gentleman who made the announcement the previous evening about Madame Brunhilde — and also because the large sign over Champ's Food Store #109 right there in Goodhope had his smiling face on it.

"Mr. Williams, I am Del Champs, president of Champ's Food Stores and of the Muddiebay Symphonic Orchestra. I am here to ask you to — to beg you to, if it comes to that — to accept a position on the Muddiebay Symphonic Orchestra's board of directors."

"That's very kind of you, but I think I'll have to pass. Thank you just the same."

"May I ask why?"

"May I speak freely?"

"Of course."

"While I certainly don't pretend to be an expert in classical musical, I couldn't help but think last night — as Maestro Woznitski led the Muddiebay Symphonic Orchestra in its version of 'The Blue Danube,' also known as *An der schönen blauen Donau* — that its composer, Johann Strauss the Second, sometimes known as Johann Strauss the Younger, never intended it to be played on two empty fifty-five-gallon oil drums, one xylophone, one steam whistle, and one jawbone of an ass. With that in mind, I don't think I'd be a happy camper on your board of directors."

"Well, let me first agree with that assessment of what Maestro Stefan Woznitski gave us last night. He tends to hate melodious Viennese music, preferring instead the compositions of modern — that is to say, painfully discordant — composers. Between you and me, Mr. Williams, I can't stand the Polack EXPLETIVE DELETED!! or his EXPLETIVE DELETED!! incredibly awful choice of musical selections. Two weeks ago, he had the orchestra play 'Ode to a Parisian Pissoir' by the Herzegovinian composer Humberto Jones. That really EXPLETIVE DELETED!! up my eardrums."

"Then why is he the conductor?"

"Because Madame Violet Tenser-Schultz McNamara likes him, and Archie McNamara is one of the major contributors to the Muddiebay Symphonic Orchestra, which usually runs at a loss."

"Well, that would explain that, I guess. What about the other supporters?"

"There's three other major contributors. One wishes to keep his support secret, because he's afraid of Madame Violet, the second is K. J. O'Hara, Senior, and I'm the other one."

"And what does Mr. McNamara think of Maestro Stefan Woznitski?"

"When Madame Violet's not around, Archie calls Maestro Woznitski 'that EXPLETIVE DELETED!! Polish Pissant.' "

"Then why does he give the money?"

"Archie said, when he sent me here today to ask you to join the board of directors, that, inasmuch as you're married to one of them, you may know how difficult former members of the Corps de Ballet of the Vienna State Opera can be on occasion."

"Ah. As indeed I do. Why do you think he told you to tell me that?"

"Archie also said that if your former member of the Corps de Ballet is as fond of Slivovitz, which I understand is a brandy distilled from Hungarian plums, as his, that is to say, Madame Violet is, he may have a solution for the dilemma."

"Which is?"

"That, to celebrate your swearing in as a member of the board, Madame Violet will have a small dinner at the McNamara mansion, which is called 'Pine Tree House' even though it's made of the finest California redwood, because Archie owns more pine tree forests in the South than anybody but Randolph C. Bruce, who with a little luck will never enter your life . . . Where was I?"

"Small dinner at Pine Tree House," Phil furnished.

"Right. At which dinner will be Archie and Madame Violet, and me as president of the symphony, and my wife, and you as the guest of honor, and of course your former ballet dancer. You and Archie will ply your respective wives with Slivovitz."

"That won't be hard. And what happens when the two ladies are bombed out of their minds?"

"You will drop into the conversation that you deeply admire Maestro Woznitski's version of 'The Blue Danube' because it is so much better than the overrated version of the original composition by that overrated Viennese composer Johann Strauss the Second. If you can get your wife to disagree with you —"

"No problem there."

"— this would cause Madame Violet to ally herself with your wife."

"That seems to be a very reasonable assumption to make."

"Then — this is where you really come in — you say that since you admire Maestro Woznitski so much that you couldn't possibly agree to fire him, despite all the unkind things he has been saying about both old and younger former members of the Corps de Ballet, even though firing him would please you, because you think that all former members of the Vienna Opera, young and old, are treasures.

"To which Archie will add, 'And I won't, either.' "

"And then," Phil responded, having had an epiphany, "Madame Violet will say, 'Archie, that miserable Polack has to go,' or words to that effect."

"Right!"

"And then Madame Brunhilde, as she now likes to be called, will say, 'You heard what Madame Violet said, Phil, that EXPLETIVE DELETED!! Polack has to go. And you will vote to get rid of the EXPLETIVE DELETED!!.' "

But then Phil had a second thought: "But what if Madame Violet and/or Madame Brunhilde asks, 'What unkind things has Maestro Woznitski been saying about our beloved Corps?' "

"Then, Phil, you would have to lie," Del Champs said. "And come up with something that would really enrage them. Could you handle that?"

"Del, old boy, *entre nous,* I have had professional training in lying through my teeth or otherwise. Trust me when I tell you that you are looking at one of the best liars you'll ever meet in this backwater of the world."

"I'm happy to hear that. So I can tell Archie you're onboard about being on the board?"

"Absolutely."

[Five]

A month after Phil joined the board of directors of the Muddiebay Symphonic Orchestra, and a week after that body announced with deep regret the resignation of Maestro Stefan Woznitski because he planned to follow his musical muse elsewhere, Rollo the Grand Hotel bell captain rolled up at the door of 105 Creek Drive in the hotel Rolls to deliver an invitation:

Mr. and Mrs. K. J. O'Hara, Sr.
Request the Honor of the Presence of
Mr. and Mrs. P. W. Williams III
At Cocktails and Dinner
To Celebrate the Institution of the
McNamara-O'Hara Chair of Classical
Ballet Dancing
At Hilly Springs College, Muddiebay,
Mississippi
Tuesday next at 4:30 p.m.

White Black Tie
Répondez s'il vous plaît, et veuillez ap-
porter votre chéquier

On reading it, Madame Brunhilde inquired, "What the hell does 'white black tie' mean? And what's that Frog all about?"

"It means a white dinner jacket with a black bow tie," Phil said. "This is going to be a classy social event."

"And what does it say in Frog?"

"Essentially: 'If it pleases you to do so, let us know if you're coming — and bring your checkbook.' "

"You mean we have to pay to get in this classy social event?"

"It means that your new bosom buddy, Madame Violet, and Mrs. O'Hara, who is throwing the shindig, are graciously permitting the affluent members of the Muddie-bay community, both those above and those below the salt, to make contributions to the McNamara-O'Hara Chair of Classical Ballet Dancing at Hilly Springs College, at which you will be an adjunct professor."

"How come you know so much about this classy social event?"

"I happened to bump into Mrs. O'Hara at

473

the Goodhope Slightly Used Children's Clothing Discount Outlet, where I was again buying shoes for Little Phil and she was buying shoes for her grandchildren, and she happened to casually fill me in."

That was not exactly true.

What had happened was that Gladys had confided in her confidant Phil that K.J. Sr. had been more than a little pissed when he heard how much it was going to cost him to fund the McNamara-O'Hara Chair of Classical Ballet Dancing at Hilly Springs College.

"Gladys," Phil had said, "I don't know how things are done here in Muddiebay, but in New York, Boston, and South Orange, New Jersey, the way things like this are done is that the people who get their names on a project, such as the McNamara-O'Hara Chair of Classical Ballet Dancing, arrange for other socialites and, more important, social climbers, to pay for it by throwing a party to which they otherwise would not be invited and telling them to bring their checkbooks."

"Okay. I'll throw a soiree. That would get the women, Phil, but what about the men?"

"You told me, Gladys, that this is a shotgun society, and that Muddiebay men will go anywhere at any time to shoot anything.

So why don't you quietly spread the word that there will be clay bird shooting off your pier while the soiree is going on?"

"You're a genius, Phil, my confidant. And . . . I just thought of this . . . it would give me the chance to put you and K.J. Junior together so that you can take him under your wing and divert him from buying exotic cars he can't afford and chasing airheaded blondes with large bosoms and tight little rear ends toward something approaching respectability."

"What the hell does this mean?" Madame Brunhilde asked, pointing to a handwritten addendum to the invitation, on the back thereof, which read *Don't forget to bring your shotgun.*

"I have no idea," Phil lied. "But if that's what our hostess wants, I couldn't leave my shotgun home."

[Six]

As Phil was taking his shotgun from the trunk of his Jaguar, which he had parked on the lawn of 1001 Scenic Highway 98, a canary-yellow Mercedes-Benz convertible pulled in beside him. A good-looking man in a white dinner jacket and black tie got out of it, bringing with him a shotgun case that Phil, because he knew a little bit about shotguns generally, recognized to be that of the Beretta Corporation, a firm that despite its being Italian made some fairly decent if outrageously priced shotguns.

"Good evening," the man said. "I couldn't help but notice the alligator-hide shotgun case you just took out of your trunk. Does it perhaps contain a Diamond Grade Browning Over and Under with full factory engraving, a gold trigger, and selective ejectors?"

"Know a little bit about shotguns, do you?"

"Actually, I know a great deal about just about everything," the man said with a smile. "In my line of work, I'm expected to. My name is Paul Twinings. And you are?"

"Phil Williams. And this is my wife —"

"I recognize Madame Brunhilde from her photographs in the press reporting the institution of the McNamara-O'Hara Chair of Classical Ballet Dancing. Welcome to the faculty of Hilly Springs College, Madame Brunhilde!"

Madame Brunhilde flashed him a dazzling smile.

"Madame Brunhilde, may I make a suggestion?"

"Of course you may, you charming gentleman!"

"I was going to suggest that, by sneaking around the side of the O'Hara mansion and going directly to the pier and busting a few birds right now, Phil and I could just about eliminate the risk of getting blown off the pier by the shotgunners there, as would be very likely later when the shotgunners get into the sauce. And then you and I, Phil, could go into the mansion and get into the latter."

"Great idea!" Phil said. "Not only has my experience with shotgunners on the sauce scarred me for life, but I have always advocated getting into the sauce as quickly as possible *ante* bird popping."

"Even though my husband thinks it's a good idea, which worries me," Madame Brunhilde said, "far be it from me to reject a suggestion suggested by a charming gentleman such as you."

There was a long line of men, each carrying a shotgun, lined up before and onto the pier. Phil's newfound friend Paul, crying, "Make way! Make way!" made his way through them onto and out to the end of the pier, where a man wielding what Phil, because he knew more than a little about shotguns, recognized to be a James Purdey & Sons Best Grade 12-bore shotgun.

"Oh, darn," Paul said. "One more proof that into one's life one must expect a torrent to pour."

"Excuse me?"

"The fellow with the James Purdey & Sons Best Grade 12-bore shotgun who just called for doubles and then missed one of them, and is saying all those crude, dirty, and sacrilegious words, is Randolph C. Bruce."

"I've been warned about him by Del Champs."

"Take heed of his warning, Phil," Paul replied, and then added, "And speaking of the devil, figuratively speaking, of course, there's ol' Del now."

Del Champs walked to them.

"I see that you've met Father Paul," Del said.

"Why do you call him that?" Phil asked.

"Because I'm polite. Did Father Paul point out Randy Bruce to you?"

"Yes, he did, and he told me to heed your warning."

"Well, maybe we'll get lucky and we can avoid him."

"Luck is not with us," Paul said as Randy walked up to them.

"Is this the EXPLETIVE DELETED!! Yankee I've been hearing about?" Randy Bruce demanded.

"Missed one, did you, Randolph?" Paul asked. "Even though I hate to judge lest I be judged, of course, I thought that might be the reason for your complete loss of temper and all that foul and sacrilegious language."

Before Randy could reply, K. J. O'Hara, Sr., and Archie McNamara both walked up to them. Both were carrying Winchester Model 12 pump action 12-gauge shotguns. K.J. Sr.'s had a rib mounted on its single barrel and Archie's did not.

"I'm not talking to you, Archie," Randy announced.

"Not that I give a goddamn — excuse me, Father, that slipped out — but why aren't you talking to me?"

"Because I suspect that harridan you're married to called my Auntie Abby and pressured her into pressuring me into coming here tonight and bringing my checkbook with me. It should go without saying that otherwise I wouldn't be here accepting your hospitality."

"I suspect that's exactly what happened," Archie said. "And I'm glad. And have you written a generous check?"

"Generous is not the EXPLETIVE DE-LETED!! word. My Auntie Abby and that overstuffed crone you're married to are not only pals but the aforementioned crone has convinced my Auntie Abby that this ballet EXPLETIVE DELETED!! is the height of culture and my Auntie Abby can't get enough of culture, which of course I have to pay for out of my Trust Fund."

A young man of about Phil's age — a Browning Diamond Grade Over and Under 12-bore with full factory engraving, a gold trigger, and selective ejectors cradled lovingly in his arms — walked over to them.

"Dropped one, did you, Randy?" he asked.

"EXPLETIVE DELETED!! you, Junior!" Randy replied, which told Phil that he was looking at K. J. O'Hara, Jr.

"Quickly changing the subject," K.J. Sr. said, "Junior, I want you to meet Phil Williams, whom my wife, your mother, tells me is a very good guy, even if he is a Yankee."

They shook hands.

"Normally, I don't shake hands with men my mother approves of, and that is especially true when they're Yankees. But I'm making an exception here because I suspect that alligator-hide case holds a Browning Diamond Grade Over and Under 12-bore with full factory engraving, a gold trigger, and selective ejectors."

"Thank you," Phil said. "Nice to meet you, too."

"May I see it?"

"Of course."

Junior examined it.

"One of the old models, I see. And, from the position of this screw, I deduce it is possibly even a prototype."

"Sometimes old is better than new," Phil replied. "This old-timer has served me well over many, many rounds of skeet and trap."

"Ha!" K.J. Jr. snorted.

"May I ask a possibly rude question, Mr. Williams?" K.J. Sr. asked.

"Why not?"

"What makes you think that that fancy shotgun of yours is any better than the classic Winchester Model 12s that Mr. McNamara and I have been shooting since we were boys?"

"Because, wielding this Browning, I am sure I can break more birds shooting at doubles than you can, even if I fire while bending over with my back to the line of flight and with my head and the gun between my knees and you firing standing up."

"That's a crock of EXPLETIVE DELETED!!," Randy Bruce said, "if I ever heard one."

"I'll tell you what I'll do, Mr. Bruce," Phil said. "I'll make you a little bet that Mr. O'Hara Junior here and I can shoot at two sets of doubles, for a total of four birds each, with him standing up and me bending over shooting between my legs, and I will do better than he standing up."

"How little a bet?" Randy Bruce asked.

"Your call, sir."

"Ten big ones a little too rich for your blood?"

"Ten big ones it is," K.J. Jr. said.

"I was asking him, Junior," Randy Bruce said. "Stop trying to steal my sure-and-in-the-bag ten EXPLETIVE DELETED!! thousand."

"How about ten for each of you, for a total of twenty thousand?" Phil said.

"I have a small problem with that," K.J. Jr. said, avoiding eye contact with K.J. Sr. "As I seem to have, even though it's only the thirteenth of the month, had to cover a number of expenses with most of this month's allowance, I don't have ten thousand dollars."

"I'll loan it to you," Phil said. "Because I know that you know how much the outcome will affect your relationship with your father in the future and that you will shoot accordingly."

"I have a big problem with this," Paul announced. "Because it sounds like a wager, which means a gamble, and gambling, while not a mortal sin, is still a sin."

"Well, I can certainly understand that," Phil said, although he didn't and was wondering how he could shut up his new-found friend. "But how about this? Rather than having the losers pay the winners, the losers will pay the twenty big ones into the McNamara-O'Hara Chair of Classical Ballet Dancing Fund?"

"That'd work for me," Paul Twinings blurted a little too quickly. "Bless all three of you! And thank you, Phil, on behalf of Hilly Springs College."

Inasmuch as the typical reader of romance novels such as this is highly unlikely to be much interested in the precise details of a competitive shotgun marksmanship contest such as this, the narrative has been trimmed to the following, where it resumes immediately after the competition previously described concluded:

"EXPLETIVE DELETED!! EXPLETIVE DELETED!! EXPLETIVE DELETED!! EXPLETIVE DELETED!! EXPLETIVE DELETED!!," Mr. Randolph C. Bruce said so loudly he could be and was heard throughout the O'Hara mansion. "The EXPLETIVE DELETED!! Yankee did it!"

"I'll be a triple EXPLETIVE DELETED!! in

EXPLETIVE DELETED!! spades," Mr. K. J. O'Hara, Sr., said.

"Perhaps, K.J. Senior," Phil said, "you will now be able to find it in your heart to be less critical of your son, K.J. Junior, than you have been in the past."

"I'll try," K.J. Sr. said.

"Phil, my newfound buddy and role model and, I hope, shooting coach," K.J. Jr. asked, "why don't we go in the mansion and have a little taste of whatever your heart desires?"

As they were having their third little taste of Famous Pheasant, two ice cubes, water on the side, the Reverend Paul Twinings, S.J., D.D., Ph.D., president of both Hilly Springs College and the Jesuit community that ran it, got the attention of the assembled guests and announced the generous contributions being made to the McNamara-O'Hara Chair of Classical Ballet Dancing Fund by Mr. K. J. O'Hara, Jr., and Mr. Randolph C. Bruce, in addition to the generous contributions they had already made.

And a good time was had by all, so good a time that as Phil and Junior and Father Paul sat by the pool — with airheaded blondes with large bosoms and tight little tails sitting on the laps of Junior and Father Paul — Phil found the courage to ask Father

Paul if he dared ask him a question.

"Ask away, after you hand me that bottle of Famous Pheasant," Father Paul replied.

"Correct me if I'm wrong, but as I understand it, members of the Society of Jesus take vows of poverty, chastity, and obedience. Yet here you are, where you showed up in a canary-yellow Mercedes-Benz 560 convertible, carrying a Beretta shotgun, with an airheaded blonde sitting on your lap . . ."

Father Paul raised his hand to silence him.

"As you know, Phil, no mortal man is perfect," he said. "And as it says in Matthew 7, Verse 1, of the Catholic Bible, and is paraphrased in Bibles used by Protestants and other quasi-heathens, 'Judge not, lest you be judged.'"

"I'll try not to."

"Bless you, Philip."

That evening, of course, marked Phil's and Madame Brunhilde's entrance into Muddiebay Society, such as it is.

XIV
TIME MARCHES ON

[One]

Muddiebay, Mississippi
Monday, September 15, 1975

Between the time Mr. Philip Williams, and his wife, Madame Brunhilde, became members of Muddiebay Society and the time when Mr. Randy Bruce called Mr. Williams and asked perchance if he would like to go pop a few pheasants with Bertie and Maggie in Scotland, quite a lot of water flowed under the causeway across upper Muddiebay Bay and out into the Gulf of Mexico.

And as someone once observed, a lot of things happen when water is flowing under causeways, some good and some bad.

For example, Phil had of course made some new friends, among them the Reverend Paul Twinings, S.J., D.D., Ph.D., president of Hilly Springs College and the Jesuit Community.

One day, when they were alone busting birds off the O'Hara pier, Father Paul asked Phil where he had acquired so much insight into the female mind, and said he was curious because it approached and even exceeded his own insight into the female mind, which he had acquired through the confessional.

After swearing the priest to secrecy, Phil showed him all three volumes of The Daily Notes of CIC Administrator P. W. Williams. Father Paul found them fascinating. After swearing Phil to secrecy, Father Paul shared hypothetically with Phil some of the really wild things he had heard in the confessional, without of course mentioning any names.

Phil was able to use some of what Father Paul told him in his creative writing, which was a good thing because he was getting close to the end of the single-spaced typewritten pages in Binder Three and didn't have a EXPLETIVE DELETED!! clue what he was going to do when that source of inspiration had been exhausted.

And truth being stranger than fiction, Phil became close to — one could almost say became a friend of — Randy Bruce. This had to do with shotgun marksmanship. Randy was determined to wipe out once and for all time the humiliation he had suffered, and the attendant financial loss attached, the day they had met.

He demanded a rematch under what he referred to as controlled conditions, by which he meant that he intended to be entirely alcohol free when he called "Pull," and that Father Paul would serve as referee. After all, if you can't trust a Jesuit to make honest calls when popping birds, who can you trust?

The first rematch cost Randy another $10,000, which, of course as a gentleman, he promptly wrote a check to cover. Phil, as a gentleman, was loath to personally profit from outshooting Randy, which was sort of like taking candy from a baby, or shooting fish in a barrel, so he endorsed Randy's check over to the McNamara-O'Hara Chair of Classical Ballet Dancing Fund at Hilly Springs College.

He thought this might please Madame Brunhilde, Father Paul, and Randy's grandmother, known as Auntie Abby, and her sister, Auntie Penny. And when Auntie Abby reviewed the checks Randy had drawn on his Trust Fund to see if she would allow them to be paid, it clearly did.

Randy's grandmother told him she was really pleased that he seemed to be making friends with people like Father Paul and Mr.

Williams. Even if the latter was a EXPLE-TIVE DELETED!! Yankee, he was married to Madame Brunhilde, the close friend of Madame Violet.

Their second rematch cost Randy $20,000, after which he bit the bullet and admitted that the EXPLETIVE DELETED!! Yankee was a better shot than he. He decided that he would make a friendly overture to Phil, learn more about him, and thus be better prepared to seek vengeance for the humiliation and loss of $30,000 in some way not connected with shotgun shooting.

He invited Phil to lunch at his favorite luncheon place, the Blue Gill restaurant on the Muddiebay Bay Causeway, which featured fresh seafood served by young women in wet T-shirts and short shorts.

Randy's idea of a luncheon invitation was to set a place and a time to meet, and then go to the rendezvous point at a time when it was convenient for him to do so.

When he arrived at the Blue Gill only an hour and a half late, expecting to find Phil waiting for him at the bar, what he got instead was one of the scantily clad food servers pointing to a message written with a bar of soap on the mirror behind the bar for the whole world to see.

Dear Randy Bruce,
Time and Phil Williams wait for no man.
                    Sincerely, Your Friend,
                        Phil Williams

Randy later made one more gesture to Phil, and this one turned things around a great deal.

What happened was that Randy telephoned Phil and said he was about to go to Uruguay to shoot *perdiz,* which is what the Uruguayans call quail, and wondered if Phil would like to go along. Surprising Randy, Phil said that he would have to ask permission of Madame Brunhilde and would get back to him.

When Phil asked Madame Brunhilde if he could go to Uruguay with Randy, Madame Brunhilde responded, surprising Phil not at all, "I don't give a good EXPLETIVE DELETED!! where you go."

So Phil called Randy back and said he would be delighted to go, providing they had a pre-trip agreement between gentlemen about who paid for what. From everything he had heard about Randy Bruce, he thought it entirely possible that once they arrived in Uruguay, Randy would announce, "Oh, my God, I forgot my EXPLETIVE DELETED!! wallet. You pay now, and I'll pay you later."

What Randy proposed was that each would pay separately for the airplane tickets, and that other expenses would be paid for on a "Your Turn–My Turn" basis. In other words, Randy would pay for their first meal on the road, and then Phil would pay for the next mutual expense, whether it was a taxi ride, or another meal, et cetera.

And so they went to Uruguay, where the *perdiz* shooting over dogs is the best in the world, the beef magnificent, the women attractive — albeit moral, which disappointed Randy — and up near the Brazilian border, where they hunted, the price of Famous Pheasant Scotch, which is about $36 per bottle in the States, was $6.50.

So they hunted and ate and drank a lot of Famous Pheasant at $6.50 per bottle, or $0.45 per drink in Uruguay's famed *whiskerías*. And then it was time to go home.

They got as far as Ezeiza International Airport in Buenos Aires, Argentina, where they would board Aerolíneas Argentinas's Flight 707 for the next leg of their flight to America's Token Third World Airport, commonly known as Miami International. From Florida they would fly directly home to Muddiebay.

There at the gate in Buenos Aires, with

tears in her dark eyes, an Aerolíneas Argentinas agent announced (a) there would be a slight delay in the departure of Flight 707, and (b) that the Gaucho Club, Aerolíneas Argentinas's club for business-class passengers that offered complimentary intoxicants and peanuts to those awaiting their flights, was temporarily closed for repairs.

She then handed them vouchers good for one twelve-ounce bottle of Quilmes *cerveza,* which means beer, and one one-ounce bag of peanuts at the Ezeiza Airport Cocktail Lounge.

"Well, what the hell," Randy announced, "let's wait over there and have a drink of Famous Pheasant. It's my turn to buy."

Four hours later, Randy and Phil learned there was a price differential in the cost of Famous Pheasant by the drink in the *whiskerías* of Uruguay and the Ezeiza Airport Cocktail Lounge. In the former, as previously noted, the cost was $0.45 per drink. In the latter, it was $13.50. And the six bags of peanuts they consumed after consuming the free one-ounce bag came at a cost of $5 per bag.

It took Phil a little bit of time to realize that Randy was having to pull twenty- and fifty-dollar bills from where he had had them cleverly concealed on his person to come up with the wherewithal to settle the tab, but he took a look at same.

"Hey, we should split this," Phil said, rather thickly, as he had been soaking up what he thought were $0.45 drinks like a blotter for four hours.

"Listen to me, Phil," Randy replied. "Although I have been royally EXPLETIVE DELETED!! raped by these EXPLETIVE DELETED!! Argentinians, I am an Old Boy of the Muddiebay Military Academy, and when we MBMA Old Boys make a deal, we keep it. It was my turn, and I will pay the EXPLETIVE DELETED!! price for not looking at the EXPLETIVE DELETED!! menu to see what these thieving EXPLETIVE DELETED!! were charging."

And he would not be dissuaded, even though he was bombed, as they say, out of his mind.

After that, Phil looked more kindly on Randy and, as the years passed, went hunting with him all over the world, and gave in, as has been previously chronicled, to Randy's pleadings to go to Scotland and meet with Charles William George Michael Bertram, the Earl of Abercrombie, who, as has been previously related, was already known to Phil as Bertie from Bertie's steeplechasing days.

There were several reasons Phil could go all over the world to hunt with Randy.

For one thing, authors do not have eight-to-five, five-days-a-week jobs with two weeks off during the summer to visit Disneyland and other vacation spots. Instead, they work seven days a week from oh dark hundred until exhaustion. They can, however, take off for a week or more whenever the opportunity to do so arises. And then, too, there was the Whorehouse Decision, which made all of Phil's hunting expenses deductible as long as he called them "research."

[Two]

Similarly, Phil developed sort of an older-brother-to-younger-brother relationship with K. J. O'Hara, Jr. They became close to the point where Junior confided in Phil that his heart had been captured by one of the airheaded blondes with nice breastworks and a tight little bottom and that he was thinking of asking her to become Mrs. K. J. O'Hara, Jr.

"Are you out of your EXPLETIVE DELETED!! mind?" Phil blurted. "That stupid bimbo is after your money, you dumb EXPLETIVE DELETED!! That's all she's after. And there's a lot more money, now that your father and his brother proved your mother and I wrong about that stupid — now recognized as monumentally brilliant — idea they had about taking the wheels off truck trailers, calling them 'containers,' and loading them onto boats."

"I'm disappointed to hear you say that," Junior said.

"You asked for the truth and I gave it my best shot."

"I meant that my intended will be disappointed not only to hear what you think of her but also that you won't be my best man at our wedding, Thursday next, as I promised her, and personally hoped you would be."

"If you promise not to tell Miss Airhead what I think about her, which would complicate our relationship post-honeymoon, I will stand up beside you while you marry your airhead."

Phil was also Junior's best man when Junior married Airhead Number Two, and Airhead Number Three, but not at Junior's nuptials to Airhead Number Four, because Number Four had heard what Phil had said about her predecessors.

Airhead Number Four had absolutely forbidden Junior — now known, after the passing of both his father and his uncle, as

K.J. the Container King — to have anything to do with Phil and his circle of friends, post-honeymoon, so K.J. the Container King had to reluctantly decline Mr. Randy Bruce's kind invitation to go pop some pheasants in Scotland with The Tuesday Luncheon Club and the boys.

Phil had some familial losses of his own.

The year that Franz Josef matriculated in the pre-kindergarten class of the Marietta Fieldstone School of Organic Education, Phil took a picture of his offspring all decked out in their new go-to-school clothes from the Goodhope Slightly Used Children's Clothing Discount Outlet and tucked it, together with a letter, into an envelope.

It read:

```
Dear Mother:
   In case you have been wonder-
ing what I've been up to since
we were last in touch, you
will find enclosed a picture of
my family.
   Pictured (left to right) are
your grandson Philip Walling-
ford Williams IV, who is six
and in the first grade at the
Marietta Fieldstone School of
```

Organic Education here in Goodhope, Miss., where we make our home. Next to Little Phil, as we call him, is Brunhilde Wienerwald Williams, Junior, your granddaughter, who is seven, and in the second grade of the same school. Next, holding Franz Josef Williams, also your grandson, in a firm grip on her lap is my wife, Madame Brunhilde Wienerwald Williams, a former ballerina of the Vienna State Opera, who is deputy chair to the McNamara-O'Hara Chair of Classical Ballet Dancing at Hilly Springs College, a Jesuit institution in Muddiebay, which is across Muddiebay Bay from Goodhope. Franz Josef, who is five, will enter pre-kindergarten this year.

In case you didn't recognize me, because of my receding forehead, I am the man standing behind Madame Brunhilde.

I have found interesting employment in the publishing industry, which supports a decent life for all of us.

    With my best regards to Dr. Michaels, I am,

Your son,
Philip

P.S.: Please tell Dr. Michaels I hope he is enjoying my late father's set of golf clubs.

After thinking it over, Phil sent essentially the same letter to his Aunt Grace, enclosing similar photographs. The first reply came three weeks later, the day Franz Josef became the first pre-kindergarten student in the history of the Organic School to be expelled. What he had done, in a skit on the grass, in which he and fellow prekindergartner Teresa-Ann Fogarty were supposed to skip onto the "stage" costumed (draped in brown cloth) as mushrooms, was to pour a gallon of gray paint over his costar and himself (he said that while he had never seen brown mushrooms he had seen a lot of gray *Agaricus bisporus*) to improve the costuming.

When Franz Josef and Teresa-Ann skipped onto the stage, dripping gray paint at every skip, his costar's mother screamed and then assaulted the skit's directoress, twenty-two-year-old Miss Penelope Greene, with the umbrella under which she had been protecting her complexion from the harmful rays of the sun.

Miss Greene then fainted, necessitating the calling of the Goodhope Volunteer Ambulance Service. These first responders responded with alacrity, and soon both dancers, the girl dancer's mother, and Miss Greene were on their way to the emergency room of Richards Hospital, which serves Goodhope.

Since there was no room in the Goodhope Volunteer Ambulance Service ambulance for Phil, he had to follow in his Jaguar, which caused him to arrive at Richards Hospital perhaps five minutes after the others.

When he entered the emergency room, he found Mrs. Helena Fogarty demanding of the medical staff that they remove the gray paint from Teresa-Ann immediately, rather than simultaneously from Teresa-Ann and Franz Josef, whom she described at the top of her lungs as "that EXPLETIVE DELETED!! five-year-old EXPLETIVE DELETED!! monster!"

"Madam," Phil said politely, "please refrain from calling my Franz Josef a EXPLETIVE DELETED!! monster."

At that point, Mr. Terence Fogarty, Teresa-Ann's father, who had been known as "Terrible Terry" when he had been a 320-pound All-American tackle at Ole Miss, entered the conversation.

"My wife can call that EXPLETIVE DE-LETED!! monster of yours anything she pleases, you EXPLETIVE DELETED!!," Mr. Fogarty said. And then, to emphasize his point, he grabbed Phil by the neck and lifted him off the ground.

This was a mistake on his part, Mr. Fogarty soon learned.

Phil, in a Pavlovian reaction, brought into play some of the wide variety of kicks and fist and elbow strikes of Taekkyeon that he had learned at the Royal Korean Archery & Taekkyeon Academy on Dried Fish Street in London and never forgotten.

Mr. "Terrible Terry" Fogarty instantly found himself begging for mercy as he lay on the ground, on his back, with Phil's foot on his groin area.

Phil thought that would be the end of it — or would be the end of it, once the emergency room staff had finished shaving the heads of Teresa-Ann and Franz Josef — but he was wrong.

The very next day, Mr. Dyson Samuels, president of the Second National Bank of Goodhope and also of the board of directors of the Marietta Fieldstone School of

Organic Education, called upon Mr. and Madame Williams and said that at the emergency meeting of the board held the previous evening, Phil had been elected to the board, and that if he accepted, Franz Josef would be allowed back into the school.

Phil was trying hard to think of a way he could decline the honor and at the same time have Franz Josef's expulsion forgiven when Madame Brunhilde saved him the effort.

"Deal," she said. "Say 'thank you,' Phil."

And so Phil joined the board.

When he went to his first board meeting, Mr. Samuels took him aside and explained the board's reasons and what Phil's role on the board would be.

"We have a little problem, Mr. Williams," Banker Samuels said. "It has plagued us for years, but has now reached something of a pinnacle, problem-wise. It deals with the attire in which our teenaged young lady students come to school to take advantage of all the educational benefits the Marietta Fieldstone School of Organic Education has to offer."

"And what is that?"

"Don't interrupt me. Bankers who loan people money don't expect to be interrupted. All they expect to hear from people like you is 'Yes, sir' and 'Thank you.' "

"Sorry."

"Teresa-Ann, over whom your son Franz Josef poured the gray paint, has an older sister, Barbara-Sue, who is sixteen. Others of our young ladies look up to Barbara-Sue as a role model."

"That's nice."

"It would be if Barbara-Sue was not in the habit of coming to school each morning dressed and made up as if she's on her way to work as a hooker. By which I mean in a short skirt exposing much of her EXPLETIVE DELETED!!, topped by a T-shirt which (a) appears molded to her bosom and (b) on which is emblazoned such witticisms as 'EXPLETIVE DELETED!! teachers' and a picture of a rooster over the legend "EXPLETIVE DELETED!! Inspector' and things of that sort.

"And because, as I said, Barbara-Sue is a role model to her peers, we have in the morning a parade of our young ladies which the casual observer would think was a parade of hookers marching to work in an economy-class brothel. This has the to-be-expected result of inflaming the hormones of our young gentleman students, to the detriment of their thinking about calculus and Modern European History, and turning it toward carnal congress outside the boundaries of holy matrimony. You taking my meaning?"

"Yes, sir. May I ask why you don't have a word with Mrs. Fogarty about proper school attire for her daughter?"

"We have tried that. The last three times we tried to do that, Mrs. Fogarty said unkind things about the three gentlemen we sent in such a loud voice that it woke Terrible Terry up, whereupon he went to his front door, grabbed our board members by their collars, and threw them off the Fogarty porch and into the shrubbery."

"I think I suspect where this is going," Phil said.

"We thought perhaps, in view of the manner in which you set Mr. Fogarty on his EXPLETIVE DELETED!! in the emergency room yesterday . . ."

"I'll have a word with him, if that is what you're asking."

"That is what I'm asking. And so far as your other duties as a board member are concerned, don't worry about them. All you have to do is join the chorus of 'Yes, sirs' when I finish telling the board what they have just decided to do."

"I understand."

Phil served on the board until Franz Josef

graduated, at which time Madame Brunhilde gave him permission to resign. During his reign, so to speak, the young ladies of the Marietta Fieldstone School of Organic Education came to school looking like happy, modestly dressed schoolgirls, as the fathers of the girls had heard and believed what Mr. Williams had done to Terrible Terry Fogarty in the emergency room of Richards Hospital and decided they would rather face the wrath of their wives and daughters than that of Mr. Williams.

As previously stated, the first reply to Phil's letters to his mother and his Aunt Grace came three weeks later, the day Franz Josef became the first pre-kindergarten student in the history of the Organic School to be expelled.

Curiously, it was from his stepfather:

Dear Philip,
    I am responding to your letter of recent date to your mother because she is undergoing psychiatric treatment under my psychiatric direction at the Seton Hall Psychiatric Institute here in South Orange and cannot do so herself.

Not only are patients at the SHPI denied for their own protection the use of sharp instruments, such as pencils, but your mother is not in a condition to use a pencil even if she was allowed to have one. In layman's terms, she is completely bonkers, and her prognosis is not good. In other words, she's not going to get any better.

In these circumstances, the Hippocratic Oath I took when I became a doctor of medicine so long ago, which included the phrase *Primum non nocere,* which in layman's terms means "First do no harm," obviously precludes my showing her your letter, which if she could read it, and she's in no condition to read it, would push her even further across that line which separates the sane from the loony tunes.

She was always worried that you would marry some foreigner and contribute to the further degeneration of the gene pool by breeding, which the photograph you sent of those ugly children clearly demonstrates you have indeed done.

The kindest thing for you to do is stay out of what's left of her life.

Under these circumstances, I'm sure you will understand that I have to withdraw my previous offer to provide you pro bono psychiatric services, even though you obviously need whatever psychiatric help you can get.

Insofar as your late father's golf clubs are concerned: When I tried to turn them in on a better set, the Pro Shop at Baltusrol Country Club seized them because your father had not paid for them when he purchased them from the Winged Foot Country Club and they had apparently shared that information with Baltusrol.

With all best wishes,
your stepfather,
KM
Keyes Michaels, M.D.

The second reply came three days after the first:

**MISS GRACE ALICE PATRICIA HORTENSE WILLIAMS
MAYFLOWER-WILLIAMS HOUSE
BACK BAY, BOSTON, MASS.**

Dear Nephew Philip:

Frankly, I always worried that when you married you would follow in the footsteps of your late father — my late brother — and take to wife someone whose position in life was below the salt, as he did.

I never in my wildest nightmares, however, dreamed that you would take to wife someone who is not only below the salt, but also below the pepper, the A.1. sauce, the Worcestershire sauce, and the Tabasco sauce as well.

I suppose it's futile of me to suggest that you should legally change your name, but I don't think it unreasonable of me to ask that you stay as far south of the Mason-Dixon Line as possible. Forever.

In case you have been fantasizing vis-à-vis inheriting any of the Williams family money, please be advised that on my

507

demise all of my worldly possessions, in other words, every last Buffalo nickel, will go to the fund for the preservation of the Mayflower-Williams House.

Sincerely,
*Grace Alice Patricia
Hortense Williams (Miss)*

[Three]

Phil of course made other friends in the years that passed as the water flowed under the Muddiebay Bay Causeway and ultimately into the Gulf of Mexico.

One of the oldest of these was Bobby "Fender" Bender, proprietor of the Foggy Point Garage & Good As New Used Parts, whom he met while still residing in the Grand Hotel, in other words, before Brunhilde was Madame Brunhilde and before Brunhilde had bought the house on Creek Drive.

Phil had gone to Mr. Bender's place of business to have the oil changed in the Jaguar, which had driven all those miles from Fort Benning. He would have preferred to take the car to a Jaguar dealer, but the list of "Your Neighborhood Jaguar Dealers" that came with the car listed the nearest dealer to Foggy Point, Mississippi, as being in New Orleans, Louisiana, which the map showed was a long EXPLETIVE DELETED!! way to go to have the oil in one's Jaguar replaced.

Mr. Bender's place of business was on a dirt road about three miles inland from Foggy Point. It was located inside a barn, or shed, that had seen better days. It was advertised by a welcoming sign mounted over an ancient fire truck:

**FOGGY POINT GARAGE & GOOD AS
NEW USED PARTS
NO SOLICITING
SALESMEN WILL BE SHOT
NO TRESPASSING**

When Mr. Bender came out of the barn, he was wearing a soup-strainer mustache, blue denim overalls, no shirt or undershirt, and an old pair of Army combat boots.

"What?" Mr. Bender greeted Phil.

"I was hoping to have the oil in my Jaguar changed."

"I don't like Yankees and I hate EXPLETIVE DELETED!! foreign cars."

"Well, I'm sorry to hear that. Sorry to have troubled you."

"Wait a minute. Maybe we can work something out. What are those cartons in

509

the backseat?"

"Shotgun shells. Specifically Winchester AA 12-gauge shotgun shells containing 1 1/8-ounce #9 Shot."

"That's what people shoot at coffee saucers, or whatever the EXPLETIVE DELETED!! they're called, for fun, right?"

"That is correct, Mr. Bender. They are called 'clay pigeons.' "

"They look like coffee saucers for midgets. But I got a buddy who does that off his pier," Mr. Bender explained. "You want to swap, say, ten boxes of them for an oil change and a lube job?"

"I would be delighted to do so."

"Okay, when I open the door, drive that ugly EXPLETIVE DELETED!! Jag-You-Are inside."

"Yes, sir."

The barn door creaked open. Phil drove into the barn and found himself next to a Maserati convertible, and with his bumper against the doors of a Lincoln and a Rolls-Royce Silver Ghost sedan. Elsewhere in the barn was what looked like half a million dollars' worth of the very latest service equipment, a half-dozen luxury cars of assorted makes, and three motorcycles in various stages of disassembly.

"Nice cars," Phil said as he got out of the Jaguar.

"The Italian Special there," Mr. Bender explained, "which is a EXPLETIVE DELETED!! nightmare to keep running, belongs to my pal Junior, the one I told you shoots at those midget coffee saucers off his pier. The Lincoln belongs to his mother, who is a great lady. The Rolls-Royce, which is a EXPLETIVE DELETED!! nightmare in EXPLETIVE DELETED!! spades to keep running, belongs to the Grand Hotel, which is owned by my buddy's father, who is married to my buddy's mother."

"I see."

"Well, let's get your EXPLETIVE DELETED!! Limey Special in the air, drain the EXPLETIVE DELETED!! oil out of the ugly EXPLETIVE DELETED!!, and see what the EXPLETIVE DELETED!! else is wrong with it. Because there's always something wrong with a Jag-You-Are, if you can get them to run. Lucas Electronics isn't called the Prince of Darkness for nothing."

Phil intuited on the spot that he had found the man to maintain his beloved Jaguar against all mechanical evil whatsoever.

And so it came to pass, even as the years passed and he hung onto the car despite the demands of Madame Brunhilde of him to get rid of what she called *das alte Gottver-dammt Cat Car.*

Phil was to come to realize that he kept the Jaguar because Madame Brunhilde hated it. It had become, in effect, his silent defiance of his wife.

XV
EVERYBODY GOES HUNTING

Muddiebay, Mississippi
Monday, September 15, 1975

On the morning of the day that everybody went hunting for whatever they intended to hunt for, Phil went to his office, which was in the house he had originally bought on a no-money-down Veterans Administration Guaranteed Loan and from which he had moved out approximately a year later.

What happened there was that Phil, after having been a member of the Foggy Point Country Club for just over a year, had asked Woody Woodson, the Foggy Point Country Club's recreation director, making reference to one of the dozen or so very nice homes on the country club property, "What's a house like that, say, the one at 102 Country Club Road, worth, Woody?"

"If you're thinking you'd like to move into 102 Country Club Road, after you bought it, of course, forget about it, Phil," Woody replied. "It's not the price that'll keep you from ever living here. It's the law of supply and demand."

"How so?"

"So few houses, so many people who would sell their grandmothers to get one of them. One of them comes on the market every two or three years. It goes to the Number One Person on the waiting list. To get on the waiting list you have to go through a vetting policy that makes the vetting policy to get in our country club look like an open-door policy. Forget it, Phil. It's just not in the cards for you."

Two weeks later, when Phil drove Junior out to Foggy Point Garage & Good As New Used Parts to pick up Junior's new toy — a Lamborghini that had died every ten miles on the way home from the dealer's in Miami, and which ol' Fender Bender was fixing — and also to sit around and shuck oysters and suck on cans of beer while listening to ol' Fender Bender deliver one of his learned lectures on the current state of EXPLETIVE DELETED!! politics and international EXPLETIVE DELETED!! diplomacy, Junior said, "There's something I forgot to tell you, Phil."

"Which is?"

"When my mother asked where I was going, and I told her you were going to drive me out here, she said, tell Phil to please call the real estate guy if he still wants to buy 102 Country Club Road. And if he's a little short of cash, not to be embarrassed, speak up and I'll cut a check to tide him over."

So the Williams family had the next week moved from Creek Drive in Goodhope to 102 Country Club Road in Foggy Point, which raised the question of what to do with the house on Creek Drive.

On the advice of Lacey Richards, L.L.D., Phil's septuagenarian local legal counsel — Gustave "Rabbi" Warblerman, L.L.D., of course was his literary legal counsel, so Phil now was pretty well lawyered up — he retained the house as his office.

Lawyer Richards had an agenda *vis-à-vis* his recommendation. He was about to draw the curtain mostly shut on his long legal career. He would no longer appeal with his famed eloquence to the mercy of jurors in the Muddiebay County Courthouse to let his clients go home despite the allegations of the merciless police that they had been driving under the influence of intoxicants. Instead, Lacey Richards would devote all of his legal skill to managing trust funds, which are a legal device by which parents can leave their children all their worldly goods and not see the hard-earned goods squandered in six months.

He would no longer need his present chambers to do this, as he could manage trusts by sitting at a desk and using a pencil. He proposed that he close his legal chambers and move into the house on Creek Drive. He would then continue to represent Phil on local legal issues *pro bono,* which means for free. This would have the additional benefit of keeping the greedy claws of the EXPLETIVE DELETED!! Internal Revenue Service out of their respective pies, so to speak.

And there was yet another benefit. There was a spare bedroom in the house on Creek Drive into which Lawyer Richards could hide from the wrath of his third wife.

The arrangement had worked out well over the years, in large measure because Lawyer Richards had thrown his paralegal, Mrs. Bonita Jones Pennyworth, into the deal. Paralegals are secretaries who know more about the law than the lawyers by whom they are employed and are compensated accordingly, providing they pretend "their" lawyer knows more about the law than they do.

In addition to providing legal advice to

Lawyer Richards, Mrs. Pennyworth could also go for the mail, and make coffee, and, when this was necessary, cook breakfast for Lawyer Richards when he was temporarily residing in the house on Creek Drive between wives.

At this point in this narrative he was between Wife #6 and Wife #7.

So in the morning of the day on which everybody was going to go hunting for whatever they were hunting for, Phil went to his office in what had once been the master bedroom of the house on Creek Drive when he lived there.

Mrs. Pennyworth brought him a cup of coffee and a chocolate-covered doughnut and assured him she would be happy to go with him in the Jaguar to Muddiebay, and then drive, very carefully, the car back to the office after dropping Phil off at Mr. Randy Bruce's home, "Our Tara," the antebellum mansion in which Mr. Bruce lived and from which Mr. Bruce would then drive Phil to Muddiebay International Airport, where they would board the airplane that would then take them to Atlanta.

Then Phil got on the telephone.

The first call he made was to Pat O'Malley, the world-famous author of *The Hunt for Gray November* and other famous literary works.

Chauncey S. "Steel" Hymen, vice president, publisher, and editor in chief of J. K. Perkins & Brothers, had introduced Phil to Pat just before the publication of *The Hunt for Gray November,* which Steel Hymen had bought, seeing in it a slight chance of making a buck with it.

Mr. Hymen wanted Pat to see in Phil how well J. K. Perkins & Brothers treated their best-selling authors, such as by buying them dinners at semi-fancy restaurants and putting them up in three — and even four — star hotels when they traveled to the Big Apple. This, he hoped, would inspire Mr. O'Malley to write a sequel to his first work, for which he would be paid another $2,500 on acceptance payment. Eventually, Steel told Pat, he, too, might become a best-selling author like Phil.

Phil and Pat hit it off from the beginning, in large measure because after Steel had gone off to deal with important authors and left Phil and Pat to amuse themselves, which they did by touring several Irish pubs in Lower Manhattan, Phil told Pat, who was then in the aluminum siding business in his native Maryland, about J. K. Perkins &

Brothers generally and Steel Hymen specifically.

Specifically, Phil told Pat that Steel was a fine editor and a good guy, but that he should keep his hand on his wallet when dealing with other members of the J. K. Perkins & Brothers management troika as otherwise, before Pat knew what was happening, his aluminum siding business would become yet another subsidiary of J. K. Perkins & Brothers, Publishers since 1812.

By midnight, Pat was so full of Knappogue Castle twelve-year-old single malt Irish whisky that Phil didn't think Pat could make it by himself to where J. K. Perkins & Brothers was putting him up at their expense at the Economy Motor Inn in Hoboken, New Jersey, as this would involve taking a ferry across the wide Hudson River. Phil took Pat to where J. K. Perkins & Brothers was putting him up at their expense, which was in an "economy class" room in The Algonquin Hotel, a historic venue located at 59 West Forty-fourth Street in Midtown Manhattan.

Phil got Pat into the right side of the queen-sized double bed with which the room was furnished without too much effort, but once his new buddy was on his back he began to snore. Worse, Pat instantly demonstrated that he was one hell of a snorer.

Phil sought refuge in the bathroom, taking with him a "bound galley" copy of *The Hunt for Gray November.* Pat had been carrying a box of the bound galleys around all night, as he had been unable to give any of them away.

An hour later, Phil, who had mastered the art of speed reading while editor in chief of the German-American Gospel Tract Foundation, had finished reading the 640-page tome.

"I'll be a EXPLETIVE DELETED!! monkey's uncle," Phil announced aloud, although there was no one around to hear him except Pat O'Malley, and he was in no condition to hear anything, "this is great EXPLETIVE DELETED!! writing. Move over, Leo Tolstoy, Charles Dickens, and Ernest Hemingway. There is a new master!"

Unbeknownst to Phil, the resident of the master bedroom in the big white house at 1600 Pennsylvania Avenue in our nation's capital had come to the same conclusion at just about the time Phil had so concluded.

He had purloined a copy of the galleys from the lap of a Secret Service agent who was sleeping in a chair outside the Presidential Apartments and taken it inside as he was having the same trouble with his wife, *vis-à-vis* snoring, as Phil was experiencing with Pat and had hoped it would bore him to sleep.

He announced this conclusion to the White House Press Corps at the eight-thirty presidential press conference the next morning.

Phil and Pat learned of this shortly after 1:30 p.m. when they were having their breakfast — vodka Bloody Mary, with triple doses of Tabasco, and one egg yolk — at the 21 Club. They learned of it through a media report on the television mounted above the bar.

Not long after, *The New York Daily News* and *The New York Times* added their versions. The former dedicated its entire front page to the story with a picture of the President holding up the bound galleys of *The Hunt for Gray November* over the cutline: WE ALWAYS TOLD YOU HE COULD READ!!!

The *Times* said, in part:

The incumbent of the Oval Office, to which office he was elected by misguided right-wingers and others of that ignorant ilk while the wiser of our citizens were apparently asleep, today announced that he had just read what he called the finest piece of literature to come down the literary pike since Tolstoy, Dickens, and Hemingway.

Even if, as some White House insiders are alleging, the First Lady had to read The Hunt for Gray November to the President, because some of the big words were just too much for the former bit player in B-grade cowboy motion pictures, his effusive praise is worthy of note.

What happened next of course is history.

The Hunt for Gray November immediately went on the *New York Times,* the *Wall Street Journal,* and other best-seller lists as #1 and stayed there for months. It was translated into sixty-one foreign languages and made into a major motion picture starring half of the members listed on the Hollywood "A-List of Stars" list.

And Pat's second book was even more successful than his first. And the third more successful than the second, and the fourth and fifth, *und so weiter.*

Phil, knowing people and the publishing business as he did, felt very sure that Pat's success would go to his head, and that the new giant of modern American literature would quickly forget he had ever met an obscure toiler in the literary vineyards named Phil Williams.

Phil was wrong.

Phil and Pat, if anything, became closer as the years passed. Phil taught Pat how to shoot, something Pat had always wanted to try and now could afford to. Despite Phil's best efforts, Pat had trouble hitting the side of a barn, although he practiced just about daily in the indoor skeet range he created in the basement of his new house, "Castle O'Malley," which he built on the site of a former summer camp for Jewish Young Ladies on the shores of Chesapeake Bay in his native Maryland.

And when he wasn't busy counting his money, or managing the Baltimore She Devils, the female hockey team he had bought, which took a lot of his time, Pat would often hop in his private jet airplane and fly down to Foggy Point to try to bust some birds off the end of the Container King's pier with Phil and the boys.

It was this — Pat's airplane — that Phil had in mind when he called Pat. If Pat had a little time to spare, going back and forth to Scotland in a private jet would be ever so much more comfortable than going through all the various levels of international transportation security EXPLETIVE DELETED!! in all those airports.

Painful experience had taught Phil that airport security devoutly believed that anyone desiring to take a shotgun with them on their travels was obviously a terrorist and to be treated accordingly.

"Sorry, Phil, old buddy, as much as I would like to go to Scotland with you," Pat said, "I'm on my better half's EXPLETIVE DELETED!! list and she wouldn't even let me go into Annapolis to watch the Navy Academy Midshipwomen running aground in their sailboats, which is always good for laughs, much less go to Scotland."

"I'm sorry to hear that," Phil said. "What happened?"

Phil liked Pat's better half and he thought he might be able to talk her into forgiving Pat for whatever he had done.

"I had a couple too many sips of Knappogue Castle twelve-year-old single malt Irish to be driving my tank."

Pat had given himself a little present when he got the check for motion picture rights to his fifth literary work. He bought an M60A1 Patton tank from Army Surplus.

"But you drove it anyway?"

"Right through my better half's rose garden. Boy, was she EXPLETIVE DELETED!!"

"I can understand that."

"But I'll tell you what I can do for you, Phil, old buddy. You'll be traveling on public air transportation, so you'll have to go through London, right?"

"Right."

"While you're in London, go to the Tower of London. I was just there and had a ball."

"Watching them execute people?"

"They don't do that anymore. What they do is lock up the Royal Jewels every night."

"That sure sounds like fun."

"You wouldn't believe all the EXPLETIVE DELETED!! diamonds the Queen has."

"I'll take your word for it."

"All purchased with the sweat of my poor oppressed Irish kinsmen, of course, but they're really something to see. And there's a great bar on the premises. Actually it's a club for those guys in the red coats."

"You mean the Yeomen Warders?"

"Right. They're all retired soldiers. Warrant officers. That's what you were, right?"

"I never rose that high in our nation's war machine rank structure."

"Trust me, Phil. Go to the Tower of London. I'll give them a call and get you an invitation. You need an invitation to get in. You'll be at Claridge's Hotel, right?"

"Yeah."

"Have a ball, Phil. Got to go."

The line went dead.

Phil next called his literary agent, Jennifer "Big Bad Jennie" Waldron, who had replaced Cushman Johns in that role when ol' Cushman had gone to that Great Book Fair in the sky.

Jennie told him that she had just nailed, figuratively speaking of course, the scrotums of David "Two Gun" Gobbet and Chauncey S. "Steel" Hymen to the wall *vis-à-vis* the new contract for his work in progress.

She told him how much money J. K. Perkins & Brothers was going to tearfully part with for the privilege of publishing the sequel to *Love and Lust in the Kremlin Necropolis,* which was to be titled *Love and Lust in the* 人民大会堂, which means, *Love and Lust in the Great Hall of the People.*

It was a lot of zeros, and normally Phil would have been very happy. But he wasn't very happy. His reaction was almost *So what?*

He thought about this. The first thing he thought was that perhaps talking to Big Bad Jennie had made him think of ol' Cushman Johns. He really missed Ol' Cushman and his blue suede shoes, even if Jennifer was much better-looking and smelled a whole hell of a lot better than ol' Cush.

And that was when he had the epiphany:

My God, am I having that midlife crisis everybody talks about?

Is that possible?

My God, I'm only forty-five years old!

A quick check of actuarial statistics maintained by the Social Security Administration of the United States Government indicated that someone of his years, and not at the moment suffering from either cancer, phlebitis, or any of the three most popular sexually transmittable social diseases, could expect to live to be 78.44 years of age.

The middle point of the lifetime of someone who will live to be 78.44 years old is 39.22 . . . 45 take away 39.22 leaves 5.78.

My God, I'm five and three-quarters years past my midlife!

Of course I'm having my midlife crisis!

I'm just having it five and three-quarters years, give or take, late!

It's all downhill from here!

I will not let this get me down!

Phil then went downstairs to the Emergency Kit and took from it a bottle of the good — that is to say, eighteen-year-old — Famous Pheasant and took two healthy medicinal pulls at the neck thereof.

Then he asked Mrs. Bonita Jones Penny-worth if she would be so kind as to drive him to Mr. Bruce's house in Muddiebay so that he might begin what he was beginning to think might very possibly be his last voyage on this earth.

XVI
En Route to Old Blighty

[One]

Muddiebay, Mississippi
Monday, September 15, 1975

Mr. Randy Bruce had given careful consideration to the solution of the problem he faced of getting Mr. Phil Williams onto the airplane — which would take them from Muddiebay International Airport to Atlanta International Airport, where they then would board the airplane that would take them to London's Heathrow Airport — without Mr. Williams learning there would be females accompanying them to the same destinations.

If Mr. Williams learned that there would be women going along, Mr. Bruce knew that Mr. Williams would be miffed and disappointed and would cancel his travel plans after causing Mr. Bruce great physical pain using the ancient techniques of Taekkyeon as he had done on three previous occasions when he had been really miffed by Mr. Bruce.

And if Mr. Williams did cancel his travel plans, this would really EXPLETIVE DELETED!! up Mr. Bruce's rather elaborate plans to get Mrs. Carol-Anne Crandall into a room in Claridge's Hotel for some non-stop romping.

There were a number of such females going along whom Mr. Bruce knew about and some that he didn't. The ones he knew about, starting of course with Mrs. Carol-Anne Crandall, were Mrs. Martha-Sue Castleberry, Mrs. Elizabeth-Anne Howard III, Mrs. Rachel Lipshutz, Mrs. Bobbie-Sue Smith, Mrs. Nancy-Jane Kingman, Mrs. "Bitsy" Skyler, and Mrs. Mary-Louise Frathingham.

The women whom Randy did not know would also be on the Muddiebay-Atlanta and Atlanta-Heathrow flights were six in number. They were Mrs. Algernon (Lucinda) Smith, whose husband was president of the Muddiebay Bank & Trust Company; Mrs. Dwight G. (Martha-Ann) Fosdick, whose husband was one of the Fosdicks in Fosdick & Fosdick, dealers in financial securities; Mrs. Ellwood (Mary-Alice) Fosdick, whose husband was the other Fosdick in Fosdick & Fosdick; Mrs. Truman (Patricia-Ann) Johnston, whose husband was a partner in the law firm of Truman, Wadsworth & Johnston; Mrs. Barton A. (Pricilla) Wadsworth, whose husband was another partner in the Truman, Wadsworth & Johnston law firm; and Mrs. Chester B. (Dorothy-Sue) Keller, whose husband was a dental surgeon specializing in the whitening and repair of molars, canines, and bicuspids.

These ladies consisted of the entire membership of the Muddiebay Chapter of the Dames of Runnymede, to get into which one had to prove that one was a direct descendant of someone who had been there when the Magna Carta was sealed under oath by King John at Runnymede on the bank of the River Thames near Windsor, England, at two-thirty in the afternoon of June 15 in 1215 A.D.

The Dames — or "We Dames," as the ladies thought of themselves — thought of themselves as somewhat socially superior to the Ladies of The Tuesday Luncheon Club and consequently were a bit distressed when members of the latter let the word slip around Muddiebay that they were off to London to shop and take tea with H.M. the Queen at Buckingham Palace and then shoot pheasants in Scotland.

Dame Patricia-Ann Johnston was selected to run this troubling rumor to ground, and she did so by contacting Mrs. Mary-Louise Frathingham, of Muddiebay Exotic & Exciting Vacations Travel, Inc., who confirmed it.

"Tell me, Mrs. Frathingham, is there among the exotic and exciting vacations you offer one that would offer the husbands of the Dames of Runnymede an opportunity to shoot pheasants in an aristocratic ambience in Scotland?"

Mrs. Frathingham immediately rose to the challenge and found "Aristocratic Pheasant Shooting in Scotland, Outfitters, Ltd." when she looked in her *Travel Professional's Guide to Scotland.*

APSSO, Ltd., offered for only £1,102.00 sterling, plus tax, per day, per person, an opportunity not only to shoot pheasants, but to be accommodated in a Ducal Castle while doing so, all meals included.

Mrs. Frathingham had no way of knowing, of course — the words "Castle Abercrombie" did not appear anywhere in the listing — that the "Ducal Castle" mentioned was in fact Castle Abercrombie, which was where the husbands of the Ladies of The Tuesday Luncheon Club were going to do their pheasant shooting.

But when Dame Patricia-Ann told her to make reservations for six couples at the Ducal Castle for a seven-day stay, it did occur to her that things might be a bit awkward if the Dames met the Ladies on the airplanes en route from Muddiebay International to Heathrow.

But then she saw a solution to this, too.

Because Mr. Randolph Bruce — whom she was now thinking of as Sir Randy Bruce of the White Panty Hose, and whom she intended to bed down with if at all possible as soon as possible once they reached foreign shores — and his friend, Mr. Philip Williams, were traveling in the aircraft's first-class compartment and everybody else in business class, all she had to do was mention this to Dame Patricia-Ann, who immediately said, "Dames of Runnymede and their mates always travel first class. See to it."

Travel for himself and Phil in first class was part of Randy's scheme to get Phil aboard the airplanes without Phil learning about their female fellow travelers.

The plan was simplicity itself.

Part of it was already fairly standard procedure for their travels around the world to shoot things. First, Randy would don over his left foot and lower left leg a massive ten-pound plaster of Paris cast, which came with a hidden zipper and had what looked like bloodstains. Then Randy would hobble down to his Mercedes and slip into the backseat. Phil would then drive them to the airport, where a wheelchair would be summoned. Phil would then push Randy to the head of the line of those waiting to be humiliated by airport security, meanwhile crying, "Make way for a cripple!"

This innocent little deception of theirs had saved them countless hours of waiting in lines to be humiliated by airport security.

And it would have worked the day everybody went to London, except that it fell to Randy to push Phil through Muddiebay International instead of Phil pushing Randy.

What happened was that when Mrs. Bonita Jones Pennyworth dropped Phil off at "Our Tara," Phil was distressed, and said something about his undergoing his middle-life crisis five and three-quarter years late, and asked where the Famous Pheasant was.

When the time arrived to go to the airport, Phil was in no condition to sit up straight in the wheelchair, much less push it, so Randy put the ten-pound zippered plaster of Paris cast with bloodstains on Phil's foot and leg, carried him to the Mercedes, drove it himself, and then at the airport loaded Phil into a wheelchair and crying, "Make way for an unconscious cripple!" pushed him to the head of the security line.

They were shortly thereafter installed in their seats in the first-class compartment.

A stewardess appeared and offered champagne.

Phil said, "Don't mind if I do. Leave the bottle as I am having my midlife crisis and need a lot of liquid courage to face it."

The Dames of Runnymede filed in with their husbands, took their seats, and ordered champagne.

The stewardess reclaimed the bottle of bubbly she had left with Phil. When she did and saw that it was empty, she went for another one.

Phil then dozed off, and Randy relaxed, convinced they were on their way and he had no problems at least for the moment.

Randy was wrong.

As soon as they were airborne, and the stewardess gave her permission, Randy went to the First Class Unisex Lavatory right behind the pilot compartment, which, because he traveled a lot all over the world to slaughter wildlife, he knew was called the flight deck.

As he exited and started back down the aisle toward Phil, Carol-Anne Crandall pushed aside the curtain designed to keep the peasants from looking at the aristocrats, and cried, on seeing Randy, "Oh, thank God! When I didn't see you before, Randy, I was afraid you missed our flight to Atlanta and London!"

Randy made a shushing gesture.

Too late.

Carol-Anne's somewhat screechy tone of voice had raised Phil from his little doze.

"I heard that!" Phil cried, as he unfastened his seat belt. "I heard that bimbo call you 'Randy' and say 'our flight.' There are women on this hunting trip, and you knew all along there would be, you EXPLETIVE DELETED!! duplicitous son of a EXPLETIVE DELETED!!, and I am going to tear you limb from skinny EXPLETIVE DELETED!! limb."

He started up the aisle toward Randy.

Unfortunately — or, from Mr. Bruce's perspective, fortunately — Phil forgot that he had the ten-pound cast on his foot, which caused him to fall into the aisle after first bumping his head on an armrest, which in turn caused a minor, but copiously bleeding, abrasion on his forehead and for him to lose consciousness.

[Two]

Atlanta International Airport
Atlanta, Georgia
5:45 p.m. Monday, September 15, 1975

When the door of the aircraft was opened onto the airway of Gate 103, Terminal Five, at Atlanta International Airport, two police officers came aboard through it.

The senior stewardess pointed an accusing finger at Passenger Bruce, Randolph, and the police saw that his visage matched closely the description the pilot had radioed ahead of the unruly passenger who had cruelly attacked a poor fellow who had a twenty-pound cast on his leg. (The pilot had repeated the description provided by the senior stewardess, who wasn't very good at estimating size, or anything remotely associated with numbers.)

The police officers read Randy his Miranda rights and led him off the airplane with his hands handcuffed behind his back. As this was happening, Randy cried out piteously, as he had so often done in the past, "Moses, my lawyer, I need you! I'm being railroaded! Or maybe airplaned!"

Moses Lipshutz, L.L.D., as he had so often done in the past, rushed to defend Randy by rising from his business-class seat, racing up the aisle of the airplane, and then chasing Randy and the cops up the airway.

Next, two Emergency Responder Medical Technicians entered the cabin and loaded Mr. Williams on a stretcher, then carried him off the airplane, up the airway, and into Terminal Five.

There two people looked down at Phil on the stretcher and said just about the same thing, but in different languages.

The male, a gentleman of distinguished appearance who was about Phil's age, said, *"Ach, mein Gott, Herr Williams, was ist mit euch?"* which Phil of course knew meant, "Oh my God, Mr. Williams, what happened to you?"

The female, who was considerably younger than Phil, and had the most beautiful bosoms Phil could ever remember seeing — and, looking down her blouse as she leaned over him, he could see them in all their glory because she wasn't wearing a brassiere — said, "Oh, my God, Master Williams, what happened to you?"

"Have we met?" Phil asked, wondering if this might be a welcome hallucination caused by the result of all the alcohol he'd consumed, the blow to his head. Or both.

"Yes, we did," the man said. "Briefly, some years ago."

538

"The master was talking to me, you EX-PLETIVE DELETED!! foreigner, butt the EX-PLETIVE DELETED!! out," the beautiful blonde snarled, and then, in far more dulcet tones, went on, "Yes, Master, we have. In Miami. You were there with the gentleman the cops just took off this airplane in handcuffs. I'm flattered that you remembered me, even slightly."

"You're welcome," Phil said, grateful this wasn't a hallucination.

"Is there anything, anything at all, I can do for you?"

"Aside from getting me a drink, everything else I can think of that you could do for me would be, because of the vast difference in our ages, at best inappropriate and probably illegal."

"Carry the master to the General's Club," the blonde ordered the EMTs. "The one across from Gate 17 in the International Flights Terminal. And do so gently."

As anyone who has ever been in the Atlanta International Airport has painfully learned, it is a long way between terminals, and as Phil made that lengthy journey he could not help but notice that as the blonde walked beside his stretcher, she not only had a very nice behind but also that beneath her somewhat short white skirt she was wearing very brief intimate undergarments onto which had been embroidered many representations of two red hearts pierced by an arrow, presumably Cupid's, along with the legend *My Heart Belongs to Phil!*

That had to be, Phil decided, surely a coincidental happenstance, and couldn't possibly have anything to do with his own Christian name personally.

He also noticed that the foreign gentleman was following them and wondered who the hell he might be.

Once they were in the General's Club, the beautiful blonde evicted an eight-member team of Japanese farm-raised shrimp salesmen from the couch where they had been telling lies to each other just to keep their skills sharp, had the EMTs lay Phil down on it, ordered a double eighteen-year-old Famous Pheasant, two ice cubes, water on the side, for him, and then began to gently dab at the wound on his forehead with her hankie.

"How'd you know that's what I drink?" Phil asked.

"I have made it my business since we first met to learn as much as I can about you," she said.

That, of course, was an interesting statement, and he would have sought clarification had not Moses Lipshutz, L.L.D., walked up to them at that moment.

"I know that as far as you're concerned what Randy did to you is inexcusable," Moses said.

"And what exactly did that miserable EXPLETIVE DELETED!! Randy Bruce do to this poor wounded man with the enormous bloodstained cast on his leg?" the blonde asked.

"And you are, Madame?" Moses inquired.

"My name is Ginger Gallagher, *Miss* Ginger Gallagher, as I am unmarried as of this date, although I confess to having girlish dreams of somehow soon changing that."

"Randy told me about you, Miss Gallagher."

"I don't give a tinker's dam what that EXPLETIVE DELETED!! told you about me. What I want to know is what that EXPLETIVE DELETED!! did to this sweet and gentle wounded genius here on the couch."

"Specifically, Miss Gallagher, Mr. Bruce concealed from Mr. Williams that there would be members of your gender on this hunting trip knowing that if Mr. Williams knew there would be females on the trip, he wouldn't go."

"Two questions," Ginger said. "One, why

would Master Williams object to members of my gender going on a hunting trip with him? Just off the top of my head, I can think of many ways this member of the gentle sex could royally entertain Master Williams on a hunting trip, especially at night when it would be too dark to see anything to shoot at."

"Excuse me, Miss Gallagher," Phil said. "Would you please cease and desist from calling me 'Master'? Master Philip was what I was called by the teachers in the many boarding schools of my childhood and youth, and it brings back many painful memories. And right now, as I am experiencing my midlife crisis, I don't think I can handle any more painful memories."

"I will cease and desist calling you Master if you cease and desist calling me Miss Gallagher and instead call me Ginger, and if you tell me what you would like me to call you."

"Ginger, I would not interpret your calling me Phil as disrespect on your part toward your elders, even taking into account the great disparity in our ages."

"Thank you, Phil."

"You're welcome, Ginger."

"Getting back to my second question," Ginger said. "Why did that EXPLETIVE DE-

LETED!! deceive Phil?"

"I haven't gotten to the bottom of that mystery yet, but I will. But I know ol' Randy well enough to suspect it has something to do with hanky-panky."

Phil said, "It probably has something to do with that bimbo who came into the first-class cabin and said she was glad to see the EXPLETIVE DELETED!! as she was afraid he had missed what she called 'our flight.' "

"That bimbo would be Mrs. Carol-Anne Crandall," Moses said thoughtfully. "My Rachel has often confided in me that she suspects Carol-Anne is far more randy — lowercase *r* — than anyone suspects. But that is speculation. The question before us is what does Phil wish to do about Randy?"

"I don't understand the question," Ginger said.

"At the moment, Randy is about to be hauled off to Fulton County Jail on a variety of charges, including attacking a cripple on an airplane while in flight. Frankly, that would not break my heart, and I know my Rachel would be delighted, but on the other hand, I am his lawyer and have a certain obligation to defend the EXPLETIVE DE-LETED!! even though my heart isn't in it.

"So the call is yours, Phil. Before you return home, do you want me to spring ol'

Randy from the slam, or do you wish to leave him in Durance Vile?"

"Two factors bear on the problem, Moses," Phil said. "One is that, inasmuch as I am going through my midlife crisis, I'm just not up to going home and having to explain to the Angry Austrian —"

"Phil," Ginger interrupted, "you're not old enough to be having a midlife crisis. And who is the Angry Austrian?"

"Actually, I'm five and three-quarters years late in having it. Although I understand how someone of your tender years wouldn't understand that. The Angry Austrian is my wife and the mother of our three children — the eldest of which is a daughter about as old as you . . ."

"How old is she?"

"Twenty-five."

"I may not look it, Phil, but at twenty-eight I'm much older than that."

"You don't look that old. But we're getting off the subject. I really don't want to go home because when the Angry Austrian hears both what that EXPLETIVE DELETED!! Randy Bruce has done to me, and also how I'm suffering in my midlife crisis, she will find this amusing to the point where she will laugh hysterically."

"That's true," Moses said thoughtfully.

"And then as I have been lying here with Ginger gently dabbing at my wounded forehead with her wonderfully smelling handkerchief, I have been considering the wise wisdom of the thirty-fifth President of the United States, John Fitzgerald Kennedy, who wrote, 'Don't get angry. Get even.' "

"How are you going to get even with Randy?" Moses asked.

"I haven't figured out all the details yet, but I know I can't get even if he's in England and Scotland and I'm back home with the AA laughing hysterically at me."

"Good thinking," Moses said.

"So I guess I'll have to go to England and Scotland."

"But Randy will be in the Fulton County Jail, where it would be difficult for you to get at him to seek the justified vengeance you seek."

"Not if you can keep him from getting hauled off to the Fulton County slam. Can you?"

"Of course I can. I'm a highly compensated attorney-at-law. I thought you knew that."

"Then do so. Tell him that out of the goodness of my heart, I am not going to press charges."

"You have a good heart, Phil," Ginger said.

"And that he can go to London and Scotland," Phil went on, "providing he rides to London in economy tourist class in the way back of the airplane, near the toilet, something he has never done before in his life."

"That's true and also very cruel of you," Moses said. "Good for you."

"And make sure he waits at the gate until he is the very last passenger to board so that as many passengers as possible will witness his humiliation," Phil added. "And en route to London, I will think of other very cruel things I can do to the EXPLETIVE DE-LETED!!."

"I'm on my way," Moses said, and left.

Ginger leaned over Phil and resumed dabbing gently at the wound on his forehead, which had just about stopped bleeding.

He closed his eyes.

"Why did you close your eyes?" Ginger asked.

Phil opened his eyes and found himself looking into Ginger's eyes.

He took a deep breath.

"Looking into your beautiful twenty-five-year-old blue eyes, Ginger, I find that I cannot lie to you. The reason I closed my eyes just now was because when they were open and you leaned over to dab at my wound, in so doing you exposed to my sight your absolutely spectacular and unrestrained-by-a-brassiere mammary glands, and I knew that as a forty-five-year-old man in the midst of his midlife crisis I should not be peering hungrily at the breastworks of someone only ten years senior of the single malt I sip, as doing so causes my heart to beat savagely."

Ginger chuckled.

"Close your eyes, Phil," she said softly.

When he had done so, she went on softly, "Ask yourself, Phil, if you really think that when a twenty-eight-year-old female leans over a slightly older but remarkably well-preserved-except-for-male-pattern-baldness man in such a way that she knows she will be giving him an unrestrained view of her naked bosom, she's doing so to chase him out of the room?"

"Let me think about that," Phil replied.

Because of the beating of his heart, Phil had a hard time hearing himself think, but after ninety seconds or so of doing so, he opened his eyes and found himself looking into the eyes of the distinguished gentleman his own age he had first seen when they carried him off the airplane on the stretcher and from thence to the International Terminal where he was now.

"If I may, Herr Williams, may I present my card?" the man said, and proceeded to present it.

Phil glanced at it:

DR. WALDO PFEFFERKOPF

HAUPTGESCHÄFTSFÜHRER,
GENERALDIREKTOR UND KÜNSTLERISCHER
LEITER UND VORSITZENDER DES
VORSTANDS

DIE WIENER STAATSOPER UND CORPS DE
BALLET

OPERNRING 2, 1010 WEIN 1

Phil, because he spoke German, knew that he was holding the professional business card of Dr. Waldo Pfefferkopf, general manager, artistic director, and chairman of the board of the Vienna State Opera and Corps de Ballet, which did business at #1 Opernring in Vienna's first district in Austria.

"What can I do for you, Doctor?" Phil asked politely, and then before Dr. Pfefferkopf had time to reply, asked, "Have we met before? You look familiar and 'Waldo

548

Pfefferkopf' seems to ring a bell in my memory."

"Very briefly, the day before you were married."

"It'll come to me," Phil said.

But it didn't for a while.

"Herr Williams, I would deeply appreciate a little of your time so that we may talk seriously about your wife, Madame Brunhilde Wienerwald Williams. Would it be convenient to have our little chat now?"

"Frankly, no. As you may have guessed, since I'm in the International Terminal, I'm about to travel internationally, specifically to London. Furthermore, I'm in the midst of my midlife crisis, and talking about my wife, Madame Brunhilde, is the last thing I wish to do right now."

"Well, then, I guess I'll have to have another shot at talking to you in London. I understand you'll be staying at Claridge's Hotel?"

"I will be, but how did you know that?"

"Madame Brunhilde told me," Dr. Pfefferkopf said. "See you in London."

He left.

"What was that all about?" Ginger asked.

"I have no idea."

"You can open your eyes again, Phil, as I am about to lean over you again while I dab gently at your forehead," Ginger said.

"Before you start dabbing and I start looking where I shouldn't be looking, I really would like to get this EXPLETIVE DELETED!! cast off my leg. We're already past security."

"If you leave it on, Phil, I can push you in a wheelchair to the gate, and we can get on the London airplane ahead of everybody else."

"Good thinking!" Phil said, and almost added, "Especially for a well-endowed blonde," but instead said, "You're going to London?"

"And Scotland. I'm hoping to show you that there are exceptions to your belief that all women on a hunting trip are a pain in that part of the anatomy on which we sit. All I need to do is make a quick telephone call to my private pilot to tell him to go to Heathrow and wait for me there."

"If you have a private plane, why don't we fly to London on that?"

"Your call. But I was thinking you wanted to see that EXPLETIVE DELETED!! Randy Bruce's humiliation as he makes his way all the way down the aisle to the last seat by the toilet in the economy tourist class cabin."

"You're right again, of course, Ginger! We really think alike, don't we?"

"Oh, I hope so! Now open your eyes and look into mine, or at whatever else your heart desires."

[Three]

Heathrow International Airport
London, England
Tuesday morning, September 16, 1975

On the flight to London, Ginger discreetly took the cast off Phil's leg just after takeoff and didn't put it back on until just after they touched down at Heathrow International Airport.

Phil didn't get to actually see Randy's humiliation as he marched to the end of the aisle in the economy tourist class cabin, but Ginger recorded the event for posterity for him with her movie camera and said if they could find time when they got to Claridge's Hotel he could watch it over and over to his heart's content.

She said anything else he might have in mind for when they got there was fine with her.

On the flight to London, they sipped champagne and held hands and dozed, with her head resting on his shoulder in a position that permitted him to inhale the delightful smell of her long blond hair.

Cripples have the same de-boarding priorities as they do boarding priorities, so as Phil and Ginger had been first to get on the plane, they were first to get off and soon found themselves standing beside one of two of London's famed red double-decker buses.

Instead of signs reading "Trafalgar Square" and "Kingston upon Thames" and "Greenwich and Lewisham," and the like, the signs on these buses were hand-lettered "Magna Carta" and "Ladies Lunch." Intuiting the latter was intended to indicate the bus on which The Ladies of The Tuesday Luncheon Club were to be carried to Claridge's Hotel, Phil bowed Ginger onto the latter.

"Go upstairs, baby," he said.

"What did you call me?"

"Uh, slip of the tongue. A man my age should not be calling a woman your age anything personal like that under any circumstances. Chalk it up to my midlife crisis."

"Don't be silly, my precious. I love it when you call me baby!"

Ginger got on the bus and climbed the stairs to the second floor. Phil followed, enjoying the convenient point of view of her tight white skirt as it ascended before him.

"All the way up in front," Phil suggested, once on the upper deck.

"All the way up in front what, Precious?"

Phil took her meaning.

"All the way up in front, baby," he said, and blushed.

"See how easy it is, Precious?"

When they were sitting in the front row of seats — which, for those not familiar with London's famed red double-decker buses, is way up front of the vehicle, even farther forward than the driver — Ginger asked why they were sitting there.

"I'll tell you if you promise not to laugh," Phil said.

"You have my word."

"I have always regarded sitting up here as a thrilling surreal experience, like Salvador Dalí and his bent clocks. When the bus is moving, you race down the street, around corners, et cetera, and you have absolutely no control of how fast you're going, et cetera. You see what I mean?"

"No," Ginger confessed. "But as I am convinced that as we skip down life's path together, I will inevitably say something stupid like that, that you won't understand, you get a pass for that one."

"There is a small problem with our skipping down life's path together, as much as I would like nothing more, in that I am a married man with a wife and three children, one of whom is only three years younger than you."

"So you keep reminding me. You know what I say, Precious?"

"No, I don't."

"*Carpe diem.* Think of what's going on between us as a thrilling surreal experience that may or may not last, but will if I have anything to do with it, and worry about your Angry Austrian and your three kids if and when that problem rears its ugly head. *Carpe diem.*"

Phil of course knew *Carpe diem* meant "seize the moment." So he seized the moment by seizing Ginger and kissing her. And she kissed him back.

Then there came what sounded at first to Phil like celestial trumpets a little out of tune, but which turned out to be the sound of the bus driver blowing the bus's horns to attract the Lunch Ladies and their mates to his bus.

As they watched them dragging their luggage to the bus, Phil said, "I feel so good, Ginger baby, that with your permission I'm going to fire up a cigar."

"You don't need my permission, Precious. I love the smell of a good cigar. As a matter of fact it was the smell of your Don Fernando Super Churchill that first attracted me to you when I first saw you with that EXPLETIVE DELETED!! Randy Bruce in Key Biscayne."

So Phil fired up a hand-rolled Don Fernando Super Churchill eight-inch *Duro* with Connecticut shade-grown wrapper. He puffed happily away on it as Ginger sniffed the aroma appreciatively as the Lunch Ladies and their mates got onto the bus.

He saw the bimbo whom Moses tentatively identified as Carol-Anne Crandall, the randy lady who was most likely involved in hanky-panky with Randy. And of course Moses and Rachel Lipshutz, whom he knew. And Pancho Gonzales, who was with a beautiful Latina.

"That's that EXPLETIVE DELETED!! fried banana eater and his so-called niece, Pilar," Ginger said.

And then Phil exclaimed, "My God, look at that gorilla! He must weigh at least three hundred and twenty pounds and stand six feet ten or more!"

He had no way of knowing it but he was referring to Mr. "King Kong" Kingman, the proprietor of the King Cadillac, Buick, Chevrolet, and Harley-Davidson Auto Mall in Muddiebay, who had been known as

"King Kong Kingman" when he had been an All-American linebacker at Ole Miss because he had then weighed 320 pounds.

That he had picked up a little weight in the ensuing years was made evident by the degree to which the bus tilted when Mr. Kingman climbed aboard.

Finally, last and least, Mr. Randy Bruce boarded the bus, and it finally started off.

No sooner had it moved than a loud voice called out, "Hey, you in the front! Get rid of that stinking stogie!"

Phil inquired of Ginger if she had seen any "No Smoking" or even any "No Cigar Smoking" signs. She replied in the negative, so he took another puff on his Don Fernando Super Churchill.

"Hey, stupid!" came the call. "You deaf, or what? Get rid of that EXPLETIVE DELETED!! cigar!"

Phil returned rudeness in kind, by raising his left hand balled into a fist save for the index finger, which remained extended. It could have meant that for some reason he was signaling the number one, but he wasn't, and the recipient of his signal took Phil's intended meaning.

"All right, EXPLETIVE DELETED!!, get rid of that EXPLETIVE DELETED!! stogie or I'll shove it up your EXPLETIVE DELETED!! and

then throw you and your EXPLETIVE DE-
LETED!! bimbo off the EXPLETIVE DE-
LETED!! bus."

Phil started to rise so that he could remon-
strate with the gentleman, but Ginger
restrained him, and limited their common
response to raising her hand as Phil had
raised his, that is, balled and with the index
finger extended.

Then a female voice was heard.

Phil and Ginger had no way of knowing,
but it was that of Mrs. Nancy-Jane Kingman, wife of King Kong, and reliably reported to be the only human being on the
face of the planet Mr. Kingman lived in ter-
ror of.

"Wait until we get to the hotel, dumpling,"
Mrs. Kingman was saying. "Then you can
tear the stogie-puffing EXPLETIVE DE-
LETED!! apart."

[Four]

Claridge's Hotel
Brook and Davies Streets
Mayfair, London, England
Tuesday, September 16, 1975

The Lunch Ladies' bus arrived at Claridge's
Hotel not quite two hours later.

From their vantage point in the front of

the bus, Phil and Ginger could see that the Magna Carta bus had won the race to the hotel, for the Magna Carta Dames were lined up on the sidewalk. They were making strange bobbing movements.

"Precious, what in the world are those old women doing?" Ginger inquired.

"They are practicing curtsies," Phil explained.

"Whatever for?"

"You see that Rolls-Royce? The one with the funny lamp over the windshield and the license plate reading 'ER'?"

"Daddy left me a couple like that," Ginger replied. "The last time I looked, there was one in the garage of my penthouse overlooking Biscayne Bay, and I suppose the other might still be in the garage of the Waldorf Astoria in New York City, which is where Daddy was when he passed on to that Great Hedge Fund in the sky. But what about this one?"

"That's what they call a Buck House Car," Phil said. "Which means a car belonging to the motor pool at Buckingham Palace."

"Oh, really?"

"That's what the funny light over the windshield means, that and the ER license plate, which does not mean 'Easy Rider,' as most think, but 'Eleanor Regina.' Which means Queen Eleanor."

Phil was taking a little pride in being able to show Ginger his insider knowledge of London culture, which he had first acquired in his youth when he had regularly stayed at Claridge's Hotel when he had been an armed CIC sergeant courier.

Before I met Brunhilde, who became my wife and the mother of our three children, he thought, *and whom, with any luck at all, I am about to betray by having unlawful carnal knowledge of a beautiful woman almost as young as our daughter.*

He forced this disturbing chain of thought from his mind and continued, "What I think is happening here is that, seeing the Buck House Car, the Magna Carta Dames think that Her Majesty, Queen Eleanor, or one of the minor Royals, is in the hotel and about to come out, and they want to be ready to curtsy should that happen."

"You're probably right," Ginger said. "But, Precious, I may be wrong, but I think that's Queen Elizabeth."

"Slip of the tongue," Phil said. "Well, let's get off the bus and see if there's room for us in the inn, so to speak."

So they went down the stairs onto the first floor, and then stepped off the bus.

Two men were waiting for them.

One was George, the top-hatted head doorman of Claridge's Hotel. The other was Mr. "King Kong" Kingman.

No sooner had George said, "Welcome back to Claridge's Hotel, Mr. Williams, and you, too, Miss Gallagher, although your unexpected presence here is an unexpected pleasure," than Mr. Kingman launched all the nearly four hundred pounds of himself at Mr. Williams with the obvious intention of causing him great bodily harm.

This was a mistake.

Seconds later, he was on the ground, moaning piteously from the pain caused to his nose and groin area by two of the Claridge's bellmen, all of whom had been trained in the Ancient Korean Art of Taekkyeon at the Royal Korean Archery & Taekkyeon Academy on London's Dried Fish Street as part of their bellman training.

Mrs. Kingman, screaming naughty words, rushed to defend her husband, which shortly afterward caused her to be lying beside him, as two tea-servers of the Sidewalk Tea Tables, on the sidewalk in front of the hotel, who were famed for the crisp paper tiaras they wore in their hair and their feminine daintiness in general, had literally leapt to defend the bellmen, their fellow alumni at the Royal Korean Archery & Taekkyeon Academy.

"Sir and madam," George then said, leaning over the Kingmans, "I must tell you that sort of behavior, even for Americans, is beyond the pale and will not be tolerated. Should you persist, you will be asked to vacate the premises."

"George," one of the Magna Carta Dames who had been in London often before and knew the head doorman pretty well, "that sort of behavior is to be expected, sadly, of white trash like those two. I say give them the boot!"

This caused other members of the Ladies of The Tuesday Luncheon Club to offer some unkind words in response and a royal brouhaha was clearly about to occur.

George said to Phil and Ginger, "Why don't we hustle you inside and get you accommodated in your accommodations?" and proceeded to hustle Phil and Ginger into the lobby.

Dr. Waldo Pfefferkopf was standing just inside the revolving door.

"Well, here I am in London, Herr Williams," he said. "Dare I hope to now have the few minutes of your valuable time you promised to me yesterday in Atlanta to discuss your wife, Madame Brunhilde?"

561

"Dr. Pfefferkopf, while there is nothing I would prefer more than to discuss my wife," Phil lied through his teeth, "now, sadly, is simply not the time. Try me tomorrow."

"I have to tell you I am determined to discuss your wife with you, sir."

"So I see. Try me tomorrow," Phil repeated, then walked quickly after George and Ginger, catching up with them at the reception desk.

"Ethelbert," George announced to the reception desk official, "we are going to have to find suitable accommodation for Miss Gallagher here, as she has again graced us with her patronage but this time without letting us know beforehand that she was coming."

"George," Ginger replied, "that will not be necessary, as I will share the accommodations of my Uncle Philip, as I am his niece."

George nodded. "Well, in that case, why don't we get on the lift to it?"

And they did, the lift being the elevator, and when it began rising, Phil asked, "George, what was that Buck House Rolls-Royce doing here? Is, or was, Queen Eleanor here?"

"Actually, sir, the Buck House Rolls carried a message for you, borne by Lieuten-

ant Colonel Sir Brathwaite T. Smythe, Equerry to H.M. Queen Elizabeth."

"A message to me from Queen Eleanor?"

"Uncle Philip, dear, I've told you twice already it's Elizabeth. Queen *Elizabeth.*"

"Of course it is, niece dear. So where's the message?"

"I will give it to you when you and your niece are accommodated in your accommodations, together with another message we have been holding for you."

"Another message? From whom?" Phil asked.

"Well, here we are," George replied as the lift door slid open. "At the fifth, or Aristocratic, floor. If you will be so good as to follow me?"

George led them down a thickly carpeted corridor to a double door on which was a shiny brass plaque identifying it as the Maharaja Jaswant Singh of Marwar Suite.

George opened the door, said, "Compliments of Mr. Pat O'Malley and the U.S. IRS, Mr. Williams," then handed him a five-page single-spaced letter.

Phil saw that it was from ol' Pat, and sat down to read it. It took him some time as the one literary flaw the Master of American Literature had was a tendency toward loquaciousness. He never said, in other

words, what could be said on half a page if he could find a way — and he almost invariably did — to write what he wanted to say over five single-spaced pages.

The nut of what he wanted to say here was that after he'd spoken with Phil and told him that the tank-tracks-chewed-up wifely rose garden had precluded his going to London and Scotland with Phil, he had spoken with their mutual friend and literary legal counsel, His Honor Gustave Warblerman, L.L.D., and told him that ol' Phil was off to ol' Blighty, where he had suggested ol' Phil pass the time by watching them lock up the Crown Jewels in the Tower of London.

Ol' Gus, the e-mail went on somewhere on page three, had then said that was a marvelous idea, inasmuch that if Phil actually went to the Tower of London to do so, they could tell the IRS he was doing research not only for himself, but for O'Malley as well, and they could deduct the entire expenses of such research, including those expenses incurred, but not yet paid, by Mr. O'Malley when he was over there watching them locking up the Crown Jewels, including the two weeks Mr. and Mrs. O'Malley had spent in the Maharaja Jaswant Singh of Marwar Suite in Claridge's Hotel; Mrs.

O'Malley's little incidental expenses in Harrods and Marks & Spencer and other such establishments; and Pat's bar tab at the Royal Yeomen Warders Club, which was in the Tower of London and which, Pat being Pat, had been a doozy.

So, Phil, ol' buddy, ol' Pat's letter finally ended, *instead of sitting around lonely and alone with absolutely nothing to do and no one to talk to in your London hotel room, you can go to the Tower of London and watch them lock up the Queen's family jewels. Fondly, your pal, Pat.*

George then handed Phil the message from Lieutenant Colonel Smythe, and announced, "I will leave you and your niece now so that you can rest from your journey. Since you were traveling with all that white trash, you must be exhausted."

**LIEUTENANT COLONEL SIR
BRATHWAITE T. SMYTHE
KNIGHT COMPANION OF THE BATH
AND
EQUERRY TO H.M. QUEEN ELIZABETH
BUCKINGHAM PALACE, LONDON W.1**

My dear Mr. Williams,

For reasons I am loath to put to paper, it

565

is absolutely essential that you go to London Tower to watch the sequestering for the night of the Crown Jewels rather than sit around the Claridge's Lobby Bar getting sloshed out of your mind as our mutual friend, Mr. Pat O'Malley, thinks you would much rather do.

If you could find it in your kind and warm American heart to do so, please do knock me up at your earliest convenience at 677-777-234, and thus greatly oblige,

Your faithful servant,
"Smitty" Smythe

Phil went looking for Ginger and found her jumping up and down on the emperor-sized mattress in the bedroom wearing nothing but the intimate undergarment with the two hearts joined by Cupid's arrow and the legend *My Heart Belongs to Phil!* embroidered all over thereon.

He averted his eyes.

He handed her Lieutenant Colonel Smythe's message.

"How do I deal with this?" he asked.

She stopped jumping up and down on the mattress, read the message, and then reached for the telephone.

After Phil had explained to Ginger that when the Brits say "knock me up," they are

566

not talking about impregnation, but rather asking to be telephoned, she got on the telephone.

"Colonel Smythe, this is Miss Ginger Gallagher, personal executive assistant to Mr. Philip Williams. How may the Master be of assistance to you?"

Since he could only hear one side of the conversation, he didn't understand what was being said from the other end, so when Ginger said, "We'll be there," and hung up the telephone and appeared to be in the act of removing her intimate undergarment, he logically asked, "What was that all about?"

"I'll summarize it briefly while you take your clothes off," Ginger said.

He began to do so, and she did so:

"At five-fifteen, a Buck House car will pick us up here and take us to the Tower of London, where we will watch the sequestering of the Crown Jewels, after which we will go to the Yeomen Warders Club, where you will be very nice to Generalissimo and President for Life Sir Montague Obango of the People's Democratic Republic of Chongo — a member of the British Commonwealth of Nations — who thinks your book *Love and Lust in the Kremlin Necropolis* is the finest he has ever read dealing with love, lust, and international intrigue, and intends to award you the order of Montague Obango Second Class in person at the Tower of London. Smitty says that if you're not willing to go along with this, you'll be threatening the entire British Commonwealth of Nations establishment. And Smitty suggests I bring along a can of Mace, as Generalissimo Sir Montague Obango has wandering hands."

She paused, and then said, "Let me help you with that zipper, Precious. The way your hand is shaking, you'll never get it down."

And here, dear reader, we must once again draw the curtain of modesty across the narrative stage of this romance novel.

[Five]

Her Majesty's Royal Palace and Fortress,
a/k/a the Tower of London
On the north bank of the River Thames
London, England
5:45 p.m. Tuesday, September 16, 1975

At 5:10 p.m. that same afternoon, a Buck House Rolls-Royce rolled up to the front door of Claridge's Hotel, and an elaborately uniformed officer, who was of course Lieutenant Colonel Sir Brathwaite T. Smythe, Companion of the Bath to H.M. Queen

568

Elizabeth, got out and went through the revolving door and into the hotel.

He came out of the hotel approximately three minutes later, which elapse of time permitted the Ladies of The Tuesday Luncheon Club and the Magna Carta Dames to leave their widely separated tables in the Sidewalk Tea Tables at which they had been impatiently waiting and to form opposing lines between the Rolls-Royce and the revolving door.

At a quick glance, the couple whom the elaborately uniformed officer ushered quickly through the lines of opposing ladies didn't look much like Royalty, but the ladies curtsied anyway.

When the Buck House Rolls had rolled away, there was some discussion about who the couple had been. At least two of The Tuesday Luncheon Club Ladies were convinced that the man had been that EXPLETIVE DELETED!! Yankee friend of Randy Bruce, but admitted they knew nothing about the blonde except that she was visibly not wearing the upper intimate undergarment without which a Muddiebay young lady would never dream of going out in public.

Two of the Magna Carta Dames were strongly convinced that they had just seen the Duke of Harlborough, H.M. the Queen's Second Cousin once removed, and his French mistress, basing their convictions on two things. First, that the duke was known to have a weakness for young French women, who have a weakness for going brassiere-less, as this blonde was so visibly doing. And, second, that the duke was known to go around with a dazed look on his face.

Mr. Philip Williams did indeed have a dazed look on his face as he passed between the opposing lines of Ladies and Dames. But he also had a look of wonderment and joy on his countenance alternatively.

The looks flashed rapidly from one to the other in the manner of the flashing red warning lights at railway crossings when a train is due to cross the crossing.

One second, he would be thinking, and his countenance would reflect:

I am the happiest, luckiest EXPLETIVE DE-LETED!! in the world.

A beautiful blonde loves me and I love her and together we have made the greatest whoopee I have ever experienced in my life!

And then, next second, F L A S H!, he would be thinking, and his countenance would reflect:

I am the most miserable EXPLETIVE DE-

LETED!! in the history of the world, who has just taken sexual advantage of a fine young woman young enough to be his daughter, which at the same time constituted infidelity to his wife of all these years and the mother of his three children, none of whom even suspect what a terrible person their husband and father is!

And then, next second, F L A S H!, he would be thinking, and his countenance would reflect:

I am the happiest, luckiest, EXPLETIVE DE-LETED!! in the world.

A beautiful . . .

Und so weiter.
Ad infinitum.

Practically any aficionado of romance novels will follow my meaning, as this isn't nearly as difficult to understand as some of the narrative I've encountered in romance novels written by others, and I'm not talking just about the lousy grammar and sometimes unintentionally hilarious spelling.

Things went well at the Tower of London, far better than Lieutenant Colonel Sir Brathwaite T. Smythe had dared hope, although on three occasions during the night when things didn't seem to go well, he nearly had a heart attack.

The Queen's jewels got safely tucked away for the night, following which everyone repaired to the Yeomen Warders Club, or as it is sometimes called, "The Beefeater's Bistro."

Generalissimo and President for Life Sir Montague Obango was already there with two of his younger wives. He was about as heavy as "King Kong" Kingman but stood only five feet five inches tall. With him were two officers, whom he introduced as Field Marshal Percy Dingo and General of the Army Ethelbert Jones. They were both the size and the height of "King Kong" Kingman.

To judge by their medal-covered chests, all three officers had served with great valor in every war from the Wars of the Roses (1455–1485 A.D.) onward.

"Please come in, Mr. Williams," Generalissimo and President for Life Sir Montague Obango said. "Sit by my side, have a little taste of Famous Pheasant, and tell me how much you're asking for the blonde."

Phil pretended to misunderstand, and said, "She'll have what I'll have, Generalissimo, which is a double Famous Pheasant, water on the side, and two ice cubes."

The drinks were produced by a Yeoman Warder, rims touched, and downed.

"I was thinking you could have your choice between these two," the generalissimo said, pointing to his wives, "plus, I will up the Order of Montague Obango Second Class I am going to award you for your distinguished literary achievements writing about love, lust, and international intrigue to First Class, which comes with a purple sash to drape over your skinny shoulders."

Again Phil pretended to misunderstand, and said, "Don't mind if I do."

Phil had hoped the first drink would turn off the flashing railroad lights.

It didn't, but the second had helped, so he held up his glass for a refill.

"Okay," the generalissimo said. "I should have known that someone of your intelligence would drive a hard bargain. Both wives, the Order of Montague Obango First Class, plus two camels. I confess the blonde has caught my eye."

The third Famous Pheasant turned the flashes off for the rest of the evening and also caused Phil to be in the condition he was in, the diligent reader may remember, the night he went steeplechasing with the naked Valkyrie in the Pferd and Frauen in

573

Berlin, Germany.

In other words, he didn't know what he was doing.

"I'll tell you what's caught my eye, Generalissimo," he said. "And if my eye catches your hand again trying to caress the gluteus maximus of the love of my life, I will tear your EXPLETIVE DELETED!! hand off and ram it up your EXPLETIVE DELETED!!"

This caused the heart of Lieutenant Colonel Sir Brathwaite T. Smythe to stop.

Generalissimo and President for Life Sir Montague Obango glared in disbelief for a moment, and both Field Marshal Percy Dingo and General of the Army Ethelbert Jones jumped to their feet to glower at Phil.

Then the generalissimo laughed.

"And what makes you think you could do something like that, Skinny?" he challenged.

"Because I am a better man than you, Gunga Din. In the sense that I am smarter and more talented in the manly arts, if not quite so fat."

"What manly arts?"

"Taekkyeon, for example."

"I have no idea what that is. What other manly art, for example?"

"How about arm wrestling, sometimes called *Bras de fer,* for example?"

"Ha!" the generalissimo snorted. "I'll have

you know that you're looking at the People's Democratic Republic of Chongo's Champion Arm Wrestler!"

"Well, Fatso, shall we have at it?"

"I would like nothing better than to tear off your arm while arm wrestling with you, Skinny, but if I did so, I would probably get blood all over my uniform, so what I suggest is that you arm wrestle with Field Marshal Percy Dingo, who took second place in the National Arm Wrestling Finals, and let him tear your arm off."

"Whatever you say, Shorty."

So Phil and the field marshal assumed the position.

Although the field marshal was not only much stronger than Phil, and a better arm wrestler, he knew nothing about Taekkyeon and Phil was a Master (Beginner's Class) of the ancient art. The result of that was that three seconds after they began their contest, the field marshal was on the floor, weeping piteously as he tried to remove his arm (still attached at the shoulder) from where Phil had put it in an upward position in an orifice of the field marshal's gluteus maximus area.

"My God!" the generalissimo said in awe. "I never saw anything like that, not even when I was Sergeant Major Montague

Obango of the People's Democratic Republic of Chongo's Regiment of Light Lancers and in charge of person-to-person combat training. How did you do that? And will you show me how?"

"Perhaps, but first you said something that has piqued my curiosity. You said you were the sergeant major of what regiment of Light Lancers?"

"That of my native land when it was still under the colonial yoke. At that time the occupying force was Her Majesty's Own Scottish Light Lancers. When the Scots left — and they were pretty good chaps, actually, despite what people say —"

"Did you," Phil interrupted, "perhaps know a —"

"I think I'm starting to like you, Skinny, but not to the point where you can feel free to interrupt me at will."

"Sorry."

"As I was saying, when the Scots left, we formed our own Army, of course, and included in it the People's Democratic Republic of Chongo's Light Lancers, which assumed the customs and traditions of H.M.'s Own Scottish Light Lancers. I was appointed colonel commanding and the field marshal here was appointed my chief of staff as a lieutenant colonel."

"That was quite a jump in rank," Ginger said.

"Yes, it was, my . . . excuse me, *Phil here's* . . . blond beauty. But ol' Percy and I were the only soldiers in Chongo who could read and write. One thing quickly led to another, of course, and soon I moved into the Presidential Palace, formerly Government House, as generalissimo and president for life and ol' Percy became field marshal." He paused, and then went on, contemptuously, "For Christ's sake, Percy, stand up and stop moaning like a woman! Think of the traditions of our beloved regiment!"

Field Marshal Percy Dingo jumped to his feet, stamped them, and barked, "Sir!"

"Better," the generalissimo said, and then turned to Phil, "You had a question?"

"I was wondering if when the heavy yoke of colonialism lay across your native land, you ever ran into a young officer of the Scottish Light Lancers by the name of Charles William George Michael —"

"Bertram," the generalissimo picked up. "Indeed I did. Ol' Bertie's the one who taught me and the field marshal here how to read and write. Jolly good chap! I've always wondered what happened to ol' Bertie."

"Generalissimo, what if I told you I know

where ol' Bertie is and would take you to see him right now, or in the morning —"

"Excuse me," Lieutenant Colonel Sir Brathwaite T. Smythe said. "That would be a little difficult, as I happen to know that Charles William George Michael Bertram the Earl of Abercrombie is in Scotland and there's no way we could go there tonight."

"Yes, there is," Ginger said. "My private plane is at Heathrow and will take my Phil and anyone he wants to take with him anywhere in the world it would please his precious heart to go to."

"You were saying, Phil?" the generalissimo asked, and then added, "Why don't you call me Sir Montague?"

"What I was saying, Sir Montague, what if I both took you to see our mutual friend ol' Bertie and taught you how to do what I did to the field marshal? What would you do for me?"

"What do you have in mind?"

"Well, off the top of my head, first things first, that you award my beloved Ginger the Order of Montague Obango First Class. I think that purple sash you mentioned will go nicely with her lovely blond hair."

"Done!"

"And that you . . . Tell me, Sir Montague, do you believe in cold-hearted revenge?"

"Phil, how do you think I rose to be generalissimo and president for life? By kissing babies? What's on your mind?"

"Well, that we get out of here, get in all three Buck House Rollses, and roll back to Claridge's Hotel and have a nightcap in the bar. As we walk to the lobby, we will pass through parallel lines of women who may curtsy. You will ignore them. Or give them a look of distain."

"Is Percy or Ethelbert going with us?" Montague interrupted. "One or the other, or both?"

"Both are essential to my plan," Phil said.

"Pray continue."

"We will have a final taste of Famous Pheasant in the bar. Ginger and I need some rest for reasons I don't wish to get into at this time and will retire. Then you and Percy and Ethelbert will leave. You will notice that the ladies in the parallel lines are not only still there, but have increased greatly in number. This is because while we were having our nightcap, the original ladies will — having noticed the purple sashes Ginger and I will be wearing, and of course your splendiferous uniforms — have notified the other Ladies and Dames that since some really important people have gone into the hotel, some really important people will shortly be coming out, and they should be there to curtsy."

"And then Percy, Ethelbert, and I again look at them with disdain?"

"Not quite. This time, while you look at them with disdain, Percy will go down the left, the Ladies' side, and Ethelbert will go down the right, the Dames' side. They will stop before each Lady and Dame, grasp them firmly by the arms and kiss them as wetly as possible on the mouth, each time saying, 'With the very best wishes of Mr. Randolph C. Bruce, who would do this himself if he wasn't too drunk, again, to stand.' "

"Phil," Montague asked. "Have you considered the possibility they might be offended to be kissed wetly on the mouth by two officers to whom they have not been properly introduced?"

"I'm counting on just that, Sir Montague."

"Phil, that's an absolutely rotten thing to do to Randy," Ginger said, then grinned and added, "You're a genius!"

"I knew that he was a genius when I read the first three paragraphs of *Love and Lust in the Kremlin Necropolis,*" Sir Montague said. "Field Marshal, sound 'Boots and Saddles.' "

XVII
BONNY SCOTLAND, FINALLY

[One]

London, England
Wednesday, September 17, 1975

The day that was remembered for a long time by many people as That Day in Scotland actually began that day for Phil and Ginger in Claridge's Hotel, which is located at the corner of Brook Street and Davies Street in Mayfair, in London, England.

It began when Phil and Ginger awoke in the emperor-sized bed in the Maharaja Jaswant Singh of Marwar Suite, looked into one another's eyes, and then had what one might call "one more for the road."

Then they had a shower, which included the washing of their hair, which they then of course had to dry. Since Ginger had far, far more hair than Phil, he knew this would take some time, and he decided to take advantage of this by calling Moses Lipshutz

581

and advising him of his, and of course Ginger's, travel plans.

Mrs. Rachel Lipshutz answered the phone.

"Rachel, this is Phil. May I speak to Moses, please?"

"Well, I guess. But thank God they didn't find you. Or that blonde you were last seen with."

"Is someone looking for me, or us? And 'that blonde,' Rachel, has a name. Miss Ginger Gallagher."

"That's not what the people looking for you with blood in their eyes and evil intent in their hearts are calling her. And since I'm a lady, I can't say out loud what they're calling you."

"And who exactly are these people?"

"Well, leading the howling horde is our acquaintance Mr. Randolph C. Bruce. Howling on his heels are the Ladies of The Tuesday Luncheon Club and the Dames of Magna Carta. I shudder to think what the latter two groups will do to you after Randy carries out his promise to disembowel you. What I can't understand is why they haven't found you. They've been prowling the hotel's corridors all night and have staked out the lobby, other entrances to the hotel, and Heathrow Airport."

"That's probably because Ginger and I

are in the Maharaja Jaswant Singh of Marwar Suite, which is on the fifth, or Aristocratic, floor, the corridors of which are off-limits to riffraff."

"What are you doing there?"

"Rachel, I don't think you want to know."

"That's what Moses and I thought you would be doing, but we didn't know where you and the blonde . . ."

"That's Ginger, Rachel. Please. She holds a special place in my heart."

". . . and *Ginger* were doing it."

"Well, now you know."

"My position on that subject, and Moses's position, Phil, is, as the British would say, 'Bully for you!' You're entitled. We're fully aware of how Madame Brunhilde has been treating you over the years."

"Thank you, Rachel."

"If you're planning on escaping the country, which would presume your getting out of the hotel alive and un-disemboweled, which seems very unlikely, I think I should warn you that two of the Luncheon Ladies are staking out the International Departure Terminal at Heathrow."

"What I called to tell Moses, Rachel, is that we, Ginger and me, are going to Scotland. I'm not through getting even with Randy, and —"

"You're clearly not thinking clearly, Phil. These people want to kill you — and yet you insist that you want to carry on with the hunting trip? At which all these murderous people will be outfitted with very expensive, and very deadly, shotguns?"

"I just had a chilling thought."

"What? Worse than an angry mob of females with loaded shotguns?"

"I'm going to have to think it through, Rachel," Phil said. "When I do, I'll tell you about it in Scotland."

"Didn't you hear what I just said about the Luncheon Ladies waiting with blood in their eyes and murder in their hearts at the International Departure Terminal at Heathrow hoping you appear there?"

"My Ginger and I will be departing through the Terminal for Rich People With Private Jets at Heathrow, so that will not be a problem."

"Only if you can get out of the hotel alive, which is extremely doubtful."

"I'll think of something, Rachel. I'm Machiavellian. I look forward to seeing you and Moses in Bonny Scotland!"

Ginger came out of the bath moments later brushing her now dry long blond hair. She was wearing only her intimate lower undergarment embroidered, this one identical to the one previously described, with hearts pierced by Cupid's arrow and the legend *My Heart Belongs to Phil!,* but in a different color, suggesting she may have a suitcase full of same.

This caused Phil to ask Ginger if she didn't agree with his premise that if "one more for the road" was a good thing, wouldn't it follow that "two or more for the road" would be an even better thing?

After thinking it over for perhaps three seconds, Ginger enthusiastically agreed that it would and they had at it, so to speak.

After which Phil telephoned George the Doorman in Chief and explained their dilemma.

George, not surprisingly, had an immediate solution.

Two minutes later, two bellmen appeared at the double doors of the Maharaja Jaswant Singh of Marwar Suite and escorted Phil and Ginger to the service elevator, which they rode down to the second sub-basement.

There they were loaded in the back of a Thames close-sided one-half-ton lorry, "lorry" being what the British call trucks. On the side of the closed-side lorry was the legend London Five Star Hotels Lost and

Found Baggage Delivery Service.

The luxury hotels of London had learned that when their guests couldn't find their luggage, it was because it had usually been sent to the wrong five-star hotel. So they formed a cooperative much like the one developed to deliver parcels in New York City by Mr. Gimbel of Gimbels Department Store with a peer at Macy's Department Store and which they called UPS, which meant United Parcel Service.

In the present instance, the London Five Star Hotels Lost and Found Baggage Delivery Service lorry made its way around London picking up misplaced luggage and seeing to it that it was placed where it was supposed to have been placed in the first place.

As the lorry drove away from Claridge's Hotel onto Brook Street, Phil, who happened to be sitting uncomfortably on a matched set of six Louis Vuitton ostrich-hide suitcases, happened to peer out the rear window of the lorry and saw that Dr. Waldo Pfefferkopf was standing with the fire ax- and shotgun-armed Ladies and Dames who were hoping to catch him if he tried to escape Claridge's Hotel. And he naturally wondered, yet again, what the distinguished Viennese Austrian wanted to talk with him about regarding Madame Brunhilde.

Ten minutes later, they were at London's famed Savoy Hotel, which is located in the City of Westminster, which is also in the City of London, which sometimes confuses people.

There three Buck House Rolls-Royces were waiting to roll Generalissimo and President for Life Sir Montague Obango, Field Marshal Percy Dingo, and General of the Army Ethelbert Jones — and of course Lieutenant Colonel Sir Brathwaite T. Smythe — off with Phil and Ginger to Heathrow.

All five of the generalissimo's wives, who were not going along, stood on the sidewalk and wailed piteously and pulled their hair out as the motorcade drove off.

An hour and a half later, five minutes after they finally got to Heathrow, Ginger's jet *Kill V* went wheels-up and then pointed its glistening nose toward Scotland.

[Two]

Castle Abercrombie
Outside Dungaress, Scotland
Wednesday, September 17, 1975

Forty-five minutes after that, Ginger's jet *Kill V* went wheels-down and landed on the ancient cobblestoned runway of Castle Abercrombie.

Phil, peering out the window, said, "Somebody must have told ol' Bertie we were coming, baby."

"Why do you think that?"

"Have a look," Phil said, and while she was looking, he explained: "That's a bagpipe band, the Scottish equivalent of a brass band. And Bertie and Maggie are all dolled up."

Charles William George Michael Bertram, the Earl of Abercrombie, was in the Luncheon Mess Dress uniform of the Her Majesty's Own Scottish Light Lancers, which is to say a shirt with a lace collar worn under a scarlet red jacket worn over a kilt, which was woven in the pattern of Clan Abercrombie.

The bagpipe band, as it was actually the regimental band of Her Majesty's Own Scottish Light Lancers, was similarly attired, except for the two men who had the Regimental Goat, whose horns were painted gold, on a leash. They were wearing trousers woven in the pattern of Clan Abercrombie because the Regimental Goat had an annoying habit of, given any opportunity at all, sticking his cold black nose and rather sharp teeth up under kilts for a sniff and a nip at what the old goat knew was under there.

The countess, as she stood beside the earl, was wearing a simple black ankle-length dress designed for her by M'sieu André of Paris, a red sash, and in her hair a tiara containing all of the Abercrombie family jewels but two.

"He's the big guy in the skirt? Next to the redhead with that bejeweled thing in her hair?"

"That's a kilt, baby, but aside from that you're right on the money."

"I'm going to get you one of those, Precious. You have much nicer knees than your pal Bertie."

"I better go say 'hi,' " Phil said, and went to the Citation's door, which he then opened and leaned out of while cheerfully crying, "Tally EXPLETIVE DELETED!! ho, Bertie!"

To which the earl replied, "Hi-Yo, EXPLETIVE DELETED!! Silver! Away yourself, old chap!"

"Bertie, have I got a surprise for you," Phil called.

The countess motioned for the earl to lower his head to hers so that she could whisper in his ear.

"Bertie, darling," she whispered, "somehow I don't think ol' Phil is going to surprise us with the six Dames of Runnymede and their husbands, which group of Americans is dumb enough to pay £1,102.00 sterling, plus tax, per day, per person, or a daily total of £13,224,00 sterling, plus tax, for the privilege of sleeping under our somewhat leaky roof."

"Now that you mention it, that would be a bit odd, wouldn't it, my love?"

"What I suspect is that his surprise for you is going to be that bloody Austrian ballet dancer he married when he was, I deeply suspect, deeply in his cups."

"That does seem to be a more likely possibility, doesn't it?"

"If that is the case, you'll be sleeping with that bloody regimental goat, and not your countess, until death do us part."

"I take your point, my love," the earl said, and straightened up.

"Phil, old chap, could you give me a wee hint about the surprise you have for me?"

"Montague Obango," Phil replied. "How's Montague Obango for a surprise?"

"I thought her name was Brunhilde," the countess said.

"Montague Obango? Surely you jest, old chap!"

"I EXPLETIVE DELETED!! you not, Bertie.

Generalissimo and President for Life Sir Montague Obango in the EXPLETIVE DELETED!! flesh, of which there is quite a bit, as you know."

The generalissimo then deigned to stand at the doorway. He stomped his feet, which caused the plane to teeter dangerously, and saluted in the British manner, and barked, "Sergeant Major Montague Obango reporting once again to Sub Lieutenant Charles William George Michael Bertram, sir!"

The earl crisply returned the salute, and with his voice breaking with emotion, called out an order: "Bandmaster! Sound the 'Regimental March'!"

The band had played it often, so they knew it by heart, so they could and did immediately break into the regimental march of Her Majesty's Own Scottish Light Lancers, which is the old Scottish tune "When Scottish Eyes Are Smiling" arranged for eight bagpipes, two tubas, two bass drums, the jawbone of an ass, and a flute.

The generalissimo came down the door stairs, followed by Field Marshal Percy Dingo, and General of the Army Ethelbert Jones, and of course Lieutenant Colonel Sir Brathwaite T. Smythe. They took up positions and raised their hands in salute as the band played and the earl marched across the field to join them.

The countess, who did not like being left to stand alone, half trotted across the field to the airplane, arriving there just as Ginger, who did not like being left to sit alone in her private plane, came down the stair door.

The countess recognized Lieutenant Colonel Sir Brathwaite T. Smythe.

"Smitty," she inquired, "what in the bloody hell is going on here?"

"Not now, Maggie. Except that the fate of the British Commonwealth of Nations is at peril if things go wrong."

"But I want —"

"Honey, you heard what Smitty said," Ginger said. "Why don't you cool it?"

"How dare you call me Honey!" the countess said.

"Okay," Ginger said agreeably. "Maggie, why don't you cool it?"

"How dare you call me Maggie!"

"Why not? Smitty just did."

"Smitty is Lieutenant Colonel Sir Brathwaite T. Smythe, a fellow aristocrat, and you're . . . I don't know who you are. Who are you?"

"I have recently become the love of Phil's life."

"Isn't that a little awkward, inasmuch as Phil is already married to a bloody awful

Viennese hoofer, with whom, I just recalled, he has a daughter about your age?"

"Phil is worth a little awkwardness."

"Actually, Phil's a pretty good chap. I like him so much that he can call me Maggie instead of Your Ladyship. Which gives me the moral right to ask this, or more accurately, to deliver this warning: If you're after Phil's money, I won't let you get away with it."

"That's my private plane," Ginger replied. "But I am touched by your concern for my Phil, so perhaps you're not quite the unmitigated EXPLETIVE DELETED!! that you at first appeared to me to be."

"And I am touched by your saying you are attracted to Phil for who he is, warts and all, than for his money, so perhaps you're not quite the expensive hooker I thought you must be when I noticed when you were getting off the airplane that you are not wearing a brassiere."

"Thank you," Ginger said. "Nothing personal, of course, Your Ladyship, but I don't need support for my boobs."

The countess started to reply, but then changed her mind and instead said, "I have an idea."

"Glad to be of help," Ginger said graciously. "If you've got them, flaunt them, I

always say."

"What I meant to say," the countess said, just a bit coldly, "is that what we were doing out here was waiting for a dozen of your co-countrymen, who are willing to pay through their bloody noses . . ."

"The Dames of Runnymede?"

"You know about them?"

"I know if they get their hands on my Phil, they are going to kill him."

"Over my dead body, they will!" the countess said. "What did Phil do to annoy them?"

"If you could dig up a taste of Famous Pheasant for me, I'll tell you all about it."

"I'll tell you all about Famous Pheasant," the countess said. "It's distilled right here on the lands of Castle Abercrombie. Most of what we distill here we sell around the world as Famous Pheasant. The really good stuff, the forty-eight-year-old Old Pheasant, we of course keep for ourselves. What do you say, Ginger, let's go in the house and have a sip, and then discuss how we can keep Phil out of the hands of the Dames of Runnymede?"

"I'm starting to like you," Ginger said, "so much that that I'm willing to go along with your 'Your Ladyship' EXPLETIVE DELETED!!"

"You can call me Maggie, Ginger. Any true friend of Phil's is a friend of mine."

[Three]

Over the next hour and a half, in the game room of Castle Abercrombie, so called because it housed the stuffed hunting trophies — an elephant, a rhinoceros, two lions, a giraffe, and an assortment of smaller fauna — the present earl had brought home from his service in the former British Crown Colony, now the People's Democratic Republic of Chongo — Ginger and Maggie got to be great friends.

Three-quarters of a bottle of forty-eight-year-old Old Pheasant helped, of course, but so did the sense of freedom the countess now felt after she had adopted Ginger's *If you've got them, flaunt them* philosophy and hung her upper torso intimate undergarment on the left tusk of the stuffed *Loxodonta africana,* or African bush elephant, which stood to the left side of the fireplace across from the stuffed *Diceros bicornis,* or hook-lipped rhinoceros, on the right.

The girls also solved between them the problem of how to handle the Dames of Runnymede, and The Tuesday Luncheon Club Ladies, and at the same time satisfy

Phil's desire for revenge on Mr. Randolph C. Bruce.

When the earl and the generalissimo and the field marshal and the general of the army and Smitty finally staggered into the small reception room, weary and thirsty from their having marched back and forth for an hour and a half, reliving the happy military days of their youth, Ginger and Maggie said they wanted to outline for them what they had come up with.

"But before we get into that, where's my Phil?" Ginger asked.

"I saw him come into the house," Smitty said. "He said the marching and saluting he'd done as a youth in his own military service was enough for a lifetime, and he had no desire to march down military memory lane with us."

"But where is he?" Ginger persisted. "Can we can send someone to look for him?"

"God only knows in which of the three hundred eleven rooms of our little home he's in," Maggie said. "When Phil wants to be found, he'll come out, but not before. That bloody ballet dancer we were talking about before once hunted for him for five days without success."

"Okay, Maggie, if you say so."

When they had finished explaining the

plans, Generalissimo Sir Montague Obango asked if he might dare to offer a suggestion that would solve all of the problems quickly and efficiently and once and for all time.

"What I propose is that Field Marshal Percy Dingo meet the plane carrying the Dames of Runnymede here and shoot them all as they debark. He will then see that all the bodies are buried on the moor. Then, when the other ladies, the Lunch Ladies, arrive at the Dungaress Royal Hotel in Dungaress, with their husbands, General of the Army Ethelbert Jones will shoot all of them and consign their remains to the moor. And as a personal favor to my new friend Mr. Phil Williams, I will personally cut the heart out of Mr. Bruce before we bury him out in the moor."

It was hard to dissuade Sir Montague from his plan. He was after all generalissimo and president for life, and back home people who dared disagree with, or even question, any suggestions he might make rarely lived more than an hour or two.

By the time they had dissuaded him, it was time for Phase One of the Plan to be executed. This was to house the Dames of Runnymede in rooms along one corridor in an upstairs wing and then to station Field Marshall Percy Dingo at the foot of the stairway leading to that wing. That would be enough, Maggie reasoned, to keep them in their rooms and from killing Phil until the banquet.

Phase One went off without a hitch, although there was a moment when one of the ladies — no names here — didn't seem nearly so terrified to see the field marshal as the others and could even have been smiling shyly at him.

Phase Two was to have the invitations to the Ducal Banquet printed and distributed to both the Dames and the Lunch Ladies when they arrived late that night at the Dungaress Royal Hotel. The invitation stated that Mr. Randolph C. Bruce requested the honor of their presence the next night at a formal Ducal Banquet under the patronage of the Earl and Countess of Abercrombie at Castle Abercrombie.

It did not mention the menu would be haggis. If anything would redirect the ire of the Ladies and the Dames away from Phil and toward Randy, haggis would do it.

"Frankly," Maggie said, "I think what Ginger and I came up with is pure genius. I'm only sorry Phil can't hear of it."

"Phil has heard of it," Phil said, and came out from behind the stuffed rhinoceros where he had been hiding. "But I have been thinking."

"Thinking of what, Precious?" Ginger inquired.

"Thinking that if that duplicitous EXPLETIVE DELETED!! Randy had not asked me to go shooting pheasants in Scotland while he was randying about with Carol-Anne Crandall, I would never have met you, my love."

"That's true, my precious."

"I'm not finished," Phil said. "So, because the duplicitous EXPLETIVE DELETED!! did invite me and I did meet you, is it fair of me to do to the duplicitous EXPLETIVE DELETED!! what he so richly deserves to have done to him? And that doesn't even get into the subject of my wife and children, including the one who is nearly as old as the love of my life and which, frankly, I don't have a EXPLETIVE DELETED!! clue how to deal with."

"One problem at a time, my precious," Ginger said. "Try this *vis-à-vis* your feelings of guilt toward Randy. He didn't know we would meet, or what would happen if we did, as indeed it did. So you owe him nothing in that regard and can sock it to the EXPLETIVE DELETED!! as hard as you want with a clear conscience."

"That makes sense," Phil agreed.

"And so far as your wife is concerned," Generalissimo and President for Life Sir Montague Obango said, "no problem at all, Friend Phil. Give me your address and the field marshal will see that she is dealt with as we deal with difficult wives at home."

"But, Sir Montague, buddy, she's the mother of my children."

"So what? What's that got to do with anything?"

Thirty minutes later, Phil was still trying to convince the generalissimo why he didn't think his tribe's traditional barbaric rituals would work on the Angry Austrian — she was indeed a formidable one — when there came the sound of a jet aircraft flying low overhead.

"I wonder who that is apparently about to land?" someone asked.

"Send someone to find out, Bertie," the countess ordered. "If it's the Lunch Ladies, tell them to take a hike into the village."

It wasn't the Luncheon Ladies.

It was Moses Lipshutz, L.L.D., Mrs. Rachel Lipshutz, and with them was Dr. Waldo Pfefferkopf.

"*Et tu,* Moses?" Phil said. "*Et tu,* Rachel? I thought you were my friends and here you are with this Austrian gentleman who wants to talk to me about my wife, which is the last EXPLETIVE DELETED!! thing I want to do right now. How could you do this to me?"

"Call it tough love, Phil," Rachel said. "Listen to what Dr. Pfefferkopf has to say."

"Moses?" Phil asked.

"Listen to Rachel, Phil. Listen to what Dr. Pfefferkopf has to say. I considered it so important that I chartered a jet to bring him here. If this turns out the way I think it will, you'll get a bill. Now talk to him!"

"Not in front of all these people, certainly!"

Three minutes later Phil was alone with Dr. Pfefferkopf, everybody else having left them alone in the game room.

"All right, let's have it, Pfefferkopf," Phil said, biting the bullet.

"May I speak frankly?"

"Why not?"

"The time has come for you to end the suffering your Brunhilde has been suffering all these years since she let her lust run away with her in Paris."

"How would I do that?"

"Sign these papers."

"What are these papers?"

"They state that you are willing to allow Brunhilde to divorce you and also to take with her to Vienna your minor child, Franz

Josef, which she can't do without your permission. Once I get the signed papers to Vienna, I am assured by the chief justice of the Supreme Court, who has always deeply regretted marrying you in the first place, that the divorce will be practically instantaneous."

"What's Franz Josef going to do in Vienna?"

"He wants to become a ballet dancer."

"Dr. Pfefferkopf, what makes you think Franz Josef wants to go to Vienna to become a ballet dancer?"

"May I speak frankly, man-to-man?"

"Why not?"

"I managed to have a chat with Franz Josef."

"Did you indeed?"

"Yes, I did. And after getting his word that he wouldn't quote me, I admitted that the rumors that most of the male dancers in the Corps de Ballet are *poofters* are sadly all too true."

"You have the EXPLETIVE DELETED!! effrontery to tell me that my son wants to become a EXPLETIVE DELETED ballet dancer in the Corps de Ballet because all the other guys are *poofters*?"

"That is exactly what I'm telling you."

"Think it through, Precious," Ginger said,

coming out from under the stuffed elephant where she had been hiding.

"You're not supposed to be in here," Phil protested.

"If we are going to skip down life's path together, Precious, you better learn not to tell me what I'm not supposed to do."

"Fräulein, having heard you call Herr Williams 'Precious,' may I assume that you're more than casual acquaintances?" Dr. Pfefferkopf asked.

"You can bet your Austrian EXPLETIVE DELETED!! we are. Not that it's any of your business."

"In that circumstance I will confide in you that since we were six years old, I have been in love with Brunhilde, and I have never stopped loving her even after she lost control of her lust and had to marry Herr Williams."

"That's very interesting, but what I want to talk about right now is my Franz Josef and the *poofters*," Phil said. "He's never shown any signs of that sort of thing that I have noticed."

"I told you before, Precious, to think it through."

"I'm having great trouble doing that."

"Try this," Ginger said. "There are six ballet dancers, three male, two of whom are really light on their feet, and one who is heavy. The other three dancers are females, all of whose hearts beat a little faster when they look at a handsome young man wearing tights who they know to be heavy on his feet. Am I getting through to you now, Precious?"

"I get the picture," Phil said. "Doctor, do you have plans for Brunhilde should I sign the documents you have laid before me?"

"I intend to marry her, of course. And she will become vice director of the Corps de Ballet."

"And how much did you say this was going to cost me?"

"Good question," Ginger said.

"Brunhilde wants nothing but her freedom," Dr. Pfefferkopf said. "But I think it would be a nice gesture on your part to contribute to the support of Franz Josef —"

"So long," Ginger interrupted, "as he doesn't get too carried away with the dancers, the female dancers, my fiancé will assume full responsibility for all of his son's expenses."

Dr. Pfefferkopf nodded. "And as we know that Brunhilde has expensive tastes, I thought perhaps a small settlement would be appropriate."

"How small?" Ginger asked.

"How does a million dollars sound?"

"Done," Ginger said. "Sign where the nice man shows you, Precious, while I go find my checkbook."

EPILOGUE

Frau Brunhilde Wienerwald Pfefferkopf is now vice director of the Corps de Ballet of the Vienna State Opera.

Randolph C. Bruce, after losing several lawsuits against him for alienation of affections, breach of promise, and income tax evasion, was reported to be in discussions with the Reverend Paul Twinings, S.J., D.D., Ph.D., concerning his becoming a member of the Roman Catholic Church and ultimately joining the Trappist Monastery at Gethsemane, Kentucky.

Mrs. Rachel Lipshutz arranged a truce between the Ladies of The Tuesday Luncheon Club and the Dames of Runnymede that provided that on their return to Muddiebay, a joint press release would be issued to *The Muddiebay Register-Press* newspaper saying that both groups had been royally entertained at Castle Abercrombie in Scotland, and making no mention of anybody being kissed anywhere by anybody.

Mrs. Lipshutz was elected by a unanimous vote to be president of The Tuesday Luncheon Club, vice Mrs. Carol-Anne Crandall, who resigned after Mr. Homer C. Crandall announced his intention to sue for divorce charging gross infidelity by his wife.

Shortly after their divorce became final, Mr. Crandall married Bobbie-Sue Smith, the stockbroker's wife, who had divorced her husband after he and Amos Frathingham had gone to New Orleans and opened Amos & Ferdie's Fine Feathered Flowers in the French Quarter.

The New York Times settled out of court a suit brought by Mrs. Charles (Magda) Whaley charging libel and defamation of character for a series of stories alleging the former Hungarian countess, now proprietor of Magda's Previously Owned Motor Cars in Louisville, Kentucky, was actually a CIA contractor paid millions of dollars by the intelligence agency to corrupt Russian military officers using "a stable" of former ballet dancers and trapeze artists. Although the settlement agreement had a "nondisclosure" provision, it is generally believed that

"Madame Magda" received upward of several million dollars.

Miss Virginia Gallagher and Mr. Philip Wallingford Williams III were united in marriage by the Right Reverend Philip Moboko, presiding bishop of the Protestant Episcopal Church in the People's Democratic Republic of Chongo (PECC) a week after the Austrian Supreme Court, by unanimous decision, dissolved Mr. Williams's previous marriage.

The ceremony took place in the Holy Trinity Cathedral in Obangoville, Chongo's capital. Distinguished guests included Generalissimo and President for Life Sir Montague Obango and five of his six wives; the Earl and Countess of Abercrombie; Dr. Jonathan Caldwell III, former director of the CIA, and Mrs. Caldwell; Chauncey S. "Steel" Hymen, vice president, publisher, and editor in chief of J. K. Perkins & Brothers, Publishers since 1812; and Boris "Tightly" Held, who had become the J. K. Perkins "Money Man" after David Gobbet had shot himself in the foot during a fast draw contest and had to retire.

The ceremony had a military flair, as the bridegroom wore the uniform of Honorary Colonel of the Republic of Chongo's Regiment of Light Lancers, to which post he had been named by Generalissimo and President for Life Sir Montague Obango for his contribution to the close combat training of the regiment.

Following the ceremony and a wedding trip to Uruguay, the newly married couple established residence in the U.S. Virgin Islands.

Several months later, Franz Josef Williams, stating he was not up to the stress involved in being, as he phrased it, "the only straight arrow in the quiver; one man just can't handle sixty-two sex-starved teenaged ballerinas," resigned from the Vienna Corps de Ballet and returned to Foggy Point, where he became Chief Lifeguard at the Grand Hotel.

He lived, of course, in his childhood home at 102 Country Club Road. He was soon joined there by his brother, Philip Wallingford Williams IV, who resigned his position as food critic for *The Dallas Afternoon Gazette* in order to follow in his father's footsteps as a novelist.

When, eighteen months later, his first novel was published by J. K. Perkins & Brothers, Publishers since 1812, the *New York Times* review said, in part:

"The best thing that can be said about

this work is that it's not as bad as what we have come to expect from the author's father."

ABOUT THE AUTHOR

William E. Butterworth III is the author of more than 150 books, most notably the W. E. B. Griffin novels — more than fifty *New York Times* bestsellers in the Brotherhood of War, Corps, Honor Bound, Men at War, Badge of Honor, Presidential Agent, and Clandestine Operations series. He lives in Alabama and Argentina.